By Christine F

CHRISTINE FEEHAN
RECOVERY ROAD

PIATKUS

PIATKUS

First published in the US in 2023 by Berkley,
An imprint of Penguin Random House LLC
First published in Great Britain in 2023 by Piatkus

1 3 5 7 9 10 8 6 4 2

A CIP catalogue record for this book
is available from the British Library.

ISBN: 978-0-349-43246-5

Printed and bound in Great Britain by Clays Ltd, Elcograf S.p.A.

Papers used by Piatkus are from well-managed forests
and other responsible sources.

Piatkus
An imprint of
Little, Brown Book Group
Carmelite House
50 Victoria Embankment
London EC4Y 0DZ

An Hachette UK Company
www.hachette.co.uk

www.littlebrown.co.uk

For Pat McGuire.
Your coastal family misses you.

FOR MY READERS

Be sure to go to christinefeehan.com/members to sign up for my *private* book announcement list and download the *free* ebook of *Dark Desserts*. Join my community and get firsthand news, enter the book discussions, ask your questions and chat with me. Please feel free to email me at Christine@christinefeehan.com. I would love to hear from you.

ACKNOWLEDGMENTS

Thank you to Diane Trudeau and JoCarol Jones, without whom I would never have gotten this book finished under such circumstances. Shylah Sparks-Diehl for taking all the work off me with the animals while I got this done. Brian Feehan for making certain he was here every day to set up the pages I needed to write in order to hit the deadline. Denise for handling all the details of every aspect of my life that has been so crazy. Pat McGuire for his help in answering questions on addiction. Any mistakes are mine alone. Thank you all so very much!!!

TORPEDO INK MEMBERS

Viktor Prakenskii aka *Czar*—President

Lyov Russak aka *Steele*—Vice President

Savva Pajari aka *Reaper*—Sergeant at Arms

Savin Pajari aka *Savage*—Sergeant at Arms

Isaak Koval aka *Ice*—Secretary

Dmitry Koval aka *Storm*

Alena Koval aka *Torch*

Luca Litvin aka *Code*—Hacker

Maksimos Korsak aka *Ink*

Kasimir Popov aka *Preacher*

Lana Popov aka *Widow*

Nikolaos Bolotan aka *Mechanic*

Pytor Bolotan aka *Transporter*

Andrii Federoff aka *Maestro*

Gedeon Lazaroff aka *Player*

Kir Vasiliev aka *Master*—Treasurer

Lazar Alexeev aka *Keys*

Aleksei Solokov aka *Absinthe*

Rurik Volkov aka *Razrushitel/Destroyer*

NEWER PATCHED MEMBERS

Gavriil Prakenskii

Casimir Prakenskii

Fatei Molchalin

PROSPECTS

Glitch

Hyde

SIBLINGS WITHIN THE GROUP

Viktor (Czar), Gavriil and Casimir

Reaper and Savage

Mechanic and Transporter

Ice, Storm and Alena (Torch)

Preacher and Lana (Widow)

TEAMS

Czar heads Team One

Reaper, Savage, Ice, Storm, Transporter, Alena, Absinthe, Mechanic, Destroyer

Steele heads Team Two

   Keys, Master, Player, Maestro, Lana, Preacher, Ink, Code

OLD LADIES

Blythe, Lissa, Lexi, Anya, Breezy, Soleil, Scarlet, Zyah, Seychelle

RECOVERY
ROAD

ONE

Everyone had a breaking point. Everyone. Kir "Master" Vasiliev was well aware he had been past that point when he agreed to take the assignment. He never should have done it. Burning out when behind bars with no backup was a bad idea, especially if he didn't give a fuck whether he lived or died—which he didn't.

The only reason he didn't kill the two guards and the four prisoners right then and there was because he had a job to do, and he never let a job go unfinished. That was drilled into him. His club, Torpedo Ink, needed the intelligence, and he had been given the assignment to get the information and then kill the four men who had threatened their president and his family. That meant the two dirty guards who were involved with them had to die as well.

The eighteen charter members of Torpedo Ink had grown up together in a place loosely called a "school" in Russia. Their parents had been murdered by a powerful man named Kostya Sorbacov. He took the children of his political enemies and placed them in one of four schools supposedly to become assets for their country. That was true of three of the four schools, although all of them were brutal.

The fourth school was located far from the city, where the criminally insane prisoners—the ones the government refused to acknowledge existed—were housed. Pedophiles. Rapists. Serial killers. These were men and women Sorbacov utilized as the instructors for the children in the fourth school. Supposedly the children were to become assassins—assets for their country. What they really were, were playthings—toys for Sorbacov and his friends. Over twenty years, two hundred eighty-nine children entered that school. Only nineteen survived.

Destroyer, the nineteenth survivor, had recently found his way to them and joined Torpedo Ink. Like Master, Destroyer knew his way around prisons, but Master had been trained to take these missions from a young age, and Torpedo Ink relied on him. Of all the members, he was the only one with a record in their new country. They all had impeccable paperwork, thanks to Code. Even Master's prison records were mostly manufactured. Still, the fact that he was officially dirty, when the rest of his club was officially clean, set him apart. Only Destroyer would understand that concept.

Torpedo Ink now spent a good deal of their time hunting pedophiles and those running human trafficking rings. None of them could ever live normal lives after what had been done to them as children, teens and young men and women. To survive, they had turned their bodies into weapons and developed what others might refer to as psychic talents. Czar had explained that he believed everyone had talents, they just didn't have to use them so they never worked at making them strong. The members of Torpedo Ink had started as young children to practice in those long, endless days and nights in the basement of their hideous torture school.

Master was positive the cameras in the laundry room where the guards had brought him had been turned off. After all, the guards wouldn't want it to be caught on film if the four prisoners about to beat the shit out of him accidentally killed him. Still, that didn't stop him from making certain the cameras weren't working. He wasn't about to take any chances. He never did. That was what kept him from ever getting caught.

Master had been sure to offend these specific prisoners several times in the yard that afternoon, even after he'd been warned. He'd done it out of anyone's hearing so that when the prisoners and the guards were found dead in the morning, and he was back in his cell, no one would think to connect him with the bodies. That was always key in this kind of mission. As the primary assassin, you were never caught with the target, not by anyone. There was nothing to connect you to the death. If you had to draw attention to yourself to get put into solitary, you picked a fight with some other prisoner, not the target.

It had taken time and expert maneuvering to get locked up near these four men so they would share the same yard and floor. Torpedo Ink had to be certain the intelligence was right about them. Once they'd locked onto them, Master had been put in place. Then it was a matter of finding out who was aiding them—passing on messages to them and allowing them out into the world when they were needed.

Master knew every classic way to hide an assassination team. Master had been placed in several prisons, hidden there, to be used when Sorbacov deemed it necessary. These four men were protected in that prison. They came and went, and they had special perks. Women were brought to them when they asked for them. They had whatever kinds of meals they wanted. Cush rooms. Master recognized it all, because he'd lived that life from the time he was a teen and could pass for an adult. It was a shit life to live. He spent a lot of time fighting, killing, getting beat by guards, pacing in small cages, trying to stay sane.

Master stood against the wall, where the guards had thrown him. Just waiting. This was such a common scenario. He couldn't count the times he'd been in it, the new prisoner, stupid enough to cross those older ones who ran the prison and bribed the guards. It was always the laundry room or some smaller concrete room with a hose to wash down the blood. Sometimes there were small windows where guards watched and bet on the action. He knew this wasn't going to be one of those times because it was probable the intention was to kill him. As if he gave a fuck. He didn't. And that was bad. For him. For them. Mostly for them.

The guards hadn't bothered with cuffs. Why would they? Four big Russians were about to beat the fuck out of him for his "indiscretion." The guards locked the laundry room doors and sat back to watch the show. They parked themselves on the long table that prisoners used to fold the laundry, grinning from ear to ear. This certainly wasn't the first time they'd brought someone for the four Russian assassins to teach a lesson to.

"He's a big fucker, Boris," Shorty, one of the guards, said. "Strong as an ox."

Boris didn't bother to answer the guard or even look at him. "You got something to say to me now, freak?" he hissed.

Master raised an eyebrow. Answering in Russian, he called him several names, including degenerate, a brainless, obnoxious pig who could only hang with monkeys. He indicated the other three men with him. He was fluent in several languages, but like Boris and the other three prisoners, he was born and raised in Russia.

He might look all brawn, but he had a brain. He was born with the odd talent of seeing in numbers. He could compute numbers almost faster than any computer. His brain just worked out any problem and spit out the answer. He had instincts for investments, and when Code, their resident genius hacker, stole money from criminals, he knew how to utilize that money to the fullest. As treasurer of the club, he oversaw the money and made the investments. He also played several instruments, and his main job was construction. He had an affinity for wood. Now, looking passively at Boris, he taunted him in a bored voice, getting creative with his insults, because he was a creative kind of man.

Boris roared and came at Master, his arms spread wide. Master stayed with his back against the wall, on the balls of his feet, shoulders loose, and as the other man came in, he snapped out his hand like a knife, driving it straight into the exposed throat. Boris choked, coughed. His eyes rolled back in his head and he went down to his knees, both hands going up to wrap around his throat. Master followed up with a strike to the back of his skull, driving him hard toward the cement floor. Boris face-planted so hard the sound seemed to reverberate through the entire laundry room.

"Damn!" Shorty laughed. "That was fast. Should have been taking bets on the new guy."

"Too late now," Longfellow, the other guard, said mournfully. He moved a little closer to survey the damage Master had done to Boris.

The Russian assassin was vomiting, but not lifting his head, so he was by turns choking and getting the mess all over his face. He lay gasping for breath, desperate to breathe around the endless retching.

The three other Russians fanned out, coming at Master from three sides. They were silent as they tried to surround him, their faces the masks they'd learned from their teachers in the schools they'd attended, but they couldn't hide the fury—or slight trepidation—in their eyes. In their experience, no one had ever bested Boris in the prison. Most likely they had never dealt with anyone as fast or as calm as Master.

Master didn't move, keeping the wall at his back and Boris on his left. That meant he only had to deal with two of them immediately and the guards. The third had to get around the body of his fallen friend before he could actually be of some help to his friends.

Kir "Master" Vasiliev had been in this scenario too many times. He knew their moves before they made them. They might be faster than any who had come before, but Sorbacov's sick trainers had forced him to learn these tactics in very brutal ways. That fourth school, the one he'd attended, had had its own prison on the grounds. The instructors had plenty of opportunities to teach a young boy how the prison system worked. How corrupt the guards could be. How complicit. How the inmates could be beaten, raped or killed by other stronger, more powerful prisoners in just such setups as this one. He'd learned all of the various setups because he'd lived through them all.

His training hadn't been simulated. Unlike other children who had been sent into the prison to be "trained," he hadn't died. He'd survived. He'd become a warped, scarred, dead soul of a man with a hefty criminal record. He was the only member of Torpedo Ink that still had that record, and it was ongoing. Absinthe could get rid of the charges eventually, but they were still out there, looking as if he had been freed on technicalities.

He waited, knowing what was coming, and there it was, without warning: the familiar adrenaline rushing through his veins like a drug. The need for violence. The only time he felt alive. He wasn't like Reaper and Savage, or even Maestro. He didn't need or want to take an opponent apart. That wasn't his thing and never would be. No, he needed the actual war, the fight, the pounding of fists, the slash of the knife, the precise blow of the foot sending so much power and energy through a human body that the shock shattered internal organs.

He had spent a good portion of his life behind the walls of some kind of prison. That had been his specialty, what Sorbacov had him trained for. He was the chameleon, able to, even as a teen, get into the right block, assassinate the right prisoner and never have an ounce of suspicion directed his way.

In order to gain those skills and accomplish the mission, again and again, he'd been beaten and raped repeatedly from the time he was a toddler. He'd learned to kill. To make weapons out of nothing. To make himself into a weapon. To endure pain and put it to use. Pain kept him sharp when he was completely on his own in those hellholes. Pain fed the anger and craving for violence so that it raged in him and made him stronger mentally and physically. Now that his companion was here, racing through his veins, he moved with blurring speed.

Master kicked Avgust, the largest of the four assassins hiding in prison, so hard in the kneecap they all heard the sickening crunch. Adrenaline-laced joy rushed through his veins. These were the only moments left to him now to actually feel, as disgusting as it might be. The edge of his boot caught the assassin in the side of the head deliberately as he swung around in a flowing motion toward Edik, one of Avgust's partners. The blow snapped Avgust's neck, killing him. He wasn't important to the interrogation anyway.

Master spun away from Edik's homemade knife, catching his wrist as he did so, completely controlling his arm with his superior strength and the momentum of both their bodies. He plunged the razor-sharp blade into Edik's throat, dropping him, and then going straight for Longfellow, who stood just one scant foot away, his mouth gaping open. Slashing the blade across the guard's throat, Master kept moving with blurring speed, having gone over and over the moves in his mind, knowing what he had to do to survive. He slammed his fist into Shorty's throat, putting his body weight behind the blow, going in for the kill.

There was one prisoner left standing, and two alive. Boris was still on the floor, unable to stand. Still coughing. Master had killed four men in under a minute.

The remaining assassin, Ludis, faced him with disbelieving eyes. "Who the fuck are you?" he demanded. He was the acknowledged leader of the group, the one Master needed to answer the questions he'd been sent in to ask.

Master calmly walked over to Boris and snapped a front kick to his left temple with the toe of his boot, again putting his body weight behind it. The angle allowed him to slam Boris' head into the concrete wall so hard they heard the fracturing, as if the skull were an eggshell. Boris tipped over, his breath coming in ragged pants, his eyes wide open in shock.

"Need you to answer a couple of questions for me," Master stated calmly. "You had a nice setup. Hiding in plain sight. Must have been paid a great deal of money to sit in prison though. Fuckin' hate these places."

Ludis was calm. He lit a cigarette and leaned a hip against the long table where the guards had been sitting. "You're the one we've heard rumors about all our lives. You slip in and out of prisons, no matter how high the security. You assassinate your target right under the noses of the guards, and no one ever figures out who you are or how you do it. You've been at it for years. Makes sense that you're Russian. One of us."

Master nodded. Ludis was thinking hard, speculating, trying to figure out how he was going to kill Master and get out of the situation alive. That wasn't happening.

"The four of you were sent out by your little mistress to wipe out a man's family in Sea Haven. Viktor Prakenskii's family. She wanted all of them dead."

Ludis' face went very still. Master walked over to Boris and slammed his boot into his ribs, deliberately crushing them, right over his left lung. Ludis straightened, but when Master turned toward him, he put his hands up and once again rested his hip on the table.

"We couldn't get near them. We were lucky to get out of there with our lives. Our intel wasn't good. You taking over the job?"

Master shrugged. "Did she pull you back or did you make the call?"

"I made the call. We don't take suicide missions. She was pissed as hell."

"Her name."

Ludis shook his head. "I can't tell you that. You know the code."

Master turned and stomped Boris' left lung. Boris gurgled, and little red bubbles appeared around his mouth.

"What the fuck?" Ludis shouted, losing his feigned cool.

"Isn't that what you had in mind for me?" Master asked.

Ludis settled with obvious effort. "I still have it in mind."

"Her name. I've got all night, remember. The guards arranged to have the room so you could take your time with me."

Ludis swore in Russian.

Master delivered another kick, this time to Boris' groin, smashing through his balls and crushing his penis. "You know when he's gone, I'm going to have to start on you. You aren't giving me much choice."

"She goes by Helena now. She wasn't Helena when she was a child, but that's what she calls herself now."

"Helena what? Where is she?" Master asked patiently.

"Helena Smirnov. No one ever knows where she is. When she wants to see you, she comes to you."

"How many teams does she run?"

"Ours and at least one other. She has access to more, but we were hers exclusively, and so is the other team. She does all the recruiting."

"For the Russian and his Ghost assassins."

"If you know everything already, why the fuck did you come here to kill everyone?" Ludis demanded.

Master could see the man was working himself up to make his play. Ludis shifted to the balls of his feet, and then sudden comprehension slid into his eyes. He swore again in his native language.

"You're one of them. From the fourth school. Sorbacov's killers. You're one of them. No one has ever seen one of you. No one believed any of you actually survived, but you're one of them, aren't you? I was just making shit up when I implied you were the chameleon; no one ever believed there was such a person. But there is. You're from that school. You are the chameleon."

Master didn't react. Didn't blink. Just stared at him with a blank expression.

"Damn you, at least give me that much. You're going to kill me. You killed my team."

"You didn't recognize the name? Viktor Prakenskii? Think about that name. Where have you heard it before?"

Ludis shook his head. "She wouldn't. Not after him. I never connected the name with him. Not once, because he had to be dead. He was a legend. Not real. Not real, like you're not real. And she wouldn't send us after him."

"She sent you after him," Master confirmed. "Viktor sent me after you. And she's going to die for what she did. He'll wipe out every one of the Ghosts if they come after his family. No one fucks with him." Master shrugged again, watching Ludis carefully.

Master rarely talked. He saw no point in conversation once he was through with them, once he was going to kill his opponents, but it was possible Ludis would give him more information simply because he was shaken or angry. Master had come to this prison to get as much information as possible and to kill the assassination team sent after Czar's family. No one tried to kill the president of Torpedo Ink's family and got away with it. No one. Master wouldn't have considered going back to prison for any other reason than this one.

Czar's wife, Blythe, was the heart of their club. Without her, none of them would have a clue about humanity. Czar had been their moral compass growing up. He'd given them a code to live by, but they were killers—they had to be in order to survive. He'd brought them home with him to Blythe. She'd taken the club members in and taught them what unconditional love was. Not a single one of them had believed Czar when he'd told them about her—what she was like. Now they believed she could walk on water.

Nothing, no one, would have ever persuaded Master to enter a prison willingly again, with this one exception. Blythe. Czar's children. All of them were adopted. Blythe had taken in the three girls. They'd rescued two from a trafficking ring; the third, their little sister, they'd gotten from the foster home so they could all be together. Then Kenny, a teenage boy the club had rescued on one of their missions. Last, little Jimmy, a boy being auctioned off to the highest bidder. She'd welcomed all of the children. Every last one of them.

"I was part of the second school." Ludis gestured toward the others. "We all were. We didn't want to be part of the Ghosts. We stuck together and went out on our own. Helena approached us and ended up hiring us for a few of her own jobs, separate from what the Russian wanted. She works for him, but she wanted her own teams loyal only to her."

"Who is the Russian?"

Ludis shook his head. "Only Helena knows. At least she's the only one who talks directly to him. Seriously, I never thought it was possible to meet one of you. I never would have gone after Prakenskii's family had I known it was him. You have to believe me."

Master waited for the attack. It was coming. Ludis was definitely working up his courage. "Why would Helena send you after them?"

"I have no idea. She started acting strange a few weeks ago. Secretive. She always talked to us. All of a sudden, she went very closed mouth. She began going to a kink club in San Francisco regularly and wanted a couple of us with her to have her back. It isn't all that easy disappearing out of here weekend after weekend like she wanted us to."

Ludis made his play, coming at Master with a number of fast snapping front kicks to drive him back and into the position he wanted him. Master simply stood still, on the balls of his feet, legs shoulder width apart, blocking every kick with a smooth bat of his palm. He moved with blurring speed, suddenly gliding on the floor with his body, catching his legs between his opponent's and rolling, taking him down in a scissor move.

Ludis hit the cement floor belly first, Master coming

down hard on top of him, his fist hammering hard several times in his kidneys. He planted his knee on Ludis' spine and trapped his head in his hands, snapping the neck with a hard jerk.

Kir Vasiliev would leave this prison very soon. The charges against him would be dropped. All evidence would be proved false. He would go back to his club and be their numbers man, bury himself in his music and working with wood, in the things that kept him sane—he hoped. Absinthe would come for him.

It wasn't like he had the information the club had hoped for, but they were a step closer—and he'd gotten this assassination team. Helena might think twice before she sent her second team after Czar's family. Could she afford to lose more of her men? She'd have to weigh that price tag. Consider what it would mean to pit her people against Torpedo Ink. She'd lose her teams, one man after another. She had to know who they were and where they came from.

Master made certain there wasn't a trace of blood on him. He'd been careful of his clothes and boots. He hadn't wanted to use a knife. Often, when one stabbed or sliced into flesh, you cut your own skin, leaving behind traces. He hadn't. He was too professional for that shit. Still, he was meticulous, going over every inch of what would become a crime scene in the morning when the bodies were discovered.

He had to make certain the guards' phones didn't contain any evidence that he had been the prisoner they were bringing to Ludis and his crew. He took his time, not hurrying, not letting nerves get to him. When he made his way back to his cell, he was just as careful, not touching anything, not allowing a camera to pick him up. He also made doubly certain he followed the exact route the guards had taken him, back through the narrow hallway only the privileged used, so no prisoner spotted him as he let himself once again into his solitary confinement cell.

It was only a matter of allowing time to pass without

losing his mind or letting anything get to him before Absinthe came to get him out. Absinthe was their club attorney, and he could work magic on paper or off, get anyone to do what he wanted. He could compel truth from just about anyone. They wanted Absinthe to get his hands on the Russian woman and find out just why she was after Czar. No one knew, not even Czar.

Master paced back and forth like an animal for the next few days in that small cell. Push-ups. Pull-ups. Sit-ups. Pacing again. Anything physical to keep his body as exhausted as possible. He didn't sleep much. He hadn't for years; that left time for a lot of physical activity, as well as reading, music and his investments.

Just as expected, all hell had broken loose in the morning when the guards and four longtime prisoners were found dead in the laundry room. The laundry room appeared to be locked from the inside by the guards. It was a mystery that the detectives and prison authorities were frantic to solve. The public—and the politicians—tended to demand answers when murders happened inside a prison.

The glitches in the security cameras were later attributed to the guards. There was money in their accounts going back several years that seemed to be unaccounted for. The rumors were rampant in the prison—as they always were. Evidence was piling up that something shady had been going on with those prisoners and the guards. Who had killed them and why?

It was a classic assassination meant to rock the system and be very public. Evidence was fed to the investigators in just the right places. Bank accounts. Tips. Other prisoners coming forward to tell of the privileges given to the dead men—how everyone feared crossing them because they were protected. It was even rumored by prisoners that women were brought in for them or they were taken out whenever they wanted to leave to party.

Master wasn't even part of the investigation. He had no interaction that anyone really saw with the prisoners or guards in question. He hadn't been in that prison for very long. He simply waited, counting the days and nights, sliding back into that well of darkness that had been his home for far too much of his life.

He was quiet and he functioned, giving the club what they needed. He played in the band, practiced with the other band members often. He worked with his hands with the wood, building whatever was needed. He was good at it; the wood revealed so much history to him. And there were always the numbers. He lost himself in numbers, and that was what kept him sane—if he was sane. He questioned that often. Too often lately. Especially when he did pull-ups in his cell.

What was he going back to? A life where no one saw him. He really was what others had whispered about him—the chameleon. He became what Sorbacov needed. And then his country. And now the club. It didn't matter that no one saw him, because if they did, they would see the killer in him. The man who couldn't feel anything but that hot rage flowing through his veins. Or hot need.

The others didn't understand that either. What happened to him when he came out of that small little cell. What Sorbacov and his friends had programmed his body to need. He could already feel that building inside. That dark lust. One more terrible difference to set him apart from the others in his chosen family.

As he paced and did push-ups and sit-ups and endless math problems in his head, he realized he was angry with Czar. He shouldn't be. Czar couldn't help seeing into people. Seeing into their souls—if one had a soul. He could pierce through your armor and get right to the core of you. He'd always had that talent, even as a boy. He would look at a child and know who would stand and fight, be loyal to the bitter end, or lie and cheat and betray. He knew the heart of you. While every other member of Torpedo Ink had been given a clean slate when they came to Sea Haven and Caspar, he hadn't. Czar had looked at him with those eyes and said no, they would need his skills. That had been a sentence worse than if Czar had condemned him to death.

Master had known he was a lost cause the moment Czar decreed that not only should he keep his prison record, but Absinthe and Code needed to make certain he looked very scary while ensuring that his convictions would be overturned, so he wasn't in danger of the three-strike law in effect. He had known there was little humanity left in him, if any, but to have Czar see into him and then expose him to the others—that was a blow beyond comprehension.

He had learned to use silence as a child to keep from giving his "instructors" more joy. He had used that silence in prison to keep from killing. He was used to it now. He lost himself in his music or working with his hands, but he had withdrawn from the human race as much as possible. He let the others handle all of the niceties. No one questioned his silence. Sometimes he wondered if they even noticed. He learned not to care.

On the fifth day after the discovery of the bodies, Master heard the guards outside his cell and knew Absinthe had come for him. The two men were talking in low tones, not at all happy that he was being released.

"Vasiliev, your fucking lawyer is here. Get your ass up and collect your things."

Barry Adams wasn't a bad guard. Surly most of the time, but he did his job, and he didn't push the prisoners around. He didn't like Kir Vasiliev, and he made that plain. He thought Master was guilty as sin of every crime he'd been thrown in prison for but somehow his brilliant lawyer kept finding a technicality, or a witness, something to overturn the conviction.

"Seems like this is a hotel for you, a revolving door," John Sippo added, gesturing for Master to walk out of his cell. "Why are you always in solitary?"

Master just looked at him. There was no point in conversing. None.

"He's a troublemaker, can't get along with anyone,"

Barry said. "Get moving, Vasiliev—you know the way by now."

Yeah, he did. He walked straight to the front desk, where Absinthe waited while they handed over his personal items, all of which were in an envelope. The two fell into step without a word, the guards walking with them to let them out.

"We'll be seeing you soon," John said.

Master didn't turn around or even bother flipping him off. He wasn't coming back. Not even if Czar commanded him to. He was done with prison. He was never going back, not for anyone. Not for any reason. They could kill him first.

He took a deep breath of freedom and then slid into the car with Absinthe.

"You okay?" Absinthe asked.

"Yeah. Just fine. Need to head to the club."

"Czar wants you to come straight home. He's anxious for any information you have, and there's a situation developing we need to take care of." Absinthe eased the car into traffic.

"Take me to the club, Absinthe, or fucking drop me off at the corner and I'll get a ride." Master pulled open the glove box and took out the wallet with his own ID, credit cards and the fat wad of cash he liked to carry. He shoved the one he'd been arrested with inside. It had his driver's license and little else personal. Prison had already taken too much of him; he wasn't giving anything else of himself if he could help it.

Absinthe glanced at him, a quick, shrewd once-over. Absinthe had a gift. He could hear the truth, even compel it. He knew Master meant exactly what he said. He shouldn't be surprised or even alarmed. After every prison stay, Master did as he was programmed to do. He found a woman and he used her hard. That was what the club was for. The women there were looking for men like Master, or at least thought they were.

"The club it is," Absinthe said. "I'm sorry it took so long for me to get you out of there."

Master shrugged his shoulders and stared out at the cars and trucks on the highway. Absinthe handled the Audi with ease, moving through traffic without calling attention to them. They did everything that way, as if they were still in the shadows. They probably always would.

"Talk to me, Master," Absinthe said.

"Don't have a fucking thing to say," Master murmured, not turning his head. He knew better than to say a word around Absinthe. He could see inside a man's head, hear truth in a voice, and it wouldn't be a good thing.

Master was feeling . . . murderous. It wasn't an unfamiliar feeling when he was first out of prison. There was always that transition he had to make. From prison survival of the fittest to the latest edition of whatever self he was going to be. He'd been an animal in a cage, with too much time to remember every single thing done to him when he was a child and teen. The moment he entered a prison, the memories were there, threatening to swallow him whole.

Master didn't just have to fight physically to stay alive, it was a mental process as well. Each time he was alone in his cell, the memories swamped him. It was impossible to push them away. He couldn't close those doors on the nightmare of his childhood, and every time Czar sent him back, it felt as if he were being abandoned to his past, to those monsters.

"You suicidal?"

Master sighed and turned his head to look at his Torpedo Ink brother. He'd known Absinthe since they were practically toddlers. They'd gone through hell together and survived. Absinthe was one of the best of them, whether the man knew it or not. He was genuine in his concern. It was the only reason Master didn't slam his fist into his face, and the hell with what happened after that, because he didn't give a damn if they crashed right there on the freeway.

"Probably." He thought about it. "Yeah. Mostly, I want to kill someone. I need to fuck someone hard. And then I want to kill someone. I'm a little psycho. So, suicidal, need to fuck, and psycho. The usual."

Absinthe drove in silence, easing the car smoothly through traffic, the speed always steady as they headed toward San Francisco and the underground club where Master could take care of his immediate need.

"That bad." It was a statement.

"I'm not going back, Absinthe. Not for anyone." Master made his own statement.

"I'll talk to Czar."

"You already talked to him. It didn't do any good. The only way I'm going to ensure I don't go back is to walk away." He kept his voice low. He always did. He'd learned it was better to speak softly or not at all. "Sooner or later, he'll need something. It will be important enough in his mind that he'll decide I have to go back."

"I'll make it clear if we need someone to go in, Destroyer will have to go."

Master shook his head. "That would be worse than asking me, Absinthe, and you know it. He can't ever go back without killing someone. He may be quiet, but he's ruthless. You ought to know that. He spent years in prison. I went in and out, and I barely can make it through. You can't keep asking a man to relive his worst nightmares over and over without consequences."

The moment the words were out of his mouth, he realized he'd said too much. Absinthe was very good at manipulating others into telling him what he wanted to know. Master had never actually come out and told anyone what it was like for him going back to prison again and again.

Absinthe continued to drive in his smooth, easy way, eyes on the highway with the lanes filled with cars, making his way to San Francisco without further protest. They were close to the club, and the adrenaline and hot blood were mixing, already pulsing through his body, a dark streaming ribbon of venomous heat that couldn't be denied.

"You should have told me what happens when you go there, Master," Absinthe said.

Master frowned at the quiet guilt in his tone. "Don't do that. Don't try to take responsibility for something you have no control over. What happened to me, happened to everyone, just in different ways. You couldn't have stopped it then, and you can't now. Czar decides he needs something, getting in and out of jail or prison for someone like me makes sense to him, and he sends me."

"Someone like you?" Absinthe echoed. "What does that mean?"

"Don't be obtuse. If he thought I was worth shit, he would have had Code set me up clean, given me a start I might actually succeed with here, but he didn't. He made sure I had a record no decent woman would ever tolerate. If I found someone and we had kids, I couldn't do half the things with them at school because of my record. You tell me how that equates to a fresh start for me, Absinthe."

Absinthe took the exit that would take them to the club. It wasn't far, and he was silent until they were in the parking lot. "You've got this wrong, Master. No one is left behind. We stick together; that's how we made it through. Every single one of us is invaluable to the others."

Master stepped out of the car, taking another lungful of freedom—of that fresh air he could never find in prison, not even outside in the yard. Absinthe locked the car and fell into step with him as they approached the archway to the De Sade.

"I'm invoking the confessional, Absinthe. This conversation is strictly between us. There's no need to take it to anyone else." There was satisfaction in being able to turn the tables on Absinthe.

"No way. You're tying my hands. I can get to the bottom of this, Master."

"The confessional," Master reiterated and opened the door to the De Sade.

TWO

"Are you coming for a drink with us, Ambrie?" Amanda Gibbs stuck her head into her boss's office. "It's Daniel's birthday tomorrow. We're celebrating, remember? The poor man puts up with the two of us all day. The least we can do is celebrate his birthday."

Ambrielle Moore looked up from the flow of numbers moving on her computer screen, blinking to bring her assistant into focus. "Is it that time already?"

"Past," Amanda confirmed, moving all the way into the small room.

There were only three people working for the small financial advising business: Daniel Parker, Amanda and Ambrielle. Daniel and Ambrie were full partners and had more than their share of clients. Both were trying to persuade Amanda to finish her schooling and partner with them. So far, they had not been able to get her to see the advantage of giving up her job as Ambrielle's assistant to work full-time as an advisor.

Ambrie's office was large enough to give clients the idea that she was successful—which she was—but small enough to make them feel very comfortable. There were several very large potted plants growing near the huge bay windows. She loved plants, and they grew with extraordinary zest in her office due to the light and care she gave them. She talked to them often, mostly about her clients.

Ambrielle really liked the people who came to her for help—at least the majority of them. She enjoyed turning their finances around for them and helping them plan for their futures.

"Computer needs to go off," Amanda reminded her firmly. "Seriously, you have to have some fun. Did you turn down that hot ballplayer that asked you out on a date? He was absolutely gorgeous."

Ambrielle laughed as she obediently shut down the computer and turned to face her assistant. "He is very aware of how hot and gorgeous he is, Amanda. I have one small mirror in the office, and he spent nearly the entire time he was in here not paying attention to anything I said regarding his future with his money but staring at himself. He winked several times at himself and made a kissy face once. He even did the muscle thing. I had to call his attention back to his finances several times. It was all I could do to keep from laughing. He had the attention span of a teenager."

"Umm, Ambrie, you aren't going out with him for his scintillating conversation or his brains. You were supposed to be after his body."

Ambrie widened her eyes, striving to look innocent. "I was? You failed to instruct me properly. I blame you."

Amanda rolled her eyes. "There's no hope for you. How am I ever going to get you to let your hair down and just plain have fun if you couldn't even go for the hottie ballplayer? Do you know how many women would have given anything to be in your shoes?"

"Why, yes, Amanda, I do." Ambrielle leaned forward, putting her elbow on her thigh and her chin in the heel of her hand. "I know because Mr. Hottie Ballplayer informed me several times that he wasn't going to wait around for me when there were a good million women eager to take him up on his offer."

Amanda burst out laughing. "I suppose it would be difficult to sleep with someone who thought so much of themselves. But he calls you three times a day."

"Because I'm such a hottie," Ambrie replied with a straight face.

Amanda just laughed harder. "Actually, you are, you just refuse to see it. You never even notice the way men ogle you."

Ambrielle sat back in her chair, legs stretched out. "Really, Amanda? Like they do you? With my long legs that go on forever? And my model's body?" She indicated her short legs, curvy hips and generous breasts, which were there no matter how hard or often she worked out and how careful she was of what she ate. "My lovely hair that will turn into a mass of frizz the moment there's any kind of moisture in the air? I suppose there're a lot of things men might admire about me." She laughed again at the sheer absurdity of her assistant's observation.

Amanda gave a little sniff of indignation. "Go ahead and ignore the fact that you're beautiful and extremely intelligent. Men like curves and brains."

"Intelligence scares the crap out of men."

"Some men, yes," Amanda agreed, "but not all men. The ones that count want a woman who can keep up."

Ambrielle flashed her mischievous smile. "Keep up? Is that what I'm supposed to do? You should have told me that. I usually bury them with my quick thinking, and they run for the hills. And that's before I get the chance to tell them about my background."

Amanda groaned and ran her fingers through her artfully styled and perfectly straight hair. "I give up on you, Ambrie. Really. You sabotage yourself before you even get started dating. Although . . ." She perked up. "My brother wants me to introduce you to him. He's already madly in love, he says. You saved him thousands of dollars with that last tip you gave us. Me. Him. The both of us."

Ambrielle frowned. "What tip? I don't remember giving your brother a tip. I've never even met him."

"Remember, I told you, Adam and I both invested heavily in stocks a couple of years ago. Recently I asked your opinion on whether or not you thought we should keep them. You said absolutely not, and to get rid of them fast. Like yesterday. To sell while they were at premium. And you told me what you would invest in. I told my brother, and he argued with me for about an hour, but in the end, we sold the stock, made a mint and reinvested it in what you suggested. Overnight we nearly doubled our money. The stock we had formerly owned began dropping in value. It keeps going down. We would have lost everything. Adam says he wants to meet you for drinks or take you out for dinner. Something to say thank you."

Ambrielle gave a little shake of her head. "You're practically family, Amanda. I had a hunch that stock was going to drop in value. It had been riding too high, and the market was getting shaky. If you hadn't asked me, I wouldn't have even known you had it. Your brother should take *you* out to dinner."

Amanda tilted her head. "He has no choice. I'm his baby sister. He must take me to dinner frequently or I whine. He despises me whining at him, so I get a free meal a couple of times a month. It's nice. I can catch up with him on what he's doing and who he's dating and feel like we're still close."

"You *are* close," Ambrie pointed out.

She'd always envied the fact that Amanda and Adam had such a good relationship. She had no siblings. Both of her parents had been in the military and were often away. She had a peculiar childhood, although not one she resented.

She'd met Amanda in college, and they'd formed a fast friendship, rooming together when neither one needed to do so, eventually getting an apartment together off campus. Later, when Ambrielle opened her own business, she asked Amanda to work for her. Amanda was still working toward her master's, but she certainly could take on clients if she wanted to do so and had filled in for Ambrie when it was absolutely necessary, but she preferred to remain as Ambrielle's assistant for as long as possible. She said she learned more by watching.

They both had met Daniel Parker in college and included him in their study group. He was impressive with his skills and work ethic. When Ambrielle could see there was going to be far too much work for one person, and Amanda was adamant she wasn't ready to come in as a partner, Ambrie asked Dan if he'd like to join her. Fortunately, he fit right in.

"We are," Amanda conceded. "But Adam is overbearing sometimes and drives me crazy when he tells me what to do. He's good at investments, Ambrie, but he doesn't have your intuition. I've told him that, but for some reason, he just has to argue with me every single time we have a conversation about what we're going to do with our money. I told him I'd pull my shares out of our joint ventures and invest the way I want on my own, but he just laughs at me and says there's no need for that. In the end he always goes with what you've suggested, even with his own money."

Ambrie tilted her head, allowing her dark hair to slide over her shoulder in a series of thick curls and waves. "He's deliberately trying to get a rise out of you, Amanda, and you're falling for it every time."

Amanda made a face. "I know. I can't help it. He's my big brother and I think he programmed me. Come on, if we don't leave now, a client is bound to call, and we'll get stuck here. I really want to go out tonight. Besides, if we don't get to the bar, Dan is going to think we stood him up." She hesitated and then shrugged. "I've just got to ask. I know you go out sometimes, Ambrie, but you're never really that interested. Why? Who are you looking for? Or should I say *what* are you looking for?"

Ambrielle smiled at her, hearing the unasked question. "My parents had a very unusual love affair, and I guess I'm looking for that same thing. I don't know. My mother says I'm like she was before she met my father. She wasn't attracted to very many men, and when she was, it was mild and didn't last beyond the first conversation. That always happens with me. She said when she laid eyes on my father, everything changed. She couldn't think of anything or anyone else and was so attracted she was willing to have sex with him within practically the first five minutes after they met, and that never changed. They barely knew one another, and he had to leave the country, so they got married. She just knew he was right for her, and they'd work it out. She said she was never sorry. I hope she's right and someday I'll run into someone who would make me willing to run off with him in a heartbeat."

"That's crazy. Your mother took a huge chance on a stranger."

Ambrielle nodded. "They're very intense about each other." She looked Amanda over, really noticing what she was wearing and how meticulous her hair and makeup were. "You're dressed for a killer night. Just who do you have your sights on, Amanda?"

Amanda did a slow spin to show off the clever way her dress draped her body, showing her figure to the best advantage without giving everything away. Then she took a step, and the slit up her left thigh opened to reveal her long, slender leg, an enticement that disappeared with her next step.

"Very nice," Ambrielle approved. "Where do you find your clothes? I swear, no one but you has anything that can look that casual, elegant and sexy all at the same time."

Amanda looked pleased. "I am so going after Marcus Phillips."

Ambrie paused in the act of walking across the office toward the door. "Marcus? Cold-fish Marcus? You dubbed him that two minutes after he acquired the entire upstairs as his offices and wouldn't deign to look at either of us when we said good morning to him on the elevator ride up to our floor."

"Yep. That's the one." Amanda looked smug. "I've already started my campaign, he just doesn't know he's in my sights yet." She laughed and indicated the door. "Women throw themselves at him. He's rich, powerful, good-looking and seems very arrogant, which draws a lot of idiot women."

"Apparently you too," Ambrie pointed out.

Amanda shook her head. "I didn't even give him a thought until about two months ago. He really isn't at all the way he seems."

Ambrie took her hand off the door. There was real interest in Amanda's voice. "You don't intend to drop him like a hot potato. You're really interested in Marcus."

Amanda nodded slowly. "I've been watching him carefully for a while now. I know that makes me sound like a stalker, but he did something really nice and seemingly completely out of character and I wanted to know which was the real Marcus." She lifted her chin, color staining her cheeks. "So I started watching him. Under his cold-fish façade, he's really a sweet man."

Ambrielle leaned against the door. "What really nice something did he do, Amanda?"

Amanda sighed, the color going from a deep pink to an actual red in her cheeks. "I was really embarrassed at first, so I didn't tell you, and then I realized I was kind of obsessing over him and that made it worse. I didn't want to admit that to you either, so I kept it to myself."

Ambrie lifted her eyebrow and continued draping herself against the door so Amanda couldn't escape.

"Fine. Do you remember a couple of months ago when it was really storming outside, and I came in looking like a drowned rat? I came into the office in my stockings because I'd broken the heel off one of my shoes?"

Ambrielle nodded when Amanda didn't proceed right away.

"I slipped in a huge puddle of water. I was running about half a block from here, carrying my books and a load of papers. I'd been at the coffee shop studying and forgot the time. I didn't exactly slip. I wasn't watching where I was going. There's a big grate where the water is supposed to drain off the road, but there was so much water, it was covered, and I didn't really see it. My heel got caught and snapped right off. I went down very hard. Not only was the fall utterly humiliating, but it hurt like hell. And my books and papers went everywhere. To make matters worse, I burst into tears."

"Oh, honey," Ambrie whispered, taking a step toward her. Amanda didn't cry easily.

"I was going to call you, but my hand hurt so bad and was shaking. I dropped my cell in the puddle. A car went by at that exact moment, which sent a wave of water pouring over me, and that made it seem so much worse. I just sat in that puddle and cried. To my absolute horror, the car pulled to the curb right in front of me and Marcus got out of the back seat. His chauffeur began to gather up my soaking-wet books and papers, and Marcus crouched down beside me and asked me if I was hurt. If I had broken anything. When I kept crying, because I was so humiliated, he wiped my tears with his hand, and he was so gentle you wouldn't believe it. He asked me again. I shook my head. When I did, he caught me around the waist, lifted me right out of the puddle, set me on the sidewalk and crouched down again to examine my ankle."

Ambrielle was shocked to think of Marcus Phillips crouching down on a sidewalk in the middle of a rainstorm examining anyone's ankle. It seemed so out of character.

"What did he do then?"

"He helped me to the car, and then he went back to help the chauffeur gather up the rest of my things. The chauffeur came up with a towel from the trunk and handed it to him. He gave it to me, and when I tried to thank him for helping me, he brushed it off like it was nothing. He was really gruff about it, like he didn't want me to know he was kind. I was too embarrassed and knew my face was red and blotchy, so I acted like an idiot and hid it in the towel. He helped me out of the car once we got to the parking garage and private elevator."

"By the look on your face, I would think he carried you," Ambrie teased.

"Very funny. He did ask me if I had dry clothes to change

into. I was shivering. I assured him I had other clothes in the office, just not shoes. I tried to make it a joke, but I failed and started crying. At least I didn't cry ugly, just silent. I didn't think he noticed because I turned away. Someone got in the elevator, and I put my hand over my face. Marcus moved so that his body was in front of mine, kind of trapping me in the corner so no one could see me. The other person got off on our floor, so they work in one of the other offices. I changed, refreshed my makeup and sat at my desk. The next thing I knew, the most beautiful pair of high heels was delivered to me, compliments of Marcus Phillips."

"You're kidding."

Amanda shook her head. "Not just any shoes, Ambrie— he has really good taste. They were Jimmy Choos. Gorgeous. Of course, I couldn't accept them, as much as I wanted them. I wrote a thank-you note and told him he was wonderful to help me when I was such a hot mess, but I couldn't accept such a thoughtful but far too expensive gift." She sighed. "He sent them back to me and said they weren't his size and if I didn't keep them, they would be going into the trash. I sent him another thank-you note and kept them. I adore those shoes. He didn't respond, and when I ran into him again, he simply nodded to me, so I followed his example and nodded to him. I realize women throw themselves at him. I've watched them do it, so I decided I wouldn't. I don't need or want his money."

"You only have that one example of his kindness," Ambrielle cautioned.

Amanda shook her head, a hint of color returning to her face. "Actually, that's not quite true. I told you I was watching him. Kind of like a creeper. I really am attracted to Marcus, and I didn't want to take a chance on him being in a relationship or being a real jerk with just that one thing. I have a pretty sizable trust fund, as you well know." She indicated the door. "We can walk and talk at the same time. We're already late."

Ambrielle obliged her. "I already called us a cab. It's waiting for us. Tell me what you've done."

"I hired a PI. Just to make sure." Amanda made her confession in a rush. "I know if he finds out he'll never forgive me, but I'm not going to repeat history."

Ambrielle couldn't blame her. Amanda had fallen hard for a man in her first year of college. He seemed like a really great person. Ambrielle couldn't quite like him, but that didn't bother her. She felt she wasn't the best judge of men. From the beginning, Geoff had been just a little too smooth and charming for her liking. Ambrie wasn't in the least attracted to that type of man. For Amanda, who was far more sophisticated, Geoff seemed perfect. He liked everything Amanda liked. They were the perfect couple, going to the theater and hitting the galleries looking so beautiful together.

That had all fallen apart when Amanda's brother had done a background check on Geoff and found out all kinds of interesting things about him, starting with the fact that he wasn't who he claimed to be. He was a con artist who was twenty years older than he was pretending to be. His name was Clarence Vaughn. He had no intentions of doing anything but robbing Amanda of every cent she had and then moving on.

Amanda was heartbroken and embarrassed. After that, she never dated seriously. Never. She didn't trust anyone, and Ambrie didn't blame her. The fact that she was interested in Marcus Phillips, so much so that she'd hired a private investigator to check him out, was a little shocking.

"Have you told Adam you're interested in Marcus?" Ambrie asked as she slid into the back seat of the cab.

Amanda gave the address of the bar and then shook her head. "Not until I know for certain he's interested in me. So far, he hasn't been. Sometimes he goes to this bar after work. That's the reason I told Dan to meet us there tonight. We both like it and go there, so Marcus isn't going to think I'm following him around. If he doesn't at least acknowledge me tonight, then I'm giving up on him. I'll chalk it up to him just being nice because I fell on my butt."

Ambrielle waited because Amanda continued to tap her fingers up and down her thigh. She had something else to say but clearly didn't think Ambrie was going to take it too well. Amanda remained silent all the way to the bar, a record holdout for her. Ambrie paid for the cab, adding a generous tip for waiting so long. She sighed as they fell into step together easily, making their way to the front entrance.

The bar was modern, encased in thick glass in order to extend the interior outside into the heavily and very beautifully landscaped patios. Fountains, smaller bars and mood lights added to the lacy green shrubbery and trees that hid spaces for either larger or smaller groups. The dance floor was inside with the main bar. Four, sometimes up to six, bartenders worked quickly and efficiently to attend to their clients. The DJs were always the best.

"Just tell me, Amanda."

"I asked Adam to come and meet you tonight," Amanda said in a little rush, not looking at her but trying to make it to the door before Ambrie could reply.

Ambrielle tried not to laugh. "As in a blind date? You set that poor brother of yours up with me on a blind date?"

"Not a date exactly. Just more like a get-together. To meet you. He's mentioned meeting you a thousand times. I'm just making it happen finally." Amanda smiled at the doorman and flashed her ID. He opened the door for them as Ambrie showed hers.

The music seemed to blast until their hearing adjusted. Ambrie spotted Dan immediately and waved to him. He had commandeered a table and was sitting with his wife, Lacy.

Amanda spotted her brother sitting at the bar. She clutched Ambrie's arm. "Adam's sitting at the end of the bar, right next to the table where Marcus and his friends are."

Ambrielle shook her head. "You have all the luck. You can order our drinks. You know what I like. I'll go keep Dan and Lacy company." She made her way over to the couple.

"Happy birthday, Dan. Lacy, it's so good to see you." She hadn't seen Dan's wife in weeks. That wasn't a good thing. She really needed to be better about having a life.

Dan leaned over and brushed a kiss on her cheek. "You work too hard, Ambrie. Lacy was just telling me we need to have you over for dinner. I told her you wouldn't come."

"I would too. I might work late, but I do have to eat."

Adam came over with Amanda, balancing more drinks, and they sat down, Amanda obviously very proud of her brother as she introduced him to the others. Ambrie found it very interesting that Amanda didn't sit in a chair where she would face the table where Marcus sat. She had her back to him and appeared to forget he was even in the same room.

Dan danced with Lacy. Adam danced with Amanda and Ambrie several times. He was a wonderful dancer. Ambrielle found she very much enjoyed the evening out. Dan and Lacy eventually called it an evening. As they left the table, Ambrie caught sight of Marcus making his way toward their table.

"Heads-up, girlfriend," she whispered, trying to warn Amanda.

Marcus bent his head low. "Would you care to dance, Amanda?"

She turned her head, so her lips were close to his ear. "I'd love that. Thank you." She took his hand and allowed him to help her from her chair.

Ambrie watched them cross the very crowded room to the dance floor. At no time did Marcus allow anyone to bump into Amanda. "She's amazing."

"She is," Adam agreed. "And she deserves the best. Thank you for being such a good friend to her." He took his eyes off his sister and studied Ambrie.

She gave him her full attention. He'd been as interesting, amusing and intelligent as Amanda, yet she hadn't been the least bit physically attracted to him. Her luck. She also knew he wasn't the least bit attracted to her.

"I have a partner," Adam announced. "We've been

together for well over a year, and he moved in with me four months ago. His name is Rashad Perry. When I say he moved in with me, he has an apartment in my building. We both have one on the same floor. He spends most of his time in my apartment, or I'm in his."

"You're talking about Rashad Perry, the singer for the Troubled Sons."

"That would be my Rashad," Adam confirmed, taking a drink of his scotch. He did so not taking his eyes off her, waiting for her reaction.

"And you haven't told Amanda because . . . ?" she prompted.

"I've tried to tell Amanda, but she doesn't want to hear me. There's a clause our father put in our trust fund. He knew I was gay, although he despised that I was. If I didn't live with another man, the money in the trust fund was shared. The moment I moved in with a man, I forfeited my share to Amanda and didn't receive any further benefits. I turned over the money to her a long time ago. I act like it's shared because she would never have it any other way, but that money is hers. When it came to running his company, Dad knew Amanda wasn't going to do it, so he put me in charge with no provisions. We both own the lion's share of the stock, so there is no way I can be ousted as president, even if the news comes out and some of the stockholders take exception in the same way my father did."

"Your father knew Amanda would never sell her share of stock in the company to anyone else," Ambrie confirmed. "She's completely loyal to you."

Adam nodded. "And she'd be royally pissed if she knew I wasn't getting money from the trust. She's like that. She'd just turn around and sign over the shares back to me. That's how she is. She doesn't like that side of things. I was surprised when she took business in college. She's got the head for it, but she doesn't like it. It isn't her dream."

"She did it to be able to stay close to you, Adam," Ambrie

said. "She looks up to you and would do just about anything for you."

He sighed. "Then why won't she let me tell her about the one other really important person in my life?"

"Because it will change everything between you," Ambrielle said as gently as she could. "She knows when you find someone, she isn't going to be number one anymore. That's just the way it works. And right now, when she feels shredded, she needs to feel like she's your number one priority. She's getting stronger. She'll come around. She knew you weren't going to sweep me off my feet. She just wanted you to check out Marcus, and she wanted me here in case he didn't take the bait. She's been trying to get his attention for a little while."

"Are you kidding me? He didn't notice her?" Adam was annoyed on his sister's behalf. "He's not nearly as bright as I thought he'd be."

"He noticed her. They're both doing some kind of silly dance, circling around, making certain the other one is really interested." Ambrielle shook her head and flashed Adam a little smirk. "That's why I steer clear of such foolishness. By the way, did you do a background check on Rashad?"

Adam nodded. "Of course I did. I told him I was going to do it. He didn't like it, but I told him I'd be giving up a great deal of money for him. It didn't matter to me, but he didn't need to know that. The bottom line is, we both have something to lose. We're taking it slow, one day at a time. I want Amanda to meet him, to come to dinner. I was hoping you could get her to do that soon."

"She loves dinners with you." Her cell phone vibrated for the third time, making it impossible to ignore. With a sigh, Ambrie palmed it.

"She always makes certain we meet at a restaurant. We have to eat in."

Ambrie glanced down at the text message from Charles

Dobbs, her father's best friend and the family lawyer. He wondered if it was possible for her to come by her parents' house even though it was so late. They were putting together some papers and were anxious to get them signed. It wasn't unusual for Dobbs to be drawing up papers at all hours of the night for her parents because her mother, Marcy Moore, sold her patents on a regular basis, making far too much money. She invented interesting little tools that made a mint. Her parents kept odd hours, and she had no problem keeping those odd hours with them. She texted that she'd be dropping by in the next half hour.

"I have to go, Adam."

"Wait. Haven't you noticed my sister didn't come back? She's with Phillips at a private table. I've been keeping my eye on them. You have to stay. You can't leave me here alone; it'll look like I'm spying on them."

"This gives me the excuse to drag Amanda to dinner at your house. You set it up and I'll get her there." She called for a cab, and they both made their way to Amanda and Marcus' table.

"I'm sorry, Amanda," Ambrielle said after introductions were made. "I have to go."

"I can make certain she gets home safe," Marcus volunteered immediately before Adam could say anything.

"You certain?" Adam asked. "Amanda, you okay with that arrangement? Otherwise, I can stay for another half an hour."

"I'm comfortable with it," Amanda assured him and kissed her brother on the cheek.

~

Ambrielle tossed her gloves onto the small table next to the coatrack by the front door of her parents' home. She almost called out to them, but her father always hated her doing that. He'd been telling her since she was a little child she needed to act with more decorum. She couldn't help smiling thinking about her father, with his perfect posture and firm-spoken commands.

He'd been certain he would have sons. At least four of them. He told her all the time. Every chance he got. The corners of his eyes would crinkle, and his face would get soft. She could see the love for her there because he never bothered to hide it. Then he'd say, four sons would never add up to his little fairy princess. He'd roar with laughter when he'd say it. She was five foot two, and there was no princess in her. Sometimes he'd call her a sprite. Sprites could be mischievous and even mean.

Her mother would gently correct him and say naughty, not mean. Ambrie knew she could be mean. She detested bullies, and she ran into them quite often. Being female, five foot two and having more than generous curves although she worked out like a crazy person—including running, which in her opinion was for nutters—she ran into more than her fair share of bullies. Fortunately, she was born with a very large brain, and her parents had insisted from the time she was a very young child that she use it. They gave her every opportunity for an education, sending her to the best schools or providing the best tutors when they moved from place to place. They also insisted she learn how to handle weapons—in the plural.

She walked down the hallway to the cozy sitting room her parents insisted on calling their library. They loved to read and had instilled that love in her. The moment she stepped into the room, she realized they weren't alone, and the tension inside could be cut with a knife.

There were six men in the room with her parents, all standing, all wearing suits, and others scattered around the house. They didn't give off a warm, friendly vibe. She could tell immediately they weren't military. Her mother's face was pale. Her father looked as if he wanted to whip out a gun and clear the room. Instead, the hand that was lying loosely on top of the arm of his chair lifted a scant inch, and he waved her off.

She hovered in the doorway, one foot already moving back. "I'm sorry, Dad. I had no idea you had company. I can come back later." She took a step back and blew a kiss to her mother.

"Stay, Ambrielle," one of the men protested. His voice was deep. Amused. "We were waiting for you. Dobbs sent for you, right?"

She had taken a second step back when four of the men followed her into the hall, two moving behind her in order to halt her progress. She frowned at them. Charles Dobbs *had* sent for her. She had the text message from him in her phone. Was it real?

"What is this?" One of the men glided close to her as if he might grab her arm. She gave him her haughtiest look. "Don't even think about touching me. Dad? What's going on?"

"Your father was just discussing how he was going to give you a huge present on your wedding day, Ambrielle. Come back into the room."

She glared at the pushiest of the men. He towered over her and smirked when she glared at him, making a show of pulling his suit jacket back so she could see his gun. She rolled her eyes, unimpressed, but deep inside, tension coiled as she returned to the sitting room. She started to go to her parents, but the man in charge caught her arm and brought her to a halt.

"I'm Walker Thompson." He said it as if she should know his name. He was medium height, which meant he still had several inches on her. His hair was brown, the same as his eyes. He appeared to be around forty. He was fit and carried himself as if he was used to everyone deferring to him.

Thompson had several bodyguards surrounding him. Those men were concerned with Thompson. The other four men were concerned with her parents—and her. The four appraising her and her parents looked to be hard, made of stone. The one closest to her clearly was the one in charge of the other three. He was the one that gave off the most dangerous vibe.

Ambrielle looked at her parents and then back at Thompson. "Have I done business with you? I'm sorry, I honestly don't remember you."

"That's too bad, sweetheart, because you should always remember the man you're going to marry."

She stared at him, laughter bubbling up. She was absolutely certain she'd never met him before. "I think you have the wrong woman. Maybe the wrong family. The wrong house. Dad, Mom, do you know this joker? Because this has to be some kind of joke."

"I assure you, sweetheart, this is no joke. You came to my casino with your parents a few months ago. You were celebrating another big sale your mother made. Toasting her. Laughing. You have a beautiful laugh, Ambrielle. It was difficult not to notice you. I made it my business to find out everything I could about you, and luckily, you fit right in to everything I need for my bride. I was just negotiating with your parents how big your dowry will be."

"I don't have a dowry, and we aren't getting married."

"Ambrielle, sweetheart. Your parents have a choice to make. Sign over their very vast fortune to you right now, or I put a bullet in your father's head. Then I have your mother sign the paper anyway. You marry me and make certain that fortune continues to grow the way you've been doing for your parents, only you do it for us, since the money will all be yours and you'll sign it over to me. If you do that, your parents remain safe."

Thompson looked at her father. "I believe your signature is required on the papers I've had drawn up."

Her father shook his head. "This is ludicrous. I don't know what Dobbs told you, but he lied. Even if I signed these papers, they wouldn't do you any good."

"Who are you?" Ambrielle asked, staring at Thompson, trying to place him. He wasn't making any sense. "Yes, I was at a casino in New Orleans celebrating with my parents a few months back, but I don't understand what you mean by this." They'd been on a riverboat casino. It had been a tremendous amount of fun. "I've never met you. Why would I want to marry a perfect stranger? And Dad's right. Why would Dobbs tell you that signing those papers would matter when—"

"Enough." Walker Thompson smiled. She'd never seen any smile so cruel. "Gleb. If you or Denis would be so kind." Thompson nodded his head toward her father.

She turned to look at the man who had been in the hallway with her earlier, the one she'd marked immediately as the most dangerous. He had a gun out, the one he'd shown her. Instinctively, she knew what he was going to do.

Ambrielle hurtled her body in front of her father, or at least she tried to. Two men caught her firmly, holding her while she fought like a wild animal to get loose as the man called Gleb pulled the trigger once. She made no sound as her father slumped over, quiet in his death, blood on his chair and running down his face to soak into his shirt. She stilled. Her mother very gently placed her hand on her husband's arm.

Ambrielle's eyes met her mother's, and then she raised her gaze to meet the shooter's. He was a big man. Blond. He was all hard angles and planes. His eyes were a light blue, almost crystal. She memorized every inch of his face. The way he moved. The way he held himself.

Gleb shook his head. "Don't." He warned her softly. Even with just one word she could hear a slight accent—Russian, if she wasn't mistaken.

She hadn't said a word. She didn't need to. He'd read everything in her eyes. If she lived through this night, she would hunt him down and kill him. Nothing would stop her. Nothing. No matter how long it took. She would find him.

The men holding her were strong, and they had her in a viselike grip. They wouldn't keep that grip tight for very long. They would buy into the fact that she was a woman, and she was small. They would think she was cowed, defeated. She just had to keep her mouth shut. Gleb wasn't buying what she was selling, but the others, they would. And Walker Thompson would. He was too arrogant to even realize he had four cobras in his very own entourage. Those four Russians might look like they took his orders, but they would kill him in a second if it suited them.

"Mrs. Moore, I believe you need to sign the papers giving the money to your daughter for her wedding present."

"Wait, Mom," Ambrielle interrupted. It was pure bullshit signing the papers. The money was already hers. She didn't want her mother to tell Thompson that. He clearly hadn't done his homework. Dobbs hadn't told him the truth. What his reasoning was, she didn't know, but at least she had the chance to keep her mother alive. "Give me your word that if she signs the money over to me, you won't allow anyone to kill her. You won't kill her. You'll keep her alive."

"You're not in any position to bargain, sweetheart," Thompson said. "Although it's cute that you think you are."

She detested him. He was looking at her size and thinking she was a child and already he could do and say whatever he wanted.

"If she's alive, then clearly I have incentive to make as much money as possible for you," Ambrie pointed out, trying to sound reasonable instead of sounding like she thought he was an imbecile. He was. She was going to cut his throat at the first opportunity. She didn't dare look at Gleb because he knew she was going to do it. The interesting thing was, he didn't care.

"There are all sorts of incentives for you to obey me, dear little Ambrielle, but yes, if she signs the papers, she won't be killed. Do get it over with, Mrs. Moore. I'm running out of patience."

"These papers aren't worth—"

"Mom, just sign them," Ambrie interrupted. "He wants them signed; just do it."

Marcy Moore looked at her daughter and then to her

husband. Her palm stroked down his arm, the pen between her fingers as steady as a rock. Her gaze flicked from her husband to Walker Thompson and then Ambrie.

Ambrie felt the protest welling up as Gleb shifted position. Time slowed down. Tunneled. She centered her attention on Gleb. He was the killer in the room. Walker Thompson thought he was the boss and safe. He was surrounded by bodyguards, but the only four that really mattered were Gleb; his partner, Denis; and the other two men standing just out of her reach. They were the real deal when it came to murder. She could see they were fast, efficient and meant business. They weren't messy, and there was no hesitation. These were men who killed for a living.

"Don't," she hissed to Gleb. "You touch her, and I swear you're a dead man. I mean it. You touch her, you're dead. It will be you or me leaving this room alive. I swear that on my father's soul."

The big Russian shook his head. "I'm not going to kill her. You heard Thompson. She just must sign the papers. The money will be yours, and you can marry Thompson. All will be well. What happens after that is anyone's guess." He exchanged an amused look with the other Russians.

"Ambrie." Marcy Moore spoke her name softly, lovingly.

Ambrie shook her head. "Mom. Please. Just sign. It doesn't matter. He doesn't matter. What he wants doesn't matter. I need you. Just please don't do this. Sign them for me. Do it for me."

"I am doing this for you. So he can't control you. You are not a puppet, Ambrie. You will never be a puppet for anyone." There was no inflection in Marcy's quiet voice. Her palm was still laid gently over her dead husband's arm. The pen was in her other hand, poised over the papers. "Remember every single thing we ever said to you, Ambrie, because each word mattered and was told to you with love."

"Mom." Ambrie whispered her name in despair. Her mother was a strong woman. Once she made up her mind, there was no changing it. She despised men like Thompson. She loved her husband and daughter fiercely.

Ambrie took a deep breath and selected her own target. If her mother was sacrificing her life, then she would do the same. The Moore women were going down in a blaze of glory. Whatever plans Walker Thompson had for her, Ambrielle wasn't about to comply. Her mother gripped the pen in one hand, and her gaze slid to Thompson, who had stepped close to watch her sign the papers.

Ambrie knew she couldn't get to Gleb, but she could get to one of his men. The Russian on her left had taken his gaze from her, alert to her mother, watching with slight amusement as she suddenly struck at Thompson, the pen going from the paper as if she were about to sign, up toward his neck. His bodyguard yanked Thompson back so that he staggered, but Marcy Moore threw herself forward, the pen embedding itself in the bodyguard's neck deep, right into the artery.

At the same time, Ambrie spun out of the hands of the Russian holding her captive and attacked one of Thompson's bodyguards watching, using the same method as her mother had done, only she had weapons: two small knives she'd hidden in her sleeve. No one had thought to search her. She buried one deep with a hard flick of her wrist, throwing it accurately and then spinning to throw the second one at another guard standing in front of Thompson, killing one guard and wounding the other. The goal was to take down anyone standing between them. To get to Thompson. His guards were trying to hustle him out of the room.

Marcy continued her forward assault as well, hand-to-hand combat, sweeping the legs out from under another bodyguard. Thompson shot her multiple times, emptying his weapon into her, all the while yelling at his men to take Ambrie down.

It was Gleb and his partner, Denis, who managed to take her legs out from under her so she hit the floor hard, landing in the river of her mother's blood, staring into her wide-open eyes. Gleb kept his knee hard in the small of her back as he did so. She didn't move or speak, but watched the life go out of her mother.

"You're coming home with me. Your clothes are already packed. The license is in place, and we've got a very willing pastor to perform the ceremony, so it will be in a fucking church. How do you like that, Ambrielle?" Walker Thompson laughed as he led the way out of her parents' home.

Gleb and Denis had to carry her because when they forced her to stand, she erupted into kicking and fighting. When she started screaming, they injected her with something that made her world turn black.

THREE

The Torpedo Ink clubhouse was usually a place of comfort for Master, a sign of freedom and brotherhood, even if at times he did feel apart from the others. He knew his brothers and sisters accepted him, whether he thought they knew him or not. To those in the club, he was one of them, and they would fight to the death for him. That was how deep their loyalty ran. He felt the same way about them.

The clubhouse was very large and overlooked the ocean. The sound of the waves breaking against sea-stacks and the bluffs was a constant melody that never faded into the background, not even when they held one of their important meetings. Czar had called them together, and fortunately, the room was spacious, a good thing after Master had spent far too much time in the small prison cell feeling as if he were unable to breathe. He still felt that way.

He was a big man, and sometimes—especially after he'd been incarcerated—he could barely stand to be inside four walls no matter how sizable the space was. The large windows facing the ocean and the crashing waves helped to create the illusion of being outside, but he still felt as if he couldn't get a decent lungful of air, especially when every one of his brothers and sisters arrived and took a seat around the large oval-shaped table.

Czar opened the meeting immediately, not waiting for them to finish their usual bantering with one another, which Master was grateful for. He didn't ever feel like talking with anyone when he first got out. He needed to be alone and get back under control. He was two people, and he needed to lock this one away. The one kept behind those prison bars wasn't fit company for anyone anymore, not even his brethren. He knew this meeting was important or he wouldn't have come.

Absinthe seated himself in the chair beside him. Master was very aware Absinthe knew him better than any of his brothers. If anyone truly saw inside him, it was Absinthe. He could hear lies. He could compel the truth. Absinthe could be a very dangerous man to anyone outside the club, but he was protective of anyone inside it. Right now, he was declaring silently that he was protecting Master should he need it. It wasn't as if Master needed the protection for himself—it was more that Absinthe knew Master needed a shield standing in front of him to keep the others safe until he could put the beast he became in that prison away, shove him out of sight where no one could see him and no one could be in danger.

Master sat quietly, inhaling and exhaling, watching his brothers take their seats, studying their faces. Czar was stressed, an unusual situation for the president of their club. They all were. Even Steele, their vice president, had those lines carved deeper than usual. No one had ever threatened a family of Torpedo Ink before—the entire family.

They were actively hunting the Ghosts, a group of assassins out of Russia from the same schools they had been trained in, but whoever was threatening Czar wasn't after him because of that. The woman was connected to the Ghosts, but she had her own vendetta against him, and her payback was to take out Czar's family. Master had gotten some information, but not enough to actually find her.

This was a first for them. They were used to being hunted.

They hadn't exactly had conventional childhoods. But once they had settled in Sea Haven, no one had ever threatened their families, certainly not Czar's. Blythe and his children were sacred. The heart of the club.

"As always when Master goes undercover for us, he comes back with something. In this case, we have a name," Czar said without preamble. "As you know, there was an attack on my family. At least the idiots tried to attack my wife and children."

Master had been there when the assassination team had come to Czar's home. His children were already in bed. Blythe was in the sitting room with Master, Czar, Savage and Maestro. The others had already gone home after an evening of watching movies and just hanging out with the kids as they often did. The first shot hit the window right where Blythe's head was. Fortunately, Czar was a man who never took chances with his family, and that window was made of bulletproof glass. Nevertheless, he tackled his wife hard, taking her to the ground while the other three Torpedo Ink members rushed out into the night to find the would-be assassins.

They found evidence of one of the assassins attempting to climb up to the second story, but again, Czar had circumvented that possibility by embedding tiny nails every so many inches up the walls of his home. It was a simple enough trick, and in the brick, there were many sharp objects inserted as well. They knew where they were and how to climb fast, if need be, but anyone attempting to break in would have a difficult time.

The assassins had realized quickly that it was useless to try when they'd been discovered and were now hunted. They'd made a run for it and had already chosen a clear escape route. They'd left behind blood from various scrapes. Preacher was their scientist, and he had no problem eventually identifying, with Code's help, one of the members of the assassination team. It was quite the shock to find out the man was in prison and had been for several years.

"A woman by the name of Helena Smirnov sent the team after my family. She originates from Russia, and she works for the man we've been trying to identify, the one we know runs the largest pedophile ring we've come across. She recruits his assassination squads for him. All those men are pulled from the Russian schools. Like us, they were trained in the schools and have various levels of skills in killing."

Steele held up his hand. "I'm not sure I have this straight. She's recruiting assassins? She isn't the actual head of them?"

Czar frowned and shook his head. "Those squads are the ones referred to as 'the Ghosts.' They are privately contracted out to work for whoever wants to hire them and can afford them. They have 'security companies' in several different cities across the United States. These men are all Russian and are lethal. Helena knows them and actively goes after them to get them to work for the Ghost Security Company. In other words, for her boss in Russia."

"So he's aware of us now," Reaper, one of the sergeants at arms and Czar's top enforcer, stated. "He knows our club is after him?"

The club members looked at Master. Master detested the spotlight. He shrugged and looked to Absinthe.

"Master doesn't really know the answer to that. Helena ran two teams of assassins that were strictly under her control. They had nothing to do with her boss. It appears on the surface as if she didn't tell her boss about Czar and Torpedo Ink. She continually referred to him as Viktor Prakenskii. Those two teams were recruited for her own use. Master eliminated one of those teams in prison. We know Helena found out about Viktor when she was frequenting the De Sade club in San Francisco. She tried to hypnotize various members of Torpedo Ink to get information about Czar, but no one was susceptible enough to give it to her."

Lana, one of the two women who had managed to survive the school, shifted in her seat uncomfortably. "She planted a suggestion in me, Absinthe. I made Seychelle's life pretty miserable for a while. If it hadn't been for

Seychelle, we wouldn't have even known that Czar and his family were targeted. She's the one who managed to remove the suggestion."

"You didn't give her any information," Absinthe pointed out.

"Still." Lana looked ashamed. She flashed a quick glance at Savage.

Seychelle was his woman, the love of his life. Everyone knew it. Seychelle wasn't that enamored with the club. She didn't trust the members yet, and no one could blame her. She always came through for them when they needed her, but they'd treated her like an outsider even when they were using her skills. Making up for that poor beginning was going to take time. When they were at war with a hidden enemy, time wasn't always a gift they had.

"We have no idea why this woman wants my family and me dead. She had opportunities to kill other members of Torpedo Ink, and she didn't take them," Czar said. "Clearly, this is a personal vendetta. I don't remember her. The man Master interrogated said Helena wasn't her original name, but he didn't know what that was. She does have a second team that's under her sole command. Along with that, we must expect that she could hire, or even simply command, any of the Ghost teams she recruited for her boss."

Steele tapped the end of a pen on the table, his eyebrows coming together as his mind tried to put the pieces together. "Master, was there any indication where the second assassination team loyal to this woman might be?"

Master shook his head. "I doubt he knew."

Czar frowned. "What kind of an answer is that? He either knew or he didn't. You should have had the time to extract the information out of him."

There was no getting back to the man he wanted to be when Czar made it so clear he preferred the beast who belonged in a cage. He flicked his dark eyes toward the president of the club just once, determined to stay in control, when he wanted to surge to his feet and turn the huge table over, dump it right on Czar and pin him to the floor. So much for loyalty. Maybe there always had to be a bottom-feeder. Too fucking bad it was him.

The roaring in his ears drowned out everything else. His heart accelerated and then slowed to a steady beat. The roaring subsided, and his vision tunneled. Marked his targets. Czar's guards, how many, who he would have to take down first in order to get to the man.

"I don't know what the fuck is wrong with me. I'm sorry, man." Czar scrubbed his hand over his face. "You went into that hellhole for me and got what information you could. I know that. I'm just so damned scared for Blythe and the kids. I've never given a shit about my own life, but Blythe? If we didn't have those windows, she'd be dead right now. I don't know how I'm going to keep her safe. But I do know I have no right taking my fears and frustration out on you, Master. Especially when you sacrificed so much for me. Believe me, man, I do appreciate it."

Master watched, with a kind of shock, as Czar rubbed his forehead with the heel of his hand. He looked around the table. The other members of Torpedo Ink were staring at Czar with the same shocked expression Master was certain he wore. Czar was their absolute rock. Absolute. He didn't ever waver. He looked . . . destroyed.

Clean air rushed through Master's lungs, driving out the burning claustrophobia that numbed him, that buried any good trait Master might have so deep he forgot he was a human being. He could look at his president in that moment with compassion. This was about Blythe. *Their* Blythe. She belonged to Torpedo Ink.

"No one can get to them," Reaper reminded Czar. "We've got them locked down tight."

Czar shoved both hands through his hair in agitation. He looked at Master, not Reaper. He waited until Master reluctantly met his eyes. Master didn't like looking directly into Czar's piercing gray gaze. That gaze could look right through you and see things better left alone.

"Blythe told me I was *never* to ask you to go back to prison. Not for any reason. That whatever information, whatever the club needed, wasn't worth what it would take from you personally."

The gray had melted into silver just as Master feared it might, but he couldn't look away. It was too late.

"She was right, wasn't she? She said she was in prison, and her cage was beautiful. She was surrounded by the people she loved. She had the freedom to go anywhere on an enormous property and visit with her sisters, and their children. But she couldn't live her life the way she wanted. Her children couldn't live their lives free either. Darby is unable to go to work or repair the damage to a relationship she clearly held dear. Blythe said if they were all miserable in such a beautiful environment, the real prison had to take pieces of your soul."

There was no hiding from that silver gaze. Czar had highly developed gifts, just as they all did. Few knew exactly what Czar could do, but they knew his gifts were powerful. Having the spotlight turned on him was uncomfortable, but it also gave Master insight into Czar. The president of the club would always have to carry a heavy responsibility with the things he knew about the human beings surrounding him. Their strengths and weaknesses—traits Czar had helped develop. Right at that moment, Czar had to see that Master didn't have a soul left, or if he did, it was black as sin.

"We'll find this woman," Steele said. "She can't hide forever. Master took out her first team. If she hid her second team in a prison, which I doubt, we have a backup in Destroyer."

Both Master and Czar looked to the nineteenth member of Torpedo Ink. Rurik Volkov, aka Destroyer. He was a big man with massive shoulders and muscular arms. He was covered in tattoos, some drifting up his neck. The tattoos were raw prison tattoos covering scars, not smooth ink work. His eyes were dark and mesmerizing. His hair was long, falling to his waist and braided in segments.

The last thing Master wanted was for Destroyer to ever go back to prison. He'd served his time in the worst prison Russia had, and he'd survived when few did. Steele had no idea what he was talking about. Master could see Czar knew Destroyer couldn't go back, but then Czar knew more about Destroyer than any of them did.

Master identified with him far too much. The two of them exchanged a long, knowing look. Destroyer knew what it was like to live inside those cages for extended periods of time. To be treated as if you weren't human until you weren't. Sometimes, often, it was kill or be killed. When he was a child, just trying to survive what the adult prisoners did to him was often the only thing left to him, and he was more animal than human for certain then.

When he was a teen, trying to survive what the adults did to him, he fought back until they nearly killed him. He wanted them to kill him. He wanted to be unconscious at least. He was never given that, but he began to hone his fighting skills, and he learned to kill with the best of them. He toned his body, built himself into a weapon, became a machine. He recognized that same cold-blooded machine in Destroyer.

There were only so many times either of them could go back and relive those times. He didn't know what happened to Destroyer in that terrible place, but he knew his own hell had started when he was just a boy. He had been seven when Sorbacov decided his fate and sent him inside, giving him to a "friend" to see what could happen to a boy trained in the way of prisons so he might be useful if he survived.

"Helena appears to be an intelligent woman," Absinthe said. "I doubt she would make such a mistake as hiding both her teams in a prison. She would want one mobile for fast deployment. This discussion is getting us nowhere. For the moment, Blythe and the children are safe, Czar. Even if they have to be in lockdown for a short while, they knew they would have to make sacrifices. We all are going to have to be extra diligent in our security. Anyone with a wife or children, you know what you have to do, whether or not they agree."

Steele nodded. "It's already done."

Master believed that. Steele didn't give his wife, Breezy, too much leash when it came to her safety, or that of their son. Zane had been kidnapped once already, and they both watched over him carefully.

The members, including Czar, looked to Savage. He gave them a shrug. "Do you think I'd take the slightest chance with Seychelle? She's in the clubhouse with Anya. The two of them are waiting for us with Soleil and Scarlet." Soleil was married to Ice and Scarlet to Absinthe. Anya was Reaper's wife.

"Player?" Czar asked. "Where's Zyah?"

"At the house with her grandmother. I've asked some of the members of our Trinity chapter to watch them while I'm here."

Czar nodded. "Then let's get down to business. We've identified one of the elusive Ghosts finally. His name is Walker Thompson, and his daddy, along with a good number of others, owns a string of casinos. Thompson and three of his friends he went to school with, all from very wealthy families, all with parents as part of the conglomerate owning the casinos, decided to do a little branching out on their own. Code can tell you more."

Master admired the way Code could handle a computer. Even as a kid, he'd had a gift for the machines. Data just seemed to flow from them straight into his brain. He was just shy of six feet, without an ounce of fat, closely cropped dark blond hair, whiskey-colored eyes, more scruff than a beard and a barely there mustache. Master wasn't positive he actually slept. He'd never witnessed it.

"Thompson and his friends are into everything. You know they're after the MCs, but I discovered they've got a hell of a human trafficking ring started. I bleed off

Thompson's money and he goes after more girls," Code reported to the members of Torpedo Ink.

Master looked around the big oval-shaped table in the large meeting room, at the grim faces that told him they all felt the same way he did about Walker Thompson.

"I just intercepted this prick's latest plot. He's decided to marry this woman." Code tossed a set of pictures on the table.

The high-resolution glossies were passed around, so everyone got one. The woman was beautiful. She looked for all the world like a fairy princess: small, lots of curves, hair that was thick and wild and all over the place. Her eyes were large, framed with dark lashes, the color of her hair. That only served to emphasize the unusual color of her eyes. She had what appeared to be blue-violet eyes, but no one really had that color, did they? Her mouth was generous, just like her hips and breasts.

"She's no slacker, this one. She's a brain. The real deal. From what I understand, she can run circles around Thompson intellectually. I doubt he's aware, or that he cares." Code sighed. "From what I'm pulling from his phone and computer, he seems obsessed with her. He must have a thousand pictures of her. He's got his men watching her every move."

"She into him?" Master asked.

"As far as I can tell, she's never met him. They were in the same vicinity only one time. She went to one of his casinos in New Orleans with her parents, but there was no exchange of phone numbers or any interaction that I could find," Code said. "I hacked into the security cameras, and I didn't see any interaction between them. That was three months ago. I think she's entirely unaware of him."

"Why does he want this particular woman, other than her looks?" Czar asked.

"Her family has money. They're rolling in it. Mother invents shit, sells it to big companies and they invest the money the way their daughter tells them to do it. She's smart, that girl. Knows her stuff. The money grows and grows. The mother keeps inventing. Keeps selling. Daughter keeps telling them where to invest. They're pushing toward the billionaire range. They live simply. Drive inexpensive cars. Dress in normal clothes. Are hardworking. Parents only recently retired."

"But Thompson found out."

"Fucking lawyer, Charles Dobbs, father's best friend, gambled a little too much and owed Thompson. My guess, Dobbs got the crap beat out of him and offered information to Thompson in exchange for his debt. He should have gone to his friend and asked for the money. Instead, he told Thompson all about his friends the Moores and the big nest egg they held for their daughter, Ambrielle," Code continued. "It's a guess, but I think it was Dobbs who talked the Moore family into going to New Orleans for their celebration so Thompson could look Ambrielle over as a possible wife. It's speculation and reading a few text messages back and forth from Thompson's and Dobbs' phones."

Steele sighed. "We knew Thompson was a pile of shit. We should have realized how low he'd stoop. He's after this woman because we're draining his personal accounts and he can't run to Daddy to refill them."

Code nodded. "He can't replace his personal money with his business money anymore. His daddy isn't happy with him. His partners aren't happy with him, so he has to find another way. Ambrielle Moore is his big plan. Thompson's in Napa with a full crew and four of his Ghost assassins right now. They've rented a large complex out in the middle of nowhere so Thompson can get away with whatever he wants to do. It's got a chapel on it, right in the middle of a garden. He's got a preacher on standby, the corrupt son of a bitch. The paperwork for Thompson and Moore to get married has mysteriously been put through."

"Can you get rid of the paperwork?" Player asked.

Code shrugged. "Easily. But as soon as he realizes, he

would just replace it. They have someone with skills. Not great skills, but skills."

Preacher tapped the tabletop. "As long as the paperwork is intact, no one is going to look at the names, right? Can you put a cartoon character's name where Thompson's is? Maybe same with the woman's?"

"That might draw his attention as well," Code said. "It would mine."

"Yeah, but you're extraordinary," Czar said, frowning. "Preacher might be onto something. Leave Ambrielle Moore on all the paperwork. Change just Thompson's name. Can't be a cartoon character. We can make up a name, but it would be our luck it would be a real person." He looked around the table, his gaze resting thoughtfully on each of the members. "If something happens to the woman, we don't want someone to come forward and say he was her husband and inherit her fortune."

"Uh-oh," Maestro said. "Everyone had better duck. Czar's got his scary voodoo mask on. Don't let him look at you."

Czar remained silent, his piercing gaze continuing to sweep the table, settling on each member of Torpedo Ink.

"What the hell are you thinking, Czar?" Keys demanded. "You going to marry one of us off to this little fairy princess? She looks like you might be able to break her in half if you looked at her wrong. She doesn't fit."

Czar turned his scary soul-searching gaze on Keys. "I've always decided who fit with us, Keys." His voice was very soft. When Czar's voice was that low, no one argued with him, particularly when he was bringing someone in with them, or passing on someone. He'd been the one to decide when they were children, and he'd always been right.

They'd started out together, children of murdered parents, ripped from their families and taken to a "school" to be trained as assets for their country. Truthfully, no one expected them to survive the brutality at the hands of criminals and pedophiles. Two hundred eighty-nine children had been taken to the school; only nineteen survived—thanks to Czar.

There was a long silence while the members of Torpedo Ink waited for their president to make up his mind. Czar picked up the glossy photograph of the woman again and studied it carefully. "You say this woman always makes the right investments, Code?"

"Every damn time, Czar."

"One hundred percent of the time?"

"Just the way Master does."

Master gave Code a sharp look. He didn't want any attention brought to him, not when Czar was going all weird on them and turning those eyes of his into some kind of instrument of judgment. They all knew once he started on a course of action, he kept on that path until it was complete.

Czar tapped the photograph, a distinct rhythm to his fingers hitting the tabletop. "No one gets it right one hundred percent of the time unless they have a very strong gift."

Alena cleared her throat to get their president's attention. He looked at her over the photograph. "Can you really decide just looking at a picture, Czar?"

"She belongs with us," Czar said decisively. "Whether or not we can get to her in time, or bring her in, that's another thing altogether. We've made the offer to so many, but they couldn't see what we were giving them."

"We're going to have to move on this fast," Code said. "I tapped into her parents' surveillance cameras. Thompson just showed up at their home with his private crew. They went in like they owned the place. It isn't looking good." He was clearly watching the feed. He sat up straighter. "He has his own security, but I think he's brought four Ghosts with him. He brought private assassins."

"There isn't anything we can do from here, Code," Czar said. "Don't beat yourself up watching. Thompson's a sick fucker. You know that. He isn't there to play nice."

He continued to tap the photograph, looking around the

table. His eyes gleamed more silver than ever. "If we're going to have any chance of saving her, one of you has to have your name on those documents. I can't tell you how I know that, only that I do know it." His gaze settled on Master.

Master's head jerked up, his dark eyes going a deep ominous black. "Not a chance. For once, Czar, your voodoo magic is totally off. You know me." He hissed the denial. "I'm no one's husband. I don't do needy women. I'm not any woman's picnic. And a woman like that . . ." He shook his head. "No. Absolutely not. I don't even know how to be gentle."

Before Czar could reply, the others burst out laughing.

It was Keys who threw a wadded-up piece of paper at him. "Don't be a bonehead. You actually have to stand in front of a preacher and say your vows to be a husband. No one's puttin' a gun to your head."

Rather absently, Master picked the missile out of the air with one hand, not even looking at it. "I suppose. Then it doesn't matter if your name is on the license, Keys."

"I don't care." Keys shrugged. "As long as that prick Thompson doesn't get her, kill her and inherit her money."

Master shrugged, a smooth roll of his broad shoulders. He glanced down at the photograph of the woman again. One finger slid over her delicate cheekbones. She was beautiful, but so fuckin' fragile looking she appeared as if he could break her in half with one careless snap of his wrist. He had a tremendous amount of hidden strength. It wasn't just that he was tall and broad-shouldered with a heavily muscled chest, it was the muscles that ran beneath his frame. Dense. Compact. He didn't need to work out in a gym, although to get rid of pent-up energy he used the heavy bags and speed bags, kicking and hitting precise targets.

Master was a man of few words. He worked hard. He played in the band. He had a good voice, but he kept that to himself. He wasn't about to draw attention to himself. He didn't need groupies. He didn't want idiot boyfriends to take exception to their old ladies throwing themselves at the band members. If someone took a swing at him, unlike some of the others who made a fight out of it, he tended to put a stop to things in a permanent way immediately.

Czar didn't give him enforcer or bouncer work. He wasn't ever given door duty at the bar, nor was he ever a bouncer. The other members of Torpedo Ink respected his boundaries and kept them. His finger traced the full lips of the little fairy princess as Keys told Code to put his name on the marriage license. Something dark and ugly moved inside him. He flicked a glance at Czar's set features. Then to Keys.

"Leave it, Code." His voice came out a low growl. "Czar wants my name on the paperwork, put it there. I follow him. I always have. He thinks it needs to be there, then it does."

He didn't know why, but already he had the feeling he was going to have to protect that little fairy-tale princess. He sighed. He just wasn't that man. Keys was better suited, and he was as tough as they came. Even Maestro would do better, and he was a dominant asshole. Both men at least could be gentle if they had to be. He had one gear, and it wasn't a nice one. Still, if Czar decreed it, he was still the man Master followed and always would.

❧

Ambrie glared at Charles Dobbs, the man who had been her father's best friend and confidant for years—all her life. "You are responsible for my parents' deaths. How could you?" She almost called him "Uncle Charlie," as she had for years.

The strain on Dobbs' face showed in the deep lines around his mouth and eyes. "I didn't know this would happen, Ambrie. I had no idea Walker would kill your parents. Are you absolutely certain he gave the order? His men seem . . . trigger-happy. One of them pistol-whipped me." He touched the mostly healed wounds on his face. "I objected to him marrying you, and the moment I contradicted Walker, his goon hit me with his gun."

Ambrie wanted to do more than hit him with a gun. "Do you have any weapons on you?"

He looked around the room and shook his head. "There are cameras in here, Ambrie. For God's sake, if he hears you, he'll come in here and shoot me right in front of you."

She shrugged. "Since you turned traitor and sold out my parents and me, I don't think that matters to me all that much." Her head ached, and she felt sick and dizzy from whatever drug they were continually pumping into her system to keep her compliant. She had taken to faking being nearly unconscious just so they wouldn't give her any more of the drug.

"Don't say that. I'm all you have now. If I'm dead, who can tell anyone that Thompson took you against your will?" He hissed the question in her ear.

"Do you think I care? Because I don't. I'm not marrying him. The moment I do, he's going to kill me so he can inherit the money. I can't trust you to make me a will, and I certainly wasn't given time to make one. My husband would inherit."

"He's not going to kill you, Ambrie. He won't," Dobbs assured her.

"How do you know that?" She couldn't help the sarcastic note very prominent in her voice. While she argued with him, she looked around the little room she was locked in.

The room had one window, far too small for anyone, even her, to escape. It wouldn't have mattered, because one of Thompson's horrid guards stood right outside. He'd peered in, leering while she was forced to dress herself in her wedding attire. It was that or let her guards dress her, and she wasn't about to give them the satisfaction. She was still fighting the effects of the drug she'd been given to make her docile.

She hated the dress she would have found beautiful if it hadn't been Thompson's choice. She recognized the high-end designer and knew he'd paid a fortune for the wedding dress and veil. The dress had been created for her specifically, sewn to her measurements, which made her sick. That meant Thompson had been stalking her for some time.

Worst of all, the dress was exactly what she might have chosen. It was crafted in a nude sparkly tulle and adorned in 3D silver embroidery. The corset bodice had a plunging neckline with thin straps, which served to emphasize her small waist and large breasts. The trumpet dress had geometric sheer back cutouts and a long train that made it impossible to run.

In another life, she would have loved the dress, but in this one, she looked for a weapon on it. A place to hide a weapon in it. Walker Thompson had no idea what he had unleashed in her when he killed her parents. None.

With both her parents serving in the military, that meant she'd grown up in that life. She'd learned how to handle weapons from a very early age. Both her mother and her father believed in their daughter learning self-defense, and she had begun training at an early age for that as well. She hadn't stopped, although she had taken dance lessons for fun. It was easier to keep up with her defense lessons when they moved so much in the beginning, but her parents worked at keeping her in dance because she loved it and they thought it was a good way to help her become more social. Glaring up at the cameras, and there were three—overkill—she thought maybe the socialization didn't take quite as well as the combat lessons had.

"I'm not marrying you, asshole," she called to the camera.

"Ambrie." Dobbs almost wailed her name. "Don't make him angry. Never make him angry. You can see the kind of man he is. Just marry him and you can live your life. He'll want you to handle the money. You're good at your job. You could make him a mint. I told him how good you are."

Ambrielle loved numbers, but it was more than that. She had an intuition when it came to investments. She had made hundreds of thousands of dollars for her clients. "Do you really think I'm going to help a man who murdered my parents? What's wrong with you?"

She shoved Dobbs away from her, or tried to. Her movements were clumsy. The drug was still in her system, making her limbs heavy and slow. She had no idea where she was. No one knew where she was. No help was coming. If she didn't save herself, she would be forced into the chapel to marry Walker Thompson.

Dobbs had to steady her by catching both of her arms. She didn't look at him, but instead looked desperately around the room in the hopes of finding a weapon. Anything that could be used as a weapon. She tore herself away from Dobbs and stumbled to the desk, doing her best not to stare at the fountain pen. That looked like a perfect weapon. Where could she conceal it on her wedding dress? It wasn't as if she had pockets in the formfitting designer dress. It clung to her curves. And then there was the letter opener. It wasn't super sharp, but it did have a point.

She reached for it, and a fist hit her arm so hard for a moment she thought her bone had shattered. Walker Thompson wrapped his fingers around her throat, nearly lifting her off her feet. She caught at his shoulders to try to ease the hold he had on her, but he only tightened his fingers in warning.

"What the fuck do you think you're going to do with that?"

She couldn't tell him she was going to stick it right through his eye if she got the chance. For one thing, he was strangling her, and she was about to pass out. For another, she didn't want him dosing her with more of whatever he'd given her to get her ready for their wedding. She tried to hang limply and not fight, but self-preservation was strong. She kicked at him and used both hands to grip his wrists when she began to see spots and her lungs couldn't get any air at all.

He flung her away from him. Ambrie hit the edge of the desk and then the floor. Walker bent over her, gripping her hair to drag her head up. "You had better cooperate if you know what's good for you."

He hit her twice on her left side, just under her eye. She was still trying desperately to drag in air, so there was no twisting away from the blows or the one that followed, his foot connecting with her hip. He straightened, his hands going to his tie.

"Clean her up and get her ready. I want her out in five minutes, compliant. You understand me? She doesn't do what she's supposed to do, you're dead, Dobbs." He looked over Dobbs' shoulder to the two men guarding the door. "Get her up, Gleb." He stalked out, slamming the door behind him.

Ambrielle didn't bother to try to sit up. Even trying to get air past the painful swelling in her throat hurt too much. It took all her effort just to try to breathe. When hard hands caught at her and yanked her up, she couldn't get her legs to work at first. It was humiliating to have to hold on to the man who had shot her father, especially when he was grinning so openly at her.

"Your future husband is not a patient man," Gleb said.

She avoided looking at his face by staring down at the shoe mark on the beautiful nude tulle, with its gorgeous 3D silver embroidery. Laughter bubbled up. Nothing like having her future husband's shoe on her hip.

"You're hysterical," Dobbs said.

She pointed to the shoe print. "At least it isn't on my ass." She tried to say it, but her throat was so swollen she mostly croaked.

Gleb and his partner got her messed-up humor. They laughed at her insanity. Gleb steadied her and gestured toward the small bathroom. "Denis, get a cold washcloth for her face. Sit in the chair, Ambrie."

He all but put her in the chair, so she didn't protest or try to fight him. She was too aware Thompson had told him to make her amenable. She wanted Gleb to think Thompson had taken the fight out of her with his rough handling. Little did they know that he had only made her angrier and all the more determined to kill him. She was far past wanting to get away. She didn't believe she would, but she wanted to kill Walker Thompson, and after him, Gleb and his partner, Denis. If she got them, then she'd go after Dobbs.

Gleb laughed softly. "Walker doesn't have a clue what he's getting with you, does he?"

She didn't rise to the bait. She knew he'd deliberately seated her at the desk in front of the fountain pen and the letter opener. She wasn't taking the bait. There were other ways to kill Thompson. If she had to, she'd wait for their wedding night. Sooner or later, the idiot would be so secure in his superiority that he'd let his guard down.

Gleb and Denis were much more worrisome. They had faint Russian accents, and instinctively she had known all along she was dealing with very dangerous men. Much more so than Thompson. Thompson might think he was in charge, but there was something about the two bodyguards that made her think they were something else altogether.

There was no doubt in her mind that Walker Thompson had hired them. He thought they worked for him. They obeyed his instructions. Still, Ambrielle was fairly certain they had their own agenda, and if it differed from Thompson's they'd kill him without hesitation. They'd kill her too, just the way they had her parents. Without thought. It had been too easy for Gleb. He'd barely looked at her parents when he'd shot her father without one iota of remorse.

Denis came back with the cold washcloth and handed it to her. She applied it to her throbbing face, leaning one elbow on the desk, right next to the letter opener just to keep the Russian bodyguards on their toes.

"If we're taking bets," Gleb said in Russian, "my bet's on her. She'll kill him inside of a week."

"He'll break her in a week. He'll beat her every day and rape her over and over until she breaks," Denis replied indifferently, as if she weren't even in the room.

"I'll take your money. One hundred thousand American."

"Bullshit, Gleb. She won't get near a weapon. He's stupid, but not that stupid."

"This one won't need a weapon. She's trained. She can kill him with her bare hands. She'll bide her time," Gleb responded. "I wish I could be there to see it."

...to threaten me. ...She switched her glare ... that you can't see he's ... I'm not doing?" ...Gleb takes out his gun ... Walker asked with his smooth smile. ...who set my parents up to be killed? ...but if you want to do it, go right ... marrying you."

FOUR

"I'm not exactly sure what you have left to threaten me with," Ambrielle said, staring up at Thompson with sheer defiance. She switched her glare to the preacher. "And you, what's wrong with you that you can't see he's forcing me to marry him, which I'm not doing?"

"You don't mind if Gleb takes out his gun and shoots your family lawyer?" Walker asked with his smooth smile.

"You mean the man who set my parents up to be killed? I plan on killing him myself, but if you want to do it, go right ahead. I'm still not marrying you."

Walker shoved her veil back over her head so he could stare directly into her eyes as he grabbed her throat again.

"Go ahead, Thompson. Choke me, right in front of the preacher. Beat me up. That's going to get me to marry you. You killed my father and mother. There isn't anyone left."

He pressed his forehead hard against hers. She could smell alcohol on his breath. "I beg to differ with you, darling. You have a very sweet friend. Amanda Gibbs is her name. I can bring her here. Right now, she's having coffee in a little café, studying the way she does every day at this time. She's very predictable. My men have been in her home while she's been sleeping. It would be so easy to pick her up and bring her to my place. I won't have to hurt you, Ambrielle, only your friend. She has a brother, Adam, doesn't she? How do you think she will feel when he has an accident, and she finds out you could have prevented it?"

Ambrie had managed to lift the stupid little pocketknife Dobbs carried with him. She knew he had it on him because he never left it behind. It wasn't a great one. He didn't use it for the knife, but he liked the opener on it so he could pop the tops off beer bottles. He'd done it in front of her for years. She wanted to stick that knife right into Thompson's throat, but his bodyguards were watching her closely, half expecting her to make a move against their boss.

Gleb, Denis, Karlin and Kesar were somewhere behind her. She knew Karlin and Kesar were on either side of Dobbs, presumably to scare her into marrying Thompson. The two men were Thompson's personal army, not part of the Russian assassination squad. She couldn't care less if Thompson ordered Dobbs killed right there. He was responsible for her parents' deaths. The wedding was a crock anyway.

"Do we have an understanding, Ambrielle, or should I make a phone call and have my men pick up dear little Amanda? She would make such a nice addition to our wedding. You do need a maid of honor. I'll bet she feels left out when you tell her you got married without her."

Thompson's voice was so irritating, and the drug in her system just amplified it, creating a disturbing echo that grated on her nerves to the point that she nearly brought up her knee with the idea she might break his neck right there in the church with the preacher looking on.

Thompson's bodyguard inserted himself between them as the groom stepped back and waved at the preacher. "I think my lovely bride will be much more cooperative. Get started."

~

"This is some bullshit right here, Steele," Master snapped, adding more weapons and ammo to his vest. "Who does this kind of thing? That son of a bitch is going to marry this woman after he kills her parents? Her fuckin' lawyer just hands her over?"

"They doped her and she's still fighting them," Lana whispered, admiration in her voice. "We've got to get in there and shut this down. They injected some kind of shit into her neck. I saw the big Russian do that to her after her loving groom smacked her in the face twice, punched her in the ribs a couple of times and kicked her when she was down."

"She's a hell of a handful. What is she? All of five foot nothing? He's like a foot taller and he's going to knock her around?"

Master was so pissed he wanted to go in and start shooting before Czar and Steele gave the go-ahead. He couldn't say he was the best with women, but he could say he didn't beat the shit out of them. Like Lana, he admired the bride. Even drugged, she was ready to do her part to kill the bastard who had kidnapped her and murdered her parents.

"It's a go. Kill every single member of the Ghosts. They're lethal. Don't miss," Steele cautioned. "Go in hot."

Master didn't need a second order. He walked right into the little church, shot two of Walker Thompson's crew in the head as he sauntered past them and went right down the aisle where the pastor was reading the vows to the bride and groom. At the sound of the gunshots, all hell broke loose. Master kept moving, eyes on the prize, gun spitting bullets. He didn't miss.

Thompson tried to grab his bride, but she resisted, pulling away from him. His men surrounded him, urging him toward the preacher and the door behind him. Master shot one of the bodyguards, and beside him, Ink shot another. The two dead guards dropped right on top of the bride. She hit the floor like a stone, her gorgeous dress now soaked red. She didn't make a sound, and Master hoped she hadn't taken a hit. He didn't have time to check because Czar's team had sealed off the escape route and Thompson's men and the four Ghosts were fighting in earnest, trying to find a way out.

Ambrielle tilted her head slightly to calculate the distance between her and the nearest exit. She had the weight of two dead bodies on her, and they were heavy. It was difficult to assess what was happening. Gunfire was loud, and it seemed like everyone was Russian. The preacher had crawled behind a pillar. Dobbs was behind a pew, still alive. She worked her way out from under one of the dead men and yanked the veil off her head. Her train was caught under the second body. She tried everything she could think of, but it seemed she was trapped by the material.

Finally, she took out Dobbs' old pocketknife. It looked rusty, but she didn't care. She began to saw through the tulle and embroidery. Sometimes she could rip it, other times she hacked and sawed as fast as she could, all the while staying low to the floor, hoping Thompson didn't see that she was alive, and neither did Denis or Gleb.

She could hear gunfire erupting all around her, and Thompson snarling at his bodyguards to get her. She heard him calling her name, but she stayed low to the floor of the little chapel, hidden behind the two dead men with her rusty, tiny blade, which could barely make it through the tulle and embroidery. She yanked and tore and then, with one last desperate roll, found herself free of both dead bodies.

From the bloody floor, she tried to assess how far it was to the nearest exit. She didn't want to go anywhere near Thompson. He appeared to be trapped between the closest door, just behind where the preacher had been standing, and a mob of shooters. She couldn't tell who was at war, but as far as she was concerned, they were all the enemy.

Ambrielle located an exit some distance from her, but she calculated she could make a run for it. There were four dead or dying bodies strewn in her path, one hanging grotesquely over the back of a pew just near the door she had spotted. The body moved once, so she gripped the small pocketknife in one hand, her trumpet skirt in the other, and rose to her feet, already running in a low crouch. She kept her gaze fixed on the door, weaving in and out of all obstacles, refusing to cower down when the gunshots sounded close and one burned right past her ear.

Without warning, a man loomed up in front of her. A solid wall of pure muscle. There was no mistaking him for anything but the enemy, with his hair falling like sin into his dark, compelling eyes, eyes that were pure ice. He had a thin scar across the top of his forehead. His jaw was strong, the angles and planes of his face all cut sharp and edgy. He was definitely Russian, and he hadn't even opened his mouth.

He was wearing a combat vest that held a multitude of weapons and ammo. There was a gun in his hand, and he carried it like he knew how to use it. There was no mercy, no compassion in that icy gaze as it slid over her, clearly assessing her. Judging her in her wedding dress, with blood all over her.

Ambrielle attacked first. She wasn't waiting for a bullet. There was no room for hesitation. She only had one shot at taking him down. He had more than a foot on her in height, and his body looked to be pure muscle. He was armed to the teeth. She hid the knife in her hand as she pushed off with her foot and leapt into the air, getting her body weight behind her for the strike. She hit at a perfect angle, embedding the knife in his neck, or at least she should have. The man casually swatted her away, and the blade broke. Actually broke. It barely penetrated his skin. There was a trickle of blood, but no more than that.

Ambrie landed on her butt, the wedding dress in complete disarray around her. "Damn it, Charlie. Of course your stupid pocketknife would be totally worthless." She looked up and found herself staring up at the man who was folded over the back of the pew. His eyes were wide open, and he stared at her. Blood dripped macabrely down the edge of the bench seat to the floor. Just under the pew was his gun, where it had dropped from his hand when he'd been shot. Triumph burst through Ambrielle.

She lunged for the gun, expecting the man she'd tried to kill to shoot her at any moment. As she gripped the gun, rolling to keep her gaze on her target, she found him just standing there, looking at her. Not moving. Not trying to defend himself. He had lowered his weapon to his side, those eyes of his on her, observing her every move. A trickle of blood ran down his neck where she'd broken the blade of that worthless pocketknife on him, and he made no move to stop it. He didn't move, not even when she stood on shaky legs and aimed the gun right at him.

A slow, taunting smile dared her to pull the trigger. He was playing with her. Around them, time tunneled. Why was it so difficult? She knew how to squeeze a trigger. She wasn't opposed to killing a man and getting out of the chapel. She had to get to Amanda and Adam. She had enough money to hide them away until she could hunt Walker Thompson and rid the world of his vile presence.

The man with the midnight-blue eyes took a step toward her. She shook her head. "Don't. Just let me leave."

He shook his head. "Can't do that, princess. Thompson got away. He's got his men waiting to pick you up."

Just the way he said *princess* set her teeth on edge. She was nobody's princess. He was asking to be shot. She took a step to the side in an effort to get around him. He countered her move, gliding closer. Too close. So close the barrel of the gun was no more than an inch from his vest, but she still couldn't make herself pull the trigger. Not when she was looking into his eyes. She'd never seen anyone with eyes like his, and even with all the dead bodies lying around her and the knowledge that he'd killed several of them, and might kill her, there was an unexpected response to him somewhere deep. A clenching that shouldn't have been. That was obscene and wrong.

"Master, what the hell are you doing?" a voice behind her demanded.

The man in front of her didn't look up. "Giving her a choice."

"What the fuck does that mean? Letting her kill you is a choice?"

"Yeah, Savage, it's a fuckin' choice. Everyone here had a choice but her. I say she deserves to make at least one choice in this mess."

Another man burst out laughing as he came up on the other side of her. He had platinum-and-gold hair and was very good-looking even dressed for war. "We came to rescue you, babe. That's rich that you want to kill the one man who would have taken the place of that bastard Thompson for you." He reached out and very gently removed the gun from her hand.

Ambrielle had no idea why she allowed him to take it. The man in front of her, the one they called Master, flicked his icy gaze toward the hapless victim folded over the pew. Apparently, he wasn't dead enough. He tried to raise a gun toward the trio. Master shot him between the eyes and casually turned back to her.

"You really came here to rescue me?" Ambrie didn't know any of the men or women still alive in the room with her. They were all wearing vests and armed like he was.

She looked around the chapel. Mostly Thompson's bodyguards were dead on the floor. The preacher sat on the floor with his hands locked behind his head, right next to the two dead bodies she'd crawled out from under. Her blood-spattered tulle with the 3D silver embroidery train was still locked under the bodies. She found that a bizarre sight. Dobbs was facedown in the front aisle, his hands over his head, fingers locked behind his head indicating he was still alive. A burst of fury shook her.

"Excuse me for a minute." Head up, she swept past two more men she didn't know and should have been afraid of, but now adrenaline had taken over. No one stopped her. She marched to the front of the chapel and kicked Dobbs hard in the ribs. "You asshole. If I still had that gun, I'd shoot you. You might as well have killed my parents yourself."

Groaning, curling his body, Dobbs turned his head to look at her. "Ambrie, I didn't have a choice. Walker was going to kill me."

"Well, now I'm going to. I'll get to you somehow. Right now, I have to get out of here and warn my friends." She turned back to the men and women watching her as if she were an actress in a play. It was Master she instinctively went to. "Thompson threatened my friends. If I don't marry him and cooperate, he'll hurt them. Or kill them."

Master shook his head. "We know he threatened your friends. We have some of our people on it. They'll protect them."

He sounded safe. Reassuring. She wasn't certain she could trust anyone. She wanted out of the bloody wedding gown. She needed to think. Thompson wasn't going to give up. This was a setback.

"All he has to do is fake the marriage certificate, kill me and he gets money he wants anyway." Ambrie murmured aloud, talking to herself more than to her audience. She began to pace back and forth as if they weren't there, paying no attention to the fact that her dress was soaked with blood or that she was surrounded by dead bodies.

"Actually, Ambrielle," the platinum one said, "he's more likely to kidnap you again and insist on marriage. Thompson's obsessed with you. I'm Ice, by the way. We were after him, and our tech found him watching you. He's got a thousand pictures of you. He isn't going to give you up easily. Although, this time, if he had married you, it wouldn't have been legal." He grinned at her. "Code, our tech, substituted Master's name on the license for Thompson's."

She jerked her head up and looked at Master. Really looked at him. He was intimidating to say the least. And beautiful in a terrible, rough, scary way. He looked powerful. All muscle. His body dense. She could barely keep from staring into his eyes, mesmerized by the intensity there. He didn't bother to hide what he was from her. He didn't give her an easy smile that would have been fake as hell. Yet he was the one who said she should have a choice, and his voice, even though it was low and gravelly, held honesty.

"You came here to kill him, didn't you?" For the first time, she believed them. This wasn't just about rescuing her. They didn't know her. They were after Walker Thompson for some reason she didn't care about. She just happened to have gotten caught in their net because they made their move against Thompson. She'd gotten in the way, and they missed him. None of them seemed upset about it.

Master nodded. "That was the plan. He had an army surrounding him, and no one wanted to take the chance of a stray bullet hitting you. We'll get him next time. He can't run forever. Even if he leaves this area, he'll head back to New Orleans. He thinks he owns that town. He feels safe there."

"He's going to make another try for me." She knew that to be true. Thompson wouldn't give up. He was very focused on the money.

Master shrugged. "I told you, I'll keep you safe." He frowned at the snicker that went around the room. "The club will keep you safe," he corrected.

As if they all thought that mattered to her. Walker Thompson had ordered his private hit squad to murder her father right in front of her. Gleb had done so. She was all about revenge, and she didn't care if that wasn't considered ladylike. And this man . . .

She looked at him speculatively. "You said that you thought I should have at least one choice. Did you mean that? Really mean it?"

Master nodded his head. "Yeah, princess, I meant it. You want that man killed, I'll do it for you."

Ambrie walked right up to him until she was so close she could feel his body heat. He was tall and solid. All muscle.

Intimidating this close up. That didn't matter to her. She tilted her head so she could look him in the eye. Those cold, midnight-blue eyes. So dark they were almost black. He didn't blink or look away. He let her see he was a killer. That didn't bother him. He didn't try to hide who or what he was from her, and she liked that about him. She needed that from him. She took a deep breath, making up her mind.

"Marry me. Your name is on the license. If it really is and you say you're willing to give me a choice, that's my choice. Marry me and make me the promise to hunt him down with me. Not just him. Those Russians as well."

"Babe, you don't have to marry me to get my promise to do that for you," Master said.

He didn't blink. He didn't react at all to her outrageous proposal. The chapel had suddenly gone quiet. There was no snickering. No laughter. His friends knew she was serious, even if he wasn't taking her that way.

"I don't want you to do it for me. That's not what I said. We do it together." She looked at him steadily so he could see she meant every word. "I do have a huge trust fund. I'll sign it over to you the moment it's done. If you have a lawyer, we can write it up so you know the money is yours."

Master shook his head. "I'm not interested in your trust fund. Money isn't an issue. You sure you're not fucked-up on the drugs they pumped into you? Because I don't want you to wake up tomorrow morning and say you didn't know what you were doing."

"I'm positive. Thompson will lose his mind if I get married. You know he will. He'll keep coming out into the open instead of sliding into the dark like the slug he is. Tell me what you want. Negotiate."

He shook his head. "You don't know the first thing about me. I've been in prison most of my life. I'm not a nice guy. You'd be tied to someone you wouldn't want to introduce to your friends."

"I don't give a damn if you spent most of your life in

prison. I'm not looking for a nice guy. I'm looking for someone to be my partner. Negotiate with me. Tell me what it
would take for you to marry me."

He reached out and traced her cheekbone and then her
lips. Just that light touch sent a shiver of awareness down her
spine. Her body responded with that same improper damp-
ness. With a clenching that was so wrong in the middle of a
war zone.

"You. I want you. You marry me, there's no divorce. There's
no walking away. We make it work. That's the deal. You give
yourself to me and you promise to stay, and it's done. Otherwise, I just go after the fuckers myself and kill them. Either
way, they're going to die. You have to know that, princess,
they'll die either way. That I can give you my word on."

Ambrielle studied his face. It was impossible to read
his expression. But his eyes. That was something else.
"Kiss me."

Master stared down at her with his dark blue eyes, those
killer eyes. They didn't soften, but they did change. They
darkened even more. He caught her around the nape of her
neck and pulled her close to him. Just the palm curling
around her nape, so large, strong, his thumb sliding up the
side of her cheek, set her heart pounding. But it was his eyes,
staring down into her eyes, mesmerizing her as he bent his
head to her.

Slow. Giving her time to change her mind, except her
mind had melted, every brain cell gone somewhere else. She
was no longer thinking, only feeling. Hot blood rushed
through her veins. Flames licked at her skin. She couldn't
look away from his eyes. The world dropped away so there
was only the two of them.

Then his mouth was on hers. She didn't think of self-
preservation. There was no more Ambrielle without this
man. She would never be the same. Flames licked up her
spine and danced over her skin. Colors burst behind her
eyes. Her nipples felt like twin flames, and between her legs
a firestorm had started. Her skin had never felt so sensitive,

as if her nerve endings were alive and aware of only him—Master.

He was the one to pull back. She stood trembling, shocked that she'd forgotten where they were. What had happened. He'd had the ability to take that away for her. For that alone she would have married him. She couldn't speak, so she just nodded her assent.

"One more thing before you make your decision. For the sake of full disclosure. I like to fuck. I fuck hard, and I'm rough. You're a tiny little thing. I'm not. You marry me, you come to me knowing what you're getting into. I'll take care of you, because you'll be mine, but we aren't going to have separate bedrooms. We marry, it's going to be damn fuckin' real."

Ambrie pressed her fingers to her lips to keep him from seeing that they were trembling. She doubted that she was doing a very good job. She had the feeling he saw everything. "I get it," she acknowledged. "You're giving up your freedom and you want something in return. If you want sex in our marriage, then we're exclusive. I'm not going to worry about getting some disease, and I'm not going to be disrespected in my own home. You be certain this is your price, because I'm not nearly as sweet as I apparently look. You cheat on me, and I won't go to a divorce lawyer. When you're sound asleep, I'll cut your throat." She kept her eyes on his so he would see she meant what she said. "So if you're a man who likes variety, you'd better negotiate another deal."

Another man intervened. "Make it fast, Master. We don't have time for much more negotiations. I get it this is a lifetime thing here, but there're a lot of dead bodies, and we don't want the cops coming around. Not our turf."

"I don't want that asshole that was going to help force my obviously sweet little princess into marriage to marry us, Czar. He can be a witness. Where's Preacher?" Master asked. He held out his hand to Ambrie.

Ambrielle put her hand in his, wondering if she'd completely lost her mind. The drug was definitely wearing off, and her body wouldn't stop with the tremors. No matter what, she couldn't control the way she shivered, and she didn't want Master to think she was afraid of marrying him. It was her idea. Her choice. If anything, she was forcing him, not the other way around.

"Preacher, just get them married," Czar snapped. "The rest of you, get gone now. We're out of time. Code, make it legal and make certain Thompson's people don't try to pull a fast one."

Master casually wrapped his arm around Ambrielle's head, covering her ears and forcing her face into his rib cage. The sounds of the two gunshots were loud, one almost on top of the other, and then he was turning her body to face the front of the chapel. She heard the thump of a body hitting the floor, and her stomach lurched. That had to be the original preacher.

"Why did you kill him?" she whispered against his vest. She was gripping his vest with both hands in order to stand up, so shaky she was afraid her legs were going to give out.

"He went for a gun. Who would have thought he had one? And why would he try it? Even with everyone leaving, he still couldn't have thought he'd make it out of here alive," Master said.

"And Dobbs?"

"He helped kill your parents. Princess, you're shaking like a leaf. I'm serious. You don't have to do this. I'll take care of Thompson, Gleb, Denis and anyone else on your hit list. Just point me in the right direction. You don't have to marry me."

The man they called Preacher had seriously curly hair. She let her gaze fixate on that while Master slid his arms around her waist to hold her up. She stood in her blood-stained wedding gown, leaning against him, feeling the guns, knives and ammunition against her back. It was a hell of a way to get married, especially when her father had been murdered and couldn't walk her down the aisle, and her mother never had the chance to help her pick out a wedding gown.

She was crying. She despised that she was crying while she said her vows. She knew Kir "Master" Vasiliev, her new husband, would think she was crying because she was marrying him. It was just that everything was beginning to sink in and she was crashing.

Her parents were really dead. She couldn't bring them back no matter how many men she killed. She was marrying a man she didn't know, the only man she'd ever really had any chemistry with, and he was some kind of hit man who had spent most of his life in prison for crimes she didn't want to know about. She'd traded her life for revenge, and she'd do it all over again in a heartbeat. There was something seriously wrong with her.

"He pronounced us man and wife. I'll kiss you in the truck. We've got to go," Master said, and swept her into his arms.

"The drug is really wearing off," she whispered. "I can't stand up."

It was a little thrilling that he could pick her up as if she didn't weigh anything at all. It wasn't as if she didn't have curves—a lot of them. She wrapped her arms around his neck and buried her wet face on his shoulder, hiding the evidence that she was acting like a baby. She didn't want him to see her looking weak. She wasn't that kind of woman. She needed him to view her as an equal partner, and he wouldn't do that if she was crying like a two-year-old.

Ambrielle snuck a peek to see where they were going as Master moved fast, his long strides silent for such a big man in combat boots. The one called Ice led the way, his automatic weapon looking too much a part of him. Preacher, his curly hair thick and wild, a guard right behind them, his rifle all business looking as well. These men knew what they were doing, and she had thrown her lot in with them, without question.

She looked up at Master as he approached a truck with its engine running, the man in the driver's seat looking like he should have been a model. Master didn't put her down as Preacher dragged open the door to the back. Master climbed in smoothly with her and slid her into the middle seat.

"Put your seat belt on." Master slipped in next to her.

Ice occupied the seat on the other side of her, while Preacher took the front with the driver.

This was crazy. She was insane to have done this. She'd traded one nightmare for another because she'd been desperate for revenge. She would have done better to have chosen for them to let her go. But looking at the four grim-faced men, all of them armed to the teeth, she didn't think that would have been one of her choices. Somehow, she would have ended up exactly where she was, in the truck, surrounded by these same four men.

"We're good, Transporter, go," Master informed the driver and leaned around Ambrie to do up her seat belt before she even reached for it. The pad of his thumb slid across her cheeks, wiping through the wetness there as he sat up straight.

Ambrielle did her best to control her breathing, to keep it slow and regular. She didn't understand how under the circumstances, everything about Kir Vasiliev, the man who would be her husband, could attract her. Not just attract her; she had to admit the chemistry was off the charts. When she'd never really experienced hot sexual attraction, and didn't even know she could under extreme duress, it was shocking and mortifying. She had the horrible feeling that chemistry had unduly influenced her decision when she wasn't thinking as straight as she should have been.

"There's a vest on the floor," Transporter said. "You may need to cover her with it. There're only three ways out of here, and we blew our time frame."

"I'd prefer a gun," Ambrie said. "I can assure you, I know how to use one."

Master caught her chin in his hand and tugged her face

around, forcing her to look at him. Her eyes met his: a challenge there. Defiance. Growing anger.

"I think my bride is having second thoughts. Putting a weapon in your hands when we're going into war isn't the brightest of ideas, princess." His tone was just that little bit mocking, just enough to set her teeth on edge.

The pad of his thumb slid over her lips, and it felt like deliberate seduction. He was taunting her. She opened her mouth, knowing he wouldn't resist. There was too much lust gathering in his dark eyes. The moment his thumb sought the moist interior of her mouth, she bit down hard, never taking her gaze from his. If she could break the skin and draw blood, that would be all to the good as far as she was concerned.

To her consternation, he laughed. He didn't wince or blink. He laughed. She wasn't certain he actually felt any pain at all.

He caught her jaw with his other hand and forced her to open her mouth by pinching at the hinge of her jaw until she had no choice. He wasn't gentle either, but he was casual. He didn't change expression, and there was no malice showing.

"What was that for?" He stuck his thumb in his mouth and slid his tongue around the wound, all the while watching her intently.

Ambrie tried not to stare. She wouldn't be mesmerized by him. She told herself he was a killer. He'd admitted it to her. Warned her. She wanted to groan aloud. He'd even *warned* her. She couldn't cry foul; he'd been truthful about what he was.

"We had a deal, you bastard, and you're already breaking your word." She tried to pour accusation into her voice, but it was a whisper of sound. What was she saying? What was coming out of her mouth? One minute she was looking for a way out, and the next she was furious at him because he was carelessly throwing her away. Breaking their deal. He'd told the others she had a choice. She had meant what she said when she took those stupid vows. When she'd married a total stranger.

She was so tired. She could see her parents' bodies slumped over. What would they think of her? Trading her freedom, her chance to avenge them, for her life? For that first shocking heat that raged through her body and caught her so unawares?

The truck suddenly spun sideways, throwing her against Master hard. The movement made her face hurt. Her ribs hurt. Mostly, her heart and soul hurt. She'd really screwed up. How was she going to get out of this one? She had no weapon. She wasn't certain she was even thinking right. Her mind was nothing but chaos.

"Don't worry, princess, I never believed for one minute you were marrying me for real or that you meant a single thing you said. I had no intention of holding you to it. I wanted to see how far you'd take it. Did you really think I'd believe someone like you would tie yourself to someone like me?"

The sheer contempt in his voice put steel in her spine. Her chin went up and flames all but crackled in her eyes. She swore she was looking at him through the leaping blaze. "I have every intention of keeping my word—unlike you, asshole. I'm not a liar and a cheat like you."

"Then why all the tears?" This time there was no denying the curl of his lip and the darkening of those blue eyes to midnight black.

"Oh, I don't know. Maybe because my parents were murdered right in front of me. That might do it. Some asshole beat the shit out of me. That could do it. I was drugged and now it's leaving my system. Good bet that might contribute. I'm married to the most insensitive, vain, thinks-the-world-revolves-around-him bastard on the planet—that might do it. I'm in a dress covered in blood. Do you need me to go on, or is that enough for you? I think it best no one gives me a gun because I'd be a widow before the wedding night."

His expression was completely unexpected again. He looked at her as if he wanted to throw her on the nearest bed and devour her. She'd never seen such stark, raw lust blazing in a man's eyes before. Certainly not when he looked at her.

The truck spun around in a circle and left the paved road to take a dirt one. The men barely moved in their seats, but Ambrielle was thrown forward and then locked in so tight against the seat she couldn't breathe. Before she could unsnap the belt, Master was already leaning across her.

The movement put his head right up against her breasts and the corset with the sheer vee down the front. She could feel his hot breath as he unsnapped the tab from the metal lock. She could have sworn his mouth dragged against her left nipple, hot and wet, sending fire straight to her clit. Her entire core clenched. Then he straightened, his hair sliding over her nipples intimately, his face turned away from her as he brought up the large bulletproof vest that had been lying on the floorboards. Had she imagined the entire thing? Color crept up her neck into her face.

The terrain was bumpy and threw her all over the seat, so that it was only Master steadying her, suddenly shoving her head down. He wrapped the vest around her, gun in his fist, window open, his large body blocking hers as he squeezed the trigger repeatedly. On the other side of her, Ice was doing the same. Up front, Preacher was firing.

Ambrielle couldn't see anything, because every time she struggled to get free of the vest and get her head up, Master's large, very heavy arm would come down on top of her, pushing her head to the seat. The truck bucked and spun, a wild ride, making her stomach lurch. The gunfire was loud. Bullets hit the doors, and twice she heard them thunk into the vest. Master grunted once and his body jerked.

"Are you hit?" Anxiety gripped her. She hadn't made her choice right away. The man, Czar, had repeatedly said they had to hurry, but Master had waited patiently, not trying to push her one way or the other for a fast decision. She didn't want to be responsible for any of these men getting hurt—especially if they had really come to rescue her.

Master didn't answer her. His arm was a heavy weight, unmovable. She shoved at it. His gun was still answering whoever was firing at them. If he was hurt, he was still fighting back.

"Are you hit? I think I can manage to put a Band-Aid on your owie without hurting you," she said, sarcasm dripping. Her struggling had managed to uncover a ribbon of view. Master's set expression. The total concentration in his eyes. The way the sky spun crazily and then righted itself as the driver maneuvered through obstacles she couldn't see. "Let me up. I promise not to let gangrene set in."

Master's gun was hot when he rested it for a moment against her arm as he slammed another magazine into it, ignoring her entirely as he once more took aim and began shooting. She didn't think there was a way to aim at or actually hit anything with the truck slewing around, spinning and bumping the way it was, but she didn't know, she could be wrong. She tried to get her head up where she could see better.

He shoved the top of her head down with his arm. "Stay down, damn it. Do you have a death wish?"

She decided it was best to just let him save her. She was tired and she hurt like hell all over. Her dress was a wreck, and so was her mind. If the truck kept spinning and bumping, she might vomit all over Master, his gun and, more important, the vest he had draped over her.

Ambrielle closed her eyes and stopped struggling. What was the use? If she survived this shootout, she was going to make Master keep his promise to her. She'd sold her soul to the devil for a reason—and she was more than certain he was the devil. When she looked into his eyes, she saw the promise of death there. He would kill without hesitation. He had promised her he would kill for her. She'd meant every single vow she'd taken in that chapel, and her husband better have meant each word as well too. She'd give him her allegiance and her body for the rest of her days, however long that might be, but he'd better find the men who'd killed her parents, and he'd better find a way to keep her friends alive. If he didn't, he'd find out very fast that the woman he'd married wasn't the princess he thought she was.

FIVE

Master swore as the hot water poured over his body, soothing the bruises the bullets had made when they tore into his vest. He didn't give a damn about them. He wasn't a saint. He'd never be one. He'd spent a good 60 percent of his life in and out of prison, and none of it had been good. He was as hard as they came. As rough. And he didn't give a damn about anyone but those in his club, and sometimes—especially when he first came out of a cage—it was difficult to remember he cared about them. So why the fuck had he tried so hard to save Ambrielle Moore from himself? And he'd tried.

He'd laid it out for her. He'd been crude. Rude. He'd backtracked. He'd tried to tell her he'd go after the fuckers who killed her parents without her having to put her body—or the rest of her life—on the line. Nothing he said or did seemed to work. She was in the master bathroom, taking a shower. Naked. That body of hers, hotter than hell. She'd been through the worst time of her life, and that didn't seem to make a difference to his body. He was as hard as a rock. Fucking titanium.

He should have let Code put Keys' name on the marriage

license, not his. The moment the thought came into his head, so did the need to beat the man to death—and Keys was his friend. He'd lost his humanity in that prison this time, but it had happened time and time again when he went back. He was unable to survive there unless he cloaked himself in that persona of a man who cared for no one. A man who could not care less about life. The problem was, it had been getting more and more difficult to find his way back. That persona had become his reality, and the other person who had cared so much about the world and its inhabitants had faded so far into the background he couldn't remember him anymore.

Bottom line, the woman he'd just married was in for a really bad time. Life often gave you a really fucked-up deal—it had him. Now she was caught up in his reality, and if she persisted in becoming part of it, he wasn't going to let her go.

He shut off the water and caught up a towel, skimming it over his body. Every muscle was locked and ready, the nerve endings close to the surface. He'd never been in such a state of pure arousal. He knew he should have taken care of it in the shower, or at least tried to, but not on his damn wedding night. Not when she was going to be in his bed with that body of hers. Those tits and that ass. Those hips. Those pouty lips that curved just perfectly, giving him far too many fantasies already. No way in hell was he going to give himself a hand job when she was right there.

He stalked out of the bathroom, the towel around his hips, barely able to cage his cock. The material rubbed along his shaft and sensitive crown, adding to his brutal hunger. It had never been like this, even when he came out of some of his longest times in a cage, when he'd been reduced to nothing more than a feral predator needing to hurt every man in sight, or fuck a willing woman so hard she might not walk for a week.

The bedroom was a work of art as far as he was concerned. Floor-to-ceiling windows, thick and framed in wood so that it looked as if windows made up one wall. The windows looked out over the back patio and landscaping leading to the forest. The bed was positioned so that the first thing he saw when he opened his eyes was the trees. Those windows were deceiving in that they were thick like walls because each was a door that swung outward, allowing him to escape easily should there be a need. Above the bank of windows, the wall angled inward slightly, and four large skylights brought in light during the day or the stars at night.

Ordinarily when he walked into that room, the hardwood floor under his bare feet, his gaze would be riveted on the forest. Now all he could see was the woman standing with her back to him, looking out the window. She was totally naked, her dark hair up in one of those ridiculous messy knots that was never going to stay because he was going to tear it loose the moment he had the chance.

All he could do was stare at the perfection of her ass. She had hips on her, beautiful feminine curves that served to emphasize her waist, but that ass was a sight to behold. Actual perfection. The moment he saw it, he wanted to claim it. He knew her body was made for him. The hell with her modesty. The towel had to go. It was rasping, sawing on the wide girth of his cock.

He stalked across the room, more animal than man, coming up right behind her, close, his body crowding hers, so she felt his heat. Felt the absolute brutal intentions of his cock. Bending his head, he nuzzled her bare neck with his nose, inhaling her clean fragrance. How could her neck look so innocent? That sweet line of her spine down to the curve of her hips and that perfect ass?

Her entire body trembled, shivering exquisitely against his. He'd never felt that before, satin skin sliding smoothly against his. It made her feel even more vulnerable to him than her diminutive size against his much larger frame.

"I was beginning to think you weren't going to come." Ambrie's voice shook, her whisper barely heard.

"Why would you think that? Were you afraid I would

abandon you on our wedding night?" He kissed her neck
and then bit her shoulder gently. Just a small nip. Damn. She
tasted like honey. Lavender honey. How the hell did she manage that? He ran his tongue over the spot to be certain. It was
there. That subtle taste of lavender honey right on her skin.

"You weren't exactly thrilled with the idea earlier."

"You didn't think so?" He pressed his cock tighter against
her. "You have any worries about whether or not I want
you?" He slid his hand down her back to caress her left
cheek. She was firm but soft. So fucking soft. He closed his
eyes just savoring the feeling of her skin before he continued
his exploration.

"Need to know if you still want me, princess. If you're
just going through with this because you think you have to."

"All I thought about while I was in the bath was what our
night was going to be like." She whispered it as though confessing a terrible sin.

The green light. That was all he needed. What he'd been
waiting for. He wasn't going to keep pretending he was some
fucking white knight because he'd never been in that role.
Not once since he'd been born. He'd been shaped into something feral and brutal, a harsh, vicious man with few re-
deeming traits.

"Put your palms on the window."

Ambrielle complied slowly, but without real hesitation.

He slid his foot between hers and widened her stance,
one hand on her back between her shoulder blades, pushing
her head down so she was forced to bend over. He kicked at
her ankle, forcing her to spread her legs more. "That's it.
That's where I want you. Don't move. Stay just like that."

He cupped her left ass cheek with his palm, stroked it and
then slid his hand lower to test between her legs. She was
already slick and hot for him. She hadn't been lying. "You
were thinking about me, weren't you, princess?" That surprised him. Maybe he'd gotten more than lucky, and his new
little wife was the kind of woman who was very turned on

by rough. He hoped so, because he didn't know—or care for—any other way.

Ambrielle could barely think, her mind in complete chaos. She had thought of her parents when she ripped the bloody wedding dress from her body and kicked it into the corner of the bathroom along with her high heels and torn nylons. She showered for what seemed hours, crying for her parents until she thought there were no more tears in her body left to shed. Then, while she filled the deep bathtub with hot water and the fragrant bath oil she'd found on the granite sink, she thought about how she was going to put a bullet right between the eyes of Gleb, Denis and Walker Thompson.

She didn't want to think about all the other women Master had brought to this particular room to have bath oils sitting right there on the sink in an ornate bottle. The tub was beautiful and located, strangely enough, right off the master bedroom, meaning she could stare right at the bed as she took her bath.

She had laid her head back and forced her mind to think about nothing but Master. She didn't want to think about her parents anymore. Or the disastrous wedding Thompson had tried to force her into. The bodies lying on the chapel floor as she'd married Master. She'd forced him into marriage. Clearly, he hadn't been happy at the idea and had done just about everything he could to talk her out of it.

Ambrie had filled her mind with the look of Master. All that dense muscle and hard strength. His eyes. Those killer eyes. There wasn't anything soft about him. He had big hands, scars on them. Tattoos on them. Tattoos crawled up his neck. There was something about the way he towered over her, the wideness of his shoulders, as if he could block out the world with his body and take over. It was the rawness of him and that feral, predatory look, almost a cruelness in him that drew her like a magnet. Just thinking about him made her slick with heat.

She had concentrated on that. Thought about the way his kiss had turned her inside out. So hot her brain had incinerated. That bulge in his trousers had been more than impressive—in fact, maybe a little intimidating, but it was all hers now. She wanted him. She was going to claim him. Have him. Keep him. This was her wedding night, and she wasn't going to sleep. Or let him sleep. She wasn't about to think of anything but sex. Raw, beautiful, hot sex, and he'd better be good at it. Good enough to keep her from thinking about anything but him all night.

"Asked you a question. Expect an answer."

The hard authority in his voice unexpectedly turned her on even more. Ordinarily, she would have told him to go to hell, but bent over, his hand on her ass and his fingers circling her clit and then stroking her scorching slit sent a fresh flood of warm liquid to coat his fingers.

"Yes. I told you I was." It was all she could do not to push onto his fingers. She was beginning to feel desperate, and she didn't even know why. Was it just the fantasies she'd conjured up? Could her own mind be making her feel this way when she'd never once wanted another man other than with a fleeting moment of interest? Nothing like this wildfire out of control?

Then he was on his knees, his wide shoulders shoved between her legs, his mouth replacing his fingers without any warning whatsoever. His tongue stabbed deep, lashing and scooping, finding her hidden secret nerve endings, already sensitive beyond anything she'd ever known or imagined. The sensation was absolutely shattering, tearing her mind apart. He wasn't gentle. He was rough in his claiming, merciless, nearly snarling as he devoured her.

Ambrielle didn't know how to feel, her body coiling tight so fast, the pressure building and building until it threatened to destroy her. She tried to buck him off, pushing back against the glass, rocking her hips to dislodge him. At the same time, she never wanted him to stop. Nothing had felt like the sensations he was giving her. He just needed to slow down and let her process, let her catch her breath. She couldn't even tell him that, it was just so much.

"Stop fighting it, princess, and let go." His tongue stroked and caressed over her clit for a couple of moments and then flicked hard. "Your pussy tastes just like lavender honey. Fuckin' amazing. I'll never get enough."

His mouth was covering her slit and clit again, and he was using his teeth and fingers as well as his tongue. He knew what he was doing. Ambrie pushed deeper into his mouth, rocking her hips as the pressure built so fast she thought she might detonate and be completely destroyed. Nothing could be that intense and not kill you.

He growled again, like a feral animal, attacking with a ferocity that was terrifying even as it was amazing and beyond intense.

"Ambrielle. Fucking let go."

If she did, if she surrendered, it might be the last thing she ever did. Who cared? She had no choice. If she didn't, she might not survive. As it was, she knew she would never be the same. She would never be Ambrie without wanting this from Master. He thumped and flicked her clit, his mouth relentless.

She came apart, just as she knew she would, an explosion that took everything she was, shattering her into little pieces like broken glass. He made those animal sounds as he lapped up every bit of the liquid pleasure pouring out of her. He sucked and licked, bit and tugged until he swallowed her down, taking everything she was or had ever been. Her legs threatened to crumble out from under her and would have, if he hadn't wrapped his arms firmly around her hips, wiping his face on her thighs, making soothing noises as he rose up behind her like a giant, all that hard muscle sliding against her skin.

"You did good, perfect, little princess," he praised, his hand stroking her back, rubbing her buttocks.

Her entire body trembled as aftershocks hit, nearly as

strong as the orgasm he'd given her. His hand kneading and rubbing her left cheek only added to her overstimulated nerve endings, and her sex clenched hard, wringing another cry out of her.

Master laughed. "That's my girl. That's what we want. You want to be nice and slick for me. So ready."

Ambrielle didn't know how she could be more ready. She tried to turn around, but he caught her around the waist and lifted her almost like a rag doll, as if she didn't weigh anything at all. The bed was close, and he simply dropped her in the middle of it on her back and went down over her, his knee between her legs.

"You have great tits, babe. Noticed first thing. Gorgeous. Impossible to hide even in the middle of a gunfight." His eyes were fixed on her breasts, his large hands covering them. Squeezing. Kneading. He was completely focused, although his thigh was pushed high, deliberately rubbing her oversensitized clit so that she found herself riding his thigh, her body coiling tight again despite her belief it was impossible.

She wanted more. Even needed more. Her breath was coming in rapid, sawing, ragged pants. His mouth was on her left breast, a tight suction, a fiery flame, tongue and teeth almost painful, and yet every flick sent lightning straight to her swollen, needy clit. His thumb and finger on her right nipple were merciless, tugging and rolling, even pinching that little bit too hard, so that she wanted to squirm away but found herself arching into him, needing more, tears in her eyes as more lightning strikes added to the delicious chaos happening to her body.

It occurred to her that he was far too experienced for her, and she might want everything he could give her, but she wasn't as ready for his brand of sex as she might want to be. She just didn't want to think—and it was impossible to think when he kept her body raging with need—he was that perfect. He gave her exactly what she needed.

Ambrielle felt the hottest, sexiest, velvet-over-steel

cockhead push into her entrance, and her heart accelerated. Fresh welcoming liquid surrounded him, and his hands slid from her breasts to her thighs, parting them farther, fingers biting deep.

"That's my princess," he murmured, focusing intently on where they were joining together.

She couldn't help looking at his face. Every line was carved with pure sensuality. Deep. It was sexy as hell. Carnal. A little bit terrifying. His chest was thick and heavily muscled, covered in scars. Deep ones, shallow ones. Knife and bullet scars. Scars from whips. Tattoos covered his chest and followed his amazing road map of muscles straight to his narrow hips and down farther.

Her breath caught in her throat. "No way in hell. No way." She whispered the edict aloud, staring at the monster trying to invade her.

The moment she caught sight of his cock, and she wasn't certain whether or not one could actually call his cock a weapon, her body reacted with a flood of hot liquid. Her heart pounded in both trepidation and a thrill beyond her comprehension. Her tongue moistened her lips and she found herself widening her thighs, pushing her body onto that impossibly thick and long monster.

"Master, it burns." It did. So much. Sizzled. Burned. Took her breath. Took away every thought in her head so she could not remember anything, couldn't think about anything but this man and what he was doing to her. To her body. It hurt like hell. "No. Stop. It really burns."

"In a good way," he countered, his voice that nearly hoarse enticement. His eyes jumped up to meet hers, blazing with lust. With possession.

She shook her head. "Wait. You have to wait."

He suddenly stopped, his eyes meeting hers in shock. His cock burned, scorching hot, the broad head barely lodged in her, but pressing, pushing against the tight silken muscles and barrier. "What the fuck? Do you think you might have told me?"

"Just give me a minute to breathe. You're huge." He couldn't stop. She didn't want him to stop. He had to keep moving, she just needed him to keep her fully engaged. She felt desperate.

Master leaned into her, his cock pressing just a little deeper, stealing her breath, as he touched his lips to hers. His breath was warm. Minty. "You're so brave. I've never met a woman like you. So damned brave." His lips feathered kisses down her chin. He nipped gently. "You positive you want this, princess? I do this, there's no taking it back. I'm not exactly a gentle man."

He was being gentle though. Ambrielle was afraid he was stealing her soul. Her heart did a strange fluttering in her chest as he nipped her chin and kissed his way down her throat, rocking his hips against her.

"I'm sure, Kir, absolutely certain. No doubts. I want to be your wife in every single way. You said you wanted me to have a choice. My choice is you." She used his real name, wanting him to know she meant what she said.

His gaze flicked up to hers, and her breath caught in her throat at what she saw there. Stark possession mixed with a strange tenderness. Raw passion. Dark, carnal lust. Her body reacted with hot, pulsing desire.

"Burn for me, Ambrielle." One hand cupped her breast, squeezing and kneading, and then his thumb and fingers were rolling her nipple and pinching down relentlessly, sending a wicked lightning strike straight to her clit. Another flood of wet heat surrounded his monstrous cock, and he mercilessly pushed another inch deeper, tearing through the thin barrier and straining the walls of her sheath until she thought she would be torn apart.

She couldn't help the cry of pain, although she tried to muffle it with her knuckles. It did hurt. God, it hurt. But it didn't stop her from wanting him. She was burning for him. She was stuffed so full she was afraid he would tear her apart, yet she wanted more. She needed more of him. She rocked her hips in an effort to take him deeper, although it didn't seem possible. His hands went back to her thighs, forcing them apart even more. Stretching her legs wider.

"Relax now, baby. That's it. Look at you taking me."

His gaze was once more fixed on their joining, and Ambrie couldn't help staring down at their bodies. The way he held her helpless and wide open for his invasion, his cock halfway swallowed by her so-much-smaller body, was somehow sexy as hell. That brought another fresh onslaught of hot liquid, allowing another inch to push through her tight folds.

"Fucking tight, baby, and scorching hot. It does burn, doesn't it? I'm going balls deep now, Ambrie. I'll go slow, but you're taking every fucking inch of me, you understand? All of me." He began a steady pressure, a relentless, merciless drive that refused to stop pressing forward, determined to bury himself in her reluctant folds, no matter that her body was too tight.

Ambrie wanted him in her. All of him. But he didn't fit. He wouldn't fit. She caught at his shoulders, burying her fingernails deep. "There's too much of you."

"You were born to take my cock, woman."

She was. She wanted it. Him. All of him. "Slow down and let me get used to it. I mean it, Master. I want this. But I have to be able to adjust to your size." Now her nails were scratching down his back, then leaving a trail on either side of his ribs.

He laughed softly and stopped moving again. "Get with it, princess. I don't like slow."

His cock, feeling the size of a log, was like the hottest steel poker filling every inch of her, pushing at soft tissue and igniting inflamed nerves, setting off a wildfire she couldn't seem to gain control of. She rocked her hips again and again, riding him, unable to stop the little moans and keening noises that insisted on escaping as her body thankfully relaxed more. That accommodated another thick inch.

She was so full—so stretched. She wasn't certain she could really handle the size of him, when she could already feel her sheath straining to accommodate him. Her heart fluttered, a part of her panicking. He must have known, because he captured her jaw in one large hand and held her still, forcing her to look him in the eyes. It was too intense. He was too intense. His cock was going to tear her in two if she wasn't careful, yet she needed him inside her. She needed him.

"You can take me, baby. All of me. Every fucking inch is yours. You want it?"

"Yes." She whispered her answer decisively.

Master suddenly leaned forward and bit down on her nipple. She gasped as fiery flames shot straight to her clit. Her entire sheath contracted and expanded. He surged forward, burying himself deep when the welcoming liquid once more surrounded him.

Ambrielle muffled her cry as he stuffed her so full, she could feel the thick vein, his throbbing heartbeat hammering in tune with her own.

Master stroked her inner thighs. "Balls deep, my little princess. You did it. You took your cock like no one ever has. You earned it. I'm going to fuck you hard, baby. That's the way I like it. Rough. Hard. You'll like it too."

She was panting, her breathing ragged, but she had to admit, her body was adjusting to his thickness and length. She needed him to move. She didn't care how. He just had to move.

"Go for it," she whispered. She didn't want any time to think. She just wanted to feel. It didn't matter to her how terrifying it was, or how much it burned or even at times hurt; it also felt amazing, and the way he looked at her was the most intense thing she'd ever experienced. She hadn't known she could ever feel this way about a man and sex.

A blaze of fire streaked through her as he pulled back with his hips, taking her breath with him, and then he drove that thick, long shaft as deep as he could possibly go. There was no way to cry out, no breath left in her burning lungs to tell him to keep going or she might die right then and there.

He had to move, but if he moved, her body might come apart.

Master pulled his hips back again, in a long, slow withdrawal that had her tensing her thighs and tightening the muscles in her sheath around his cock to prevent him from leaving her.

"You're killing me, princess. You're so fucking tight I think you're going to strangle my cock—if it doesn't go up in flames first." His voice was so hoarse, a husky, sensual sound.

Lightning seemed to fork through her body, and flashes of color played behind her eyes. She dug her fingernails into his back again, crying out as the tension coiled tighter and tighter. Her head thrashed on the mattress, and she couldn't seem to control herself. She felt wild and abandoned, aware of every nerve ending in her body. On fire. Insane with her need of him. She wanted more. All the time more. He could never stop. If he did, the world would end for her. It would end and she would end with it.

He was taking her to the stars, climbing there with her, showing her the way. All around her the pinpoints of light scattered like a crazy out-of-kilter galaxy he was sending her soaring into. "Don't stop," she begged, scraping down his back with her nails, tears running down her face.

Her body betrayed her, clamping down on his, taking him with her, strangling his cock. She could feel the way the crashing waves rolled through her, so powerful and demanding, the silken muscles like tongues lashing and sucking, milking him dry. His cock pumped and jerked while ropes of hot semen coated the walls of her sheath, triggering more and more waves.

She couldn't breathe. Couldn't think. She drifted there, with his body collapsing over hers, his cock buried deep, still jerking with every squeeze and contraction. His arms went around her, holding her to him. His face was buried in her neck. She kept hers buried in his shoulder.

Don't think. Don't think. Don't think. Just about Kir. Her husband. She could think about him. That was acceptable. *Please, please, please, please.* She had no idea what she was pleading for, but that beautiful euphoria she had been drifting in was leaving her mind and she was coming back to reality. That couldn't happen. Panic began to set in. Her only savior was the man she clung to.

She managed to lift one hand and bury her fingers in his hair. He'd been incredible, although it had hurt like hell at first and she was probably never going to walk again. He was still lodged in her, joined with her, skin to skin. Making them one. His arms were around her, holding her tight, holding her together when her entire world was gone and there was nothing left. Nothing. She had him. Kir Vasiliev. He was her husband, her partner.

He felt huge inside of her, stretching her in spite of the mixture of his semen and her blood and cream. She was still so wet. Was he still hard? Was that even possible? She was certain it wasn't, but she wanted it to be. She swirled her hips experimentally, trying not to wince when he hit a sore spot.

"You all right?"

"I think so. I'm not breathing."

He rolled them over fast so she was sprawled on top of him and he was still buried deep. He was hard. On top of him, she could feel him differently. He felt like a pole, his wide girth stretching her tender tissues, and each time she moved even a little, the friction radiated through her body with shocking intensity.

"Um, Master, you're still, um . . ." She trailed off lamely and lifted her head. Hopeful. Needing him to want to go another round with her. Go all night. The next day. Just never stop so she never had to think again.

"Hard as a fuckin' rock, princess. That happens to me. Lucky for you, although you're going to be sore. Sit up— you're going to ride me this time. Then you can take another bath with some salts to help with the soreness."

"Ride you?" She was already sitting up, her knees on

either side of his narrow hips. He was built strong. All muscle. A lot of him. Tons of scarring, now that she got a good look at him. She could see the tattoos on him. He seemed to favor Russian prison tattoos.

His hands went to her hips. "Yeah, babe, like a horse. You ever been on a horse? Look at your tits. So beautiful."

He lifted her hips, and she didn't need a second urging. She wanted to bliss out again. She needed it more than she needed anything else. He guided her into spirals and then leaning back and forward, then harder and deeper. Her breasts bounced and jiggled, drawing his attention so that he sat up, capturing her left one and drawing it into the hot cavern of his mouth. Searing heat rushed through her veins. She couldn't take her eyes off him devouring her breast. Pulling, kneading, using his teeth and tongue ruthlessly on her nipple, sending those amazing lightning strikes to her clit.

She ground down on his cock, rocking forward and back as she did so, not caring how sore she was, chasing after the magic of mindless pleasure again. It wasn't working. Nothing was working. Panic began to set in, and she grasped at Master's arms, her eyes finding his.

Shit. He'd never taken a woman before who had no experience with sex. He had no experience with intimacy or decent sex. He fucked. He didn't know any other way. He'd done his best with her, but he could see the desperation in her eyes. His lady was unraveling. He didn't blame her. He'd even expected it. The trust in her as she looked to him to save her settled in his heart. That trust wasn't something he had expected. It was a gift.

He slid his hands from her breasts to her rib cage and then down her belly. "You too sore to keep going, princess? I'm not going to be upset with you if we have to stop."

Real panic hit her. She shook her head. She ground down on the thick length of his cock, sending waves of shimmering heat through his body. She was tight and scorching hot. The fact that she was his and so willing to take his monster of a cock when she shouldn't want anything to do with him made it even more necessary for him to find a way to aid her.

Master's fingers settled on her hips, taking control back. He lifted her easily, pulling her body off him, and then surged into her as he brought her down. Her eyes widened. Yeah. She liked that. He did that several times and then settled her, guiding her body with his hands, so that she was riding him hard, just the way they both seemed to need. Her lashes drifted down.

"No, baby, you look at me. Right at me." He made it a command, not taking a chance that she'd turn inward again. To make certain, he captured her jaw with one hand, holding her face still, forcing her to stare at him as she rode his thick cock.

With every surge of his hips, he felt her liquid heat surround him, felt her tight sheath bite down so the friction was growing hotter and hotter. He surged upward as he slammed her small body down over his shaft. Harder. Deeper. Bucking. Driving into her. She caught the rhythm, her hips meeting his. Streaks of fire raced down his spine to his groin. Settled there. Burned. His cock expanded until his girth pushed that silken sheath as far as it could possibly go.

Her eyes glazed. Her lips parted. Her breath came in rapid pants. Her magnificent tits bounced up and down as her body suddenly clamped down violently on his, squeezing and milking, taking him with her so that his cock erupted in a frenzied explosive rocketing of semen across the walls of her sheath.

She sprawled over him like a rag doll, her body still working his, the aftershocks nearly as strong as her orgasm, sending spears of pleasure arcing through his body. He'd never experienced anything like it with any of the women he'd ever been with. He held her, stroking caresses in her hair while both of them worked at getting their breathing back under control.

"I'll run you a bath, babe," he offered. He knew he sounded gruff. He wanted her soaking. He knew he wasn't going to be able to leave her alone for very long and she was going to be sore.

She just nodded without lifting her head, too exhausted to answer him.

—

Master was careful to tuck the blankets around her once she was out of the tub. The temperature on the coast was cold. Living in San Francisco, she was most likely used to the colder weather, especially at night, but he wasn't taking any chances. She was completely naked under the covers. He liked knowing she was, even if she was sore as hell. She propped two pillows under her head and stared up at him with her large blue-violet eyes.

He figured he might as well get the talk over with. If they were really going to do this, he was going to lay it out for her. "So, here's how we're going to start off, princess. We're going to establish a few house rules, because this marriage is going to be real, and I'm not going to have one of those shit relationships. We're going to be a solid couple. You'll have my back, and I'm going to have yours. That means we're on the same page and we gotta talk shit out."

Ambrie's long lashes fluttered. The tips, dark and thick, framed her amazing eyes, even though her eyes were dark and bruised and beginning to swell. She looked a little amused. "I'm listening. I want the same thing."

"I'm telling you up front, I don't know what the fuck I'm doing, so you have to spell it out when you want or need something. Don't think I can read your mind. You want space, say so. You want me close, you need to let me know. I'll learn fast, but you gotta direct me. It isn't that I don't want to do for you—I do. I don't do well with uncertainty."

"That's fair. I can do that."

"You want to go shopping, you can't go alone right now. It isn't safe, but you aren't a prisoner. Say what you want, and I'll go with you. Any kind of food, we'll make a list and get it in. You like to go out for dinner, Alena has a great little restaurant, and I'll take you there."

"Before anything else, I want you to keep your word and make certain my friends are safe. Amanda and her brother, Adam. My partner, Daniel, and his wife, Lacy."

"That's been taken care of. I'll take you to them after you get some rest."

"I could call Amanda tonight," she countered.

He made an effort to push down his temper, but he knew it showed in his eyes. "You callin' me a liar?"

She frowned. "Why would you think that?"

"I just said I'd take you to them after you get some rest. I thought that would be better than calling them. Do you think I'm lying and haven't secured them?"

"No, I just wanted to hear Amanda's voice."

"Later, after you get some rest. It's fuckin' late. I expect honesty. I fuckin' hate liars. No leaving shit out; that to me is the same as lying. You don't flirt with other men. That's a good way to get someone killed. You don't cheat. That will get someone killed, and you'll feel it a long, long time. You get pissed at me for something, you tell me, straight up. Right then. Don't brood about it, just say it. We can make this work if we both put effort into it, and we want it to work. You don't say no to sex unless there's a damn good reason. Understand? If there is, you state what it is. And if something hurts or scares you when we're havin' sex, you say so."

"And do all those same rules apply to you?" Ambrielle challenged.

"Yes. I won't lie to you, or cheat. If I'm pissed, you'll know. I won't say no to sex if you're asking." He gave her a faint smile, fairly certain that wasn't going to happen.

"I don't know much about sex, other than I expect you to make it really good for me. When I say really good, I mean spectacular. You want it all the time, then make it great. Teach me to make it great for you. I'm all for learning. I want a good marriage with you. I do. I meant what I said when I said I'd commit for life. That means I'll give it my best."

"Good. I expect you to treat me with respect when we're out in public, which means don't argue with me. You want to argue, do it here or when we're in the truck together. I'll listen to you. You don't give me respect, especially around the brothers, there's going to be hell to pay. You got that?"

"Yes. I expect the same."

"You'll get it."

She tilted her head to one side and studied him. "I know what I wanted out of this, but you said you didn't care about the money. You told your man to do some kind of prenup so you wouldn't get it. I'm going to get my own lawyer and do a workaround so you get the money anyway. I'm not taking any chances that Walker Thompson finds a way to get his hands on it. But why would you tie yourself to me? Did your club president force you to in order to find that Russian woman? Am I part of some deal you're going to make for her?"

He could see real fear in her eyes. He hadn't expected her to think that, but it made sense. She couldn't understand why they'd bothered to rescue her. She was trying to reason it all out.

"First, as my wife, no one is going to take you away from me. Not ever. There will be no using you as bait or exchanging you in a deal. And second, no one can ever force me to do anything I don't want to do, Ambrielle. I had enough of that done to me when I was young. I swore never again."

"But you went to prison."

"That was always my choice. I went there to get a job done, always knowing it was for a set time. Then I was out again."

She propped her head up on the heel of her hand. Her eyes had gone nearly violet as her gaze drifted over his face. "Could any of the others have been put on that license, or just you?"

He shrugged his shoulders, hesitant to tell her. He didn't

want her to look at Keys, not even for a moment. Keys was a brother, but Ambrielle was his wife now. No one touched her. No one flirted with her. She was off-limits.

"Not just any of them. Keys volunteered to have his name put on it, but I said no."

"Why?"

He sighed, but he wasn't going to lie to her. They weren't going to start out that way, not after his big fuckin' speech. "Because that asshole Thompson wasn't going to lay a finger on you. I knew I could stop him."

"Why would you marry me, Master?" Ambrie persisted, her voice soft.

"Because I wanted you to belong to me. And you do. You're mine. Your body and soul belong to me. Now I just need to win your heart. That's going to be a little more difficult. I've never managed to win anyone's heart. Not ever. I've got a big fuckin' challenge in front of me." He gave her that same faint smile that never reached his eyes because smiles in his world weren't ever real.

Ambrielle's small white teeth bit down on the side of her lower lip and chewed at the mark he'd put there. The tip of her tongue touched it as if soothing the bite. "You really married me because you wanted me? Why?"

He let out his breath. For the first time he wanted to laugh. Really laugh. "Look at you, woman. You're so fucking beautiful it hurts. And you're pure class. The way you move, the way you talk. You look like something out of a magazine. You're smart. You can actually think for yourself, and you're not afraid to look me in the eye when you're pissed at me. I could go on, but it doesn't matter. A man like me doesn't stand a chance with a woman like you. I approach you in a bar and ask to buy you a drink, you'd tell me to fuck off."

Those strangely colored eyes drifted over his face and then down his bare chest. She shook her head slowly. "You're the first man in my entire life I've ever been physically attracted to." Her smile curved her full lips, drawing attention to the mark he'd put on her. His mark. "I saw you and the chemistry was off the charts, even when I knew I was going to have to kill you. It was such a shame. Then you kissed me, and you melted my panties off. I would have taken the drink in the bar. I probably would have gone home with you if we made it that far. That's how classy I am."

She could make his cock hard just talking about her panties melting off. Shit. He was acting like a teenager without the least bit of control. His jeans weren't even halfway buttoned and already the material was too damned tight. You'd think he hadn't seen any action in years.

"Tell me what you need from me. What kind of marriage did you envision when you thought about it?"

Her gaze dropped to the front of his jeans and her breathing changed. He kept back the grin of pure satisfaction. His princess liked his body, especially his cock. He hoped she had no inhibitions when it came to sex, because he didn't have any.

"I always thought I'd find a man who loves me, but things change, you know. I can accept that."

He didn't know what the hell love was, and they'd just met. It wasn't as if he could reassure her. But he would do his best to give her a good life with him. "I'll do right by you." That was the best he could give her. "Keep talking, princess. What do you want out of our marriage? What kind of life are you looking for?"

If she kept looking at his cock with hunger in her eyes and that little tongue of hers kept darting out and moistening her lips until they were wet and gleaming, he was going to palm the back of her head and bring her mouth right where it belonged. There wasn't going to be time for any more talking. He didn't want to do that right now. Well, he did, but she needed sleep. Desperately. She was on the verge of a breakdown. She had all the signs.

"I like working with my partners and had always hoped my husband would be interested, at the end of the day, in what I do and have no objection to me continuing with my work."

"What is it you do?"

"I help people with their finances. People come to me, usually unable to figure out how to save money for retirement, or they want to buy a house. They can't manage to get their credit score where it needs to be, or they aren't happy with the way their money is being managed. I help them get all that under control."

He was listening to her voice and watching her expression as she told him. The animation and joy let him know she needed to keep her work in her life. She liked the people she worked with, and she liked her customers.

"Sounds good. I'm all for that. I'm fairly good with numbers myself. Do that sort of thing for our club and help Code every now and then. I'd like to see where you work and check out what you're doing when we have the time to settle in. The house has an office space that will be perfect for you when you need to work from home, although I will prefer you keep your work away from here as much as possible so it's the two of us at home. I'll do the same."

His phone rang, telling him it was Czar calling. "Gotta take this, babe. Be right back. You try to go to sleep, and in the morning, we'll eat, get clothes for you and go see your friends."

He didn't wait for her reaction, but answered the phone and strode out of the room. Czar was concerned because Code was beginning to get rumors on the woman identified as Helena Smirnov, that she was running a second team of private assassins and pointing them toward Caspar.

"It isn't as if we weren't aware of that team, Czar. I handed you that information."

"Code said it was possible they were coming out of San Quentin."

Master stared in silence out the window of his great room at the leaves rustling in the trees. Finally, he sighed. "I don't care what Code's rumors are saying, Czar. They aren't in San Quentin. Even if they were, I'm not going back to prison. I told you, I'm done. You need someone to go, you find someone else."

"It's Blythe and the kids, Master," Czar said.

"I know who they're after. It's my sanity. I'm telling you, the second team isn't in prison. She wouldn't be that stupid. They have to be mobile at a moment's notice. If Code is hearing rumors, she's clever enough to be starting them. Trust me on this."

This time Czar was quiet for a long time. "I guess I'm going to have to, Master. This has thrown me. They missed by a mile last time, but I can't keep the family under wraps forever, and the woman knows it."

"We'll be ready." Master hoped he was right. He slipped his phone into the pocket of his jeans and went back to the master bedroom.

She wasn't in their bed. He glanced toward the bathroom, but he already knew she wasn't there. She had to be totally exhausted. He'd fucked her two times. Hard. She'd been up for a good forty-eight hours, drugged, kicked around, traumatized—she needed sleep. Now he was going to have to go after her and drag her ass back, scare the crap out of her instead of treating her the way he wanted. Like the princess he called her. Damn it.

SIX

Ambrielle was crying. Well, damn. Master stood on the deck listening to her heart-wrenching weeping, feeling as if he'd just stepped into a very private moment that was defining in some way. A big way. He could slink away and pretend he hadn't found her. He wanted to take the coward's way out, tell himself she'd left their bedroom to be alone to cry. She had the right to privacy. Most people didn't want others around when they cried. Ambrielle was most likely one of those. She was a compassionate little thing and wouldn't want to disturb him.

Yeah, right. He could talk himself out of anything. He didn't know the first thing about relationships because he'd never been in one, but he watched Czar and Blythe, and it seemed the little things Czar did for Blythe were worth far more to her than any grand gesture. Ambrielle might not feel the same, but Master was determined he would find the right path with her. It was just that . . . tears were manipulation.

He'd been taught that shit in prison. In Sorbacov's school for his "assets." Code word for assassins. Master was a damn good assassin. His woman wanted someone dead, he'd kill the son of a bitch for her, but tears . . . He'd never done tears very well. He'd never done them at all.

He half turned to go back into the house but stopped abruptly. He'd never backed down from anything he wanted in his life. He'd never walked away. He fought hard for everything he'd ever gotten—and that wasn't very much because, truthfully, he wanted very little. But Ambrielle . . . he wanted her. And he wanted her happy. She wasn't a manipulator. He had sized her up before he'd ever agreed to marry her. Then he continued to assess her character before he took the entire marriage seriously. Now he was serious. He was her husband, and she was crying. It might be a small thing to someone else, but to him it was enormous.

Master caught up the blanket she'd discarded on the glider facing the forest and approached her silently. She nearly jumped out of her skin when he wrapped the blanket around her shoulders and pulled her tight against his body. "Too cold out here. Your muscles are going to get stiff. You won't be able to walk."

She dashed at the tears on her face as if afraid to be caught crying, convincing him he was right—this was no manipulation. "I can't go back inside."

He pushed down his visceral reaction to her shaky statement and concentrated on her shivering body instead. He wasn't going to make this about him. He didn't need her to say she was regretting her decision to marry him. That he was far too rough for her. That he was a killer—anyone could see that, and she couldn't live with him. He didn't need to hear her regrets. He only needed to support her. She'd been through hell. He knew what hell was like.

He caught her up, wrapped in the blanket like a burrito, cradling her close to his chest, and carried her to the glider, where he settled his ass down, her on his lap, arms tight around her. Pressing her face to his shoulder, he began to rock her gently. "Cry all you want, Ambrie. No one can hear you but me. We can stay out here for the rest of the night if you prefer."

She pulled one arm out from the blanket and wrapped it around his neck. "I don't know why you're so good to me when I can't stop crying. I promised myself I wouldn't cry until after I killed Walker, but I can't stop. When we were together, I could put the way they murdered my parents out of my mind and just fill my world with you, but the moment I'm alone, I can't stop seeing them with blood all over them. I couldn't get to them in time to stop them from being murdered."

The anguish in her voice was heartbreaking. He wasn't the kind of man to let that kind of thing get to him. He was stone. Steel. He had to be. But she was twisting him up inside. He kept the chair moving gently back and forth and let her talk. She needed to get it out. Her body was shuddering, although her weeping was quiet. He felt the tears running down his chest, so he knew she was shedding them. Just silently.

"Then what do I do? I enjoy myself. Not just enjoy myself, I lose myself in you, totally, completely. I can't think of anything but you. I'm so mindless, so wrapped up in the orgasms you give me, that there's nothing but us. You and me. I want more. Your body. Anything you can give me. Teach me. I just want us alone right here, in a little cocoon where no one can reach us. What does that say about me? What kind of person am I? There's blood all over my wedding dress and my parents are murdered and all I can think about is having more sex with you."

She lifted her head, and this time her voice ended on a condemning wail as her tear-drenched eyes met his. Her lashes were spiky and her face swollen from crying. She was still the most beautiful woman he'd ever seen. She looked at him with guilt, expecting him to condemn her.

He wrapped one hand around the nape of her neck, his fingers finding the knots of tension there. "When I was a boy, my parents were murdered in front of me." He never opened that door. Never talked about it. Some things were best unsaid, but she needed to know she was human. Traumatized.

He exerted a little pressure, telling her silently to put her head on his chest so he wouldn't have to look at her when he said the things necessary to calm her. She resisted. Master sighed. He was a fucking idiot for starting this in the first place.

"I know it's not the same thing. I was a kid. This man, Sorbacov, my parents' enemy, took me to a school run by pedophiles. There was a prison on the same grounds. Quite a few of the instructors at the school came from the prison. Sorbacov claimed he was going to shape us into assets for our country, assassins. I didn't want to think about my parents and how they died. I wanted to learn how to fight and kill. I wanted to shape my body into a killing machine in order not to ever think about how my parents were murdered. A very wise man told me that was the brain's way of protecting me. That's what's happening to you. You've got to let it happen. Let your brain process the information at the pace you can handle without making you insane."

It was the most he'd said at any one time to someone outside the club that he could remember. Her eyes searched his and then she leaned into him, resting her head against his chest again. "Thank you. You didn't have to tell me, and I know you didn't want to."

"You're my wife. You have a right to know about me. I would have told you eventually." He continued massaging her neck, thinking about it. "That might be a lie. I don't know if I would have told you."

A little muffled laugh mixed with a sob escaped. "I love that you're so honest."

"I'm rude and crude and you're going to be embarrassed by half the things I say or do when you're around your fancy-ass friends," he corrected. His voice. He wished he could control the gravel in his tone that caused his voice to sound like he was going to commit murder any moment.

Again, her reaction shocked him. The arm around his neck tightened and she pressed closer to him, almost as if he were her lifeline. "That would show I have shocking taste in friends, and I don't think I do."

She made him want to smile. He kept gliding back and forth, listening to the wind in the trees, willing her to listen too. His fingers found the knots of tension in her right shoulder, worked at easing them.

"You would have liked my parents, Master."

"If they were anything like you, I'm certain I would have." He knew they would have been appalled that their beautiful, intelligent child had been placed into the path of a man with a prison record as long as his.

"My father pretended to be very exacting and strict with me. He was career military. So was my mother. She was the same way on the outside. Both were marshmallows with me on the inside."

With her free hand she began to draw little patterns on the muscles of his thigh. He was covered with denim, and she had the blanket separating them, but she might as well have been licking his skin with her tongue the way his cock reacted, coming to life and pushing a demand against the backs of her legs.

Ambrie's laughter was muffled against his chest. "You're amazing. Really, really amazing. I'll bet you could set some kind of world record for always being up for sex." Another giggle escaped. "Do you see what I did there?"

She was killing him. He liked her. He hadn't expected that. Admire. Respect. Crave. But actually like? He bent his head and found the sweet spot between her neck and shoulder with his teeth, scraping lightly. She reacted with a full-body shiver.

"I want to." Her whisper was very sincere. "I'm not sure I can ever walk again though. I'm pretty sore. Maybe I can take care of you another way?"

He suppressed a groan. Naturally, she would tempt him. He wasn't going to let her turn this into another marathon sex session. He didn't want their entire relationship based on sex, and that could happen so easily for both of them. He could see himself letting it because it would be so much easier than putting in the work, learning to understand her needs.

"Maybe you can relax and let me just hold you for a little while. I'm going to be hard anytime I'm around you or thinking of you. That's the way it's going to be. If you weren't so damn sexy it might be different, but you are, and we're both going to have to live with it." It came out gravelly, as if he might be annoyed with her.

Another sound, somewhere between laughter and choking, bubbled up. "I can't imagine that I'm so sexy right now. Bruises on my face. I'm an ugly crier. I've got bruises on my hip too. You're just pretending not to see, and I'm grateful for that."

"You're sexy. Settle down. You need rest."

The slight smile faded immediately. She turned her face fully up to his. "I'm afraid to close my eyes. Talk to me. Tell me about that horrid school. At least it sounds horrid. And the man who gave you good advice."

"He was a kid when he gave it to me. That was Czar. He was about thirteen or fourteen. He often came out with good advice, although at the time, when he said it, I usually wanted to punch him in the face. I was a pretty violent kid. Had a lot of rage in me."

"Czar was in that same school?" She rubbed her wet cheek along the heavy muscles of his chest like a kitten.

"Yes. All the original members of Torpedo Ink were in that same school with me. All of them lost their parents in the same way. Sorbacov hated their parents and had them murdered. He hated Czar above all else. He did everything he could to break him." Master stroked his hand down her hair. She had amazing hair. Soft as silk. How did women get their hair to be so damn soft? Or maybe it was just Ambrielle. He didn't make it a practice to bury his fingers in women's hair unless he was fisting it and dragging their heads back while he fucked them.

He tried to puzzle out why he felt so different about Ambrie. He barely even saw the women he paid in the clubs. He registered their faces because he looked for ones that had been around the block a few times. There weren't a lot of words exchanged. No promises made. No building up to any kind of intimacy. He didn't kiss. Mostly there was hard, rough fucking. He got them off because he wasn't a complete dick, but when he came out of prison, that was all he wanted to do, and frankly, he didn't give a damn who he did it with or even how. Until now.

"Sorbacov sounds like he's far worse than Walker Thompson, and I didn't think anyone could be worse."

"Sorbacov is dead. He was a serial killer drunk on his own power. He was the worst kind of pedophile. He enjoyed brutality, torture and rape. Watching it, doing it and leading others down that same path. The more brutal, the greater his enjoyment. He would get some of the kids in the school to believe he was benevolent. That he would give them extra food for ratting out others for infractions. He never spared them the punishments, but he always convinced them he would. He enjoyed seeing how often they would believe his betrayals. It amused him."

"Were all of you trained as assassins?"

"All the survivors. Out of two hundred eighty-nine children taken to the school over twenty years, only nineteen survived. I'm one of them. All of Torpedo Ink are survivors of that school."

She suddenly lifted her head, her eyes meeting his. "Master, do you think Gleb and Denis are survivors from your school? They're Russian and they weren't in the same league with Thompson's other men. Most of Walker Thompson's personal protectors were bulky men who relied on everyone seeing they had guns. Gleb and Denis and the other two men with them weren't like that at all. They were very quiet and ten times scarier. Thompson thought he controlled them, but he didn't. I know he didn't. They would have turned on him in a minute if he said the wrong thing to them."

"There were four schools that children were taken to. Three of the schools were legitimate, although extremely violent, and all the children were subjected to brutality while they trained. There are men for hire, they call themselves 'Ghosts.' We've run across them many times. We believe these men are from one or more of those schools and have banded together and have offices in various major cities where they offer their services."

"So Gleb and Denis would be from one of the other schools." She looked to him for confirmation.

Her eyes had gone that incredible shade of electric violet that didn't look real. Beautiful. Unusual. She reminded him of a glamorous movie star who didn't belong with a dirty biker who had spent more time in prison than he had out of it.

"Not certain yet, but Code will find out. He can track anyone, given enough time. We're working on it, princess. I made you a promise, and I don't break my promises."

Her gaze didn't leave his. "I'm counting on that. On you. I think the others will want you to go their way, Master. I could see it when some of them looked at me. They thought you were crazy to agree to take me with you. I think they thought you were humoring me so you could get . . ." She trailed off.

He grinned at her, leaned in and nipped her lower lip. "Pussy, baby. Your sweet ass and pretty little pussy."

He not only saw the blush moving up her naked body, he felt her skin heat. She buried her face against his chest instead of pulling away. He liked that a hell of a lot. Nothing he said or did seemed to offend or scare her off. She might look like a fairy princess, too ethereal for his world, but she was tough.

"I keep my promises too, Master. I'll make you a good wife." A little giggle escaped. "I'm really good with numbers. I have a feel for investments, so if you need any advice, I'm your girl. Domestically, that's hit-or-miss. I make a mean potato salad. And I can make an omelet. Sort of. If you don't mind it sometimes mushy in the middle or turned into a scramble at the last minute."

Master's laugh surprised him. It was the real deal escaping, along with a strange happiness he hadn't ever experienced before. She was giving him a few very unexpected firsts. His fingers tunneled in the silky mass of her hair. So beautiful. So classy. His classy little princess. She detested him calling her that, thought he was making fun of her. He was calling it like he saw it.

"I'll eat whatever you cook for me and appreciate it. I'm decent enough and can help out, especially with the cleanup and prep. We can learn together."

She gave him a little smirk, leaned into him and astonished him by pressing her mouth to his bare skin. "Are you a good assassin?"

"There isn't any such thing, baby, as a good assassin. I kill people. Don't try to make me into something I'm not. If you're wondering about my skills versus Gleb and his friends, I have no doubt I can take them on. That's why you're with me."

He had to remind himself, for him, the marriage might be real. She would always be his choice. This might be his wedding night, but he'd bought his wife with blood. She wasn't going to love him. Respect, yes. He would earn that. He knew he would.

She rubbed her face against his chest again, back and forth, as if in protest, but she didn't deny it. She couldn't. He was her killer, paid for with a life sentence. She was a prisoner, and even though she'd put herself in prison, imposed that sentence on herself, that was what she'd done. Traded the lives of the men who'd killed her parents for her own. She'd done so willingly, with her eyes open and with full knowledge and consent. He respected her for that. She wasn't going to pretend otherwise. She wasn't going to whine about it. She planned on making the best of her life with him.

"Tell me more about your life, Master."

Changing the subject. He heard the reluctance in her

voice. She didn't want to change the course she'd set out on for both of them, but she didn't want to call him out and name him a killer. She was gaining his respect with every minute they spent together.

"I think it would be better if you told me about your life. We're trying to keep you from having nightmares. My life was crap up until I laid eyes on you. Now I've got a shot at a decent life, and I'm taking it." He gripped her hair again and tugged until she looked at him. "Tell me about your friends."

His phone jingled. The sound was overly loud in the sudden silence. Immediately, he tensed. What the hell was he supposed to do now? He had to take the call.

"Gotta take this, princess. Wouldn't call this time of night unless it was an emergency." He pressed the talk button even as he stood and gently deposited Ambrie on the glider, blanket wrapped around her body. "Give me a minute. Alone."

Instantly, Ambrielle's chin went up, eyes narrowing suspiciously. "Who is that?"

"No one important. I'll be right back." He started for the door.

Ambrie was up and out of the glider, her much smaller body trailing after him. "If they aren't important, why can't you tell me who they are? You said we're communicating. No secrets. The first thing you do is break your own rule," she accused.

"Babe, really? It's no big deal. Give me a minute to take this, and we'll talk."

"Hand me the phone." She held out her hand, snapping her fingers, glaring at him.

She was five foot two at the most. He towered over her. She stood there, wrapped in a blanket, the picture of outrage. She made him want to laugh. Almost. "What the fuck is wrong with you, Ambrielle?"

"It's another woman, isn't it? Our wedding night and already you've got another woman, don't you?"

"Hell. You aren't kidding. You've gone from my cuddly little princess to psycho woman in two seconds flat." He put his ear to the phone. "Hang on, Reese. I have to talk to my wife for a minute. Yeah. I said my wife. Hang on."

She continued to stare up at him, but those long lashes of hers were fluttering now. She'd heard what he'd said.

"Don't have another woman. Have you heard anything I said to you tonight?" He made it an accusation when she was so damn cute he wanted to put his arms around her and pull her close all over again. "Now, I've got to take this call. It's important."

That stubborn look he was coming to recognize came over her face. He sighed and wrapped his arm around her as he once more lifted the phone. "Reese, you're on speaker-phone. My wife is listening as well. Don't hold back. Whatever you need to say, she can hear. What you tell me, you're saying to her. She wouldn't repeat anything she hears. You have my word on that."

"How do I know if she can be trusted?"

"Because I just gave you my fuckin' word. You interrupted our wedding night, so spit it out."

A sob could be heard in the background. Master frowned. "Reese? Is Tyra with you? Is the baby? Put Tyra on. I have to know she's all right."

"I didn't hit her if that's what you mean. Broke a few dishes."

"Scared the baby and Tyra," Master corrected, dropping his arm and stalking across the deck, unable to contain the adrenaline rising. "What the fuck, Reese? You're supposed to call me before you get to that point."

"I called you before I took a drink. Bottle's sitting right here in front of me. I haven't touched it yet. I need you to come now, Master. Everything's going to shit, and I can't put it back together." There was panic in Reese's voice. "You have to get over here now. I'm afraid to talk on the phone."

"Did you call your sponsor?"

"Yes, before I called you."

"Put Tyra on, and then I'm on my way. Don't you touch her or the kid. I'll be there."

A woman's voice came on. "Master?"

"You all right?"

"I'm scared. Not of Reese. Hurry, Master."

"Be there in ten. Keep him away from the bottle."

Master ended the call and then texted Ink to stop by Reaper's to pick up some clothes for Ambrielle. Anya was closest in size to his woman. He already knew where that stubborn look was going to take them.

"You catch up on your sleep and I won't be gone long," he suggested, guiding her back into the house.

Ambrie went with him without a fight. "You're not going without me. I don't want to be separated from you."

"You aren't the clingy type, princess."

"I *wasn't* the clingy type," she corrected. "I wasn't the psycho type either, but evidently I am now. I can wear one of your shirts, Master. I promise I won't lose my temper again, but I have to go with you. I've lost too many people I care about. I can't lose you too."

He fucking loved that, but he didn't let it show on his face. "Babe, you're worn-out." He traced her high cheekbone with the pad of his thumb, a gentle caress. "This could be a huge mess and take time to sort out."

"I know you must think I'm one of those silly women who has to be with their man every second. I swear I've never been like that in my life. I'm independent, but I'm so scared to be away from you. Just for a little while, I'm asking you to please let me tag along with you."

Master detested making her beg, but he honestly didn't want to take her because he was a little embarrassed. He knew he was going to have to answer questions. "You can come with me, princess. I've texted Ink, that's Reese's sponsor, to stop by Anya and Reaper's to pick up some clothes for you. She's close to your size. Tomorrow we'll get your clothes."

Before she could respond he walked her through to the

master bedroom. He needed his boots, shirt and jacket. Ambrie sank onto the bed, gripping the edges of the blanket so hard her fingers turned white.

"I'm sorry." Her voice was a whisper—a thread of sound. "I don't know what's wrong with me. I can stay here. I've got my big-girl panties on. I was thrown just for a minute, but I'm fine now."

He turned to face her, watched her press the pads of her fingers to her trembling lips. Her gaze refused to meet his.

"Babe, don't do that. Don't lie to me. We promised each other we wouldn't do that. We're not going to be those people. You're coming with me because I want you to come. I don't mind you having panic attacks. You just lost your parents, and you have some asshole forcing you to marry him. Oh. Damn. That asshole would be me." He tried to make her smile.

She didn't smile. Instead, she lifted those long lashes and finally looked him in the eye, her gaze searching his. He let her see he meant what he said. He wanted her to go with him or she wouldn't be going, no matter the circumstances. He might be uncomfortable admitting what he was doing, but she'd find out sooner or later.

He dragged on his shirt and jacket and, sinking down beside her, pulled on his socks and boots. "I told you, I don't do anything I don't want to do. I'm taking you with me because I want to, not because you're forcing me to."

The sound of a motorcycle drawing close had him standing, reaching to pull her close to him, catching the edges of the blanket and tightening it around her. "That's Ink. I'll get the clothes from him, and you can get dressed and ready to go. Whatever you hear tonight stays confidential. I mean it, princess. You act like you don't see it or hear it. Understand?"

"I'm a financial advisor, Master. I'm used to keeping things confidential," she assured him. "Thank you for being understanding. I'm all over the place and not making much sense."

"You're doing fine, Ambrielle," he corrected.

"Coming in," a voice called.

"In the bedroom," Master answered, positioning his body in front of Ambrie. He didn't exactly understand why. She was covered up by the blanket, and he wasn't a man concerned with his brethren seeing her naked, at least not as a rule. So, what the hell?

Her hand found the back of his jacket, fingers curling into a fist, and then her forehead rested on the small of his back as she leaned into him for support from her place at the edge of the bed. His heart reacted physically with a strange jerking. A curious melting sensation he'd never felt before. Emotions welled up. Protective. Beyond strong.

"Ink." His Torpedo Ink brother came through the door, eyes cool, sweeping the room, his dark hair disheveled from the ride on his silver Fat Boy Softail, with its custom images in scrolling Russian Cyrillic and Celtic symbols. Ink was covered in tattoos, all his own art, mostly animals and reptiles, giving the appearance of moving across his body as if alive when he took even the smallest of steps.

Master took the bag from him. "Thanks, man. She'll only take a minute."

"You sure about her going with us?"

Ambrie's fingers in his jacket fisted tighter. She'd gathered the skulls that rested in the roots of the tree in the patch on his jacket into her palm. Her head turned once, giving him a silent signal that she didn't want to be separated.

"Made her a promise, Ink."

"This could get ugly."

"Her wedding wasn't? Wading through dead bodies to get to Preacher? She's seen ugly. Give her five."

Ink shrugged. "Your call."

"Her choice."

Master waited until Ink had walked into the next room before he stepped forward to loosen Ambrielle's hold on him. He'd known all along the breakdown was coming. He wasn't about to blame her. She wasn't nearly as hysterical as she could have been. Should have been. He crouched down in front of her.

"Listen to me, princess. Ink is right. This could get ugly. I'll take you with me if you want to go, but we could be walking into a mess. I've got some cabins on my property and I let some people use them now and again. Sometimes they're in trouble and working their way out. Reese Fender is a good man. Has a good family: wife, Tyra; little girl, Sandree, about one or two. He's a damn hard worker, talented as hell. He was set up, for reasons I don't need to tell you right now, and sent to prison. We can get into that later. The thing is, he's an alcoholic. Made it easy for him to take the fall. I met him in prison, liked him. Knew he didn't do what they said and got my brother Absinthe to get him out. He's out on parole while we're trying to unravel everything."

"I need to stay with you." Her voice was very firm. "I might be good for Tyra and her daughter."

He framed her face with both hands and brushed a kiss on top of her head just for being brave. "Get dressed. Hurry. I don't want Reese to have too much time to think."

She nodded and Master quickly strode from the room to find Ink draped against the front door. That didn't surprise him. Ink was calm most of the time. When he moved, he could explode into action very quickly.

"She okay?" Ink asked.

Master shook his head. "Ambrie is one tough woman." He let admiration leak into his voice. "She's determined to keep her word and make this a real marriage. I gave her every out."

"You up for that? Having a woman in your life permanently? You never saw yourself like that before." Ink's tone was mild. Inquiring. Nothing more.

"With her? Yeah. I can do it with her. Don't ask me why, because I couldn't tell you, but I know I can. She makes me want to. There's something valiant about her." He felt like an idiot for even saying it, but Ink nodded as if he understood.

"Yeah, I kind of thought so too, when she stood there in

that wedding dress of hers with her shoulders straight and that gun in her hand."

"Reese tell you what his fuckin' parole officer told him he had to do, or he was going back in?" Master changed the subject.

Ink sighed. "Yeah, he told me. I said to put the bottle down and wait for us. That he needed to call you and we'd sort it out. Someone wants him back in prison, Master. We're going to add this to our long list of priorities."

"I have the feeling that if they manage to get him back in, this time, he won't be coming out alive. They'll arrange for an accident inside." Master scowled. "I should have been pushing harder to figure out who was behind these charges. I just thought some bitch was pissed because he turned her down, so she accused him of rape and battery."

"That never made sense to me. An MMA fighter goes down for rape and battery charges, although his wife maintains adamantly that he was with her the entire time and it was impossible, but the jury is persuaded he's guilty even though she can't identify his penis with the multiple piercings?" Ink said. "Not to mention the tattoos?"

"Absinthe felt the same way. I knew he wasn't guilty just talking to him. But he has a temper, he drank, and more than once he had an outburst in court."

"Because they accused him of cheating on his wife," Ink recalled.

Master nodded. "Yeah, that set him off every time. Reese has a real thing about honor and integrity and his wife. He's got a code. They called him the 'Knight' in the ring, because he was always so honorable. He never cheated on the rules. I never could understand why he started that descent into the bottle when he was so careful. It was evident his family meant the world to him. He made a fortune every time he stepped into the ring."

"The promoters began to pressure him to take a fall. He also had someone in his past putting pressure on him. He wouldn't tell me about it, but I suspect that's the person behind the woman who insisted he beat and raped her," Ink said. "You'll have to get him to open up, Master. He hasn't to me. Tells me all about the fight scene, training, the scandals, what the promoters and even his trainer did to him, but not the one thing we need to protect him."

Master sighed. "I'll do my best. I don't know why he's shielding this person, but essentially, that's what he's doing."

"You'll have to make him see he's trading his family, his freedom, and possibly his life if he doesn't help us," Ink said.

They both turned to watch as Ambrielle entered the room. He knew how small and curvy she was, but seeing her dressed in soft leggings and a clingy top that emphasized her full breasts, he could see how diminutive she really was in comparison to him. No wonder he felt like he could break her in half when he wrapped his hands around her.

She had pushed her feet into flip-flops that were far too big for her, and she was going to trip trying to walk in them. As it was, she was walking gingerly. He knew Ink noticed, because he did. Hopefully, Reese and his wife wouldn't.

"Lose the shoes, princess. We'll have your things here tomorrow. I'll carry you to the truck." He should have felt like a fool carting a woman around, but he liked cradling her in his arms. He knew she needed to be close to him, and that gave her an excuse.

"I can't go into someone's house barefoot." She looked horrified.

Ink lifted an eyebrow. "Some kind of law I'm not aware of?" He turned his head to look at Master. "You know about this law?"

Before Master could respond, Ambrie gave her appealing laugh, the one that sounded a little like perfectly tuned bells skipping over water. He was a music lover and knew a perfect pitch when he heard it.

"Are you always such a smart-ass, Mr. Ink?" She kicked off the offending flip-flops and made her way across the hardwood floor.

She looked a little like an injured ballerina. Master scooped her up. She smelled liked heaven. He was already getting used to that scent of hers. She was winning him over so fast it was a little on the scary side. He thought the explosive chemistry between them was what he was going to base his entire relationship with her on, but there was something else, something emotional and equally strong—maybe stronger—growing in him for her.

"Why, yes, ma'am, I most likely am," Ink agreed with her. "And you can drop the 'Mister' and just call me Ink. Everyone does."

"Are you responsible for all the beautiful tattoos on Master as well as on yourself?"

"Don't be looking at him." Master tried to sound like he was growling at her. He had that deep rasp in his voice, and apparently it worked very well, because she started that little musical laughter again. He deposited her in the passenger front seat of the truck, leaving Ink to sit in the back. "Seat belt," he added. "Not a damn thing on that man is beautiful."

"I think you need glasses, old man." She didn't back down for a second. "Did you even look at that sleeve?"

"Ink, you can run to the cabin. Get the fuck out of the truck."

He was rewarded with another burst of laughter, this one a little longer. She made his chest ache. Ink ignored him, but when he glanced in the rearview mirror, Ink had the beginnings of a little grin on his face as well. The woman was magic.

"Do you have very many cabins on your property you rent out to people you meet in prison who need chances?" Ambrielle asked.

Master made a face. His hands tightened on the wheel. "It's not like that. I have a few cabins. Nine I've renovated. They're in use now. There are six other cabins that are in bad shape that I'm still working on."

"Your property must be huge."

He didn't comment. It was. The cabins were tucked away in the forest. It was a pretty piece of land in heavy woods with several springs, a large pond and a smaller one on it. He liked working with his hands, and renovating the cabins, making each one different and as beautiful as he could while keeping them practical, had been his goal. His brothers had come often to help him, and he'd enjoyed the comradery while he worked, shaping each dilapidated cabin into a future home for someone in need.

"Wait until you see what he calls a cabin," Ink said. "And it's exactly like that. He finds some prisoner who can't find a job, is struggling to find a place to live, is a recovering alcoholic or drug addict, and they wind up here. Half the time, they don't pay much rent."

"You really do want to walk, don't you, Ink?" Master shot him a warning look.

It was too late. Ambrielle looked up at him from under those impossibly long lashes with far too much admiration. "You do have a heart of gold, don't you?"

"It's black, baby, all the way through, and you'd do well to remember that."

SEVEN

Master reversed the truck, backing into the space, blocking Reese's Jeep but facing forward for a quick escape. He texted two of the others in the Torpedo Ink club where they were and what they were doing, just in case they needed backup.

"Listen to me, Ambrielle. This is the perfect time for you to start learning to work with us. Hopefully, everything is cool and we have no problems, but if I give you the signal to hightail it out of there, you get to the truck however you can. Don't worry about Ink or me, just get in the driver's seat and get back to the house. Hit the lock on the security code and it will slam all armor in place. There are several caches of weapons in the house. The easiest for you to access is in the master bedroom in a panel in the wall directly behind the headboard of the bed. Text Czar. Tell him you're alone and need backup immediately. Tell me you understand the order."

She nodded. "I will, but I don't have a cell phone."

He handed her a burner. "Everything you need is in there. Stay behind me and stay quiet until I let you know it's okay to speak. If for some reason I can't direct you, take orders from Ink. Tell me you understand."

Ambrie nodded again. "I understand."

"That's my girl. Right behind me."

"You should be wearing a vest."

He couldn't help the little smile that came out of nowhere. It was rusty, but it broke through at her censure. "Yeah, babe. I should be. Wanted to get to him fast, before he did something really stupid. Just go along with anything I say."

Ambrielle nodded again.

Master wasn't altogether certain he should trust her when she was being so perfectly obliging. He didn't think it was in her nature, but he had no choice. He knocked on the door, angling his large frame so Ink could cover whoever answered the door easily as well as block Ambrielle completely from sight.

A tall, shapely woman opened the door instantly, as if she'd been waiting. Her face was swollen and red from crying. She had dark hair, and quite a bit of it had escaped the simple ponytail, so it hung in sad ringlets around the sides of her face. Her chocolate eyes lit up the moment she saw who was there. "Master. You came." There was relief in her voice.

Ambrie's fist twisted in his jacket right at the patch embroidered into it. She chose the exact same spot she had before—the skulls at the root of the tree. He felt the sudden tension in her when Tyra flung herself into Master's arms.

Shit. This was not good. His woman was making it very clear it was not good. He was the one who had laid down the rules to her on other men being around her. He sure as hell wouldn't like her flinging herself into another man's arms, or having some man just walk up to her and hug her. He awkwardly patted Tyra.

"I need you to meet my wife, Tyra," he said, before he could think it through. "I brought her with me because, hell, it's our wedding night."

Very gently, he put Tyra an arm's length from him and reached behind him to capture Ambrie's wrist. "My wife, Ambrielle. Everyone calls her Ambrie. This is Tyra, baby."

"Your wedding night?" Tyra was horrified. "We called you out on your wedding night? Oh my God, Master, Ambrie, I'm so sorry. This gets worse by the moment." She pressed her fingers to her mouth, her eyes welling with tears.

"Don't you dare cry, Tyra." Master turned very stern. "Where's Reese? And Sandree? Is she doing all right?"

"Yes, I asked Callie to keep her for the night."

"Callie and Braun live in the next cabin over, Ambrielle," Master explained. "Nice couple. They have a child around the same age as Sandree, a boy, right? Jarod."

Tyra wiped at the tears on her face, nodding. "Yes, he's such a sweet boy, like his mother." She straightened her shoulders as Ink came into the cabin before she could close the door. "I really am sorry about disturbing you on your wedding night."

It was Ambrie who waved the apology away. "We thrive on adventure, don't we, honey?" she asked, slipping her hand into his back pocket. "No worries at all. I love what you've done with your home. It's really quite beautiful. Our house is very rustic. I can see Master all over it and didn't think there was much room for me, but I can see how you've woven feminine touches into the wood."

The enthusiasm sounded genuine, and looking down at her face, Master was certain it was. "Tyra, is Reese in the sitting room?"

She nodded. "He's waiting for you. There's a fresh pot of coffee. If you don't mind, Reese asked me to stay out here."

"I would prefer that. You can get to know my wife."

Ambrie's brows came together in a quick frown. She looked up at Master with a small shake of her head, her fingers once more bunching in his jacket. "I thought I'd be staying with you, Kir."

Once again, his given name was spoken in a whisper of

sound. There was that plea in her eyes that got to him when nothing got to him. He was stone. Sheer fuckin' stone, and yet she could tear his heart out already with just that look she had in those strange-colored eyes. She looked . . . lost. Scared.

He wrapped one arm around her, nearly swallowing her as he brought her close to him. "I'm not going anywhere, princess. Just into the other room."

Her fingers curled into the front of his jacket this time. She went up on her toes, and her lips touched his jaw as she spoke in a whisper against his skin, so the words went deep. Sank into bone. "I can't lose you too. Not one more person who belongs to me. I just can't."

His knees nearly gave out—nearly dropped him right to the floor in front of her. He was looking right down into those violet eyes, lashes spiky with unshed tears, and he knew she wasn't playing him. He had far too much experience to be taken in by a show. This was raw. Stark. All too real. His princess had placed all her eggs in one basket. That basket was her sanity. She was looking to Kir "Master" Vasiliev to save her. To keep her together. He was *hers*. And by all that was holy, she was *his*. He knew it wouldn't last forever. His little princess was going to wake up one morning whole again, not needing him anymore, but for now he was going to take what he could and give her every single thing she deserved, if he could figure out how.

He framed her little face with both hands and bent close. "Look at me, beautiful woman, in the eyes, so you see I'm telling you the truth. I'll be right in the next room. Nothing will happen to me. I'll leave the door open, and I'll stay in your line of vision so you can look in and see me at all times. We're in this together, remember?"

She nodded. Swallowed hard. "He's dangerous."

"So am I. More than he is. He has no idea what I am. You do. I let you see because you're mine. He's the one in the room in danger, not me, princess. You do what you were doing. It was perfect and helping me. Let Ink and me do what we need to do."

"Stay in sight."

That was an order. Issued as one. He didn't smile, even though he desperately wanted to. The thought that she was worried for him and not for Reese was a joke. Ink would be in the room with him. Two lethal men who had trained as assassins practically since birth. He nodded his head, brushed a kiss into all that dark, glossy hair and stepped back. She reluctantly dropped her arms and let him go.

Master sent one wary glance toward Tyra, who had pressed herself against the front door. He didn't like her cutting off Ambrie's escape. "Tyra, move away from the door. You want to take Ambrielle to the chairs and get her comfortable. She's had a long, very trying day." He made it an order—easy enough to do when he put a growl in his voice.

He waited until she complied, sweeping her hands toward the two most comfortable chairs they had in the room. Ambrie took the one facing the room Master was about to enter. She smiled gratefully up at Tyra. "Thank you. I really did need to sit down." All the while, her gaze continued to flick toward her husband. One hand rested just inside the jacket Master had given her to wear. He knew the gun was inside that jacket. She looked relaxed, but she was on alert. He was proud of her.

He nodded to Ink and moved ahead of him. "Coming in, Reese. I've got Ink with me. My wife, Ambrielle, is going to stay with Tyra out here." He believed in stating things just the way they were. He also believed in being prepared. When he moved into the room, he was very aware his wife was in the line of fire if Reese was armed, so he didn't step to the side as he might have normally, clearing the doorway for Ink. He gave Ink just enough room to take a shot if he had to.

Reese sat in a large cloth-covered chair, one he and Tyra had found at a secondhand store and both fallen in love with. Reese was a big man, and the chair suited his large, muscular frame. He'd worked out before he went to prison and while he was in prison and continued to do so. It was part of his daily routine, and it showed. Between his big hands, he rolled an unopened bottle of Jack Daniel's back and forth. On his lap was a revolver.

Glass lay broken on the floor in colorful pieces where lamps were shattered. Books were knocked from shelves that had been torn from the walls, so the shelves hung suspended upside down or sideways.

Master walked all the way into the room, deliberately stepping on what had been Tyra's favorite stained glass Tiffany lamp, the one she'd found at a garage sale and talked about for weeks. The shattered glass crunched under his boot. Master grunted loudly as he smashed the glass, going straight toward the chair, keeping his body between the former MMA fighter and the door. Ink slipped into the room and stayed along the back wall, to one side, a silent shadow, arms folded across his chest. He looked relaxed, but his weapon lay hidden along his arm, the barrel aimed straight at Reese's left eye.

"Stop right there, Master," Reese ordered without looking up.

"Fuck you, Reese," Master said, not even slowing down. He kept the same pace, stalking across the room in his motorcycle boots, not fast or slow but purposefully, a kind of fury building in his chest. He'd dragged his woman, suffering from a real trauma, out in the middle of the night to help this man, and he *dared* to threaten him? That was so not happening. "You do this with Sandree in the house?"

He towered over Reese, snagging the revolver, putting the safety on and tossing it to Ink, who caught it one-handed. "Did you? You tear up your home with that little girl here?" He had the presence of mind, even in his fury, to stay out of range of Reese's feet. The man was a hell of a fighter, and you had to respect that.

"What's it to you?" Reese snapped belligerently.

"You're not worth shit if you don't protect your woman

and child from yourself when you're in this state, Reese. I told you that from the beginning when I told you I'd get you out and help you. So you fuckin' answer me. You want to drink yourself to death, damn well do it—that's between you, your God and Ink. I take care of the other shit for you. But not if you pulled this temper tantrum in front of your baby. You did that, you can go rot in prison, because you aren't the man I thought you were." He kept his voice low, the way he always talked. There was never a point in raising his voice.

Reese raised pain-filled eyes to Master. "No, man. I had Tyra take her to Callie. They're coming for me again. There's no way out for me this time, Master. Even you can't help us. I either do what they say, or I go back to prison. Those are my choices."

Master sighed. "You sent for me because you know I take care of that shit, Reese. Stop feeling sorry for yourself. That doesn't get you anywhere. You want to know who can feel sorry for herself? My wife. She saw her parents blown away, murdered, right in front of her, two days before our wedding. Then you call on our wedding night. Now knock off the shit, talk to Ink while I step back and then we'll talk this out and get it fixed."

Reese stared at him, the bottle loose in one hand. "That true? What you said about your wife? You telling me straight?"

"Bastard had them both killed right in front of her. Tried to force her to marry him. He's not long for this world, and neither are the men who were with him. I told you, Reese, I fix things. You don't throw temper tantrums. They don't help you do anything but look like the maniac they named you. And that bottle of booze you're looking at nearly lost you your wife and helped to put your ass in jail. You remember that."

Master turned his back on Reese, only because Ink never once changed the aim of that gun. He remained in the shadows, as still as a statue while Master read to Reese from his own personal bible. He looked at his woman sitting in the chair, talking to Tyra, who had made them both a cup of tea. She was watching him without trying to look like she was. He gave her a little nod, to show he was paying attention. She gave him a half smile in return.

He signaled Ink, and his Torpedo Ink brother moved into him, passing the weapon as he made his approach to Reese. Ink didn't make the mistake of standing directly in front of the former MMA fighter. He crouched down to the side of the armchair, leaving Master a direct shot if Reese made a single move against Ink. He was fairly certain the fight had gone out of Reese, but he wasn't taking chances with Ink's life.

"Where's your higher power in this picture, Reese?" Ink asked softly.

Reese continued to hang his head, not meeting Ink's eyes. His face flushed a dull red under his pale skin. Even his spiked hair seemed to glow a little redder. The freckles scattered across the nose that had been broken more than once stood out in stark relief.

He heaved a sigh and placed the bottle of Jack Daniel's on the floor, as far from the chair as his arm could reach.

Master leaned back toward the door but didn't take his gaze from Reese. "Tyra. Come in for a minute and remove this bottle, please. Dump it down the drain and rinse out the bottle. Take it to the outside trash and bury it deep. You know the drill."

Tyra was up and rushing into the den with a little cry of joy. She snatched up the bottle and ran back out without even looking at her husband or the others. That made Master's gut knot up all over again. Tyra was a good woman, a good wife. She'd stuck with Reese through his alcoholism and his imprisonment. She'd fought for his sobriety. She worked tirelessly to find a lawyer who would help prove Reese's innocence. She deserved better than having her husband destroy her home in a fit of rage and scare her the way Reese had so obviously done.

"There is no higher power in this, Ink," Reese finally answered.

"Did you ask for help from your higher power, or did you expect to find it in a bottle?" Ink's voice was very soft. In inquiry. No accusation. No judgment.

Reese shook his head. "I didn't ask. I put the phone down after listening to what my parole officer had to say and knew I was completely screwed. My life was over. There was no way out. I just lost it. I barely managed to tell Tyra to get Sandree out of here. There was so much adrenaline, and it had to go somewhere."

"Look around you, Reese. What did this accomplish? How did being out of control serve you? What did it do for you? Did it make you feel better? How do you feel right now?"

"Like shit."

"You gave them power over you. You gave your disease power over you. You're letting your disease have its way with you."

Reese took a deep breath. "I feel as if everything in my life is spinning out of control."

"All of us have that happen to us. We've talked about it, and how it will continue to happen. We go through the steps, Reese. We can't control others. That's an illusion. We can only control ourselves. You call on your higher power for help."

Reese nodded. He turned his hands over and curled them into fists. "They took my life away once, Ink. I was scared."

"You're so new to the program, Reese, you haven't gotten rid of the way you've handled things in the past. You can't let that be an excuse to do this kind of thing." Ink stood up slowly and gestured to take in the room.

Reese rubbed his temples as if he had a headache. "I know. I do know. I knew when I was hurling things around it was wrong. I called you, Ink, and I didn't take a drink, but I shouldn't have brought the bottle into the house in the first place. It was in my truck on the front seat under my jacket. I found it when I got home from work. The phone rang, and it was my parole officer with the news that I was to help this crew rob a series of small convenience stores all in one night. They wanted to hit them hard and get out. That was the plan. It's not like someone looking like me, even wearing a mask, isn't memorable. It's a setup."

"What were you doing with the gun?" Ink asked. "You're on parole. You get caught with that, you go directly to prison."

"It was on the seat with the bottle, under my jacket, fully loaded."

Master shoved his own weapon in his harness and stalked across the room, wanting to smack Reese. "What the hell is wrong with you? Why would you pick that gun up and get your fingerprints all over it? For all you know it was used to murder someone. If you know you're being set up, the last thing you want to do is have a gun someone put in your truck. You don't have the damn thing on your lap and your fist around it. I think you took too many knocks to the head when you were fighting in that ring."

Reese nodded. "I did think about that, after Leonard called me. He's the parole officer, Leonard Stoddard. It was already too late. I had my fingerprints on the gun and the bottle of Jack in the house. Stoddard told me I had to help out his crew or I was going back to prison. He'd see to that personally."

"Has Stoddard always been your parole officer?" Master asked.

Reese nodded again. "Yeah. He seemed all right. He did his job. Checked to make sure I went to work, and I'd informed the boss that I was on parole. He dropped by the cabin several times to make certain there were no drugs here and no alcohol. He walked around our house like he owned it, but other than that, he left me alone. I thought he was a pretty decent guy."

"Until now."

"Yeah. I didn't see this coming."

"You certain it was him?" Ink asked. "His voice? Just because he identified himself as your parole officer, doesn't mean he was."

Reese went quiet, thinking it over. He was calm now, his breathing back to normal. Ink was that way, calm in every situation, bringing down the tension. He wasn't a man given to violent outbursts until pushed beyond a breaking point, and then no one wanted to be around a nuclear bomb exploding. That was Ink. Complete and utter calm until the ultimate explosion.

Master took that moment to look at his woman, to ensure she was doing fine. Tyra was back, gabbing away. Ambrielle looked like the little fairy princess she was. Regal. Elegant. Sitting there in that shabby-chic chair, her hair a mass of dark, glossy waves, the leggings showing the luscious curves of her hips, but the jacket he'd given her hiding her full breasts and narrow rib cage. There were bruises on her face, smudges under her eyes, but to Master, that underscored the beauty he saw in her.

She looked straight at him and smiled. Her entire face lit up. Her eyes turned that strange shade of inky violet. Her long lashes fluttered, and she looked so drowsy, as if she might fall asleep right in that chair with Tyra talking her ear off. He knew she'd be mortified if that happened. He gave her a small salute and mouthed, *You all right?*

Tired.

He pointed to her phone and then texted. I can take you home so you can sleep.

She looked down and then shook her head and indicated for him to pay attention to what Reese was saying to Ink. Master did so, but reluctantly. Ambrie really needed sleep. For that matter, so did he.

"Yeah, it was Leonard. He did sound stressed though, not himself."

Master stalked across the room, right up to Reese. "You want out of this mess, you tell me the entire story this time.

I listened to you, knew you didn't touch that woman and she lied her ass off to put you in prison. I believed you got a raw deal, but you still were protecting someone. That's why Absinthe couldn't clear you. Isn't that the truth, Reese?"

Reese hesitated and glanced covertly into the next room. Tyra stood up, abandoning all pretense of entertaining, of pretending she wasn't listening. She walked to the open door of the den and stopped, and then leaned against the doorjamb to look at her husband. Master could see she was shaking.

Ambrie immediately padded across the room on her bare feet to slip her arm around Tyra. She looked very small beside the taller woman, but she was strong and supportive. Tyra leaned on her.

"You don't understand," Reese began.

Master took a step closer. "No, you don't understand. You called me out in the middle of the night. I got married tonight and I still came. My bride still came with me to help you out. Your wife is still with you. Ink is here supporting you. We're all here, offering you a way out of this mess, but there's a risk to us. A big one. I'm willing to take that on for you, but there are no conditions you get to put on me. You tell me everything this time, Reese. I need to know what I'm dealing with. You don't tell me everything, you go back to prison and they're going to kill you, just like you said. No one does this elaborate of a setup without the payoff they're looking for."

There was a small silence. Tyra let out a little sob and jammed her fist in her mouth. She put her head on Ambrielle's shoulder. "I won't stay, Reese. If whoever you're protecting is worth more to you than Sandree and me, then go ahead and stay silent. I'll leave tonight." Her words were muffled, but clear enough that everyone heard and knew she meant it. Just the fact that she was clutching a stranger and crying in front of her, making her line in the sand, was enough.

Reese froze. All color seemed to drain from his skin. His

eyes locked on his wife and stayed there, as if somehow he could keep her with him by sheer will alone. Very slowly he stood up, revealing his size. He was a huge man. Tall, over six and a half feet. His shoulders were like ax handles, his arms ropes of defined muscles. His chest was thick with muscles. He shook his head.

"No." A single word.

Ink moved to one side of him, a subtle motion, barely seen, silent but deadly. Ink didn't make a single sound, but then he was a real predator. He had muscle moving beneath that frame, not as showy, but it was there, and he was lightning fast when he needed to be.

There was nothing at all subtle about Master. He was deliberate when he stepped in front of the women, blocking Reese's view of Tyra and Ambrielle. "Don't even think about threatening her, Reese. She told you what you needed to do. I did as well. Man up. This is your truth moment. You need to know what's important to you. Is it this life and the people in it you're with right now, or the ones you're protecting from your past? That's what this comes down to."

"You always act like you're not afraid of me," Reese said. "Everyone's afraid of me." He glanced at Ink. "You don't ever act scared either. Just the two of you. Everyone in prison, the guards, the other prisoners, everyone wanted to see me fight, or they ran from me. But you two, you don't ever act like you're afraid of anything."

Master didn't respond. There wasn't a need. He didn't believe in talking. Or fighting, for that matter. If Reese made one move toward the women, he was a dead man. He was an experienced fighter, and he should be able to sum up an opponent with no problem. Master could. He could walk into any bar and with one look around tell his fellow club members who the real rivals would be. Any of the Torpedo Ink crew could do that. He waited.

"I would never hurt Tyra."

"That's the thing, Reese. You *are* hurting Tyra. Look

around this room. Your reaction hurt her. The fact that you're allowing these people or this person to control your life is hurting Tyra." Master folded his arms across his chest. "If you continue to allow them to use you like a puppet, putting a gun in your hand that most likely killed someone, setting you up to take the fall for a string of robberies, that's your prerogative, but know you're hurting Tyra. You're taking her down with you."

"My mother."

The whisper was so soft that even in the silence of the room, Master nearly missed the admission. He stood facing the man like an idiot, without a word to say, his mind blank, unable to comprehend what that even meant. Ambrielle slipped her hand up his back, under his jacket, along his shirt, fingers bunching, making that fist she did in the small of his back, connecting them.

"Maybe it would be a good idea if Reese came into the other room, where he'd be more comfortable, and had some coffee or tea and told Tyra and you about his mother." Ambrie's voice was gentle but carried an authority, as if she was part of Master and Ink's team.

Reese nodded. "Yeah. I need to get out of this room. I can't breathe in here."

Master immediately stepped out of the way. Tyra still leaned against the doorjamb, her gaze jumping to her husband's face. As he approached her, he hesitated and then swept his arm around her. She curled into him immediately and they went to the sofa together, where she settled very close.

Master breathed a sigh of relief. "Thanks, princess. I was caught off guard." He bent down and brushed a kiss on top of her head.

Ink came up behind them. "I'll help Ambrie make coffee. I know where everything is. Maybe open the front door, but get that gun out of here first. I've got a bad feeling about that gun. If he gets raided and they find that, he's in trouble."

Master nodded and went back to Reese and Tyra. "You two lovebirds relax for a minute. Ink and Ambrie are taking care of things in the kitchen. Who knows, they might be inclined to clean up a bit in the den if you're making up in here when they come back. I'm going to see to it that if you get visitors looking to find anything wrong, nothing can possibly be found. It will take a few minutes, so just relax. Do you want the door left open for air? It's pretty cool outside this time of night."

Ink paused in the doorway of the kitchen, turning to look back at him, a puzzled look flitting across his face, making Master aware he was talking too much. Making a damn fool of himself. That was why he preferred not to talk. Never to engage. Not to ever be part of this kind of shit. He was a fixer, not a soother. He didn't do what Ink did. Ink saved people. Master cut them down. He turned and shoved open the door, escaping into the night.

Cool night air hit his face. Soft drops of rain felt good on his skin. What the fuck was he thinking marrying a woman? A good woman at that. A woman with a father and mother who actually loved her? She knew about family. She knew about love. She knew about mothers. What they were like. What they were supposed to be to a child.

He walked to the truck, set the gun out and took pictures of it from every angle and sent them to Code, zooming in to ensure he was able to get any markings he could. He carefully broke it down and then made his way into the forest with long strides. His property was large, nearly forty acres, surrounded by close to a thousand acres of state forest land. He needed the time away from everyone to sort out his emotions.

Shit. He was stone. He didn't have emotions. He didn't let things shake him. What the fuck was wrong with him? So, Reese had mommy issues. Ink could deal with that problem. That was Ink's wheelhouse. He dug a hole deep in the roots of a pine tree and buried the first small piece of the gun he'd broken up. He was careful to cover the ground with pine needles and vegetation, so it looked as if it had never been disturbed.

He heard her, although she walked softly. It was just that he would always be aware of her. Always. Like the photograph of her he'd been inexplicably drawn to. There was no explanation, but he knew irrevocably he belonged to Ambrielle Moore Vasiliev.

"Kir?"

He closed his eyes. That voice. The way she said his name. "Right here, princess. I ought to spank your ass for coming out here in the rain barefoot." His voice, that low register, managed to sound like a growl. Annoyed even, when he wanted to gather her into his arms. It didn't work. He should have known.

She laughed softly and came right to him, putting her hand on his hip. "My feet are all muddy now. I should spank your ass for getting out of my sight. We had a deal. In any case, I could tell you were upset."

Instantly, he shut down, jerking away from her. "We fuck a couple of times, and you think you can read me?"

The rain fell softly, steadily, into the silence, like tears on her face. On his. Her hair was slick and plastered back, dripping now. She stood very still, a small little defeated fairy in the dark forest, the beast snapping his teeth at her.

"Ambrielle . . ." What the hell was he supposed to say after that outburst?

She shook her head and gave him a half smile that was pure bullshit. Never reached her eyes. Didn't light up her face. "No, don't apologize. You're right. You're completely right. I'm going to go back. It's cold out here and I'm really tired. I might sit in the truck and sleep while you do your thing with Reese and Tyra."

"Don't go. I don't want you to go." He didn't stop her physically because he believed she needed choices. She hadn't had them when Thompson had her parents killed or when he tried to force her to marry him. Master was determined that she would always have choices if he could give them to her and still keep her safe. "Please, Ambrielle. I was pushing you away because for a minute there, I was being a fucking pussy."

A ghost of a smile touched her mouth. One eyebrow quirked at him. "Please do continue."

This woman. How could he not find her the most interesting, cool, sexy, everything woman on the planet? She just was. He held out his hand. "We have to walk some more. Can you do it on this ground without hurting your feet?"

"It's soft enough. Why don't you just bury all those pieces in one spot?" She walked with him another hundred yards, and he began digging under the roots of an extremely tall cypress.

"I don't want to take any chances that they'll find this thing. I think it's hot."

"Start talking."

He sighed. He owed it to her. "You don't share this shit. And I'm only telling you because I acted like a coward. I let you in, and when I felt that, the door opening on my past, something I never let happen, I wanted to push what I was feeling for you away. Instead, I pushed you away hard. I didn't mean what I said to you."

His tone was low, but both shame and sincerity came through. She didn't answer until he finished scattering the dirt, leaves and needles over the ground and straightened, finally looking at her. She was a mess, but still so beautiful he ached inside.

"I understand feeling like that. The thought of losing you terrifies me just as much as holding on to you does. If I count on you and believe in you and you let me down, I know I won't make it through. I do understand, and in some ways, it helps that we're kind of in the same boat, so to speak."

He didn't see how, since he was the jackass that had taken the last little sparkle from her eyes. He started walking again, choosing a path of soft dirt that would make it easy on her feet. He was carrying her back, whether she liked it or not.

"Talk to me, Kir."

Had she called him Master, like everyone else, he might have been able to resist, but she insisted on using his given name. "You have the wrong impression of me, you know. Ink's the one who takes care of those men. He makes sure they don't drink and they stay on the right path so they can have decent lives. I don't do that. He does." He was stalling. He knew it. Evidently, so did she.

"Those people are staying on your property, in cabins you renovated for them. You found them in prison and decided to help them when they got out."

He winced a little as he stopped to dig the next hole. "It wasn't exactly like that. I had fifteen cabins on the property, all needing work. I like to work with my hands. With wood. It brings me peace." He shoved the gun parts deep and pushed the dirt over them. "I didn't fix them up with the idea of having anyone stay in them. I didn't want neighbors. I bought this property to be away from everyone."

She remained silent. Waiting. He sighed and straightened again after he strewed dirt and pine needles over the covered hole. "I don't know how to do this, Ambrielle. I want to, I just don't know how."

He reached for her, not caring if she was going to protest. She was shivering constantly. The rain came down steadily, and she was soaked. It was cold, and the wind had enough chill in it to make her miserable. She didn't complain. Not one word. The moment he cradled her close to his chest, she turned into him, her arms going around his neck.

"I can tell you how, Master, if you really want to know." Her eyes met his.

Those long lashes of hers were wet and spiked, but not with tears. With rain. She blinked off the drops and kept looking at him. Straight. Unafraid. Damn her, she had courage. Did he? Was he going to have less courage than Ambrielle? He felt the air move in and out of his lungs, felt his heart beat and knew this was one of those defining moments of his life.

"Yeah, babe. I want to know." He meant it.

"My parents were military. When I say that, I mean full-time, all the way, military. They raised me to believe when you made a commitment, you went one hundred percent, all the way in, and there was no room for failure. You charged the hill, you had a hundred bullets in you, you made it up that hill. I made a commitment to you. I meant every single word. You are my choice for life. That means there is no room for failure. They said when the tough times come, it is the commitment that will see us through, but we both have to have that same level of all the way in. No holding back."

"You think you have that kind of commitment to me." He made it a statement, but it was really a derisive sneer. There was no way. She didn't know what the fuck she was talking about.

"Absolutely, I do. For life. I gave you my word. I took a vow. I meant every word I said. I thought you did too."

"And when I kill those fuckers for you? How are you going to feel then, Ambrielle, when you're tied to me for life, and you realize I'm no picnic? That I don't fit in with your fancy friends and I like to have you with me all the time? That I still want sex every time I look at you? What then, after they're dead? Because they're going to die."

"After they're dead, Master, we're going to live together. We're going to have a life together just like every other married couple, but we're going to have our commitment to keep us together. And we're having children, because I want them, so be prepared for that."

Master stared down at her in shock. She meant it. He could see the absolute determination in her eyes. He heard it in her voice. Pain gripped his chest, squeezed like a vise and kept squeezing until he could barely breathe.

Slowly, he lowered her feet to the ground, but he kept his arm locked around her back so she couldn't escape. He caught her face in one large hand, his grip rough. Hard. The killer settled in him, the one that always protected him so he wouldn't go insane or shatter into a million pieces. "You'd better mean what you say, Ambrielle. If I let myself believe you and you're lying to me, you hold back and I give you everything, I don't know what I'd do when you walked away." He meant that. Just the thought of letting her all the way in was so terrifying, his hand slipped from her jaw so his fingers could settle around her throat.

She didn't so much as flinch. Those violet eyes stared straight into his. "I didn't choose you just because I knew you could kill Thompson and his crew. I think any of Torpedo Ink could do that. I chose you because you're a good man. I don't make mistakes, Kir, not even under duress. I could see into you, and I chose you because I knew you were the right one for me. I'll stay. The real question is, will you?"

She was so fucking mixed-up. He wasn't a good man. What in the hell gave her that idea? He was standing in the rain with his hand wrapped around her throat because he was a coward. "I lied to you. Well, I did and I didn't. When I said Sorbacov murdered my parents and took me to that school. He did murder them, but not for political reasons."

The door in his mind creaked and groaned, opening slowly in spite of every protest. He was letting her in and possibly making the biggest mistake of his life.

EIGHT

Master leaned down and once more caught Ambrielle's legs behind her knees and lifted her into his arms. "You're freezing. I'm going to get you to the truck and out of these wet clothes. We can warm you up, and I'll get a flannel from Tyra."

She rubbed her face against his chest as she linked her hands behind his neck. "Pretty soon I'm going to have clothing from everyone within a fifteen-mile radius or more."

"Your feet are all muddy."

"I'm very aware. I don't suppose you have a fetish for muddy feet. Some men do, you know. I could probably make money showing them off on various sites on the internet. I should probably take video before I wash them."

"I'm not sharing your feet with some dumbfuck who gets off on muddy toes. Even virtually. *Bog*, woman, you're going to turn my hair gray." Despite his chest hurting and his head screaming at him to stop the door to his past from opening, she made him want to smile.

Ambrielle had a way of making him feel as if they were together, entwined already, impossible to separate. Whatever they faced, they faced together. It was odd to feel that way when he barely knew her. He didn't believe in miracles or magic. He didn't believe that he had chances in life that others who he thought were better men didn't, and yet here she was—in his arms and married to him.

He managed to get her to the truck and into the passenger seat with the heater going without making more of a fool of himself. "Get everything off but your underwear." He tossed her a lighter club jacket he kept rolled up and tucked down beside the driver's seat. "Wear that until I get back with clothes and something to wash off your feet. I'll hurry."

"You're soaked too."

"Yeah, but I won't melt." He started toward the front door of the cabin.

She stuck her head out the window. "Are you implying I'm the Wicked Witch of the West?"

"I don't know, you could be. You give me a lot of trouble, and right now, you're a little green around the gills."

Master shook his head and hurried into the house. His woman was shivering uncontrollably. It didn't take him long to get a sweatshirt and pants from Tyra, along with warm washcloths and towels. After promising the others they'd be right in, he went back to her and climbed in on the driver's side. The heater, on full blast, had done its job, warming the truck, and Ambrie had stripped off the wet clothes.

She took the towel and began drying her hair immediately, holding her head down in front of the heater while he washed her feet for her. There were a couple of scrapes on the soles of her left foot and one on her right. She hadn't said a word about them. Her hair became a mass of wild dark curls.

"Kir," Ambrie began softly, keeping her head down as she shook out her hair. "I've been sitting here thinking about something. It's occurred to me that I sort of railroaded you into not only marrying me but also agreeing to keep me. So . . ."

She took a deep breath and sat up, flipping her hair back as she faced him. She looked determined, but he could see fear in her eyes. She moistened her lips. "I thought maybe I'd give you a onetime offer. You know, to get out. We could still have great sex but agree to part ways at the end of the time when we get the ones responsible for murdering my parents."

Master was fairly certain she was unaware she was shaking her head *no* even as she gave him his "out." He wrapped his palm around the nape of her neck, leaned down and took her mouth, kissing her. Thoroughly. Pouring heat. Fire. His heart. Right down her throat and into her body. When he lifted his head, he looked into her eyes. "Yeah, princess, that's not happening. We done with all doubts?"

She gave him a faint smile, but he got the full effect of those large indigo eyes, already moving toward violet. She shrugged off the jacket, pulled on the sweatshirt and put the jacket over it. Holding up the sweatpants, she started laughing. "Master, what am I going to do with these? The sweatshirt comes almost to my knees. These are so long I'd have to roll them up into foot-thick cuffs. I'm not even going to talk about how she's tall and thin and I'm short and . . ."

He yanked her to him again and took another kiss. "You've got tits and an ass, woman. Perfect. Don't go complaining about perfection."

He turned off the truck and went around to gather her to him so they could go inside and listen to whatever Reese had to say. This time, he'd better tell the truth and give them the full story. Master wasn't going to lay his freedom on the line, or his life, not now when he had a woman to come home to, for a man who wouldn't fight for his own life.

Reese gripped Tyra's hand as Master settled in one of the larger armchairs with Ambrielle tucked in the one closest to him. Tyra had made hot chocolate for her.

"That should help warm you up," Tyra said. She indicated a blanket. "And that's for you too, Ambrie."

"Thank you, Tyra," Ambrielle said as Master tucked the blanket around her.

He looked at Ink to get things started.

Ink nodded to Reese. "Let's get this done. Reese did say to me, while you were out, that the more he thought about it, the more he felt Leonard Stoddard did sound under duress when he spoke with him on the phone."

Master nodded. That made sense to him. Reese had been out of prison for over two years. Long enough to get his wife pregnant, start drinking again and then get sober with the help of the program Ink ran. In that time frame, his parole officer had never once asked him to commit a crime. So why now? What had Reese done to call attention to himself? He'd lived quietly, worked hard and suddenly someone was trying to put him back in prison, and they were being aggressive about it.

"Start talking, Reese," Ink said. He used his gentle voice, but he meant business and it came across that way. "We're all tired, and Ambrielle needs to go home and sleep. We still have to come up with a plan, so get to it."

Reese brought Tyra's hand to his lap as if she were going to save him. "My mother is married to a very wealthy, influential man. He's not my father."

"Don't do that," Master snapped. "Give me a fucking name."

Ambrie laid her hand on top of his arm, the pads of her fingers brushing back and forth along his forearm in a little soothing caress.

Reese glanced at him and then nodded. "Taylor. Colonel Corey Taylor. My mother is Sherry Taylor."

Ambrielle sat up straight and leaned close to Master, her fingernails digging into his arm. He looked down and she mouthed, *I know them*. His nod was barely perceptible. She went back to running her fingers along his forearm.

"My mother has been married to Colonel Taylor since she was eighteen years old. I have a half brother, Robert, older than me by ten years. Colonel Taylor is a very abusive and controlling man, and eventually, my mother ran away. She met someone, had an affair, got pregnant and, after she had me, was found by Colonel Taylor. He insisted she give me up. He didn't want a reminder of her, and I quote, 'lack of morals.' Her younger sister, Veronica, raised me."

There was a short silence while they all took in Reese's short explanation of his past. Reese brought Tyra's hand to his chest and rubbed her fingers over his heart. "Veronica was very good to me. I had a good childhood, and my mother would visit often. It wasn't like she abandoned me altogether. She brought Robert in the beginning, when I was little. Later, in my teens, he didn't come around, and when I'd ask Veronica, she would tell me the colonel was getting ugly about Mom coming and he had forbidden Robert to ever come again."

Reese wrapped his large hand around his coffee mug and brought it to his mouth, most likely to give himself a bit of a reprieve. He looked down at Tyra. "I didn't want to tell you about Sherry because I felt like I was betraying her. She's had enough betrayals in her life. And she's sacrificed a lot for me."

Master wasn't certain what she'd sacrificed, but he remained silent. The woman lived in a mansion, drove brand-new cars, wore fancy clothes and traveled all over the world. She didn't seem like she lived in a prison. The colonel didn't always travel with her. When they were together, she appeared to be happy with him. He knew that kind of thing could be faked, but for nearly forty years? Why didn't Reese's mother get a high-powered attorney if she wanted out? These days women had places they could run to. She had enough money to get away, when so many other women didn't.

As if she knew what he was thinking, Ambrielle slid her hand under his and threaded her fingers through his. Maybe she was thinking the same thing. She was shrewd and intelligent, and she'd met these people. Hopefully, she would be able to give him some clear insight into them. Already, he'd texted Code with names to start an investigation.

"I started martial arts training when I was five," Reese continued. "I really loved it. By the time I was eighteen, I was kickboxing and had won national championships numerous times. It wasn't a big jump to get into mixed martial arts. I had a love of the sport and I enjoyed training. I saw less and less of my birth mother. Mostly, I would get short letters from her. At first everything was good. I was winning, had a good coach, good friends. Then Veronica got sick. Real sick. I wrote to Sherry, told her Veronica needed her, but she said the colonel wouldn't let her come."

Master tightened his fingers around Ambrie's. That was the biggest crock of shit he'd ever heard. What woman wouldn't go to her sister—the one who had taken her baby and raised him as her own—when she was seriously ill?

"The colonel took Sherry out of the country on a trip and Veronica died. I buried her without her sister ever telling her good-bye." There was the first note of bitterness in Reese's voice. "I had no idea, but the colonel had gotten his teeth into the franchise I was fighting in. I was making them so much money, and I was making it every fight. At that time, there wasn't a fighter they could put in the ring with me that I couldn't defeat." He tapped Tyra's hand on his chest. "I guess there comes a time when you can make a lot more money betting against your best fighter if you know he's going to lose."

Master went still. There it was. Reese had been told to take a dive.

"My manager told me I was to wait until the third round and then take a kick to my head and go down and stay down. I was shocked. I just stared at him. I couldn't believe what I was hearing. We'd been together for years, and all of a sudden he wanted me to cheat. All I had was my name. My integrity. Once you start down that road, you don't go back. They'd own me. I didn't know, at that time, it was the colonel calling the shots. I didn't say a word to my manager, I just walked out. When the fight came, I knocked out my opponent with a roundhouse kick to the head in the third round." He snickered. "I pretended I'd gotten the instructions wrong, and I'd been shocked that he wanted me to wait if I could take the guy sooner."

"It isn't like they could beat the crap out of you in retaliation, Reese," Ink pointed out.

Reese nodded. "Yeah, I thought the same thing. They didn't. But the colonel sent my mother to threaten me. She said if I didn't do everything they told me to do, he would punish her and he would ruin my reputation and see me in prison. So I quit fighting. That's when I started drinking and getting in bar fights."

"Which helped you so much," Tyra said.

"Yeah, babe, but it dulled the pain. The colonel was so pissed, he had that girl make up all that shit. The only problem was, I'd met Tyra by that time, and we were together that night, all night. I was told not to refute the woman's testimony or Mom was going to be hurt. So I just gave up and took the prison sentence."

"Were you contacted in prison?" Ink asked.

Reese shook his head. "Nope. Never heard a word from anybody, not even my former manager. When I got out, the only person waiting for me was Tyra." He brought her hand up to his mouth and kissed her palm, smiling at her. "She's the one I can count on."

"Best you remember that," Master said. "When your parole officer called you, did you say anything to him? Did you agree to go and meet this crew, or did you just hang up?"

"I didn't say a damn word," Reese said. "I wasn't going to agree to anything that stupid. I know a setup when I hear one."

"Good for you," Master said. "That gives us a lot of room. What set them off? What did you do recently that you hadn't done before?"

"You have the gym for all of us, and I've been using it every day since we moved here. I hired a good trainer, and I've been looking at the contenders in my weight division for the MMA. I believe I'm still competitive. I wanted to give it another try. I started actively looking for a manager."

Master exchanged a look with Ink. They waited, but the silence continued. Finally, Master shook his head. "This is bullshit, Reese. I told you, you want help, you tell us everything. That's not everything. You stood up to this fucker before, even though it cost you. What the hell happened?"

Reese looked at the floor and shook his head.

"Damn it," Master exploded. "Your mother contacted you, didn't she? After not hearing from her all those years after Veronica died, and while you were in prison, even after you got out and were struggling, you suddenly got a call from her, didn't you?"

Reese looked up. "Don't say it like that."

"Like what?" Master demanded. He knew what. Suspicion was in every word. Not just suspicion. Condemnation. The woman was so guilty Master wanted to strangle her with his bare hands, and he didn't hurt women. He left that to others whenever possible. He might make an exception in Reese's mother's case. "She called you, didn't she?"

"Yes." There was genuine grief in Reese's voice.

Master should have felt bad, but damn it all, Reese was a grown man with a family to protect.

"She called and told me to do what my parole officer demanded. She said that sacrifices sometimes had to be made in life, and wouldn't I do anything for my child the way she had done? Then she hung up."

Tyra yanked her hand away from Reese as if she'd been burned. "Oh my God. Oh my God. She threatened our baby." She leapt up and turned to face him, shock and horror in her eyes, tears filling them, accusation and censure in every line of her face. "She threatened Sandree, and you were going to get drunk and leave me to face these horrible people without even knowing they were going to hurt or even kill my baby. How could you, Reese?"

"I didn't, Tyra. That's why I called Ink and Master. I know them. I'm a fighter. Fighters have to observe everything about an opponent. When Master came to me and offered us this house and Ink told me about the program, I knew if I accepted, I accepted on their terms. Master had very specific terms. You think, because I'm a trained fighter, that I can't be beat, but honey, that isn't so. Look at him. Really look at him. They came here armed. They came here with the idea they might have to take me down, and they intended to do it if necessary. I counted on them. I knew they'd come. I didn't open that bottle because I knew they'd come."

Tyra wrapped her arms around her middle and began to cry. "I don't even know what to think. This is the worst night. The worst."

"Come here, baby. Please. We're going to get through it," Reese promised. "We'll do whatever they say, and we'll get through it."

Tyra looked to Ink. "Are we going to have to hide Sandree? Run? I wouldn't know where. I don't have relatives."

Master answered her. "You won't have to run or hide. You'll be safe here. Our club will look into the colonel and his wife, but Reese, I'm telling you, you're a grown man. You had better be willing to accept whatever happens without question. You've got a family right here, Tyra and Sandree. You've got good friends willing to stick their necks out for you. Whatever childhood fantasy you've got going, you just might have to let go of it, and you're going to have to come to terms with it. If you can't, you need to say so, right now, because I can't guarantee things are going to turn out like in the good fairy tales."

Reese nodded his head slowly. "I get you, Master. Tell me what you want us to do."

"I want you to go about your business as if nothing has happened. You go to work and do your job the best that you can. Tyra, you do your work just the way you have been from home. Someone from the club will be watching out for you both. We might be calling on another chapter for help, but we'll introduce them to you first, so you know who's watching over you. Other than that, if anyone calls, listen to them and record the conversation so you can send it to Ink or me. Don't respond no matter what they threaten you with. That's important. Don't respond."

Reese and Tyra nodded.

"Reese, this is important. After you were out of prison, did you ever have contact with your birth mother? Did you call her? Did she call you?"

"No." Reese looked grateful when Tyra sank back into the sofa beside him. He wrapped his arm around her. "Tyra stuck with me, and I wanted to build a life with her. I struggled, not really knowing how or what to do because all I knew was fighting, but I didn't want to get back into that world of uncertainty with Sherry and the colonel. That makes me look so bad, but I already was overwhelmed with trying to get my life back together."

Master was certain Reese knew, deep down, that Sherry wasn't being held hostage by her husband so much as she was part of what the colonel was doing to her son. He didn't want to recognize that his mother was dirty as sin, so he hadn't tried to contact her.

"She initiated the contact out of the blue. Your cell number was brand-new. Not anything you had before, correct? And it is a private number, unlisted and unpublished?"

Reese nodded. "Yes. Because we haven't been able to get the charges off my record, we thought it best not to have the number where anyone can get it."

"But Sherry was able to," Ink said. "Did you give your private number to one of the managers you were considering?"

Reese nodded. "I had an appointment with Harold Baker. He's been around for years, and his reputation is impeccable. That's one of the reasons I went to him. I told him everything about the charges against me and that I'm trying to get them dismissed. I hoped he was considering taking me on." Defeat crept into his voice again.

"We'll investigate and find out whether he was the source or not. If he contacts you, act as if nothing has happened and just go forward with your plans," Master advised. "I'm taking my bride home. Trust us to take care of this. It will take a little time to sort through the mess. Always keep Sandree close. The club will watch over you."

He stood up, reached down and gathered Ambrielle into his arms, cradling her against his chest. "Tyra, we're stealing the blanket and clothes, although I promise I'll get them back to you."

"No hurry," Tyra assured him. "We appreciate you coming."

Master nodded. He didn't like long farewells. He just turned abruptly and walked out, taking Ambrie with him. Ink would talk for a few minutes with Reese, telling him everything the man needed to hear that Master couldn't give him.

Ambrielle cuddled into him, both arms linked around his neck. Master had never liked anyone touching him. He really didn't like needy women. He wasn't a man who wanted to bring a woman home and have her clinging to him. It made no sense that he never wanted to put Ambrie down, but he didn't. He inhaled her scent and wanted to keep her in his lungs. He liked the way she felt against his body. He couldn't wait to get her home and into his bed.

"You're so warm."

That came out muffled against his chest. He opened the passenger door and reluctantly placed her on the seat, tucking the blanket around her. "Yeah, my body temp tends to run hot all the time."

"I'm always on the cooler side, and my feet are cold. Wait until I accidentally put them on you. You'll scream like a baby."

That teasing note got to him every damn time. He closed the door and went around to the driver's side. Ink was already out and heading their way.

"Babe, gotta get this over with, so you know what's going on with your parents." He turned on the truck so he could kick on the heater. "Put your seat belt on." He didn't want her to bolt on him, and the moment he mentioned her parents, she looked like she might jump out of the truck and run.

Ambrie huddled deeper into the blanket. "Can we talk about it in the morning?"

"I don't know when the cops will be contacting you and

we have to get our stories straight." Ink was in the truck and Master set it in motion. "You have to be believable when you talk to them, princess. Absinthe has been in touch with them this entire time. He contacted them on your behalf, identifying himself as your lawyer. At any time, you can change that. You can find a lawyer of your choice, although Absinthe is a damn good attorney and can get you whatever you want."

"He didn't clear your record, Kir," she pointed out, her tone belligerent. "If he's the lawyer for the club, do any of the others have a record?"

"Ambrielle." He said her name. A warning. They weren't alone.

"She's right, Master," Ink said. "Everyone in the club has a clean record. Well, I don't know about Destroyer, but even Savage does. All but you. I've never even thought about it. Why is that?"

"We're talking about Ambrielle's parents and what she needs to say to the cops. If Jonas Harrington and Jackson Deveau show up to talk to you, wait for me and Absinthe. Don't say anything until we're right there with you. Both have gifts."

Ink leaned forward over the back of the seat. "We all believe Jackson can detect lies. You have to be very careful how you word things to him."

Ambrie turned her face away from them and stared out the window, pulling the blanket to her chin. She huddled inside of it, for the first time since she'd married him really looking as if she'd separated herself from him. She looked so alone, it was heartbreaking. Master tightened his hands on the wheel and refrained from speaking. They could discuss it when they were alone.

She couldn't think about her parents and their death. She was compartmentalizing, and the moment she even thought of them, she turned to something else and frantically threw herself into that in order to avoid facing the one thing she couldn't deal with.

Master indicated for Ink to put his Harley in the garage. "You take the truck. I've got a couple of other vehicles we can use if the rain continues. No use in you getting drenched." He waited for Ink to put the bike away in the huge garage before handing him the truck keys and collecting his wife by simply sweeping her off the seat and carrying her into the house.

He went through the large front room. He would have slowed down to show it to her, hoping she'd like it as much as he did, but she was exhausted and needed to go to sleep whether she thought so or not. She didn't stop with the continual shivering until he put her feet on the floor of the master bath—familiar territory.

"Get ready for bed. There's not much to it. You don't need a lot in the way of clothes. Tomorrow, first thing, I promise, we'll get clothes, food, see your friends, and take care of any loose ends you have with your clients. That will leave you free to hunt."

Her chin jerked up and her eyes met his. The tip of her tongue wet her lips, making his cock ache. "You really meant what you said, didn't you? About taking me with you when you hunted them."

"I always mean what I say." He turned away from her. The way his master bath was built, the old-fashioned claw-foot tub sat on a field of charcoal and gray river rock that swirled out of the bathroom right into the master bedroom, making the two rooms one. The rooms of his house had an open floor plan, so they flowed one to the next, and he particularly liked that everything in it was made of natural wood or stone.

He gave her a little privacy by leaving to use the second bathroom on the main floor. He was wet from being in the woods and needed to peel off the soaked clothing and take a hot shower. He would have preferred to use the one in the master bathroom, with the jets that sprayed him from every direction. The shower stall was much larger and made of the same charcoal and gray river rock.

This one was made of the same rock, but just a bit

smaller, without the jets coming from all directions. Still, the water was hot and poured over him, feeling good on his surprisingly sore muscles. He hadn't realized he was as tired as he was.

Ambrielle was curled up under the covers, turned toward the long bank of windows, watching the rain come down. She sent him a little smile as he flipped back the covers, wrapped his body around hers and turned off the only light in the room. Master curled one arm around her waist and laid his head close to hers.

"We got to talk about this, princess. It's important or I'd let it go."

"I know. Can we make a bargain? We talk about my worst nightmare, and you give me yours."

He closed his eyes and rubbed his face against the nape of her neck and all that silky hair. "I've got too many worst nightmares, babe. One at a time or none at all might be best just so you can sleep at night."

She turned her head and looked at him over her shoulder. "Really, Kir? You have too many really bad things that happened to you?"

His fingers bit into her waist. No man wanted to talk to his woman about certain things that happened to him, but he wasn't going to lie to her. "You aren't putting it together, baby," he said as gently as possible. "I was taken to a place run by pedophiles. Sorbacov thought it would be a great experiment to see how many skills a child could develop if he could survive in prison with his so-called instructors being the inmates. What do you think happened to me on a daily basis? Usually more than once a day."

Ambrielle froze as if she'd stopped breathing. Her body tensed, then she hunched into herself as if she'd taken a body blow. One hand slid over his, the one he had over her waist. Her nails bit into his wrist.

"You told me you were taken there when you were just a little boy. I thought maybe younger than five. Were you younger than five?"

Was she crying? He didn't want her to cry for him. That damn door in his mind was creaking open. He could hear it, that squeaking of the rusty pins telling him the memories were getting too close for comfort. He couldn't have her crying, or there could be a river flooding his home.

"Yeah, princess, when the bastard came for me, I was younger than five." He waited a heartbeat. Yeah. She was crying. Her fingers bit down on his wrist in protest. "You sure you want to talk about this?"

"I don't understand human beings, Master. I really don't. The things they do to children. Or to one another." She rubbed her face against the pillow. "And you go back into prison because you have these skills you developed as a child under those horrific circumstances." She whispered to herself, but he heard. "You say you aren't a good man, Master, but you are. No one would do the things you do, even to help out your club."

He groaned, his lips on the nape of her neck again. He scraped his teeth along her sensitive skin and then kissed the spot. "Don't. I could barely keep from hitting Reese. I don't do well talking to people, Ambrielle. I think they're all idiots. I have enough patience for three seconds of their whining and then I'm out. Ink is the one with endless tolerance. He goes into difficult situations and talks people off the ledge when I want to shove them off it."

Her response was muffled, somewhere between crying and laughing. "You're so bad."

"I just never developed the kind of compassion Ink has. I want it, but don't seem to find it in those situations. His mother is in on this scheme, whatever it is. She's as rotten as her husband. Why they're targeting Reese, I have no idea, but he can't seem to let his fairy tale go. He's got a wife and child, Ambrielle. Why the hell doesn't he see he shouldn't be considering exchanging what's right in front of him for some vague, pretend relationship that never happened? He's like a little kid that never grew up. I find it sickening."

"Some people need to feel their parents loved them."

"Well, some people ought to grow the hell up and accept what life gives them." He snapped it, and then realized how it could sound when she'd just had both parents murdered in front of her. "I didn't mean that the way it came out. See what I mean about talking to anyone? I'm not so good with words, and I know it. I'm trying to say, I think a person needs to understand they're responsible for their own shit and just deal." He tried to clarify but thought he'd made it worse.

Ambrielle was silent for a long time, but she moved her body even closer to his, pressing back against him instead of moving away from him.

"I think you say what you think just fine for me. You said you didn't tell me the truth about Sorbacov taking you. When we were together in the woods, you were really upset and deliberately tried to push me away. You said it then, but he did take you from your parents. Did he kill them, Master? Or did he just take you?"

He knew it had been coming. He had known ever since he'd made the blunder and opened his big fucking mouth, but she deserved the truth. He tightened his arm around her because for right now, he had her. His princess.

"Just so you know, you might be my fairy-tale princess, and you are, but the world really isn't a fucking fairyland."

To his consternation, she rolled over and framed his face with both hands. "I see you, Kir. The real you. Not just the one you hide behind to protect the real you. I see all of you. Every part of you that makes up the man."

She leaned in and brushed her lips over his. His heart nearly stopped beating. She was so gentle. Tender, even. Everything he wasn't. Everything he didn't know how to be but wanted to learn to be for her.

"No, the world isn't a fairyland, and I know more than most people it isn't. But when we're together, I'm always going to be your fairy princess if you want me to be because I like being yours." She laid her head on his chest and wrapped her arm around his waist. Waiting.

"I don't know the first thing about mothers, Ambrielle.

Not the kind of mother you seem to have had." He slid his fingers in her hair, deep, all that silk, massaging her scalp. He meant to soothe her through his explanation, but found he was soothing himself. "My mother was more the kind Reese has. That's probably why I recognized right away she's one hundred percent a part of whatever the scheme is against him."

Master let his fingers move through the soft silk of her hair. So much of it. She had her own scent. A subtle fragrance he'd know anywhere that clung to her skin and hair. That would be home to him. Strange that she found her way in so fast. He didn't understand how or why, only that she was already there.

"My parents didn't want children. My father despised having a kid around, and when he was home, my mother would lock me away from them in another part of the house. I wasn't to make any noise. If I did, there were beatings. I didn't understand why, because I was too young, and I'd be hungry or need to be changed. I'd be afraid by myself in the dark. She would come in and be furious, slapping and hitting. She would tell me how much she hated me and wished she could get rid of me."

"Oh my God, why didn't they just give you to people who wanted children? There're so many who can't have them."

"I don't know if that would have been some black mark on their reputation. Who knows? In any case, she had a lot of men around when he wasn't home. One of them was on Sorbacov's private security force. Later, I found out he told her Sorbacov was always looking for little kids for his schools. He wanted assets to be trained for the country. Some of them were turned into toys to entertain his friends, and they were purchased at premium prices. Not to mention, if you got in Sorbacov's good graces, you were in with the society's elite, their inner circle."

Ambrielle was intelligent and quick on the uptake. "She *sold* you to that horrible man? She *sold* you? For money?"

"Not only did she sell me, she told me I deserved

whatever happened to me for ruining her life the way I had. Sorbacov must have insisted my father be present as well in the exchange, because he was there. They talked and laughed while Sorbacov patted me and then handed my mother this big envelope. She laughed, but she didn't once look at me. I was feeling so confused and angry. I knew what she was doing, and I didn't understand when I had always tried to be so good for her. Then the security men took out their guns and shot them. Sorbacov stood there for a few minutes, kind of patting me before taking out a gold pocket watch. He put me in a car and took me to that school."

"I don't understand how you managed to turn out sane, Master."

"I was lucky. I met Czar. He gave me a code to live by. He made me believe I could be a human being. I wouldn't have survived without him. None of us would have." He knew that was the truth, and he wanted her to know it was. She had to understand how important Czar was to him, to all of them. "So many of the children who came to the school during the years I was there died. We banded together and survived because Czar taught us how. We survived not just the physical assaults but the mental ones as well. Emotionally . . ." He gave a little shrug. "We stay together because that's how we did it. We wove ourselves together and we became strong enough to live. Even now, we're not that good away from one another."

He'd told her, briefly, one of the things he worried most about. Those who'd found partners had told the others that the club was something the women had a difficult time accepting. They all realized why when Seychelle, Savage's woman, had joined him. The club needed her to help them in various situations, but they didn't share information with her, and she resented it. Not only did she resent it, it interfered with her relationship with Savage and nearly tore them apart. Master wasn't going to let that happen with Ambrielle.

Ambrie turned back over, pressing against his body, reassuring him she was rejecting the things he'd told her.

"I had no idea you'd gone through so much, Master, or that the others in your club had. I felt bad for Reese and Tyra, but at the same time, I continually had to push away the images of my parents being murdered right in front of me. I don't know if it's because it happened so recently, but I struggled to have compassion for him and the way he handled things, just as you struggled. I was impressed with Ink, mainly because he was very firm, but he clearly said what Reese needed to hear."

"We don't have those addictions that Reese has," Master said. "We don't come from that place, and we can't understand what he's going through any more than he can understand us. We don't understand his choices. We see a clear path one way. He sees another that makes no sense to us. Ink can explain it better than I can."

Ambrie rubbed her face on the pillow. "I'm grateful I found you, no matter how I did it, and that you wanted me, even in my hysterical and obviously needy condition. Tell me what to do when the police question me. Tell me the story and I'll make sure I have it down."

Master tightened his arm around her. He was certain he'd gotten the better of the deal between them, but he didn't say so. They'd both made the commitment to go full in, all the way. He chose to believe that she was going to keep her word. He had to believe that if he was going to, for the first and only time, trust someone outside of Torpedo Ink.

NINE

"Master, oh my God, who is she? She has the most beautiful voice I've ever heard." Ambrie sat in the back of the mostly empty bar staring in awe up at the stage, where a woman sat on a bar stool, mic in hand, singing, facing a man with a mic.

The woman with honey-colored hair and vivid blue eyes stared into the eyes of the man. He had a shaved head and tattoos everywhere she could see skin. He began to sing back to her.

"He's got a beautiful voice as well. Not like she does though. Who are they?"

"That's Seychelle Dubois and Savage. She's his fiancée, and she sings with our band. Sometimes he sings with her when they're alone, but he never sings in public. I think he'd rather we pull out his fingernails one by one."

"Why? He's got a fantastic voice."

"Savage is the type of man to stay in the background. He doesn't like the spotlight at all. Never. When the band plays, he fades into the shadows and acts as bouncer. Anyone gets rowdy, he throws them out. Or just gives them one of his looks and they settle down pretty fast."

"He should sing."

"He should, but he won't. Seychelle's got him doing a few things none of us ever thought he'd do. She watches out for a lot of the elderly in both Sea Haven and Caspar. Makes sure they have groceries and medicine. Keeps them company. Does repairs on their houses. Now he does those things with her. Got the club doing them too. The older group, especially the ladies, have all fallen for him. They bake him all sorts of things, bring them to the clubhouse, or even here to the roadhouse. He takes it all in stride, but we give him such a bad time. If those old ladies knew he could sing . . ." He broke off, laughing. "Savage has gone from a scary tiger to a little favorite kitten."

"Do they know about you and the work you and Ink do helping prisoners get back on their feet?"

Master sobered instantly. "That's different. And no. No one knows. And they aren't going to."

Ambrie hid her smile. "Who are the band members?"

"The ones you see up there." Master indicated the three playing on the stage. "Keys, Maestro and Player. All of us can sing, but we like to concentrate on our instruments. That's why we looked everywhere for the perfect singer. We found Seychelle, but Savage had beaten us to her. That means he calls the shots on her care, which is a good thing. We might get carried away because she's so good. Never heard a voice with such a perfect pitch."

"I don't suppose she would sing something for my parents' memorial." Ambrie was wistful. "Not that I have any idea how to put something together."

"Torpedo Ink will help with that, princess. Alena and Lana were discussing what the club could do for you already. Absinthe said we could claim the bodies as soon as the coroner releases them. He's staying in touch. You don't have to do anything." He slipped his arm around her, and Ambrie immediately leaned into him, grateful for his care.

She detested talking about her parents. The minute she did, images poured into her mind of the two of them slumped in their favorite chairs in the den, blood soaking into fabric, staining it forever. She didn't want to remember them that way. They had always been alive, vibrant and animated. They were passionate and decisive. Both were strong-willed and given to long debates. What they weren't was slumped over in chairs, blood soaking their clothes and skin.

The music began again, and Seychelle began to sing. Immediately, she felt lighter, as if a great sorrow had been lifted from her and carried away. She could almost feel her grief lessen. She listened to the words of the song, expecting them to strike some chord with her, but it was more the notes the singer hit. The purity of her voice called on wings to attach themselves to the deep grief and float it away from Ambrie so she could breathe. Then Savage's voice joined in, singing counterpoint to Seychelle, while Master took his guitar from the case.

"You've got to get him to sing onstage once in a while," Ambrielle said. "He's really that good."

"It would never work. He'd never do it."

Ambrie listened to the duet as the two sang back and forth and then harmonized together. "Well, he should. At least with her." She turned to look at her husband. She found him terribly attractive, not in the accepted sense of the word but in a rough, very edgy way. She'd had no idea that was her "type" until she laid eyes on him. Master was the epitome of her type, since she didn't seem to see anyone else.

"Do you sing too? On the stage? You said all of you *could* sing but preferred not to. Do you ever sing in front of an audience?"

He did his best to scowl at her. She did her best not to laugh. He did that a lot: tried to look all tough and scary. She supposed it worked on most people. She couldn't help rubbing at the fierce lines on his face with the pads of her fingers and leaning in to brush a kiss along his too-strong jaw. That earned her one of his half smiles, the ones that never quite made it to his eyes but told her he liked what she was doing.

He tried to bite her finger. A little shiver of excitement slid down her spine. She found him incredibly sexy. He was rough. Her body could attest to that. She was sore. She didn't mind being sore, because every step reminded her of the ways he had taken her, his body moving so brutally but so completely in rhythm with hers. His eyes had been on her the entire time, so completely focused on her, as if she were the only woman in his universe.

"Seriously, Master. Do you sing in front of an audience?"

He sighed. "You're such a persistent little thing. I have. Don't like it though. I play music. I write songs. Mostly, if I sing, I do it for the old ladies at this little church, but if you ever tell anyone I'm going to strangle you."

She laughed softly and rubbed her face along his arm like a little cat. "You mean tell anyone you do good deeds? I'd never destroy your image as a badass, Master."

"I don't do good deeds, princess."

"Of course not. Tell me about this church where you sing."

"Why do you say 'church' in that tone of voice?" he challenged.

It was everything she could do not to laugh, and that made her want to kiss him. They'd come to the Torpedo Ink roadhouse to meet the sheriff to answer questions about her parents' murders. The band was there rehearsing, and the singer, Seychelle, and her man, Savage, were up on the stage together, but only a couple of others were in the bar. Ambrielle thought she would spend the entire time crying, but somehow, Master made her feel centered and strong. The singer's voice added to the calm, cutting through her grief, allowing her to feel as if she could handle whatever came up in the questions as long as she didn't have to look too closely at what had happened.

"I wasn't aware I had a tone," she lied. She had a tone. Total amusement. "Unless you mean I thought the building might tremble and fall when you walked in because of your complete badassness."

"Woman, you are going to get yourself into all kinds of trouble."

The threat was empty, and they both knew it. For the first time, his smile wasn't a half one. It was real and actually lit his eyes for all of a split second or less, but it took her breath and she wanted to be able to do that over and over.

"Tell me about the church where you sing, please." She fluttered her lashes at him, changing tactics.

Master pulled her closer. "There's a group of old ladies from Sea Haven and Caspar who have this little church they go to. They like to have music, and there just aren't very many people who attend. Zyah, Player's old lady, told us they were upset because most of the time they can't get anyone to play the keyboard or sing. It's only for one fucking hour a week. So our band goes to their one-room church and plays. Not all together—we take turns singing for the most part, so each person only goes once a month."

"Master, I love that you do that. I really do. My parents were nondenominational, but they went to church often. They said it brought them closer. I'd love to go with you the next time it's your turn." She was going whether he wanted her to or not. She had turned into the needy, clingy type overnight. She'd always been independent, but losing her entire family had thrown her completely. She didn't want Master out of her sight.

He stroked his throat. "I've had this throat thing going on for a little while. Was going to see the doc about it. Kept putting it off, but it's really bothering me. It's my turn this coming Sunday. My voice is already naturally rough. I don't think it would sound all that great with the added rasp, nor do I believe my throat's up to handling an hour of singing. Was going to ask one of the others to handle it for me. Maybe I can do it though. We'll see."

"What throat thing?" Anxiety gripped her. "You didn't tell me about a throat thing."

Master immediately wrapped his arm around her and touched his forehead to hers, creating instant intimacy.

"Breathe, princess. It's nothing. Just been sore for a little while. I'll talk to the doc today. He'll be stopping by the clubhouse to check up on you. We'll be heading there after we talk to the sheriff."

"Me? Why would a doctor want to talk to me?"

"Babe. Really?" He touched the bruises on her face. "And you've got a few more on your hip. I just want him to check you out, that's all. Some of the others will be there to meet you as well. After, we'll head over to Crow 287, Alena's restaurant, to meet up with your friends."

"Ambrielle Moore?"

Master didn't so much as blink. Ambrie realized he had known the sheriff had come up behind them. She turned, Master with her, the protection of his body close and, in that moment, needed. Not only did she feel she needed her new husband, but she felt she needed Seychelle's singing as well. Savage had gone silent, but his woman continued, her voice like an angel's pouring a melody of strength and resilience into the air around Ambrielle like a blanket surrounding her. She needed it. The moment she heard the sheriff's voice, her stomach began to churn, and the images of her parents' deaths crowded into her mind.

"It's Mrs. Vasiliev," Master corrected, his tone firm. "Her name is Ambrielle Vasiliev. She's my wife."

He did have a rasp to his voice. He sounded rough. Scary even. On the other side of her, Absinthe, the lawyer, appeared. He must have been sitting in the bar, somewhere close, and she hadn't noticed because her focus had been on Master. She found she was gripping his vest in her fist, but she couldn't let go. Once again, he was her lifeline. She wondered if she was ever going to be herself again. Right then, she didn't care what anyone thought of her. She even glanced over her shoulder to look at Seychelle, silently begging her to keep singing. To never stop, not until the interview was over. Seychelle had the bluest eyes, and she was looking straight at Ambrielle. She nodded at her, as if she knew Ambrie needed strength.

Looking at her, Ambrie realized in one burning flash what could be the truth. Seychelle took on emotions. Her emotions. Her sorrow. The terrible grief that threatened to bring her to her knees. Ambrielle looked around the bar at every single Torpedo Ink member there. She believed in psychic gifts because she had them. Seychelle obviously had a powerful one. It wasn't a coincidence that she was in the bar practicing for a gig. She was there because Ambrielle, a perfect stranger, had to speak to the sheriff about the murders of her parents.

Savage, Seychelle's man, knew what his woman was doing. The lines in his face had deepened since the first time she'd noticed him. He was a very scary man, and now he looked even more so. He was taking some emotion on his shoulders as well. These people. Absinthe. Player. Keys. Maestro. Preacher behind the bar, acting as if he was simply wiping everything down. They were all contributing to making her feel as comfortable as possible. Especially Master.

What was she doing? Her parents would be so disappointed in her. She raised her chin. She would not let a sweet woman like Seychelle shoulder a burden meant for her. She loved her parents, and that sorrow belonged solely to her. She could take it. She would. She would let the grief slowly turn to something else as it aged in her. Memories of all the good times, so grief became the ache of missing them. The burn of anger would smolder until it needed to explode into rage at those who took them from her.

She was Ambrielle Moore Vasiliev. And she was strong. She had an amazing man as her husband, mostly because she'd lucked out, but then again, it was that psychic gift that had been passed down from her mother—maybe from her father as well. She just knew she'd chosen correctly.

Another man walked into the bar. Tall, straight, broad-shouldered. He had black hair streaked with silver and wore it pulled back in a longer ponytail that didn't in any way detract from his looking rugged. His eyes were steel blue, almost a silver. She knew immediately this was Czar.

Two other men came in with him, one looking like an older version of Savage. She was certain she remembered him from the chapel. He had to be Reaper. The other one was a huge man, all muscle with long hair and prison tattoos covering a multitude of scars. She had no idea who he was, and she didn't ask Master, not with the sheriff so close.

She gave herself permission to lean on her husband; after all, her parents had been especially close all their lives.

"Mrs. Vasiliev," the sheriff corrected himself. "I'm Jonas Harrington. This is Jackson Deveau. We're very sorry for your loss. I know this is a terrible time for you, but we really do need to ask you some questions."

It was Master who waved his hand toward the table where they were seated. It was large enough to accommodate the two law enforcement officers, who murmured a greeting to Absinthe, who was already sitting on the other side of Ambrie, and also Czar, who joined them. Reaper and the newcomer took up positions at the door.

Ambrielle bit down on her lower lip, but nodded her head.

"When were you told of your parents' murder?" Jonas asked, his voice unbelievably gentle.

Ambrie's gaze flicked to Absinthe. She'd been told it was the deputy, Jackson, who was the human lie detector. She had to be very careful how she handled the question. "Master, and I think it was Czar"—she looked at him as if for confirmation—"first discussed the murder with me on my wedding day." She *had* discussed her parents' murders with Master, making it clear she wanted revenge. That had been her original motive for carrying through with the marriage. That and ensuring Walker Thompson didn't get the fortune he was so certain he was going to end up with.

"Before the wedding?" Jonas asked, his voice as gentle as ever.

She nodded. "Yes. I remember being very upset. I could barely think straight. Master said it was my choice what I wanted to do."

"It was important that Ambrielle was safe and in a protected environment," Czar contributed. "She was going to need a family more than ever."

All of that was the truth. If the deputy was a human lie detector, no one had said anything to set off warning alarms.

"Why weren't any of your friends at the wedding?" Jonas asked.

"It wasn't like it was my real wedding day," she said, lifting her lashes and looking straight at Jonas. "I hadn't planned the wedding. My parents weren't there. My father wasn't walking me down the aisle. Master married me because I asked him to." Tears filled her eyes. "I asked him. And Preacher married us."

"Master's name was on the license already," Jonas pointed out.

"I wanted to marry her," Master said. "It would have been nice to have been able to give her the wedding of her dreams."

He wrapped his arm around her, nearly swallowing her with his size. He made her feel safe and even loved in that moment. He leaned his head down and brushed a kiss on top of her head. She didn't realize she was trembling until he began to run his hand up and down her rib cage in a soothing caress.

"Did your parents have enemies?"

"Not that I knew of. Both were retired from the military. They never mentioned having problems with anyone in particular."

"Your mother was quite inventive and apparently made a tremendous amount of money," Jonas continued. "Who inherits?"

She had known the money would come up. Money was a huge motive for murder. She leaned toward Jonas and looked him right in the eye, ignoring Absinthe's restraining hand. "I would give anything to have my parents back. Any amount of money. But the truth is, I inherit everything, although most of it was already in my name. When my mother sold a patent, she would transfer the money into my name immediately. They had their retirement, but all the rest of it was just fun for her. Neither cared about the money. If you check, which I'm sure you will, you'll see she had been doing that since the time I was a small child."

Jonas simply nodded his head, as if he had checked off another question instead of knowingly struck at her with the implication that she might have murdered her parents for money. The images of their dead bodies rose up, swimming in front of her eyes. Her chest hurt so bad, she was afraid it might explode. She turned her face against Master just for a moment, a small reprieve to collect herself. Breathing him into her lungs, taking his strength, that natural masculine scent of his that seemed to steady her, she straightened her shoulders again.

Master shifted his body just a little more, turning so that he more than blocked the sheriff and his silent deputy from viewing very much of her. Very gently he caught her chin in the palm of his hand and tilted her head to him as he bent to her.

"I can stop this if it's too soon. We're all here, princess, but I promise you, always it's your choice. You don't have to do this if it's too difficult."

"No, I want to find whoever is responsible." That was the truth. Her teeth nearly snapped together, and she did her best to sound frail instead of fierce. "They have to pay."

"Are you aware that Master has a prison record as long as your arm?" Jonas asked. His voice was the same, that gentle, low tone. She nearly didn't make out the question because it didn't make sense, it was so out of context.

There was silence in the bar. The band ceased playing at that exact moment, as if they heard the question and couldn't believe it was asked.

Ambrielle dug her fingers deep into Master's thigh as a surge of anger swept through her. She had been so grateful to Czar for saving his life, but in that moment, she wondered why Master didn't have the clean record all the others in

Torpedo Ink did. She knew they had committed crimes and were still committing them. She'd seen them very efficiently gunning down Walker Thompson's men in the chapel. They'd ambushed those men, *killed* them, yet they didn't have records.

Her eyes met Czar's, and there was no way to keep the accusation from her expression. Someone in Torpedo Ink was able to forge excellent paperwork. With Absinthe's ability to compel others to do as he wished, it would be easy enough to wipe out crimes on paper, yet that hadn't been done for Master. That meant her man wouldn't be allowed to attend certain school functions with their children. She was certain Czar could attend anything with his children.

"How is that pertinent?" Absinthe asked.

Czar returned her look with his piercing silver eyes. She would have had a stare-down and won in order to have Master's back, but a weird little frisson crept down her spine. Icy little fingers of eeriness, of warning, pulled her gaze to the deputy. He was watching her closely. She was supposed to be having anger issues, wasn't she? Wasn't that part of grief?

"I'd like the question answered," Jonas persisted.

Absinthe bent his head toward Ambrie, giving her a reprieve from the deputy's laser-beam stare. "You don't have to answer him, Ambrielle. That's not part of this discussion."

Anger became rage. A wall of it. Hot and red and terrible. The emotion washed over her and through her like a tidal wave. She realized it wasn't her emotion—it was Master's. He held her, his body seemingly relaxed, but that fury moved through his body as surely as the blood moved through his veins. It was too violent to be contained. Far too enormous. The room grew hotter by increments, the walls pressing outward as if they might explode.

"What Jonas fucking means, Ambrielle, is you married a man he thinks committed murder once and was thrown in prison. He's out now and may have married you for all that money you have. To clear the way, he murdered your parents, so you were sure to inherit everything before he put the fuckin' ring on your finger."

Master's voice was lower than ever, the growl more pronounced. His fingers bit into her arms where he circled her biceps as if he might put her from him.

"Thanks for putting that in her head so she can wake up one morning and think maybe the man lying next to her put a bullet in her mother's and father's heads. Good to know what you really think of me, Jonas, when I thought you knew me better than that."

Master wasn't acting. What Jonas had implied hurt him. Struck deep. Ambrielle felt her heart breaking for him. She didn't care if the room was filled with people, and the cops were right there watching. She turned in his arms, crawled from her chair onto his lap. Sliding her arms up his chest to link her fingers behind the nape of his neck, she tilted her head back until she was looking up at him.

"Kir, look at me." She whispered the order. Low. Between them. Knowing the others at the table might hear but not caring. "Honey, look at me."

He did. She knew he would. He always came through for her. His dark eyes, filled with so much anger and resentment, so much guilt and sorrow—so much hurt he didn't even know was there—stared into hers. She slid one fist into the short spikes of his hair.

"No one could ever, under any circumstances, make me believe you murdered my parents. Never. My choice is you. Always. You're my choice. I'm yours." She framed his face with her hands. "I took those vows, and I meant every word. I know you. Inside, who you are. I see you. They don't ever have to know that man because he's mine. He belongs to me, only me."

He stared into her eyes for several long minutes. The anger receded just enough that she could see he was with her, centered on her. His hand fisted in the back of her hair. Tight, hurting her scalp the way he did. Rough. She didn't care. She didn't so much as wince. He was hers, and she'd take him any way he was. Right now, he was hurt by the things the cop had implied. He'd thought the man was a friend. She got that. He hadn't shown hurt. It wasn't even in his voice, but she felt it. That was how connected they were.

His mouth came down on hers. Hard. An invasion. A takeover. She let him. She gave him everything. When she was losing her mind, he'd given her everything. He hadn't held back, and she didn't now, not when she felt he needed her. She surrendered to him. He was pure fire. Her rock.

The fingers in her hair slowly loosened, began to stroke soothing caresses over the places he'd been so rough right before he massaged the little points of pain from his rough handling. He lifted his mouth from hers, just barely, brushing little flames back and forth over her lower lip, his eyes looking down into hers as he spoke. "You're as necessary as breathing."

It was one of the most intense moments of her life. She'd never felt so connected to another human being. "That's exactly the way I feel about you."

"Are we finished, Absinthe?" Master asked, not looking at the sheriff.

"Just one or two more questions," Jonas answered using the same gentle tone. "Your family lawyer, Charles Dobbs, seems to have disappeared. Do you know if there was a falling-out of any kind between your parents and this man?"

She nodded. "My father and Charles were best friends for as long as I can remember, but over the last few months, they argued quite a lot. Charles had no idea of their financial situation. He used to handle all of that for my parents and wanted to again, but my father refused to turn over the estate planning to him. Dad said he was family, and that wasn't a good mix. Charles exploded over that because I help with my parents' finances. I'm a planner and I do investment counseling."

At the last moment she realized she had switched to

speaking as though her parents were still alive. She twisted her fingers into Master's vest and held on as if he were her life jacket.

"That's something Master and Ambrielle have in common," Czar said. "Master handles the club's money and decides the best way to invest for us. He's made us fortunes."

"Charles gambles," Ambrielle added. "Dad didn't like it and didn't want to tempt him by giving him access to a lot of money. We talked about that, not with Charles, of course, just Dad, Mom and me."

"Were you aware Charles had accrued a tremendous amount of debt at some of the casinos? Did he talk about that to your parents?"

Ambrie shook her head. "If he talked about that to my parents, they never spoke of it to me."

"Do you have any idea where Charles would go?"

She frowned, trying to really think what he would do if he were still alive. In the end she shook her head.

"Has he contacted you since your parents' deaths? Left messages for you?"

She shook her head. "Charles hasn't left any messages for me." She pressed three fingers to her lips to stop any weeping from escaping. It was so difficult to even talk anymore. No matter how hard she tried to distance herself from the images of her parents' deaths, she couldn't.

"I'm sorry I had to speak with you under such disturbing circumstances, Mrs. Vasiliev." Jonas stood up. "I'm truly sorry for your loss. I can promise you, I'll do everything I can to find whoever murdered your parents." He nodded to the others at the table and left.

Jackson turned to follow him and then stopped to look back. "You know, Master, Jonas does his job. He's damn good at it, and he's thorough. He asks the hard questions because he's going to find the son of a bitch that murdered your wife's parents. In order to do that, he has to get every suspect out of the way. That's her, and you and anyone else that should be looked at. He might not like the job, but he does it in order to catch the criminal. It isn't personal. It was never personal. You should know that."

Without waiting for Master's reply, the deputy turned and followed the sheriff out the door of the bar. There was a small silence. Czar broke it first. "I'm sorry you had to go through that, Ambrie. The loss of your parents is bad enough, but to lose them the way you did was terrible."

"Yes, it was." Ambrielle looked around the bar. "Master tells me there is someone trying to kill your wife and children. That must be a nightmare for you."

Czar rubbed his temples. "It is. I've always managed to stay calm and think through any crisis, but knowing there's a threat hanging over their heads has thrown me a bit. These aren't just some idiot thugs from another club; these are trained assassins coming after my family." His piercing gaze switched to Master.

"Blythe got a call this afternoon from Violet, one of her friends who teaches yarn-spinning classes with her. Spinning yarn isn't something most people know just walking in off the street. Blythe's been doing it for years. She started teaching a class locally a few years back and has a loyal following. I had her call in sick and get a substitute the last couple of weeks. It seems the class had a visit from a 'good friend' of Blythe's, a woman who used to spin yarn with her years ago and wanted to reconnect with her."

The tension in the bar suddenly seemed to stretch unbelievably thin. No one moved or spoke. Ambrie found herself more anxious than ever, and she wasn't certain why.

"When Blythe didn't show to teach and the substitute came, her so-called old friend was quite upset, according to Violet. It was clear this woman didn't know a thing about spinning yarn and had never seen it done, let alone tried doing it. She had no interest in learning to spin and had come to the class with the sole purpose of seeing Blythe."

"What did she look like?" Absinthe asked.

"She matched the description of the Russian woman in the De Sade club in San Francisco. A little taller than Lana, so around five eight. Thin, but nice figure, looks like a model. Dark hair and eyes. No lines in her face. Very pretty, Violet said. Said it twice. In fact, Violet mentioned she worried the woman would get her clothes dirty just walking to the parking lot, she was so pristine," Czar continued. "She also called me Viktor when she referred to me as Blythe's husband. No one calls me that who is a friend of the family. Violet didn't correct her, but it was a red flag."

Again, there was that feeling of tension winding even tighter. Ambrie looked up at Master. He was definitely affected by the things Czar was describing. She tried to think back if she'd ever encountered a woman who looked like the one Czar was describing. She was extremely good with details. She knew her talent with finances came partially from a psychic gift, intuition and the fact that her brain thought in numbers. But she had a rare gift for remembering details, almost like a photographic memory.

The details Czar had given were thin. There were many women tall and thin with model-like features. "You say she has dark hair. Is it brown? Black? What is the length of her hair? What color are her eyes? Did she wear her fingernails long? Were they fake nails? Was she in a dress or pants? Can you get specific details? I know it sounds silly, but it helps."

Seychelle came up to the table, Savage one step behind her. "I'm Seychelle, Ambrie, it's so nice to meet you. I haven't actually met this woman, but I've heard some things about her. She seems to be a shadowy figure in the background."

Savage pulled up a chair at the table for Seychelle and then dropped into the one beside her. Ambrie was grateful for the couple's presence.

"You have such a beautiful voice, Seychelle. Thank you for coming to my aid when I was falling apart earlier. I could feel you lifting my burden. I didn't like you having to shoulder my grief for me, but I really appreciated it with the sheriff being here." She leaned into Master. "I don't want my new husband to think I'm an eternal faucet." She made a small attempt to smile up at him.

Master swept his arm around her. Like a great bear surrounding her with a fortress. It felt protective—good. He rarely smiled and he didn't now, but his eyes, looking into hers, said he didn't mind her falling apart.

"I can take on physical healing, bullet wounds, diseases, things like that, and I can change moods to some extent," Seychelle confessed, "but unfortunately, I can't take on emotional pain."

"But someone . . ." Ambrie began.

"We need to get back to the subject of the Russian woman," Savage interrupted. "Master, you got us a name, correct? Helena Smirnov."

"That's what she was calling herself, but he said it wasn't her real name. I gave the report to Czar and Code. They gave it to all of you."

Ambrie looked up at him curiously. There was a caution in his voice, a reluctance, and she knew it had something to do with her.

"I'd like to see it, Czar. If this woman is hunting you and your family, she may frequent the clubs I go to with my friends. That's why her clothes and nails are important. If she calls you Viktor, not Czar, she may be hitting all the various clubs in an effort to find you. The business district has cafés and restaurants as well as clubs. She may have her tentacles reaching into those places, looking for you."

"She has a point," Master said. "Helena didn't know you belonged to an MC at first; she was trolling for information at the De Sade, not about you, but your name came up; that's how she got onto you in the first place. She may have looked for you everywhere. You're not listed anywhere. The farm is. She can't find you through normal channels."

"That's true," Ink said, his voice rough, very unexpected. "But the children make you vulnerable, Czar. Especially Kenny and Darby."

"They know to keep it tight," Czar said, instantly defending his oldest children.

Maestro took up the argument. "They're not babies you can lock up anymore. They both have jobs. They have phones and friends outside our circle."

"I want to circle back to Ambrielle's question about Helena's appearance," Absinthe said. "I questioned those who saw her and spoke to her in the De Sade club. She had very sleek hair—most used the word *dark* but a few recalled brown, but dark, dark chestnut brown. All of them included the word *shiny*. Her hair was in a bob style to her chin. Very sophisticated. She wore earrings—small, very expensive gold with real gems. She wore one ring: a snake made of gold coiling around her index finger. I was told it was beautiful and very detailed, a work of art. The ring was delicate, and the snake had diamond eyes."

Ambrie frowned. "I haven't seen her, but that's a very distinct piece of jewelry. If it means something to her, then she'll wear it again." She turned to Seychelle. "Right?"

Seychelle nodded. "For sure. Especially if it was an exclusive designer piece. The diamonds for eyes would be unusual. Ice might know. I think there are a lot of snake rings, but Ice is really up on the artists." She seemed to take a deep breath before she looked at Czar. "I'm really sorry this is happening to your family, Czar. I hope Blythe and the kids are all right."

"Thank you, Seychelle. Thanks to you, we had a heads-up that somebody might be coming after us. Blythe was shopping with Zoe, Emily and Jimmy, our youngest, and someone rigged the brakes on the car. That was the first attempt. It was terrifying for Blythe, but she handled it like a pro. Highway 1 is no joke to drive without brakes."

Ambrielle couldn't imagine trying to maneuver the deadly switchbacks and curves along the coastal highway, with its amazing views of the ocean but also lethal drop-offs.

"The second attempt was just plain stupid. A few idiots

attempted to shoot at us. Our farm has so many warning systems built into it, thanks to Airiana working for the government, and the women having their powerful built-in grid; we're covered. I actually would have felt sorry for the gunmen, but they scared the kids." Czar raked his fingers through his hair several times in agitation. "Then the professional assassins came after my wife and children. We were lucky they tried again at our home. We were able to track them back to, of all things, Pelican Bay Prison. There were four of them. They were long-standing inmates there."

Ambrie looked up at Master. He avoided her gaze completely. *Were.* They *were* long-standing inmates. Master was the one Torpedo Ink member with a record. He had been given by Sorbacov to the prison inmates when he was just a little boy. He had learned to be an assassin. The information ran through her mind fast, looping quickly. Her husband had gone into that prison. He had eliminated the men who had tried to kill Czar's family, but not without extracting information from them first.

A burst of excitement went through her. She had married the right man. She had wanted a man who would track down her parents' killers and help her kill them. She wanted Master to teach her everything he knew. She sat next to him, adrenaline racing through her, listening to the talk swirling around her but not hearing it, when she became aware of Master's stillness. He wasn't taking part in the conversation. He seemed distant—apart from everyone else.

Ambrielle detested his distance, and she didn't want to be a part of it either. She liked him. She hadn't expected to. She hadn't expected Master to be anything like he really was. She found the more she was in his company, the faster he seemed to find his way inside. She had the feeling he thought his one use was to go into prisons and kill for his club. Now she was using him for the same thing, maybe not to go into a prison, but still, to be her weapon. He'd confided to her that even his own mother hadn't wanted him. She wanted to be the one person he knew would want to be with him for himself, but how could that be true when she was using him like everyone else was?

"I know we've got a lot on our plate, Czar, but I've got a personal thing that came up unexpectedly," Master said. He looked at Ink.

Ink immediately took over. "One of my guys, Reese Fender, had an incident. Parole officer called him and threatened him that if he didn't join a crew robbing a series of stores, he was going back to prison. There was a gun in his truck and a bottle of alcohol. He's an alcoholic. The thing is, the parole officer has always been tough but fair. Reese said he sounded off to him. Master and I need to look into this."

"Bad timing," Czar said. "Did you send everything to Code?"

Ink nodded. "Code's going to need someone with some computer skills to start helping him out. Any of the kids seem inclined in that direction?"

"Zoe, but she's a little young for the things Code is investigating," Czar said with a small grin. "She'd volunteer though. In the meantime, you'd better get it done. Steele? You want to take that on?"

Steele sat at the end of the table. The doctor, she recognized. "Yeah, no problem. I'll get together with Master and Ink, and we'll take care of it."

"Ambrie is welcome to stay with Blythe and me while you're gone, Master," Czar said.

She tried not to react. She'd promised Master she wouldn't argue with him publicly, and she meant to keep that promise, but she wasn't going to be left behind.

"She goes with me, but thanks, Czar. I appreciate the offer. We've got to go. We're meeting her friends at Crow 287, and I don't want us to be late."

TEN

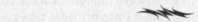

Master was both grateful and pissed at Czar for reminding him that his marriage to Ambrie was really a sham. It didn't matter if both declared their commitment and vowed they were going to stay together. The bottom line was, she married him to ensure he would find the men who had killed her parents. He was to hunt them down and kill them. He was her weapon, just as he was the club's weapon. The only difference was, he didn't have to go to prison to kill Walker Thompson.

She was a woman who would honor her vows. That didn't mean she was with him because she wanted to be with him. Any of the others would have done for her if she had seen the killer in them first. She hadn't looked at him and fallen like a ton of bricks the way he had. He was intelligent enough to know she'd come along when he was hanging on by his fingernails, and there she was—his dream woman. She'd given herself to him, and he was more than willing to accept the fantasy. But he was handing over his fucking heart like some teenager, and he was going to get it shattered. It was probably too damn late already.

Ambrielle sat in the truck on the way to the restaurant looking like a million bucks, casting little anxious looks at him. She didn't know what she'd done wrong. She could sense his withdrawal. She was very sensitive to those around her, and especially him. They'd formed some kind of connection, and he needed to find a way to break that connection as quickly as possible before she tore his heart out.

It wasn't her fucking fault. He wasn't blaming her. She'd always be his fairy princess. But he was going to have to do something to save himself. He always thought he'd die from a bullet. It never occurred to him a little princess was going to be the one to take him down.

He parked the truck in the back parking lot reserved for Torpedo Ink. They had a separate entrance they often used when they were entering the restaurant. He glanced at his watch. Her friends were already there. Several of the other members of Torpedo Ink were there having dinner and keeping an eye out. Czar and Blythe were joining them for dinner, and no one was taking a chance with Blythe out in public just in case the Russian woman had sent another assassination team that had slipped into Caspar without them being aware.

"Ink," Ambrie said as Master opened her door to help her from the truck. "Would you mind going in? I need to talk to Master in private for a minute. I don't mean to be rude, but it's important."

"I can give you privacy," Ink agreed, "but I'll wait over there." He indicated the door into the restaurant, across the parking lot. "I have to watch over you two lovebirds."

Master winced but refrained from reacting. He didn't even give him the finger. He just stood, wedged between Ambrielle's thighs, wondering if there was a special hell for men like him to serve right there on earth. Most likely, because he was in it. He couldn't stop himself from pushing back stray strands of dark hair falling around her face.

Ambrie waited until Ink was completely across the parking lot before she looked up at Master, her strangely colored eyes darkening to that almost violet that got him in the gut every damn time. He tried to keep his armor on, but just looking into those eyes of hers could turn him inside out.

"Princess, your friends are inside waiting. You've been anxious to see them."

She ran her palm up and down his forearm and then switched to her nails, so they were lightly moving over his skin. "I need us to be together, Master, and we aren't. The things Czar said to you really upset you, and you applied them to us."

She'd made that leap. He couldn't help but be proud of her. His woman was damned intelligent. Made it difficult for him to put anything over on her. He shook his head. "Czar didn't say anything that wasn't true, Ambrielle. I don't get upset over the truth. I learned to live with that shit a long time ago."

She continued to run her fingernails lightly up and down his inner forearm from wrist to elbow, sending fiery arrows straight to his groin. "I did marry you because I wanted *us* to hunt Thompson down and kill him. That's true, Master. Not just you. The two of us. Now, I don't know exactly what I want. I'm a little confused because, honestly, I didn't expect to develop feelings for you so fast. I knew I could, or I would never have agreed to a long-term marriage."

"You knew I would have let you out of it."

She nodded slowly. "But I wouldn't. I gave you my word, Master. I meant every single word of the vows I said. I mean to keep them. I know you think I look at you like everyone else does, but I don't. We have a chance at something good. Don't take that away from us before we have time to make it work."

He wrapped his hand around her neck, feeling her heart beat into his palm. His hand looked enormous, a dark stain of guilt against her skin. That heartbeat didn't accelerate in the least. The trust in her eyes didn't change.

"Do you know what it will be like living with me long term, Ambrielle? The reality of living with someone with a record like mine? We'll get harassed every time our car is stopped in traffic, and believe me, baby, it will be stopped. If we have children, I won't be able to go with them on some of their school trips or volunteer in their classrooms. You'll always get those looks, and so will they. You're going to have friends who will give you looks and talk behind your back. Being married to me could impact your business in a very negative way. If you were madly in love with me, trying to live with all that would be difficult enough, but having what is virtually a marriage of convenience, over time, there is no way you will be able to stay."

Ambrielle sighed. "You're determined to sink us before we have a chance, Master. I want this to work. I want you. I can't tell you how I know I'm supposed to be with you, but I do know. I also know I can't make it work without you. I can't be the only one fighting for us. It is an uphill fight. It takes work to hold a relationship together, and we've gotten together under terrible circumstances. I'm so traumatized I don't know what I'm doing half the time, and I'm terrified to let you out of my sight. You have to make up your mind. You do."

He'd already made up his mind. "Never thought I'd be a fucking pussy over a woman."

Her brows came together. "I don't know what that means."

"It means I know you can break my heart when I didn't even know I had one. You're supposed to be the one falling apart all the time, not me. Get out of the truck, princess. You ever tell the others I'm making a fool of myself over you, I'll strangle you with my bare hands."

Her eyes searched his again, not, he was certain, to check to see if he meant the threat but to make sure they were good. Then she gave him her little half laugh, half giggle that got him somewhere in the gut, put her hands on his waist and shifted to the very edge of the seat, clearly expecting him to lift her out. He did, because when your lady wants you to put her on her pretty little feet on the parking lot asphalt, you do it. He'd already looked like an idiot once too often.

She slipped her hand in his as they made their way to Ink. "Do I look all right? You didn't say if you thought this outfit is good enough for this restaurant. I've actually heard of Crow 287, but I've never been here. Mom and I talked about driving up the coast to try it out. She loved finding great out-of-the-way restaurants."

He liked that Ambrielle's voice was clear. She could talk about her mother without falling apart. He needed to be able to come to terms with their marriage, to believe in them the way she did. Who knew that he was going to have so many issues? He tightened his fingers around hers and reached over her head to open the door for her as Ink stepped back to allow them entrance first. He was guarding their backs— or rather Ambrie's.

She didn't seem to realize that it was more than probable that Walker Thompson had an army of mercenaries out in force looking for her. He would go looking for Kir Vasiliev, the man Ambrielle had married, and that would lead Thompson to the Torpedo Ink club in Caspar. He would send his men to kill Master and acquire his widowed bride. Thompson was really hurting for money, and no one was going to help him. Not his father and not his partners. Not anymore.

Master had stacked the deck the best he could in his favor for the dinner with Ambrielle's friends. He had two band members coming to round out the table along with Ink. Maestro and Keys were good at fielding questions. Ink could charm the socks off a roaring lion—or lioness. Czar was bringing Blythe. There would be several other members of Torpedo Ink dining at tables surrounding the longer one they had reserved.

Master halted before they were in sight of the tables. "Princess, one last thing. Sooner or later, your friend is going to get you to go with her to the ladies' room so she can be alone with you." He bent his head close to hers, to ensure she understood him. "If there is anything at all you don't like, you find disturbing, you signal Lissa or one of the other Torpedo Ink women. They'll go into the room at the same time. You'll be covered, just in case."

"Do you think Amanda is going to hurt me? She's been my friend for years."

"No, but I think it's possible Thompson has gotten to her and scared the crap out of her. She isn't going to trust us. She'll be too scared. Is she a good actress?"

Ambrie nodded. "Very good. She took years of theater."

"Can you tell if something isn't right with her?"

"I might be able to." Ambrie moved closer under his shoulder.

Master felt like an ass for saying anything to her when she'd been looking forward to seeing her friends, but he considered it likely that Thompson had found a way to get to Amanda. She worked from home, using her computer. If Code said he could easily get a message to her, there was no doubt that Walker Thompson could.

As they approached the back room, where their table was set up, Amanda Gibbs leapt up, nearly knocking her chair over, and rushed toward them. Her group rose as well and followed her, surrounding them, making Master uncomfortable.

"Oh my God, Ambrie, I was so worried when I heard about your parents, and then I couldn't get through to you on your cell." Amanda threw her arms around Ambrielle, nearly knocking her off her feet.

Master kept her from falling by standing solidly behind her, providing a wall for her to rock back against. Amanda's eyes flicked up to him and then went wide with shock. Her arms slowly loosened and then dropped to her sides.

"Ambrie? Who's this?"

Master steeled himself for the inevitable hesitation and signs of embarrassment. There were none. Ambrielle half turned, laying her palm possessively on his forearm. "My husband, Kir Vasiliev. He belongs to the local club, Torpedo Ink, so everyone calls him Master."

Amanda's eyebrows shot up. "Master? Husband? Wait. What? You're going way too fast for me, Ambrie."

Master indicated the table. "Let's sit down, and Ambrie can explain everything while we order. If we don't get to it, Alena will be out here giving us a lecture."

Amanda looked to her brother for direction. "Adam, I'm so confused I don't know what to say. This is my brother, Adam, and a friend of his, Rashad Perry. Rashad is a member of the band Troubled Sons. And this is a friend of mine, Marcus Phillips."

Master held out his hand, first to Adam. "Nice to meet you. Ambrie has spoken of you. Marcus, it's been too long since we've seen you. And Rashad, we've met a couple of times, good to see you again."

Master kept them moving toward the table reserved for them in the back room. Several members of Torpedo Ink were already at the smaller tables surrounding the one they would be using. Ice and Soleil were seated with Storm. Casimir and Lissa were having dinner with Scarlet and Absinthe.

"You all *know* him?" Amanda asked as Marcus pulled out her chair for her. "Am I the only one who doesn't? Where have I been all this time?"

Ink winked at her. "Since no one saw fit to introduce me, my friends call me Ink. I own Black Ink Tattoo—I don't use a lot of color, which is why the name, although now Lana and Alena are giving me hell over it."

"Your artwork is pretty damn famous," Rashad said. "And Master, Crows Flying is one of the best bands out there. The music you play is unbelievable. You want to jam with us anytime, man, you're welcome."

"Thanks." That was about his quota for talking for the day. He was grateful when Keys and Maestro sat down and then Blythe and Czar entered the room. The moment they did, it was as if royalty had entered. A short hush fell before several of the members called out a greeting. Czar held out a chair for Blythe across from Ambrie and Master. Ink introduced everyone.

Amanda sighed. "I just want to know how you came to be married. For real, Ambrie?"

"Yes, we've known each other awhile, broke up because, well . . ." She trailed off.

Master shrugged and brought her hand to his mouth, kissing her knuckles.

It was Czar who explained. "When you find the love of your life, it's difficult to believe you're worthy. In fact, you know you're not, so you do the honorable thing no matter how much it hurts, and you let her go."

"*He* broke up with you?" Amanda looked incredulous. She turned to Marcus for support. "Can you imagine how insane you would have to be to break up with Ambrielle? I mean, look at her."

Ambrie blushed, the soft rose color sweeping up her neck into her face. "Amanda."

"Yes," Marcus replied solemnly. "It's called love, Amanda. If you truly love someone, and you don't think you're going to enhance their life, you do let them go. Or you hesitate before you make your move because you know you really shouldn't."

At once, Amanda's face went soft. She smiled at Marcus. "That's so sweet to think that way." She turned her attention back to Ambrie. "How did you get back together?"

Ambrie laid her palm against Master's jaw, stroking gently. "I saw him and sort of flung myself at him and point-blank asked him to marry me."

Adam and Rashad laughed openly. Amanda gasped. "You did not."

"I did. I convinced him I really wanted to make it work, and then once he heard the news about Mom and Dad, he married me. I suspect he didn't want me to be alone in the world."

Amanda narrowed her eyes. "You aren't wearing a ring."

It was an accusation. More, she sounded as if she believed they were lying to her.

Master rubbed Ambrielle's naked ring finger. "We need to do something about that, princess." He brushed a kiss across her temple and then turned his head, raising his voice. "Hey, Ice. Get it finished for me?"

Ice stood, his chair scraping on the floor. "As a matter of fact, I did. Brought it with me. I hope I got the sizing right."

"Ice?" Amanda whispered.

"As in *Ice*?" Rashad echoed. He gripped Adam's shoulder. "Do you have any idea who that is?"

Adam shook his head. "I don't have a clue."

"He's only one of the most famous jewelers in the United States," Rashad said. "Very few people ever manage to get their hands on one of his pieces of jewelry, let alone meet him. I had no idea he was a biker."

They watched as he handed Master two jewelry boxes. "Thanks, brother," Master said.

"Hope you love it, Ambrie," Ice said. "Let me know if there's a problem."

Master opened the small box and took out the wedding band. It was made of platinum, a simple band etched with words in Russian. He slipped it on her finger and then took out the engagement ring. The gem was round cut, a deep, deep purple, the stone sparkling under the lights in the room.

Ambrie looked up at him as he slid it onto her finger. "I've never seen a stone like this. It's so beautiful. What is it, Master?"

"It's a purple diamond from Russia. Ice had it, and when he showed it to me, I knew it was the perfect stone. Your eyes change to that color sometimes."

Master didn't know anything at all about diamonds, but Amanda did and apparently, so did Rashad. Both let out a little gasp.

Rashad nearly threw himself across the table to get a better look. "Is that real? As in not from a lab?" There was awe in his voice. "You said from Russia. There're two mines in Russia that produce a small number of purple diamonds. They're so rare."

Ice shrugged. "Master wanted the stone because it matched her eyes, and it comes from Russia. That's the significance, not how rare it is. It's what he's saying to her." He leaned down and brushed a kiss on top of Ambrie's head. "Welcome to the family, little sister."

Ambrielle smiled up at him. "Thank you, Ice. I love my rings."

He sauntered off, acknowledging the others with a nod.

"May I see your rings?" Blythe asked.

Ambrielle held her hand across the table. Master slid his under hers. The rings looked perfect on her delicate finger.

"Speaking of rings, Amanda, do you remember going to one of the clubs and there was a woman who came in a few times wearing a very unusual ring? I was trying to describe it to Master so he could tell Ice about it. I thought he'd know the designer. It was a snake made of thin gold with diamonds for eyes, and she wore it on her index finger."

"Yes, of course. She came in with her brother to the club right down from our office. He was a big blond man. Had a scar on the side of his face. He always wore gloves on his hands. I thought that was odd in a club. She was gorgeous, tall, with dark hair and eyes. Looked like a model. I thought she was by the way she walked and held herself. She didn't look anything at all like her brother. I flirted with her brother at the bar, but he didn't respond. He kept scanning the crowd, obviously looking for someone. She was friendly. He wasn't."

"You talked to her more than I did," Ambrie encouraged. She smiled at Marcus. "Amanda is extraordinary with our customers. She can remember names and faces. She's the friendly one and puts everyone at ease. If it was left to me, we'd lose all the clients. I'd stare at my computer screen all day."

Amanda laughed her first genuine laugh. "That's not

exactly true. You remember the faces and names, but you do stare at your screen."

When the laughter died down, Ambrie continued, "What was her name? Who was she looking for?"

"She said her name was Helena Vorobyev. She was looking for a man named Viktor Prakenskii. She thought he'd been in the Bay Area business district at one time. None of us knew a Viktor Prakenskii, but she was very persistent and kept coming back," Amanda said.

Master's eyes met Czar's. The woman had been at the clubs looking for him weeks earlier. Vorobyev was derived from the name of a bird. In Russian, *vorobey* was "sparrow," often used by Sorbacov as the code word for his female assets. That could tie Helena Smirnov/Vorobyev to the schools in Russia for certain. Why would she have such a vicious rage toward Czar? So much so that she would want to kill his entire family?

Master dropped his hand under the table and rested his palm on Ambrielle's thigh. She'd gotten them prime information.

"Do you remember her brother's name?" Ambrie persisted. "The blond? His scar was unusual, wasn't it?" She sounded puzzled, as if trying to remember it.

Master noted that Ambrielle didn't say what was different about the scar; she allowed Amanda to recall it. His woman was clever.

Amanda put her fingers up to her cheek and traced a crescent like a half-moon from the inside corner of her eye to the inside corner of her mouth. "It was a perfect crescent moon. Wide in the center and taking up most of the right side of his face. I've never seen a scar that was going from the inside corner of an eye and curving to the outside of the face and back in. I couldn't imagine what made that scar so deep like that."

Ambrielle touched her own face, her fingers covering her skin. "It was very odd."

"His name was different as well," Amanda continued.

"Titus Ustrashkin. I thought that was strange even for a Russian name."

At the table beside theirs, Casimir straightened from leaning toward his wife, Lissa. He tapped his fingers on the table, drumming them seemingly to the music playing softly in the background. Master listened to the code. Casimir had attended one of the other schools where Sorbacov had taken children to be trained as assets. A Titus Ustrashkin had attended that particular school with him.

Master curled his palm tightly around Ambrielle's thigh, squeezing down to let her know she had done exactly what they needed.

The waitress arrived to take their orders, and Master was able to sit back and let the others carry the conversation so he could observe his woman interacting with her friends and the members of Torpedo Ink. The uneasiness sitting in his gut wasn't letting up, even though everyone seemed to be relaxed and buying the story of their hasty marriage.

As always, Blythe and Czar took control if a subject came up that appeared as if it might take things in an awkward direction. The other band members and Ink kept Rashad, Adam and Marcus entertained and laughing. At no time did Ambrie try to force him to take part in the conversation. She seemed content to carry their share of the banter. Occasionally, she brushed her hand over the top of his, or leaned into him. Twice she stroked caresses over her rings.

Master generally avoided anywhere he had to listen to inane conversations. He didn't like arguments. In the bar, he was playing music, not listening to the voices talking. He could get lost in the music. He had an ear for pitch, for sounds, and the wrong notes could easily grate on him. Ambrielle had a beautiful speaking voice. He could listen to her all night, and he tried to concentrate on just her voice, hoping to unravel some of the knots tied so tight in his belly—always an indicator of impending trouble.

He found himself exchanging uneasy looks with Maestro and Czar. They felt it too, that strange tension creeping into the room. He eased back in his chair and took a slow look around the room. Casimir and Lissa were on alert, along with Absinthe and Scarlet. The four were eating dinner, but they were checking out the diners in the room through the archway. Master didn't have a good angle on the other room.

A jarring note in the laughter made him wince, so much so, he wrapped his fingers around Ambrie's hand and held on tightly while he sorted out what was wrong. The sound tripped the acceleration switch on his heart. Yeah, something was very wrong. He had all the classic signs warning him. His gaze touched on Amanda.

Ambrie's friend moved restlessly in her chair. Twice she looked at her watch, then looked around the restaurant, the expression on her face shadowed, anxious. Then she would look at Marcus and Adam. She couldn't seem to settle or relax. Her voice had gone to a higher pitch, that jarring note that was off whenever she laughed. It wasn't a real laugh at all.

"We should hit the ladies' room before our food gets here," Amanda suddenly announced. "Come on, Ambrie." She stood up, looking at Master almost defiantly, daring him to stop Ambrielle from coming with her.

He wanted to stop her. His fingers shackled her wrist, unseen, beneath the table. Ambrie immediately turned to him, her free palm cupping his cheek. She leaned close, breath to breath. "We're good. I'm good."

She wasn't though. Amanda wasn't going to talk her into annulling the marriage. That wasn't Master's concern. The woman had something else in mind. He put his lips against Ambrie's ear. "Be safe, princess. Don't trust her." He kissed her temple and reluctantly let her go. As he did, his gaze went straight to Lissa and Scarlet. He was counting on them. He couldn't go with Ambrie into the women's room, although that wouldn't stop him if he felt she needed him.

Ambrielle stood, his little fairy princess, dressed in the clothes they'd retrieved from her apartment. She was so damn beautiful, so courageous, his heart ached. Amanda's gaze dropped to her watch as she followed Ambrie toward the restroom.

Blythe sighed. "I suppose I should go as well."

"You suppose wrong," Czar said. "Something isn't right. If you really need to go, I'll take you back to the kitchen. You can use the one Alena has for her employees."

"What do you mean, something isn't right?" Blythe's voice turned anxious. "Czar, do you think that horrid woman is here? In the restaurant? You don't think she's going to try to hurt me or the children again, do you?"

"I don't know what the problem is, baby, only that something is off. Until I know what's wrong, you're staying in my sight," he decreed.

Master stood up. There was no staying seated when he was feeling that dark dread building in his gut the way it was. Amanda was up to something. He didn't bother to explain himself to the others. He'd never done it before, and there was no starting now. He just walked away from the table.

<hr>

"Ambrie." Amanda nearly pounced on her as she washed her hands. "We have to go." She looked at her watch. "We only have a few minutes. There's a car waiting for you outside to get you out of here. You'll be safe."

Ambrie lifted her gaze to meet Amanda's in the mirror. "What are talking about, Amanda? What have you done?"

"I know you were forced into marrying that man. I know all about it. Right after your parents were murdered, and you disappeared, I was contacted . . ."

Ambrielle swung around, crossing her arms over her chest. "Stop right there, Amanda. I've known you for *years*. You can't lie to save your soul. You aren't saving me, so drop the bullshit. What are you doing? Who contacted you, and what did he say?" She poured steel into her voice.

Amanda's face crumpled, just as Ambrie knew it would. Her friend burst into tears. "He's going to kill Adam. He's got a sniper rifle on him. Somebody sent me an email and told me when I was contacted by you that I was to let them know. When you said to meet you at a restaurant, I was to inform them where it was and the time you would be there."

"You told them I'd be here tonight?" Ambrielle repeated, more for Lissa and Scarlet's sake than to memorize what she was told. She knew the two women had entered and gone into the stalls.

"I *had* to tell them. They said they'd kill Adam. They sent me pictures of him coming and going from his apartment. One was right outside his apartment door. I was so scared for him." There was a little sob in her voice. "I didn't know what to do, Ambrie. They were going to *kill* him. They did say this man took you and that he and his club were responsible for the deaths of your parents. I wanted it to be true. I wanted these other people to be rescuing you."

"You knew better." Ambrie wasn't going to let her off the hook. "No one rescuing me was going to threaten to kill your brother. You were trading my life for his."

"No!" Amanda wailed. "I was saving you. I was trading that horrible man's life, Master, the one who took you and killed your parents. He was supposed to die, not you. You were going to be saved, and my brother was going to be saved."

Ambrielle went very still, the air leaving her lungs in a long rush. For a moment the room spun, and a red haze shimmered behind her eyes. Kir. Master. The only person she had left in the entire world. Her husband. Amanda had just shrieked that she had set her husband up to be killed.

She forced herself to keep from leaping at her best friend and attacking her. "Amanda, how are they going to kill him? Master? How are they planning to kill him?" She kept her voice very calm. It shook, but she managed to keep her cool. Somehow. She wanted to run out of the now-way-too-small bathroom and find him. See for herself that he was safe. Where was he?

"I'm sorry, Ambrie. I didn't know what to do. I honestly

had never heard you talk about him. When you said you were married to him and you looked so happy, I tried to make myself believe you were making it up or you were, like, a victim of Stockholm syndrome. Tell me what to do to make this right. I don't know what to do."

"You have to tell me how they planned to kill Master," Ambrie insisted.

Amanda shook her head. "I don't know exactly. Only that I was supposed to take you out of the restaurant at a certain time and they knew he would follow. They have a sniper waiting to kill my brother if I don't comply. I guess they'll kill Master when he follows to get you back. That must be the plan."

Ambrielle covered her face for a minute before raising her head and looking at her friend. She'd known Amanda a long time. She'd always known Amanda had a difficult time making decisions. She just hadn't realized how hard it was for her to really think things through when no one helped her. "These people are ruthless, Amanda. They could come into this restaurant with guns and kill innocent people. It wouldn't matter to them how many they killed to make their point."

"What are we going to do?"

Lissa and Scarlet emerged from the stalls to wash their hands. Amanda jumped and let out a little surprised squeak.

"We're going to make certain everyone is safe," Ambrielle said. "I have to find Master."

"Ambrie," Lissa cautioned, "if he's not inside, don't go outside. Stay with Casimir or Czar. We need to get Blythe out of here first. The others will find the sniper, or if there's more than one, they'll clear them. Just go back to the table like nothing's happened."

"I'm going to find Master," Ambrie reiterated. "Hopefully, he's at the table."

She didn't wait for Amanda. She didn't care if the other women were angry that she didn't listen to them or if later

Master gave her a lecture because she didn't follow their advice. She hurried out of the restroom and made her way to the entrance of the back room. She could see that the chair Master had been sitting in was vacant, and her heart began to pound. Had he gone outside? He didn't like to be with a lot of people.

Where was he? She turned to survey the main dining room as Amanda seated herself beside Marcus. She watched as Lissa whispered to Czar. Master wasn't in the main dining room. The restaurant wasn't all that big. If he wasn't in either of the rooms, had he gone outside onto the large patio area, where there was outside dining? The area was covered and there were gas heaters. She made her way through the tables to the double doors that led to the outdoor seating. Just as she went to open the door, a very large tattooed man with long, thick hair stepped in front of her.

"Whoa there, little sister, where are you going?" His voice was low, a hoarse rasp, as if his vocal cords had been permanently damaged.

Ambrielle looked up at him and should have been terrified. He was covered in prison tattoos. There wasn't anything soft about him, and yet she wasn't in the least afraid. He was wearing Torpedo Ink colors, and he had called her *little sister*. That was enough for her.

"I'm looking for Master. Amanda just told me Walker Thompson's men are here to kill him with snipers. The plan was for Amanda to get me to go outside with her, knowing he would follow. They were going to shoot him."

"Then going outside isn't a good idea, is it?" He had his hand around her arm. Gentle. A shackle. There was no moving.

"I can't find him." She tried not to sound as if she was panicking. "Wait. If they were here to kill him, if that was the plan all along, it stands to reason they would have sent someone inside. A team. They have these assassins. Not like regular mercenaries. They're different. Master thinks they were trained at the same schools you were." She was so afraid for Master that she was talking too fast, the words tumbling out, falling over one another.

The huge giant was gently pulling her away from the door and in the direction of the kitchen. "I'm Destroyer. You must be Master's woman. There's no mistaking the fairy princess description." All the while he kept directing her away from the patio doors. He was such a large man, and so incredibly strong, it was easy for him to block her with his body and move her where he wanted her to go without making it seem as if he were being overbearing and pushy.

Ambrielle was so close to panic she was ready to sink her teeth into the giant's arm to get him to see her. She was no fairy princess, and she never would be. Her man was in trouble, and if these men were so damn full of themselves they couldn't stop and listen to her, she was going to take matters into her own hands. She was close enough to Destroyer that she felt the scabbard under the jacket he wore.

Sliding her free hand beneath the loose leather as she matched his step, she felt him automatically loosening his grip on her as she complied. She slid the blade from the scabbard, turned and was free, sprinting toward the patio door. Destroyer bit back a curse and caught her by her hair just as she was opening the door.

"What the fuck, woman?"

"Let go of her," a man's voice said from behind them.

Destroyer half turned to face her savior. She slammed the palm without the knife on the hand in her hair, pushing it hard onto her scalp, and dropped low, spinning around to face him and then coming up fast. He was far taller than her, and the move didn't work as well on anyone that much taller, so it didn't break his hand, but he did release her.

"Not your business," he snapped at the man standing behind them.

The man kept coming at them. He was not as tall as Destroyer, but he was lithe, and the way he moved told Ambrie he knew how to fight. His hair was light colored, and he wore a goatee on his square-cut jaw. She froze, turning the blade of the knife up against her wrist so it was impossible to see.

"He's one of them," she whispered unnecessarily to Destroyer and stepped back to give him a little room.

Destroyer remained in that same relaxed, loose-limbed stance. He didn't look down at her, and instant knowledge came to her. The restaurant, which was so popular one couldn't get in, had been scattered with only a few occupants in the front room. The back patio was lit with dim LED lights, but no one was dining out there. Although, when she glanced outside, there were shadowy figures toward the far corner beyond the last tall propane heater.

The room she and her friends were in had been loaded with Torpedo Ink members. Master had told her to be careful, that it was very likely Amanda had set her up in some way. He and the others had prepared for just this possibility.

ELEVEN

Where was Master? That was the question. The stranger increased his speed, his facial features hardening, hand sliding inside his immaculate suit jacket. Destroyer exploded into action, moving so fast he was almost a blur, pinning the hand that tried to draw the gun, one elbow slamming so hard into the man's jaw that Ambrielle heard the audible crack.

Inwardly wincing, she realized this was her best shot at getting away from Destroyer. He didn't need her to help take care of the assailant. She caught at the patio door and slipped outside, stepping immediately to one side, where the best cover was. The flooring was unexpected. It appeared to be hardwood but was actually a tile that could withstand the fog and wetness of the coastal weather.

Three striped black-and-white high-backed bench seats defined each space. The seats were wrapped around a table, with three wooden chairs on the other side. Three of the groupings of bench seats formed a triangle, creating a semi-private space for diners. In between the seats were stairs with potted plants on them, further adding to the privacy of each space and giving Ambrielle something to hide behind.

For once in her life, she was happy she was on the smaller

side. The plants at each of the stations were tall and lush, giving her adequate cover as she snuck closer to the small group of men huddled together at the far side of the patio. She realized that the overhead ceiling was retractable and that it was open, allowing the cool night air in. Around the edges of the rectangular opening was lacy fringe, and growing up the walls and the parts of the ceiling that didn't pull back were vines with beautiful, healthy green leaves. She used the large blue pots on the floor to move between to get even closer.

Five men surrounded Master. Blood ran down his face above his right eye. He sat in a chair while the others stood. His hands were free, and so were his feet. That was a huge mistake on the part of his captors. Either they had no idea of what kind of man he was, or they were waiting for him to make his break.

"Call her out here," the tallest man ordered. He had dirty-blond hair and hazel eyes. His chest was thick and his arms beefy with muscle.

"Do you really think I'm going to just turn Ambrielle over to you so easily, Yuri? You can go back to your boss and tell him I have no reason to give him such a prize. She's worth millions. He'd better make me an offer that makes sense. I'm well aware of who he is and what he does. My club wants in on his business. He gives us a cut, we give him his bride."

Ambrielle went very still. She had never even considered that she might be used as a bargaining chip to give Torpedo Ink a cut into Walker Thompson's business. She knew he owned casinos with his father, but he had illegal businesses as well. She had no idea what they were, but they had to be lucrative.

Her gaze fixed on Master's face. She knew every line. Every scar. The cut of his mouth. The way his eyes crinkled around the corners. Her mother had always told her she would know when the right man came to her. It was a family gift, handed down through her mother's line, and she had known. She hadn't just known with her body—and the chemistry between them was astounding—she'd known with her soul. No way was she going to believe he was selling her out. She believed in him. In herself. In the two of them.

"I'm not here to negotiate a deal with you, asshole," Yuri snapped.

"You mean you have no authority. Call him. Tell Thompson the offer's on the table."

Ambrielle kept her gaze fixed on Master. Waiting. The other men around him waited for a signal from their leader. Destroyer would be coming after her once he disposed of the man who had attacked them. No doubt, that man hadn't been alone.

"Kill the son of a bitch and let's go in and take her," a man in a red shirt snarled.

The leader regarded him with cool eyes. "Kuzma, if you try to kill him, I guarantee, you'll be dead either by his hand or by the sniper who has you in his sights right now."

"Her," Master corrected. "Lana never misses. You all know her reputation. He didn't tell you who you'd be dealing with, did he?"

"You'd still be dead," Kuzma snapped.

Master shrugged. "You're welcome to try. I came out here to talk in good faith. I even let your partner, Artem"— he indicated the man standing beside Kuzma in a dark blue jacket—"hit me. I warned you if any of you tried it again, I'd kill you or Lana would. I think that was fair. I've delivered my part. Call Thompson."

Yuri pulled out his phone with a sigh and walked a few steps away from Master, toward Ambrielle. She went still, afraid even to blink. She kept her gaze on Master rather than Yuri, knowing if she stared at him, she might attract his attention. She had the feeling Master already knew she was there. He didn't exactly look at her, but his fingers were on his chest over his heart, and he seemed to be tapping out a beat.

"Yeah, the club wants to make a deal. They'll hand over the bitch for a cut. The club president is here, and he'll negotiate. Yeah, we can do that, but I'm going to tell you, I know these men from way back. These aren't men you ever want to fuck with. Better to get them on your side. No, I'm not afraid of them. I'm just letting you know what they're like. Yeah, I can do that. We'll get the president out here, kill him and kill the rest of them." He ended the call, closed his eyes and shook his head as he sighed. "Fucking idiot," he whispered aloud.

He paused, his back to Master and the others, lifting his hand to his mouth. "Take out the sniper. Do it now. We're going to wipe them out." He whispered the command and then turned around, walking back to where Master was still ringed by his men. "He's willing to negotiate with your president, but only over the phone. You want to bring him out here? You want to do it inside? We got to get this over."

Ambrielle was slightly shocked at how Yuri could sound annoyed, resigned and amicable at the same time. She realized he'd probably used a similar ruse many times, luring his victim into believing he was going to give them whatever they wanted before killing them.

"I suppose it's best to go inside and talk to him there. Czar's with his wife and a few friends. They're having dinner." Master had a note of caution in his voice. "Not all of them are Torpedo Ink."

Blythe. Never in a million years would Master put Blythe in jeopardy. Not one member of Torpedo Ink would. Ambrielle saw the way they all treated her. She heard the note in Master's voice when he said her name. Blythe was sacred. He would never allow these men near her. The tension hadn't changed in Master. He appeared exactly the same as he'd been when he was seated, but she knew he was close to exploding into action.

"I don't know, Master," Yuri hedged. "Maybe it would be better if you called him out here. I've got more crew inside.

I'll call mine out as well. We don't want any nosy civilians recording on their cell phones."

Master subsided with a shrug of his shoulders. "Yeah, that might be best." His hand went to his hair, and he swept his fingers through it.

Ambrielle found herself smiling at the easy, casual way Master had manipulated the other man to do exactly what he wanted him to do. He wanted Yuri to insist that Czar come outside, where Lana and possibly others could have them under the surveillance of their rifles. Yuri clearly thought his assassins were taking care of that threat to them.

Should she have found a way to warn Torpedo Ink that they planned to kill Lana, their sniper? She had no means to communicate the threat to her. She had to believe that if Torpedo Ink had considered that Amanda would betray her by telling her enemies where to find her, then they already had a plan in place, and that would include protecting themselves against assassins attacking their sniper.

"I'll call him. He won't come alone, Yuri. He'll have Savage and Maestro with him."

There was something about the way Master said the two names that sent a chill down Ambrie's spine. She'd met both men briefly. Savage had been with the singer, Seychelle, and he'd had a beautiful voice. When she'd heard him sing a duet with his woman, he'd sounded like a man with a beautiful soul. Ambrie had observed him being so solicitous of Seychelle, and yet now, his name seemed to conjure up something else altogether.

Maestro was in the band Crows Flying with Master. She knew he played all kinds of instruments and owned 287 Construction Company with Master, Keys and Player. He'd helped to build the beautiful cabin Reese lived in with Tyra and their daughter. Still, suddenly his name seemed to be uttered as a warning, just as Savage's had been. She didn't understand what she was missing.

Master was already on the phone. "Yeah, Czar, they want

to talk. He's calling his men outside so no civilians are in the way. You're needed for negotiations with his boss."

Ambrie saw Yuri visibly wince at the word. He didn't consider Thompson his boss. That was interesting to her. Gleb and Denis and the other two Russians who had worked with them were independent of Thompson's main security people. They followed Thompson's orders—to a point. She was aware—where Thompson didn't seem to be—that the four men could easily turn on him at any time.

Thompson had drawn these men from that same pool. Gleb and Denis weren't among them. Why? She couldn't see either man taking orders from Yuri. Gleb was the kind of man to give them. Her heart sank. What if he was the man hunting Torpedo Ink's sniper? The skin itched along her inner wrist where the blade lay flat against it, as if to say she needed to be in on the action. Part of her wanted to slide right off the patio and go hunting herself. Could she do it?

Very slowly, because movement drew the eye, she turned her head slightly to view the drop-off from the patio to the ground. There were no stairs close to her hiding spot, and she didn't dare move, especially now that three more of Yuri's men had come outside.

"Where are Jaska and Karp?" Yuri demanded, sounding impatient, his gaze on the door.

The three newcomers shook their heads. "Looked everywhere for them. We thought you gave them orders to patrol outside."

Yuri spoke sharply into his radio, switching to Russian. There was no answer. The door opened again and Savage, Maestro and Destroyer emerged. Czar was nowhere in sight. She should have known they would protect their president. Master had known all along Yuri was setting them up.

Master stood up again, this time, his hand moving to his left shoulder, and then he was striking out so fast he was a blur. Ambrielle didn't take her gaze off him, but she had trouble seeing him move. From his shoulder the right hand continued to move, his fingers jabbing straight into Yuri's throat, going deep. Yuri gagged, choked, went to his knees, both hands going to his throat, as his eyes seemed to burst.

Master whirled toward Kuzma before Yuri had even dropped to the floor of the patio. His boot swept the gun from Kuzma's hand and then went straight up to his head and took him to the floor with a sound that sickened Ambrie. Master's boot had to be steel toed, and he drove that steel right into Kuzma's temple, straight through the skull. The foot was back on the floor, driving toward Artem.

Master had killed two men in under five seconds. Ambrielle still had her mouth open in shock. She wasn't even sure if five seconds had passed. It could have been three. He was already on Artem, slamming a palm on the wrist holding the gun, and then somehow taking possession of the weapon. He tossed it away as he whirled the man around, all in one smooth motion, as if the two men were dancing. His knee came up between Artem's legs hard, doubling the man over. At the same time, he caught Artem's head in his hands as it came down toward him. Master spun around, taking the head and body with him, so Artem hung over his shoulder. There was an audible crack and Master dropped the body on the patio floor. The moment he did, his gaze lifted straight to her hiding spot. He didn't look happy.

Ambrielle glanced quickly over to the others to see how they had fared. Torpedo Ink had just as quietly disposed of those men as well. The bodies lay on the floor. In the dim light, it was difficult to make them out.

"Would you like to tell me what you're doing out here, Ambrielle?" Master loomed over her. His eyes seemed even darker than usual, and he looked intimidating as hell.

She rose slowly to give herself time to process what had just happened. "I came out to rescue you. No one was listening to me. I knew you were in trouble. Amanda gave me her bullshit story and I was afraid these idiots were going to kill you. She actually told me that was part of the plan. I wanted to strangle her, so I ran out of the restroom, looking for you. When I couldn't find you, I knew you had to be outside. The big man, Destroyer, stopped me at the door, but then he was attacked, so I was able to get free to help you."

She followed up her explanation with a faint smile, hoping that would help placate or appease that extremely intense look on his face that didn't bode well for her.

"You came outside because you knew I was in trouble, so you thought you'd rescue me?" he repeated.

Ambrielle nodded, not liking the way he muttered the words as if he couldn't quite comprehend what she said.

There was a snicker behind him coming from Savage. A burst of outright laughter came from Maestro. Destroyer stalked right up to her to stand shoulder to shoulder with Master. He didn't look any happier than Master.

"You going to return my property?" His voice was that rough, low sound that was gruff and scary.

"What property?" Master asked.

"She stole my knife."

There was instant silence, and Ambrielle was aware of all eyes on her. She sighed. "It wasn't like he needed it. He was doing just fine defending himself, or I would have given it back or helped him. I thought Master might need it. Is it sacred or something? Did I break some kind of Torpedo Ink rule taking his knife?" She focused on Master. "You're really going to have to go over all these rules with me."

"She stole your *knife*?" Master repeated, shock in his voice.

"Oh, this is the best," Maestro said. "She fucking stole Destroyer's knife. Was it on him? Was he wearing it?"

"I could break your neck," Destroyer said, throwing the threat out casually.

Ambrielle wasn't certain if he was talking to her or to Maestro. Either way, she stepped closer to Master just in case. She was glad she hadn't handed the knife over immediately.

"Might be worth it," Maestro said. "Was it?" he persisted.

"Yeah." Destroyer sighed and opened his jacket to reveal the scabbard. "She lifted it, and she got away from me."

"You were a little busy killing someone," she pointed out graciously, hoping to buy some points with him. She took the knife carefully and held it out to him. "I'm sorry if it was against the rules to take it, but I didn't know it was sacred. I was just trying to rescue Master. You really should have listened to me."

Master wrapped his arm around her waist. "Woman, you are insane. Certifiably insane. I didn't need rescuing, but I appreciate that you would come for me. On the other hand, I'm a little upset that you would put your life in danger unnecessarily."

"It wasn't unnecessary," she argued. "If you had been in trouble, then I would have been able to help you. You needed to communicate with me that you had a plan. That's the point, hotshot. Communication."

He nuzzled her neck and instantly hot blood rushed through her veins. She tilted her head just a little to give him better access.

"Did you call me 'hotshot'?" his lips whispered against her earlobe, and then he caught it between his teeth and bit down.

She gasped as the little sting gave way to something else altogether. She always seemed to react to anything he did in a sexual way. "Yes. And you're in *such* trouble for not letting me know you expected Amanda to betray me."

"I did let you know."

She was silent a moment, not because he was telling the truth but because he was leaning down, his breath warm in her ear, his body pressed tight against hers. Ambrie could feel the hard outline of his cock against her back, and right away, her body reacted. Goose bumps erupted. Nerve endings fired. Her blood went hot. She couldn't quite catch her breath. She was back to the night of their wedding, where there were dead bodies all around them, and all she could see was Master.

"Stop distracting me," she admonished. "Seriously. You should have told me, Master. I was worried sick about you."

His teeth bit down on her shoulder, this time much harder, and she stilled, ignoring the flash of pain, recognizing that the tension was coiled tight in him.

"*You* were worried sick about *me*? You were exposed out here," he rasped against her shoulder. "Those men were trained assassins. They were focused on me, or they would have seen you. They should have. They knew a sniper was on them, but they thought their man was hunting her. Still, the four of them kept checking with him to ensure they were safe. That divided their attention as well. That was why they didn't spot you."

"Or maybe I'm good at hiding."

"I was aware the moment you slipped out onto the patio," he corrected. "Let's get back inside. They're going to start cleaning up out here, and we have guests. Czar and Blythe can only hold the fort for so long."

"I would have thought your club would hustle Blythe out of here the moment you knew for certain those assassins were here." She hated that he'd dropped his arm from around her waist, but he took her hand and they made their way across the patio floor.

Savage held the door open for her. "Nice job, Ambrie, welcome to the family."

"Don't encourage her, Savage," Master snapped. His voice came out more of a growl, and he coughed.

Ambrielle looked up at him, worried. Savage followed them inside. "Did you tell Steele that throat thing is back?"

"What throat thing?" Ambrie demanded, when she noticed Master trying to subtly warn Savage off.

Master glared at Savage. "It's nothing to worry about, princess."

She stopped moving right in the hallway of the restaurant,

a difficult feat when he was such a big man. "Tell me right now."

Savage turned away, but she caught a flash of what could have been a smirk he exchanged with Destroyer. She didn't care what they thought. Master had made a promise to her, and as far as she was concerned, he'd already broken it. She wasn't having him do it again.

Master sighed. "This relationship crap is getting out of hand. You're supposed to do what I tell you in front of the brothers, not the other way around, remember?"

Ambrielle hastily looked around to make sure the members of Torpedo Ink had abandoned them before she put her hands on her hips and tilted her head to look up at him, narrowing her gaze so he knew she meant business.

"I have not disrespected you. I haven't even argued with you. If anything, I've backed you when you were in trouble."

Ambrielle held her breath, seeing the struggle in him. He wasn't used to sharing his life with anyone. He didn't want to talk about his health. He'd just kicked ass, taking out his enemies in seconds, yet he didn't want to appear weak in any way. A quick overview of his childhood, growing up in a prison surrounded by sadistic, cruel men, forced to learn to survive in such a place—she could only imagine the smallest hint of weakness would mean death.

Ambrielle slid her palm along his forearm. "We're partners, remember?"

"Yeah, I remember." He all but gritted his teeth.

She had the feeling he was regretting his decision.

"I get nodules on my vocal cords sometimes. Growths. Always benign. They're caused by tension or stress. Most likely going to prison. It's nothing big." His voice really did sound gruff, and his eyes avoided hers.

That meant this had happened repeatedly. She wanted to have a conversation about it, but clearly this wasn't the time or place. She just nodded. "Thank you, Master. I would have been worried if you hadn't told me. I guess we'd better go back in and pretend nothing happened. I can't believe my friends wouldn't have been aware of what's been going on out here all this time."

"How could they? Everything happened outside, other than the one man Destroyer had to dispose of, but he was fast and he took the body out through the kitchen."

She took a couple of steps toward the dining room and stopped again. "Are you certain Lana is all right? If she was the one on the roof covering you?" She put her free hand to her throat defensively when he refused to relinquish her other hand and looked down at her from his superior height, giving her his frown.

"Yes, Lana was watching out for me. I wasn't worried though. I'm telling you, princess, these men were second rate."

"I believe you. I saw you in action. They didn't know what hit them. It's just that Thompson has four men with him—Gleb, Denis, Simon and Stas—who I think are elite Russian assassins. They were hired by Walker Thompson, but they would have killed him and his entire security team in a heartbeat if Thompson threatened them in any way. There was no hesitation at all with any decision they made. They didn't make mistakes."

"Did they underestimate you? Because, you know, Destroyer let you take that knife. He had to deal with the assassin and figured you could handle yourself. That's a rare compliment."

She nodded. "At first, but just at first. Then they watched me like a hawk. Gleb, especially, was the leader, and he was on it all the time. He knew Mom wasn't going to do what Thompson wanted and that I planned on helping her kill as many in the room as we could before they killed us. I just want to know for certain that he isn't here waiting to step out from a closet or somewhere else to kill you."

"I'd know, princess. I have gifts. Or curses. Whichever you want to call them. That's one of them. If an assassin is lying in wait, I know. That's one of the things that I worked on developing over the years in order to survive." He transferred his grip from her hand to her upper arm. "Why are you stalling?"

"Because I want to punch my best friend, Amanda Gibbs, right in the nose. She's in there, practically sitting on Marcus' lap, giggling and acting like she's so innocent when she brought those killers here to have them murder you and take you away from me. She knew my parents were dead, and she still was going to let them kill you. She *knew* that was their intention, Master, and yet she was willing to trade your life for her brother's."

"Ambrielle." He said her name gently, as if that smooth growl could calm the gathering storm building in her. "What would you have done if someone threatened to kill your parents, and all you had to do was point them to a stranger—one who had been in prison on murder charges?"

Her eyes met his. "You don't exchange one life for another, especially if that other person is innocent. Which you are, whether or not you killed that man. You served your time. Isn't that supposed to be how the system works? No, I wouldn't have done what she did. She should have consulted with me and allowed me to help her. At the very least, she could have told Marcus or Adam. She did neither. She willingly brought these assassins to a place of business where they conceivably could have killed innocent people."

"Because she doesn't have good judgment in a crisis. Let it go this once. Everyone makes mistakes. She won't have the chance to make a second one like this. I'll make that clear. Go talk to them and enjoy your evening. The waitress is here with the food. You don't want your dinner to get cold."

Ambrielle had a million things she wanted to say to him, a million questions to ask him, but he was right: now wasn't the time. She found herself liking him even more now that he wanted her to be with her friends and have a good evening despite what had just happened. He treated the attempt on his life as if it were nothing—an everyday occurrence.

She had a lot to learn in order to fit into his world, and she was determined to fit in.

She nodded and walked into the dining room with her head up, even though she was unable to keep her heart from pounding. She didn't look at Amanda. Instead, she concentrated on Adam, who was laughing at something Rashad was saying to Savage, who was seated at the table with Seychelle. Ambrie hadn't seen Seychelle come in, but she was very happy she was there.

"What have we missed?" she asked as Master pulled out the chair for her.

"Savage was just telling us that Rashad should jam with the band right here in the restaurant. They brought instruments, and apparently Alena closed Crow 287 for a private event so we could have the entire place to ourselves," Adam explained.

"I'm down," Rashad agreed. "The food, by the way, is excellent. Adam, if you aren't finishing those prawns, I'm going to. We can't waste any of this."

Adam laughed again. "I'm eating, I'm eating. If you touch the prawns, you'll lose your hand." Even as he threatened Rashad, he forked two of the very large prawns and put them on Rashad's plate beside his filet mignon.

Seychelle had a salad that looked excellent. Ambrielle wished she'd ordered that until she took her first bite of the assortment of seared mushrooms tossed into creamy pasta sauce. She loved mushrooms and pasta, especially Alfredo sauce, and this was made with fresh Parmesan, lemon and black pepper, making it the perfect blend.

"Master, this is amazing. You have no idea. You have to try it." She turned to him, slightly shocked that food could be this good in a small restaurant out in the middle of an extremely small town. "I heard Alena was an excellent chef, but this is truly amazing."

Rashad nodded with great enthusiasm. "It's well worth the drive. She could have a restaurant in San Francisco and be at the top if she wanted. Why haven't we come here before, Adam?"

Adam turned his attention to his sister. "You know all the good restaurants, Amanda. I count on you for these things. Were you keeping this one to yourself?"

Amanda shook her head. "I didn't know." Her voice was very low, and she kept her head down, her attention on her plate.

Adam frowned. "Are you all right? Is your food good?"

"Yes, it's delicious." She glanced up at him with a forced smile and then looked guiltily at Master, blinking back tears.

"Everything is fine, Amanda," Master assured her. "We're all having a good time. Ambrielle's been telling me about her business and how she can't do without you. You're the one who remembers everyone, their families and what their interests are. Like the woman with the interesting piece of jewelry and her brother in the club."

Amanda's gaze switched to Ambrielle. Ambrie nodded at her, willing her to cooperate and go along as if nothing were wrong. Amanda had been her friend too long not to read the message. She squared her shoulders, blinked away the tears and composed herself.

"Ambrie is very observant. Don't let her fool you."

Ambrielle forced herself to smile at Amanda, although the best she could do was fix her gaze at a spot on Amanda's forehead. Marcus leaned back in his chair and put his arm around Amanda.

"You're very good with people, sweetheart," he said. "I noticed that right away. You greet everyone in the building by name and ask after their families. I don't think to do that. Just in the last couple of days, I've been making an effort to be better and remember the names of the workers around me."

"I did notice the woman in the club with the strange ring," Adam said, "but only because you pointed it out, Amanda."

Marcus frowned and rubbed his cleanly shaven jaw. "The pair of them came into a couple of the clubs downtown I frequented after work before I moved my offices. The man she introduced to everyone as her brother wore platinum ghost cuff links. I noticed them because they were so unusual. He always wore gloves but had them off in the restroom once. His hands were covered in tattoos. His knuckles and fingers. One finger had a snake coiled around it the same way the woman had the ring."

Ambrielle felt the immediate tension in the room. She glanced up to meet Czar's piercing silver eyes. It felt as if every member of Torpedo Ink in the room stared at her, willing her to do or say something. She just wasn't certain what it was she was supposed to be asking. Master's hand dropped to her thigh and squeezed hard. She didn't look at him but pushed what was left of the food on her plate around in a little circle.

"That's weird," she said. "Don't you think that's strange, Seychelle? Why would the sister have a ring with a snake and the brother have a tattoo?"

"I don't think they were sister and brother, at least I hope not," Marcus said. "I left the club late one night, and they were in their car, all over each other."

"Eww." Amanda gave a little sniff. "You didn't really see them going at it, did you?"

"They were steaming up the windows," Marcus confirmed. "She was the aggressor. She practically threw herself into his lap. In all honesty, I was shocked enough to stop and stare for a minute. I'm usually not thrown by much."

Seychelle's delicate brows drew together. "Why would they pretend they were siblings?"

Savage took the fork from her. For the last few minutes, she'd been mostly pushing the food around on her plate. "Probably so they could pretend to pick up other men and women in the bar and dance or have conversations with them." He took a bite from her plate. "This is really good, Seychelle."

"It's always good, Savage," she agreed. "Alena made it. How could it be anything else?"

"You're not eating." He took several more bites, clearly enjoying the food.

"I ate."

There was the smallest note of amusement in Seychelle's voice, but for some reason, the sound lightened Ambrielle's mood, just as it had earlier in the bar. She managed to push the feeling of Amanda's betrayal to a distance as well as the awareness of the bodies being "dealt with" on the patio while they ate and talked and laughed as if nothing at all had happened.

Keys and Maestro left the table to go to the very small area set in the far back of the room where they had a small keyboard and other instruments set up. It wasn't long before they began to play. Player joined them.

Master leaned down, his lips against Ambrie's ear. "If I pick up my guitar, you aren't going to turn warrior woman on me and annihilate half the room, are you?"

She couldn't help but laugh as she turned her head so her lips brushed his, sending a little ripple of heat walking its fingers down her spine. "I might, but I'll signal you first."

He kissed her, his form of gentle that was mostly rough, his fingers bunched tight in her hair so that it pulled on her scalp, creating a little bite of pain, so hot it was scorching, so addicting she wanted to kiss him all night. The world faded away when Master kissed her, and she let it, sliding her arms around his neck and pressing her body into his. He felt safe and comforting. He felt like her refuge. Add to that hotter than hell and she couldn't resist.

"Hey, you two," Storm called. "You're burning down the restaurant."

A wadded-up napkin came flying across the table. Master caught it with one hand before it could hit the back of her head. The room erupted into laughter. Master left her while she covered her mouth with one hand, watching him take his guitar and join the others. Before long, most of Torpedo Ink were singing. Seychelle joined the band on the small stage. Rashad followed her.

Rashad's band was extremely popular, playing sold-out concerts across the country. His voice was recognizable anywhere. Adam beamed at him and jumped up, dancing behind his chair. That gave the women the excuse to get up and dance as well.

The break had them all laughing and pouring a few drinks as Savage handed each of the band members a new song to play. "Here it is. Mechanic and Transporter say it's a go, but we have to do it tonight. Can you get this recorded now?"

The band crowded close together and burst out laughing. Czar pushed his way into the group. "What has you all howling like hyenas?"

"The song. Savage is retaliating against Jackson, and Seychelle scribbled this little jingle for us to record tonight. His truck is in the body shop to be repaired. Some kid keyed it. You know how he loves that truck."

"You did not key his truck," Czar stated as he took the paper.

"No, that wasn't us. Jackson caught the little monster. But it did create the opportunity. We've got to get this done tonight."

Czar frowned as he read the lyrics.

"Read it out loud," Blythe said.

"I didn't have a lot of time," Seychelle said. "Savage told me tonight."

"Who is Jackson?" Rashad asked.

"He's a deputy sheriff," Ice explained. "Great sense of humor."

Savage turned his killer stare on Ice.

Ice cleared his throat, although his eyes were laughing. "I mean, a really horrible bad sense of humor. He pranked Savage because he believed Savage pranked him."

"Did you?" Rashad asked.

Savage shrugged. "I overheard some of the ladies asking questions about his birthday and they seemed upset. I may have given a suggestion to them, but if they took it seriously, I can hardly be blamed. He touched my bike. In a permanent way. I now have a sequined red hat welded onto my Night Rod special."

"It's really beautiful," Seychelle said.

"Not sequins," Ice corrected. "Those are real gems."

Savage threw his arms in the air. "That makes all the fuckin' difference in the world, doesn't it?"

"Read the lyrics," Rashad encouraged when the laughter had faded.

Czar cleared his throat again. "Okay, here goes.

I'm a legend of a lover

A man for undercover

A thirst trap in disguise

The women see me comin'

That silver truck of lovin'

That no one can deny

They need a red-hot hero

Not a poser or a zero

Deputy desire

You know I'm your live wire

Of fun . . .

Red Hot Jackson

Get your 911 of fun

And I'll let you hold my gun

Because I'm . . .

Red Hot Jackson"

There was a small silence, and then the room erupted into laughter again. "Seychelle, you are brilliant. That's exactly what I needed," Savage said. He slung his arm around her neck and kissed her.

"It sounds great, but . . ." Czar continued to stare down at the paper. "What the hell is a thirst trap?"

The women burst out laughing. Rashad and Adam joined them. Czar glared at Blythe. Savage did the same to Seychelle.

"It's something trendy on the internet," Blythe said. "Someone posts a flirty, sexy picture with the intention of getting attention. They can look one way, say, all buttoned up tight, and then a second later not have a shirt on, revealing muscles and sexy abs. That's a thirst trap."

Seychelle nodded. The men continued to look blank. "Or, you know, when Savage is giving me one of his million lectures on me not eating right, but he's slowly taking his shirt off, so I can't hear a word he's saying. I'm secretly recording him and then all those hot tattoos are revealed, and he moves and his muscles make them come alive and I put that on the internet, and everyone thinks he did it. That could constitute a thirst trap, couldn't it, Blythe?"

Savage wrapped his arms around her from behind and bit down on her shoulder, making her yelp in the middle of her laughter.

"Blythe, show me one of these 'thirst traps,'" Czar demanded.

"Blythe's in trouble now," Anya, Reaper's woman, whispered to Seychelle.

Blythe nonchalantly handed Czar her cell phone. Czar glared at the screen. "You watch this shit when I'm not around?"

"Honey, I have to keep up with the latest trends on the internet. We have children." She looked wide-eyed and innocent.

Again, everyone erupted into laughter. Ambrie couldn't help looking at Master. He wasn't laughing huge the way some of the others were, but he was watching her and smiling. She knew he was enjoying himself because she was.

"Let's do this," Master said. "I'm still on my honeymoon."

"And after you get the song recorded, we have to get it in Jackson's truck," Mechanic said. "That has to be done tonight. They'll have his truck painted by tomorrow."

"How will it work?" Adam asked.

"It isn't going to go through his radio, so he can't just turn it on or off. When he hits different speeds going through town, say, around five miles an hour, it will start playing and get louder as he picks up speed. So if he's going ten miles an hour it will get louder. At fifteen miles an hour it will start to get softer and at twenty shut off. If he's idling, once he starts it, it will continue to play. So at a stop sign, it will just keep looping, playing for everyone outside his vehicle to hear," Transporter explained.

"He'll never find it," Mechanic said with complete confidence. "He'll look in all the wrong places."

"How in the world can you put it in his truck to play like that and not go through his radio?" Rashad asked.

Mechanic and Transporter exchanged a small grin. "We have our ways. He'll have to come asking for help."

"He might come to lock you all up," Blythe warned. "But I get to help sing the chorus."

TWELVE

Master stood to make his way up to the small stage again, where the instruments were. Ambrielle rose as well, her hand tucked in the back of his jacket the way she seemed to like to do whenever she walked behind him. He paused and turned to her, wrapping his arm around her and bringing his head close to hers.

The tingle of unease that had been with him had grown. He felt eyes on them, knew others watched them. Her friends. His. He didn't look to Czar, the one man he'd depended on his entire life. Ambrie was his to care for, and the realization that she was in trouble may have come slow and with a sinking heart, but he got it. For as long as he had her, he would do his best for her.

He kept what he had to say between the two of them, sheltering her from the others with his much larger body. His Torpedo Ink brothers had his back, keeping the conversations and the laughter going to add to the noise, so no one could hear what he had to say to his woman.

"Now might be a good time to have a talk with your friend, Amanda. Let her know she's off the hook and you two are good. She's miserable and hurting, and there's no need for that."

Ambrielle peeked under his arm at her friend but made no move to let go of him. "She would have let them kill you, Master. She was trading your life for Adam's." There was a note of venom creeping into her voice.

He caught her chin, forcing her head up so her blue-violet gaze had to meet his. The pad of his thumb slid across her lips. "I lived for years down in that basement, Ambrie. Everything down there was blood and death. It was all compromise. We had a code we tried to live by, but we couldn't save everyone, and we knew it."

"I don't understand what that has to do with Amanda."

"Torpedo Ink was born down there. We became woven together tight through blood and the sacrifices we made for one another. The terrible choices we had to make, often daily. Princess, we had to make those decisions; we used our bodies, our souls, giving up everything to keep each other alive. Did we sometimes know by doing that, others died? Yes. Absolutely. Did that suck? Did we feel guilt? Yes. But it came down to survival."

Her eyes moved over his face, not comprehending. Not putting it together. He couldn't help but brush his lips over hers. He had thought he was incapable of feeling for anyone anymore. This little firecracker had turned him inside out without even trying. She was slicing his soul into tiny pieces when he hadn't known it was intact. It would be one of those slow deaths, bleeding from the inside, where no one ever saw the leak until it was too late. He'd take it—for her.

"We chose each other, princess, Torpedo Ink. We became a family. Amanda has Adam. She had no idea what to do. We kill for one another. We do more than that for one another. I'd do it for you. Trade anything for you. My life or anyone else's. You can't condemn her for something we would do—that's the point."

The music swelled in volume as the band and the others tried various ways to come up with a tune to go with the lyrics for Jackson's song. They were definitely on point, the beat catchy and melodic. Master's mind automatically began to add in little riffs and runs, even as he noted every expression flitting across Ambrie's face. She didn't like what he'd said. She understood, but she didn't like it.

"It isn't the same thing."

"You know it is, princess." He rubbed his thumb across her lips again. She had the softest lips. The fall he was taking was only getting longer and deeper. His chest hurt right over the vicinity of his heart. "She was trying to save her family, just the way we're trying to save ours."

"I'm not leaving you to make her feel better. If someone comes in to try to kill you, I'm not letting that happen."

His pint-sized little fairy princess was decisive as hell, staring up at him with large eyes, framed with those sweeping dark lashes that added a dramatic effect. It was all he could do to keep a straight face. Fuck if she didn't mean it.

"I get that, baby, but we have to convince them that we're solid. More than anything, Adam and Rashad have to believe you love me with every breath you take. Marcus and Amanda have to believe the same. I know you can pull it off for us. I have no choice. I'm expected to play with the band, so you're the one who has to do all the convincing." His thumb stroked her chin, and his gaze never wavered from hers.

Her teeth tugged at the side of her lower lip, and a frown appeared. "Are you just saying that so I'll be nice and make up with Amanda?"

"No. Torpedo Ink has them under our protection. We have to let them know what's happening. We're counting on you to get them to trust us. The only way you're going to do that, Ambrielle, is convince them you trust me."

"I guess that makes sense."

She was such a beautiful disaster. *His* beautiful disaster. He bent his head and took those pouting lips, indulging himself just for a moment. His stomach did a slow roll, and his cock went into a frenzy of need, hard as a fucking rock. His stone-cold heart, the one he'd been certain had long fallen silent, was beating strong just for her. She did that to him without even trying, just looking at him with her *Bog-damn* eyes and that sinful mouth of hers.

Tiny flames flicked over his skin and ran down his spine, igniting his nerves and spreading like a wildfire through his bloodstream. He groaned and wrapped one arm around her, pulling her body tighter against him, wondering how close the nearest restroom was.

"Enough, you two. You might be on your honeymoon, but we need your guitar and genius on this one, Master. Ambrie, lend us your man for just a few minutes. We'll give him back," Keys teased.

Master lifted his head and looked into her eyes. She looked a little dazed, but she had that sense of humor that got to him every time. If she laughed, that silly giggle, he couldn't help feeling it. He found himself giving her an answering smile.

"Make them believers, princess."

"Go be a genius, Master, but no one better try to hurt you."

He shook his head and left her side, going to the band, wondering how a woman half his size would think he needed looking after. It felt—good. Too good. He'd never been cared for, and it felt too close to that.

"She's really traumatized, Master," Czar said, his voice soft, his strange silvery eyes on Ambrielle.

Master resisted the urge to step between Czar and Ambrie. "Yeah. I know."

"She needs help."

"I'm well aware. If you're trying to say in a subtle way that she can't possibly really be in love with me, I'm very aware of that as well. I realize why you were so insistent my name be on the marriage license. Any of the others would believe they had a real shot with her." He kept his gaze fixed on Ambrielle.

"That's not at all what I meant," Czar denied.

The band started up again, the members, Rashad and Seychelle calling out for Master to hurry and join them. "She's extraordinary, Czar. I'll see her through this, and I'll let her go when it's over. You don't have to worry. I'll do the right thing."

Master turned his back on the president of his club, unable to look at him. Unable to face what he'd known all along—he wasn't what the others were. He never was. He'd been thrown into the prison by Sorbacov when he was a little boy, and he'd never really managed to get the filth off of him from that place. He'd been taken back to the basement, used, beaten and bloody, only to be returned the moment he was deemed healed enough. He'd learned tears didn't matter. Pleas didn't mean a thing. Promises meant nothing.

He picked up his guitar, laying the familiar wide strap around his neck, keeping his gaze on the strings while he tuned an already tuned instrument. Music poured into him, through him, found its way inside until it ran like wildfire through his bloodstream and gave him back life the moment thoughts of prison had taken all humanity away.

The darkness faded to the background in him, leaving him able to hear the notes needed to drive the music under the catchy lyrics Seychelle and Rashad sang in harmony. The band was close to the right melody, a pop beat that would bring most people to their feet, or at least make them want to sing along. Still he turned inward, melded with the music flowing in him, spreading through his heart to his arteries and veins, carried to his tissues throughout his body until he was the music.

The perfect notes found their way to the strings of his guitar, flowing like gold from the symphony in his bloodstream to his fingers. He played the way he always did, the music streaming from him to his fingers to the guitar. His band followed the way it always did, catching the notes, enhancing them, so they sprang to life and soared. Seychelle and Rashad did the rest. Within minutes the entire room was singing the chorus to Jackson's song:

They need a red-hot hero

Not a poser or a zero

Deputy desire

You know I'm your live wire

Of fun . . .

Red Hot Jackson

The moment "Red Hot Jackson" was sung, it was loud and emphasized, just the way Savage had hoped. Seychelle and Rashad sang the verses, and Torpedo Ink and their spouses took up the chorus with enormous enthusiasm. Savage led them with his extraordinary voice, encouraging them all to be boisterous and ecstatic, as if partying. They wanted the song to be distinct, to be remembered once heard.

Master finally managed to look at Ambrielle. She had dutifully joined Amanda, Marcus and Adam. Clearly, she'd been talking with them until the music had really taken off and then they'd been singing—the others, not her. She watched him intently with those eyes of hers, eyes only for him. The moment their gaze met, she smiled, and that smile was for him alone.

His fuckin' treacherous heart lurched. He could tell himself to be cautious and not let his emotions go any further, not let her wind any tighter around his insides, but she'd already pierced his skin and sent her little demonic arrows deep. There was a special hell for men like him. He thought he might have a chance after watching Savage find Seychelle. Savage was a dangerous man. A bad man, some might even say. Savage was the club enforcer. He killed for the club. Took men apart for information for the club. Like all of them, Savage ruthlessly hunted pedophiles and took back children anytime he found them.

But Master knew the reasons he was never climbing out of the muck he was buried in. He didn't feel remorse for the things he did. When he became that man without feelings, that stone-cold killer in prison, capable of taking apart human beings, he didn't feel a damn thing and he didn't look back. He never would. That child they raped over and over so brutally, the one they kicked and forced to perform vile acts for their pleasure and amusement, had learned their lessons and become the master.

He knew every con in prison. The smallest scam. The largest corruptions. He knew how to get in and out of cells without detection and how to kill without anyone's knowledge. Most of all, he knew how to protect what was left of his humanity with that ice-cold man who never felt remorse. That man deserved the hell he was living in now.

Master allowed his gaze to drift over his princess, with her hourglass figure and wild, untamed hair. Her hair fell in a dark waterfall of waves around her face and down her back, reminding him of the way it looked spilling across his pillows or over his arms when he fucked her. She was worth it—worth every single second of the agony he would be facing after she was gone—because he had her now, that intensity of her single-minded devotion. He'd never thought he'd ever have such a thing in his lifetime.

Ambrielle's devotion to him might not be real, but she certainly believed it was real, and for as many days or weeks as he had with her, he was going to live every moment as best he could. She was his. She always would be, long after she was gone and living her life with someone far more deserving than he was—if he didn't kill the man. *Bog*, he hoped he was a better man than that. He hoped he could hold to a code of honor and give her everything she deserved.

Ambrielle sang the chorus with the others, but her gaze

stayed on him, shifting only to check the entrances to the room, ensuring no one was coming to do him harm. His little warrior. She didn't know she was supposed to be a princess, and he doubted if she ever would view herself that way. That made him smile despite his dark thoughts. *Bog.* That was her gift. She could make him smile no matter the circumstances. Hell or heaven, she could do that, make him smile.

Czar took the stage as the band put their instruments away. "We need to make it very clear that a man by the name of Walker Thompson is out to harm both Ambrielle and Master. We believe he's responsible for the deaths of Ambrie's parents, although we can't prove it. He's capable of using you or your loved ones to try to draw her out into the open and away from our protection. We can protect you if you stay in your home and work from there, or when you must leave, let us know, so we can provide security. If you're contacted, you need to let us know immediately. If you choose not to accept our protection, we ask that you break off all contact with Ambrielle and with us."

Amanda looked down at her hands. "Adam, I was contacted by these people already. They wanted me to set up Master to be murdered in exchange for them not killing you."

"Amanda." Adam wrapped his arm around his sister's shoulder. "You should have told me right away."

"I know. I just was so scared I'd lose you." Tears began to run down her face all over again.

"Is that why Ambrielle was so angry with you?" Marcus guessed.

Amanda nodded. "She had every right to be."

Adam sighed and rubbed his knuckles on top of his sister's head, although he did it gently, a reminder of their childhood. "You should have told me."

"I know. I should have told her. Instead, I played right into their hands like an idiot."

Master jerked his chin toward Amanda. The last thing

they wanted was for her to talk too much and have Marcus curious about what might have taken place while Master and some of the others were missing.

"Everything is fine," Ambrie cut in, tone upbeat. "You all need to hear what Czar has to say. He's the president of Torpedo Ink and really can help you if that horrible man tries to intimidate you."

"Rashad, this is going to be particularly difficult for you with your schedule," Czar continued.

Rashad shook his head. "I have a friendship with Adam because he lives in my building, but that's all. If Thompson attempted to blackmail me into anything, I could shut him down easily."

"Adam?" Czar asked.

Adam nodded. "I'd contact you," Adam said. "Most likely they'd threaten Amanda, not Rashad, but if they threatened Rashad, I'd tell them I'd call the police and his security company."

"Good. We have your building under surveillance. If Walker attempts to send his people to your apartments, stay inside; someone will be there. Most likely, it won't be one of us, because we're too far away, but we have friends who will get to you. They'll use *Torpedo Ink* as a code, so you know it's safe to let them in. I doubt that will happen, but just in case. This should be over soon. Walker is on the run, but if he is the one who murdered Ambrielle's parents, the police will know soon enough."

Master always admired the way Czar could sound so completely reasonable in every situation. There was truth in what he said. The Moores' murders were being investigated, and it was entirely possible that sooner or later Walker Thompson might come under suspicion. More likely, the family lawyer would. Already, he was named as a person of interest and his whereabouts were sought.

"My people will help, Czar," Marcus volunteered.

Amanda's gaze jumped to Marcus' face. "You have 'people'?"

Marcus wrapped his arm around her shoulders. "Yes, Amanda, I have people. They'll help protect you until this is over. Czar's right. You'll need to keep working from home—or you can stay at my place. I have excellent security, and you can have your own suite. I can have you set up in a couple of hours. No one can get to you there. Your brother is welcome as well."

"I'm fine where I am," Adam said. "Thanks, Marcus. Amanda, I was going to suggest that you come stay at my place, so we'd be together, but Marcus probably has better security."

"You work it out on the way home," Czar said, "and let us know."

Marcus rose, helping Amanda up. "We'll do that, Czar. Thank you for an entertaining evening."

Adam and Rashad said their good-byes, and Ambrielle allowed them all to hug her. Master came in close, as she seemed uncomfortable with them touching her. He knew what that was like—until Ambrielle, he hadn't liked anyone putting their hands on him.

After they were gone, Torpedo Ink once more gathered around the larger table. This time, Alena came in from the kitchen, and Lana joined them.

Czar immediately got down to business. "The biggest thing we learned tonight, thanks to Ambrielle very skill-fully questioning her friends about the Russian woman, was that the piece of snake jewelry is some kind of symbol and is meaningful to her. The men she uses as her personal as-sassins might be part of the Ghosts' business assassins, but they have a distinctive tattoo on their index finger. At least we hope all of them do. Ice." Czar turned to their jeweler. "You're good at identifying custom pieces."

Ice nodded slowly. "There was a young Russian jeweler who had designed similar pieces. He hadn't broken out yet, but I saw his work online at an event only a few of us were privy to go to. Our work wasn't for sale; we were discussing where to get Russian gems for the best quality and prices or trading what we had with each other. At the time, he mentioned he was working on a commissioned piece for a woman he was very much in love with. He wanted to match the eyes of the snake with her eyes."

"Did he happen to mention the name of his lover?" Master asked.

Ice nodded again. "Said her name was DeeDee. DeeDee Devin. He was killed in an accident not long after that."

Alena tapped out a beat on the tabletop, drawing everyone's attention. She frowned, but no one interrupted her as she obviously tried to remember something from long ago. "Absinthe, Demyan mentioned the name DeeDee once. Do you recall that? I think he did. In passing. He'd given his report to Czar and came back to talk to us. I was . . . upset and he rocked me and just started talking. He said that name. I swear he did, but I don't remember the context."

Absinthe threaded his fingers through his wife Scarlet's hand and pulled it to his chest, heart high. "I have a difficult time recalling anything of those days when Demyan is involved," he admitted, pain in his voice. "I'll give it some thought, and if I recall anything, I'll let everyone know."

"It's important, Absinthe," Czar said. "This woman is targeting Blythe and the children. We have to figure out who she is in order to track her down."

"I understand," Absinthe said. "I really can't recall."

"Was anyone else there, Alena?" Czar asked.

Master understood, but it was difficult to see Czar without his usual calm demeanor. It was so unlike him to be pushing the Torpedo Ink members when they clearly stated they couldn't remember something or they were having issues. Czar was always respectful of them. Master knew when it came down to it, any threat to Ambrielle was going to be dealt with hard and fast. He didn't blame Czar in the least; in fact, he admired the man's restraint.

"I honestly can't remember, Czar, I'm sorry," she said.

Blythe stood before Czar or anyone else could respond. "Thanks, everyone. We appreciate what you did for us tonight. We don't know what we'd do without you."

She smiled at them, a genuine, loving Blythe smile that radiated warmth. Master remembered the first time he saw her smile at the three little girls she'd taken in when they'd been so fucked-up, terrified and definitely afraid to trust anyone. Blythe was genuine. Everything she said and did was so real, so kind, caring and loving, it was impossible not to feel it, even when you didn't want to. In the beginning, Torpedo Ink had been like those three girls, terrified to believe in her. Blythe had been the one to give them hope.

Czar stood as well, wrapping his arm around his wife, his love for her stamped into every line on his face. "Stay safe, everyone. Remember, we're not the only targets. Master, keep Ambrielle under close watch. Clearly, Thompson isn't going to stop."

"She's good."

"Ink, you and Master get this thing with your boy Reese taken care of fast," Czar continued. "We have too many irons in the fire as it is."

"Tomorrow," Ink promised.

"Any of the brothers you need," Czar added.

"Volunteers only," Ink responded. "We don't know what we're facing."

"Could use some action," Absinthe said.

"Me too," Scarlet agreed.

Absinthe laughed. "Every now and then I worry what would happen if we didn't have these little side battles to allow you to let off steam, woman."

"I suppose we shouldn't find out," Scarlet said with an exaggerated mock sigh.

The tension in the room was gone just like that, dispelled by the Torpedo Ink women. Blythe and Scarlet hadn't been down in the basement with them, torn into pieces. They hadn't been woven into one fucked-up mess in order to survive, but they were part of their soul now. Master wanted

Ambrielle to be in that revered few. For him, she would be. The others wouldn't accept her. Like him, she would always be held apart, just a little space between her and them because they understood she'd fucked up, and when she got right, she would take one look at the mess she married and she'd run as fast as she could.

"You're doing it again," Ambrielle whispered as he wrapped her in her jacket.

"What am I doing?" He zipped the jacket up, ignoring the frog in his throat.

She reached up to frame his face with her hands. Whenever she did that, his heart clenched hard in his chest and his cock went to full alert. He couldn't help looking into her eyes, which was always a mistake. They'd gone violet on him, soft and loving, melting that stone in him that was his only protection against the devastation she was going to wreak when she left.

"Looking so sad you make me want to cry."

"It's a trick of the light, Ambrielle."

"You promised we wouldn't lie to one another," she whispered, her eyes searching his, seeing too much.

"Get in the truck. Let's just go home. I want to be alone with you." He didn't bother to try to keep the weariness out of his voice.

She slipped her hand into his and turned toward the door, waving toward Seychelle as they went to the parking lot, Ink and Keys walking on either side of them. Ink opened the passenger-side door for Ambrie and closed it after her.

"I'll catch a ride home with Keys. Meet you in a few days at the Stoddard home after I get the intel from Code."

"Sounds good to me," Master agreed. "Be safe." He was grateful he wasn't on dead-body detail. There were a lot of them to get rid of.

The ride home was quiet. Ambrielle tipped her head back against the seat, content to listen to the music filling the cab. She seemed to accept that he needed the silence after being around so many people. She didn't make him feel guilty that he wasn't entertaining her or answering a thousand questions. She just listened to the music and tapped out a rhythm on her thigh. Master appreciated her even more for giving him space.

He liked to take different roads to his home. His property, a one-hundred-acre parcel, was surrounded by thousands of acres of protected private ground and state forest land. His property was completely surrounded with ten-foot-high fencing, mainly to keep humans out, not animals. He asked that those he rented the cabins to patrol the fence and maintain it—which they did.

He took a longer way in, a dirt road leading through a mixture of tall redwoods, evergreens and hardwoods. There were a few switchbacks, but there was beauty unrivaled on this particular drive. Two gorgeous waterfalls, one high and rolling over a series of rocks to fall into a large stream below, and the other, much smaller but no less beautiful, ran over boulders and fell along a short bluff before spilling into a narrower part of the same stream. Ferns lined the silvery water, and great redwoods rose up in groves as sentries. Ambrie sat up straighter and stared out the window, at one point even rolling it down as they drove slowly past.

They came up to the back side of his house, passed the sprawling, cavernous shop and garage with three bays, the shed filled with wood and the pump house. He drove straight to the back entrance and parked. The back deck was wide and covered. The hot tub was there and behind it the nearly floor-to-ceiling windows that gave him the illusion of being outdoors, so he was able to stand being inside.

The large bathtub sitting on the gray tiles jutting out into his bedroom could be seen through the thick glass. Behind the glass door panels making up one side of the room facing the deck was the master bedroom. He could be in his bed and look out at the forest and know he could escape through any of those three doors in a matter of seconds.

"You go ahead, Master," Ambrielle said. "The clouds have blown over, and for once the stars have come out. I think I'll sit out here for a little while in the hot tub and just stare at them." She didn't wait for permission. She wasn't the kind of woman who thought she needed permission from a man. She unzipped and shrugged out of her coat and went to the hot tub to unbuckle the straps securing the top.

"Unless you need alone time, Ambrielle, I'll join you," he decided. "Tell me if you prefer some time alone. I'll understand."

She tilted her head up and smiled at him, instant joy brightening her features. "You know I always prefer to be with you. I'll go in and grab us a couple of towels. I'll put up my hair." She caught up her coat and took his when he handed it to her.

Master stripped off his shirt and then opened the hot tub. He'd gotten a nice one. He needed the heat on his body. There were times when his muscles knotted up, complaining no matter what he did. He stayed active and kept fit to counteract the damage done to his body, but oftentimes he hurt like hell. He stripped off his motorcycle boots and peeled off his jeans. Steam rose from the hot tub into the night air.

Master climbed in and sank down into the extremely hot water. A sigh of pure pleasure escaped. He should have gotten himself a drink before he indulged though.

As if hearing his thoughts, Ambrielle opened the middle glass door to the bedroom. "Would you like me to make you a drink?"

It never occurred to him to ask her. Others didn't do for him. "Depends on whether or not you're any good at it." He couldn't help teasing her.

She tossed her head, making the topknot go a little wild. One hand went to her hip. "I *rock* at bartending. Usually, I'm not so bad at stealing knives off people too, but that Destroyer might have more than two eyes. What do you want me to make you?"

"Yorsh," he replied soberly.

Her eyes went dark and that little chin of hers went up as if she'd challenged him. She wore a little robe and nothing else. He could see her nipples hard and tight in the cold. Those breasts and her tucked-in waist with the flared hips were enough to entice him, but once you added that chin, he was a goner.

"Coming right up," she said and turned and went back inside.

Just like that, she'd turned his dark mood around. It felt good not to be alone. It felt especially good to have someone want to do things for him, like get him a drink. It took her a little longer than he thought it would, and when she returned, she had two drinks with her. She had them in cocktail glasses rather than in beer mugs, which made him smile. *Bog*, but she was perfect. There was a little cucumber garnish on the edge of the glass. She handed him one of the cocktail glasses, looking more anxious than nonchalant.

"I'm not sure how it turned out. The lager you have, I hope is what you really prefer in this drink. I tried it and it tastes okay." She made a little face.

He didn't give a damn how it tasted. She made it for him; he'd drink it. If it wasn't right, he'd show her how to make it later. "Get in here, princess." His voice had gone husky, almost a growl.

"I want you to drink that one, Master. If it isn't good, I'll go make another one."

"I want you to get in here with me. On my lap. Stand over my cock." Deliberately, he circled the growing monster with his fist.

She moistened her lips, leaving them gleaming, already shedding the robe. He loved her body. Loved looking at it. All those feminine curves. His. He wanted his marks on her. She climbed over the edge of the hot tub, gasped as the heat engulfed her, but she came right to him and threw one leg over him, as if he were a motorcycle. As if she were already Torpedo Ink.

"Stand right there, baby," he ordered softly and picked up

the cocktail glass. Her tits were jutting straight at his mouth, right where he wanted them. *Bog*, she was beautiful, and he didn't deserve her, not even for these fantasy moments.

He drank the Yorsh, shocked that she'd been able to get the mixture of lager and vodka right. He drank the second one, got rid of the glass, caught her by the waist and pulled her forward so he could indulge himself, his mouth around her left breast while his fingers found her right one, kneading and massaging. She was sensitive, crying out and catching his hair in one fist, holding him to her.

When he lifted his head, his gaze burned over her. "On my cock now, princess. I want you to ride me slow. Put your hands on my thighs behind you." He could barely get the command out.

Because she was his fairy princess and he was living his fantasy, she did exactly what he said. Water sloshed over the top of the hot tub. He worshipped her tits. Kissed her over and over until the fire grew so hot between them it was explosive. All the while she rode him with a slow, exquisite silken friction that threatened to make him lose all control. His fingers bit into her hips and he began to guide her faster. She resisted, keeping that slow, steady pace designed to drive him out of his mind.

As always, if he initiated a slow burn, doing his best to show her he worshipped her, in the end the ride was rough and wild. He held her for a long time with the bubbles bursting over their skin after she'd collapsed against him. He just breathed her in before regaining his strength enough to carry her inside to the bed.

~

Lying in bed with a woman curled up like a sleepy little kitten was the last thing Master ever thought would be exactly what would make him relax and feel he had a home. He stared out the glass walls that led to the forest and thought about how different his life was, how it had changed in a single moment of time. A breath. A heartbeat. All because of this one woman. Few things shocked him, but Ambrielle did. He knew he had to protect her—even from herself.

"I'm going with Ink in a few days to pay a visit to Leonard Stoddard, Reese's parole officer, to ask him what's going on. A few of the brothers will come along as insurance that things go the way we want them to go." He introduced the subject casually.

Ambrie's head went up alertly, her eyes darkening as they moved over his face. "I'm going with you." That was decisive. "I can stay in the background, but I have to learn."

"You don't have to learn anything. When we catch up with Thompson, and we will, I'll call you in at the last minute and you can finish him off if that's what you still want to do. The rest of it, Ambrielle, it isn't easy to live with. You don't have to spend the rest of your life with that kind of shit fucking up your brain."

"You do." She reached out to him, very gently rubbed along his shadowed jaw.

When she made gestures like that, as small as they were, they turned him inside out. He caught her hand with his and kissed her open palm. "That's how I know I don't want any part of this life for you." He didn't break eye contact, wanting her to know he meant it.

She pressed her palm against his lips as if to silence him. "It's because you have to live with the kinds of things you've had to that make up who you are. I need to know and understand them, Kir."

She sounded so reasonable, when he knew what she was asking wasn't reasonable. He pulled her hand down to his chin. "I want you to open your eyes just a little bit and see the real me, not the one you're making up in your mind. See reality. I'm dirty. Not clean. You persist in looking at me as if I'm some kind of hero, Ambrielle. If you don't open your eyes, sooner or later, when you do wake up, you're going to be so shocked at what you see, you'll run."

Ambrielle responded to his utter despair with a small

shake of her head. "My father used to tell me to wake up from my dreamworld and see reality. He wanted me to see that the real world was dirty and gritty, not clean and black-and-white. I think I woke up when those men killed my parents right in front of me. Everything he'd told me over the years was suddenly right there in front of me. All the times he drilled it into me that I needed to pay closer attention to my surroundings, that the world wasn't a nice place."

Master wrapped his arms around her and rolled over, so she was sprawled over the top of him. In this position, he didn't have to meet that steady gaze, the one that was beginning to look at him with an emotion he was becoming addicted to. "No, princess, the world isn't always a nice place, but you don't have to live down in the dirt. I can keep you safe." He nuzzled the top of her head with his chin.

"Master, I had the perfect example of parents who loved one another and made it work, even though they had very different personalities and sometimes even views. They knew one another, inside and out. That was how they had complete confidence in each other. My mother told me I would know the right man when he came along. I waited. I knew you'd come. You came. I want to know everything about you. If that means getting into the dirt with you, then I will."

Master closed his eyes, his heart sinking. His princess. So determined, but she didn't know what the hell she was talking about. "This throat thing." Was he really going to discuss this with her? Tell her one of the most painful things he'd gone through?

Her hand moved up to his throat, her fingers stroking caresses gently, until his eyes burned, until his soul wept. *Bog*, she was killing him slowly. Piece by piece.

"Steele wanted me to go to this specialist the minute he told me he saw the nodes and polyps growing on my vocal cords. We both were afraid it was cancer. I don't smoke and don't abuse alcohol, but I spent a lifetime as a child in prison with pedophiles. HPV, the human papillomavirus, is a sexually transmitted disease, and it's definitely on the rise for oral transmission. I knew, because I had all the symptoms and I read that shit online. I was terrified to go to a specialist and discover, after all that time I'd finally escaped and thought I was free, that those men had left behind something slowly eating me alive."

He fell silent, willing her to understand what he was saying. Giving her the picture without having to describe his childhood and the multiple assailants, week after week, month after month. Year after year. She didn't stop stroking his throat. She did turn her face to his chest and press a kiss over his wildly beating heart, nearly stopping it.

"I was lucky. I don't know how. According to the doc, I don't have HPV. The nodes are caused by the stress of going to prison." He caught her messy topknot in his fist. "You have no idea how much I detest the word *stress*. What the hell does it even mean?"

"It means you can never go back to prison," she replied firmly. "We're going to have to discuss that soon as well. The prison thing, I mean. Right now, I want to know about your throat. Are you going back to your doctor?"

He hesitated. Sighed. "I suppose. Steele made me a fuckin' appointment. The day after tomorrow I'm supposed to go. I thought you could go to the tea shop with Seychelle and a couple of the others and wait for me there. If you don't want to, I can cancel the appointment and reschedule for a better time when you feel as if you can manage without me."

Ambrielle's fingers found his jaw and traced along the outer edge. "Does the doctor do a biopsy every time?"

"Yes, but if I had cancer, it wouldn't be from HPV, Ambrielle—you don't have to worry about that."

"I'm not worried. In any case, I'm vaccinated. Hopefully, that would protect me if I was exposed. I'm worried that you could be in trouble. I can manage for an hour or so, especially if Seychelle is there. I want you to take care of this."

"It's settled, then." He went quiet for a moment, trying to

think how best to get his way. "What do you think of counselors?"

Ambrie started to lift her head to look up at him, but his hand fixed in her hair held her in place. She settled against his chest, ear to his heart. He felt her breath on his skin. Waited.

"I believe in counselors." There was a wary note in her voice. They had promised each other honesty, and she was doing her best but feared a trap. "I think everyone needs a good counselor to help sort things out now and then."

He sighed. "I was afraid you'd say that."

"Why?" Puzzlement.

His little princess. He could feel her body gathering energy as if it could protect him from whatever was worrying him. He would take that caring. Live in that moment. Let himself feel the intensity of her emotions for him. To a man drowning for care, having it shown to him was fucking everything. He savored every moment with her, just let himself imprint these moments onto his soul. He was far past trying to hold back his heart. It was long gone.

"Absinthe wants me to go to a counselor. Says I need to. Blythe has this one she knows, but I'm not going to go spill my guts and shock some little woman with gray hair by telling her my life story. Just the thought of going and hearing words like *stress* and *trauma* makes me feel like a fuckin' pussy. Not to mention, after I got through confessing how many people I've killed over the years, being an assassin for the government, I think I'd go right back to prison."

Ambrie laughed softly. "Silly man. You're not supposed to confess you've killed anyone, unless Torpedo Ink has their own counselor, which, in my opinion, they need. But if they really do have one they trust, Master, it would be a good thing. It doesn't make you a, well, you know, what you said, if you go."

He tugged at her topknot. "Do you plan on going to a counselor? You have to be stressed. Traumatized. You're intelligent. You know you are." He closed his eyes and waited. Let his hand settle so his fingers stroked her scalp, soothing him more than her.

"I'm definitely traumatized. I'm checking my behavior all the time," Ambrielle admitted. "I'm not normally a clingy person, but I'm afraid to let you out of my sight. I know that isn't natural behavior for me."

"Neither is seeing several men killed and going back into a dining room and facing your friends as if nothing happened. Coming home, fucking like rabbits and not even talking about all those dead bodies. That's not normal either for you, Ambrielle. That was never your world." He kept his tone even, quiet. He didn't want to have the conversation, but she was his to do his best for. His best meant healing her, even if that meant ultimately having to give her up.

She rubbed her cheek on his chest. "I take time to process things. All I cared about was keeping you safe. Once I found out Amanda had led those men to the restaurant with the express purpose of killing you . . ."

"And kidnapping you," he interrupted.

"I sort of overlooked that part. I can't lose you, Master. That's the traumatized part of me talking. I know that. Not the one that's numb to what you and the rest of Torpedo Ink did so efficiently for survival. That part I understand, probably because my parents raised me to realize you do whatever it takes when you're threatened. I knew those men were there to kill you. I expected you to fight back, and you did. I was impressed with how fast and competent you all were, but knowing you were trained from the time you were so young, I'm not surprised."

"Let's go back to the traumatized part talking. What do you mean?"

"I was almost hysterical when I was looking for you. Very single-minded. I would have fought Destroyer. I would have done anything to get to you. Right now, you're my entire world. I feel as if I don't have anyone else. You're my center. My anchor. I'm lost without you. I know that isn't healthy for either one of us. I'm trying to find a balance so I'm not so dependent on you, but I can't seem to do that yet. You've been extremely kind to me, letting me lean so heavily on you when I know that's not normal for you either."

She was right. It wasn't. He hadn't thought too much about that and why he didn't mind his princess clinging to him when if it was any other woman, he would have shrugged them off without a thought.

"Maybe we both need a fucking counselor, princess." He poured humor into his voice.

"We do, Master. I'll go with you and make sure you don't say anything that lands you in prison. And you go with me and make sure I don't say anything that puts me there either."

"Why in the world would you think you would be going to prison, Ambrielle?"

She brushed a kiss onto his chest. "Because I'm not letting you kill Walker Thompson for me. You aren't doing that. You can find him. I need you to find him because I don't have those resources and you do, but you're done with killing. Nothing is going to send you back to prison. I'll kill Thompson because he deserves to die. Not you, Kir. You're mine to protect, and I'm going to do it."

Holy shit. His heart exploded in his chest. That was the last thing he expected. What did a man do with that? She wasn't killing Thompson, but he wasn't arguing with his woman. His cock was suddenly as hungry for her as his heart.

THIRTEEN

Ambrielle paused to look at the wooden sign carved in the shape of a hat hung outside a charming shop declaring its name was the Floating Hat. The tea, bath and lotion boutique was situated between a clever little wine shop and a very popular gift shop. From the outside, the combination tea and lotion shop looked on the small side, with bay windows jutting out on either side of a heavy, ornately carved wooden door. But peering through the windows, Ambrielle could tell the sense of smallness was only an illusion.

One display held an assortment of teas and stacked caddies of delicious-looking scones and cakes along with other baked goods. Another display was of lotions and bath products, all organic and beautifully packaged.

Ambrie slipped her hand into the crook of Master's elbow. "Isn't it sort of odd to have a tea shop where you actually serve tea and scones, but you sell bath products as well?"

She found the store intriguing. The more she stood looking into the windows, the more she felt a pull to go into the shop. In fact, a sense of peace descended on her when she stayed close to the windows, where before, just the thought of being separated from Master, even for a couple of hours, had her feeling secretly agitated. She tried hard to hide her nervousness from him. It was silly to be so clingy, but she couldn't get over the feeling that she needed to be with him all the time or he'd be taken from her. She knew she couldn't bear to lose him. She wouldn't survive intact.

"There is nothing usual about Hannah Drake Harrington's Floating Hat tea shop," Master said. "And there's nothing usual about her. She's married to the local sheriff, Jonas. You met him. Hannah was a model at one time and some nutcase attacked her, slashed her up with a knife, nearly killed her. No one really knows how she managed to survive, but Jonas never left her side. I don't think he does much leaving her side as it is now."

He gave her one of his slow, genuine smiles that reached his eyes and warmed them. When that happened, Ambrie melted inside. Master didn't smile often. Even if he did, it wasn't ever real. Not like this. Not looking straight at her and letting her know she was his everything. She liked when he shared little things with her, little pieces of information on people and places he knew in the community.

"You like the sheriff."

"We won't say that. We definitely won't say I like his deputy."

"Jackson. The hot deputy we sang about."

"*Never* admit we did that."

She burst out laughing. "You don't think he's going to recognize Seychelle's very distinctive voice? Or the band? Or Rashad? Seriously? Most of Torpedo Ink sang the chorus. And they did it loudly and with great enthusiasm. I think Jackson, the hot deputy, is going to know."

"He'll know, but we never admit to anything," Master counseled. "As for the tea shop, this is going to be your favorite refuge. According to all the women, Player, Preacher and Savage, it's the only place to come for anything you need."

"Player, Preacher and Savage come here too?"

"Yep. Often. Player claims that's how he got out of trouble with his lady. He came here for advice and got the right gifts for his woman."

"And Preacher?"

"He's our chemist. He has a gift and recognized that Hannah has a very powerful gift. Apparently, he drives Jonas crazy by coming around looking for lessons in the craft."

"Why the name Floating Hat?" Ambrielle indicated the chain of bells hanging on the door in the shape of little hats.

"There's talk that Jonas likes to wear hats, which I do know is true. When his woman gets annoyed with him, his hat seems to get blown off his head in a wind and taken down the road just out of reach or out toward the bluffs."

Ambrielle pressed her lips together to keep from laughing at the idea of it. "Handy trick to have. I wonder what she could teach me."

He wrapped his arm around her neck and pulled her close to kiss the top of her head. She loved when he did that. She felt as if she belonged with him, not to mention her body immediately reacted in a good way, making her very aware she was alive.

"You don't need any more tricks. You've got me wrapped around your little finger as it is. The brothers are going to start giving me a bad time if it gets any worse." Master nuzzled the top of her head with his chin so that strands of her hair got caught in the stubble on his jaw. "Let's go in."

The compulsion to go inside had continued to grow stronger as they stood in front of the shop. The owner sounded so intriguing and cool. Ambrie wanted to meet her, and she was really looking forward to seeing Seychelle again. It was just that, once inside, Master would leave her and she wasn't certain she could breathe without him. She tightened her grip on his arm, an automatic reaction she couldn't stop.

"Princess, I really don't mind canceling or postponing the appointment. It's bullshit anyway. I've had so many of these. They're just going to biopsy the polyps and tell me they're benign. Most likely I'll have to have them removed. It's a thing, that's all. Nothing to worry about."

His voice was a hoarse rasp. Sexy, yes, but not good when she knew why it was that way. Still, he was the same. Ready to push his health problems aside in order to reassure her.

Ambrielle leaned into the tower of his strength. He was solid. All muscle. But it really wasn't about the way he was built. She was coming to understand that. It wasn't even about that stone-cold killer she'd first recognized in the chapel when she'd chosen to marry him. It was the real strength in him—that quiet dependability she could always count on no matter what was happening around them. No matter what chaos ensued. He was the calm in the middle of a storm.

His throat was something to worry about. The doctor wouldn't take biopsies if cancer wasn't a concern. She reached up and stroked his throat with the pads of her fingers, wishing she could cure him with a touch. With the intensity of her feelings for him.

"You go to your appointment. I'll be just fine. I've really wanted to get to know some of the ladies, so this is a good opportunity for me." That was the last thing she wanted. Well. She did like Seychelle. Blythe seemed really nice. Soleil had been quiet, but she was married to Ice and probably had interesting stories. Ice seemed quite a character. She had no idea who was going to meet her for tea because she hadn't really been paying attention.

"You have to stop shaking so I know you mean it, princess," Master said, smiling down at her. Even his eyes smiled. Maybe not smiled. But they were bright.

She tilted her chin at him. "I'm not shaking." She was, but she couldn't stop.

He reached over her head and pushed open the door to

the shop. The little hats swung wildly, setting off the bells
so they played welcoming notes, announcing their arrival to
the shop owner. Just the sound of the bells lightened her
mood as Ambrie stepped into the tearoom with Master. The
moment she inhaled the wonderful elusive scent that filled
the interior, she felt as if she'd entered a magical realm.

On one side of the shop, tables and chairs were set up.
There was a large table that could seat six to eight people,
but most tables were for four. Some were for two. The mauve
chair seats were round and cushioned, and the curved backs
were white striped. There were some booths but mostly tables, and those were set far enough apart that it added to the
illusion of space. The building went far back from the street
and utilized every inch of space for customers.

The other side of the shop was taken up with the most
amazing-looking lotions, ointments and displays of various
oils and salts. Ambrielle immediately wanted to spend time
exploring the riches she was certain were there.

A tall blond woman, extraordinarily beautiful, came toward them, a welcoming smile on her face that managed to
turn her blue eyes into sparkling gems. "I'm Hannah," she
said simply. "You must be Ambrie. Master called ahead and
said he was bringing you. It's so lovely to meet you, although I wish it were under better circumstances. I'm so
sorry for your losses."

She extended her hand, and the moment Ambrielle took
it, she felt a surge of power unlike anything she'd ever experienced. The energy, completely feminine, seemed to rush
over her in a wave. It felt as if Hannah Drake Harrington saw
inside of her, into the very mess that even Ambrie couldn't
sort through, where that little girl was still screaming and
screaming as she watched her parents die in front of her.

Hannah laid her other hand on top of Ambrielle's for the
briefest of moments and when she did, Ambrie felt some of
that terrible turmoil quiet. "Thank you," she murmured, unable to think of anything else coherent to say.

Hannah turned to Master, her blue eyes now filled with

concern. For the first time, Ambrie realized there were others in the shop. A very small woman was at the counter. Jonas Harrington was standing just a few feet away from them with his deputy, Jackson. Two women were across the shop, looking into a basket of soaps.

"Master, you should have come in when your throat first started acting up. I would have made you something to help right away."

He hadn't even spoken. How did she know? Ambrielle turned her full attention back to Hannah. And Master came to the shop? He knew Hannah? She couldn't imagine him coming to the shop.

He shrugged carelessly. "Didn't have time to talk to Preacher about it yet, ma'am."

Ambrie's heart clenched. His voice sounded worse. Had it been that raspy all along? Had she ignored it because she didn't want him away from her? Was she really that selfish?

Hannah's large eyes moved over the Torpedo Ink member, not in the least intimidated by his direct, expressionless stare, which was all but telling her not to talk about his throat condition in front of his new wife, the sheriff and his deputy.

"You can't let that go this long. It's dangerous. I'm going to fix you something right now that will soothe it. Anat and the others have been going on and on about you singing in their big upcoming church event, but you can't. You know you can't. You have to tell her, Master. You'll ruin your vocal cords."

"I'll let her know. I'm looking into finding someone for her," Master said. He used the same bored tone. Gave her the same look. He *really* didn't want to talk about his throat.

Hannah nodded. "Let me just fix you that throat soother while you and Ambrielle look around the shop. I won't be long."

"I have an appointment today. Can't eat or drink anything." Master sounded very abrupt, almost aggressive.

Out of the corner of her eye, Ambrie saw Jonas take a step closer, although the deputy put a light restraining hand on his arm.

"Right, of course." Hannah completely ignored the warning in Master's voice. "They're going to do a scope and biopsies. That's good to know. I'll make sure this will feel good on your throat after. They won't allow anything like Advil. Any blood thinners." She sounded thoughtful, as if the two of them weren't standing in front of her; she had already turned inward and was searching for something elusive. A little frown flitted across her face. "Would you mind if I put my hand on your throat for a moment?"

Ambrielle felt Master's entire body tense, although outwardly, he didn't change his demeanor at all. She leaned into him, her body tucked close into his side, one arm wrapped around his waist.

"What does that do, when you put your hand on his throat?" she asked casually to take the spotlight from Master.

Hannah blinked several times as if she'd forgotten anyone else was in the room with them. "I feel energy is the only way I can describe it. It would help me find the right ingredients to help heal his throat."

Ambrie tilted her face up toward Master's. She smiled, an intimate, just-between-the-two-of-them smile, conveying she needed him to be on the same page with her. Her fingers curled into his vest. "Sounds good to me. Anything to heal your throat, right, babe?"

She wanted him to comply. She could feel power flowing around the woman. Surely Master had to feel it as well. If he didn't stop the growth of those polyps, sooner or later, he wouldn't be so lucky and one or more wouldn't be benign.

Master looked down at her for what seemed an eternity, then he turned his gaze on Hannah. "Sure. Do your worst."

As Hannah reached toward Master, Jonas took another protective step toward his wife. Ambrie made a note of it, but her attention centered on the woman as she moved close to them. Heat surrounded them, but it was more than heat. The energy Hannah projected was so strong, the hair on Ambrielle's arms and the back of her neck stood up. Electrical charges snapped over her skin, not hurting but energizing her.

Hannah laid her palm very gently on Master's throat. She had closed her eyes, turning inward, but suddenly, her eyes flew open, going wide in shock, a gasp escaping. She bit down hard on her lip and shook her head. Tears glistened in her eyes, and she dropped her hand to her side. She looked visibly shaken, so much so that Jonas moved right up to her and circled her waist with his arm.

"I'll make you something that will help you for after your appointment. You're coming back, right? To get Ambrie?" Hannah's voice was low and a little unsteady, as if she were trying not to cry.

"Thanks," Master replied, sounding gruff. He turned away from Hannah. "Princess, I've got to go or I'll be late."

"I'll be fine. I'll wait here for you." Ambrielle did her best not to cling to him when she wanted to. Fortunately, Seychelle and Savage had entered the shop and she knew she could go over to them and feel as if she had support. It wasn't about someone being with her, it was about someone trying to kill Master. "Is Ink going with you? Who will be with you?" She tried to keep the anxiety out of her voice, but knew she failed.

"Ice will be with me, Ambrielle. You have fun. I'm going to be fine." His kiss was very gentle, a mere brush of his lips against hers.

Jackson came up behind them. "I overheard you might need to find someone to sing at a church gig you've got going for the ladies, Master. Inez has been talking about the event for weeks now. She's really excited about it. I think I can get someone for you. I just have to make certain his schedule is clear. Give me a day or two to see if I can take that off your shoulders." He glanced at his watch and then looked over his shoulder at Jonas.

"I know," Jonas called out. "Hannah, I'm taking Jackson to get his truck this morning, but I'll be back. Are you going to be all right?"

"Of course." Hannah still sounded shaken.

Ambrielle wished she knew what had upset Hannah. She'd touched Master's throat. Had she been gifted with the power to "see" if he had cancer? Was that what she saw? Ambrielle was going to straight out ask her once Master left.

Jonas and Jackson walked out of the shop and the little bells in the shape of hats chimed merrily. Master looked at Savage and the two of them exchanged a grin. Ice and Storm just broke into laughter.

"I do feel a little guilty," Master admitted as Ambrie walked him to the door. "After he was nice enough to volunteer to find someone to sing at the church event."

"I thought the church was tiny."

"It is. But they're hosting a get-together for a large number of other churches. It's a potluck. The ladies like that sort of thing. That's why it's a big deal to make sure someone is there for them."

Master dropped another kiss on top of her head and sauntered out as if he didn't have a care in the world. Ice fell into step beside him. Ambrie blinked back tears as she watched him walk down the sidewalk.

"Please tell me you didn't see cancer in his throat," Ambrie whispered to Hannah. "He's been through so much already. I don't want that for him. I know you saw something."

"I didn't see cancer," Hannah answered, "but I don't see things like that. It isn't my strength. I'm sure he's going to be fine, especially now that he has you."

Ambrie pressed her lips together. Hannah wasn't a woman to lie. "Thank you for that. I hope I make his life good and him happy. That's what I want."

Hannah tipped her head to one side, her blue eyes going crystal blue. "I believe you can make him very happy, Ambrielle. Come with me. I know your friends are here, but I want to show you some things."

Ambrie followed her through the various beautifully appointed displays. There was so much to see that she wanted to slow down and look at everything. Incredible scents wafted up from various purple and blue woven baskets. Hannah reached a long counter with various items on it. She pulled an empty basket and began to fill it with lotions and oils.

"This oil is really good for massage. Rub it directly into the muscles when they're sore or knotted. It's edible, so no worries if you both suddenly get in the mood. This lotion is for his throat. Start with his neck and shoulders and massage it into his skin. When you move around to the front, use a gentle downward stroke like this . . ." Hannah took Ambrielle's arm and turned it over to expose her inner wrist. Very lightly, she used the pads of her fingers to demonstrate the proper way to carefully rub the lotion along Master's throat.

"It's important to do this every single day, Ambrie, if you want to make certain those polyps don't return, especially if he's under any kind of stress." Hannah continued to put items in the basket. "Most of these are going to be for you. He's the kind of man who will want to do for you, and if you're always giving him massages and he can't reciprocate, he isn't going to be happy. He'll like these different oils."

"Hannah, I see you've met Master's wife, Ambrielle. What are you fixing there for her?" Preacher came up behind them.

He had very thick curly dark hair and striking blue eyes. His white teeth flashed at them as he smiled, but that smile didn't quite reach his eyes. Like all the members of Torpedo Ink, he was muscular and looked as if he could handle himself in a fight.

Hannah didn't stop filling the basket with items. "Just a little wedding gift for the two of them. I'm going to fix a soother for Master's throat. Do you want to help me?"

"Absolutely. I thought I'd make it before Master and Ambrie arrived, but I had a little problem with my truck this morning." He glared at the woman behind the counter.

Ambrielle followed his stare to look at the woman. She appeared to be a little like a sprite with her wealth of black hair, small pixie face and large eyes that were just a little too big for her face.

She leaned on the counter with a wide smirk. "What's wrong, Preacher? You look . . . disgruntled."

"A man's truck is sacred, you little she-devil."

She raised an eyebrow. "I have no idea what you're going on about. I was here all morning. In fact, I arrived early and unpacked all the baskets." She smiled big at him. "You seem to be having all kinds of trouble lately, Preacher. Last night after work you couldn't get the door open to the back room."

"Sabelia, I swear," Preacher began, taking a step toward the counter.

"If you need a break, Preacher, I can help Hannah with that soother while you sit and have a cup of tea. In fact, I'll make the tea for you myself," Sabelia offered, her tone oozing sweetness.

"The only break I need is breaking your little neck," Preacher muttered under his breath.

"I take it she won the battle round," Hannah said, amusement tingeing her voice.

"*Two* out of three," Preacher conceded. "You're creating a monster, Hannah. You might want to think twice before you teach that little demon child anything else."

Sabelia's laughter was infectious. Ambrielle found herself smiling, and she didn't even know what kind of game had been played between Preacher and Sabelia. Whatever it was, it amused Hannah and took the shadows from her eyes.

"Don't be a sore loser, Preacher," Sabelia said. "You were the winner three weeks in a row."

"Yeah, but you didn't have toad crap and slime all over your truck."

"Only because I don't own a truck."

Seychelle and Savage came up behind Preacher. "Don't tell me that woman figured out how to get toads in your truck, Preacher," Savage said.

"She did," Preacher affirmed. "Filled the cab with them."

Ambrielle looked at Sabelia with an entirely new respect.

Savage's hand shaped the nape of Seychelle's neck. "That's the end of you taking any of those crazy lessons with your Purple Hat Club or whatever your ladies call themselves."

Seychelle laughed, her amusement melodious, perfectly pitched. "Have you forgotten that you're a member of the Red Hat Society, Savage? You even have a Red Hat Society symbol right on your bike to prove it."

Savage groaned. "Never speak of that sacrilege, woman. Never. Talk about sacred. A man's motorcycle is sacred. Preacher, these women are out of control. Hannah, I'm blaming you."

Hannah turned her blue eyes on Savage. "I didn't put the toads in Preacher's truck. I put them in Jonas' bedroom when we were kids and maybe in his patrol car a few weeks ago. And his truck. But he deserved it. I had nothing at all to do with your beautiful red hat with all the diamonds and rubies sparkling so beautifully in the sun, the one on your motorcycle. I think it's the envy of all the other bikers who see it."

Ambrie desperately wanted to see the little sparkly red hat that made Savage a member of the Red Hat Society.

"I don't believe this," Savage said. "There isn't one ounce of remorse in your voice, Hannah. All this time I held out hope that you were a sweet, kind woman who would show leadership qualities to those out-of-control rebels." To Ambrielle's shock, Savage seemed to indicate a group of four older women sitting at the large table watching the exchange with interest. All of them were wearing purple or red hats. "Instead, you're teaching them how to put toads in men's sacred trucks."

"Don't forget to include the worst one," Preacher muttered, gesturing toward Sabelia, who had gathered up menus to bring to the women seated at the table.

"Sabelia is by no means the worst," Savage declared, "or

the scariest. Take a good look at the women seated at the table over there." He gestured toward the four older women talking animatedly at the large table, dressed in their bright clothes and brighter, large-brimmed hats. "Hannah is giving them lessons as well."

"Technically, I'm not, Sabelia is," Hannah denied.

"Can anyone really do that?" Ambrie asked. Who knew when learning how to manipulate toads into doing whatever you wanted them to do might come in handy someday? At the moment, Master was being truly sweet, but he might develop a penchant for being overbearing. It looked to her as if several of the members of Torpedo Ink had that trait. She could see how tempting it might be to dump toads into their sacred trucks. How anyone would dare put a sparkly red hat on Savage's motorcycle was beyond her. That seemed as if they were taking their life into their hands.

"One has to have an actual talent for it," Hannah said, as if being able to fill someone's truck with toads were the most natural thing in the world.

Ambrielle choked back laughter. Hannah looked normal. Everyone did, but they'd all gone a little bit crazy. She wasn't certain the toad part was real. She took the basket Hannah extended to her.

"Thank you so much. I really appreciate it. Please let me know how much I owe you." It occurred to her she hadn't checked to see if she had her credit cards or cash on her or even asked if it was safe to use her cards.

"It's a gift, Ambrie, a wedding gift," Hannah assured her. "I'm going to make a large bottle of soother for Master. Preacher, would you like to see how it's done? You can teach Ambrielle later if need be."

Preacher saluted Ambrie and followed Hannah around the displays, behind the counter and then behind a closed door before Ambrielle had the chance to properly thank her again.

"Come meet my friends," Seychelle invited. "You'll really like them, Ambrie."

"I'll just be sitting at the table across from you, hoping you aren't figuring out how to put frogs in my coffee," Savage informed Seychelle.

"Savage." Seychelle looked shocked, even a little outraged. "I would never hurt a frog. Hot water would burn them."

Keys grinned at Savage. "Notice she didn't seem to worry about using frogs to get at you. You might consider they could be jumping down your shirt."

"I wouldn't use frogs for that, Keys," Seychelle denied. "Lizards would be better. Or snakes. Something that is much flatter than a frog and would crawl or slither, not hop."

"You're a wicked little thing." Keys nudged Savage. "You'd better look out, brother. She's liable to really do something like that. It just goes to show you what a bad judge of character I am. All this time, I thought she was such a sweet little thing."

Savage sighed. "I've seen her when she gets riled up. I live with her, remember?"

"Ignore them," Seychelle said. "They like to annoy me for some reason." Seychelle turned away from them, but Savage caught her arm.

"Really? You think you're going to get away with that? You'd better rectify that mistake immediately."

Seychelle rolled her eyes but then burst out laughing again, tipping up her face, one palm sliding up Savage's chest as he leaned down to capture her mouth with his.

The moment went from fun to intimate in the blink of an eye. Savage might seem a powerful, dangerous man, just as Master seemed—and was—but it was obvious to Ambrielle that he truly had feelings for Seychelle. That made her happy. She was drawn to Seychelle, felt a connection with her, mostly because she knew the woman had tried hard to draw her heavy sorrow away when the police were questioning her by sending her soothing vibes with her music.

It was Savage who finally broke the kiss. As he escorted Seychelle and Ambrielle to the larger table where the older women were seated, he deliberately spoke in a louder voice. "Now you're really going to get into trouble with that crew."

The women broke into laughter. "Savage, you're so terrible. Come here, please. I have a huge favor to ask of you."

"Mama Anat." Savage leaned down and brushed a kiss on her cheek. "Your favors always get me into huge trouble."

"Mama Anat," Seychelle began introductions, "this is Ambrielle, Master's new bride. Ambrielle, Mama Anat Gamal. She's Zyah's grandmother. Zyah is married to Player. This is Inez Nelson. Inez owns the local grocery store. Doris Fendris and I have been friends forever. She makes amazing cookies, and I walk miles to keep from gaining weight after I visit her, but trust me, it's well worth it. This is Lizz Johnson. She's new to our group and a wonderful addition, although too good at cards and I'm losing all the time."

"Lovely to meet you," Ambrie whispered, suddenly wishing Master was right there with her. She didn't like the spotlight on her. She didn't know how much these women knew about her, but they had too much compassion in their eyes. They couldn't talk about her parents' deaths. No one could say anything. For a moment her lungs refused to work.

"Savage lives to do you favors, Mama Anat," Seychelle said. "Especially carpenter work when he's using my tools. The pink ones."

That brought another round of laughter and, with it, air that managed to make its way into Ambrielle's lungs. Whether Seychelle knew it or not, she had successfully turned the focus away from Ambrie, allowing her to just be part of the group without having to be the center of attention in a way she wasn't yet prepared to handle.

"Ha ha, angel." Savage nuzzled the top of Seychelle's head with his chin. "What can I do for you, Mama Anat?" He indicated the chairs to Seychelle and Ambrie.

Seychelle took the seat close to the window and Doris, leaving Ambrie the one beside her and across from Mama

Anat. Ambrie felt an instant brightness just sitting at the same table with the women.

"We have a little church service that is nondenominational. Someone from the Crows Flying band comes every Sunday to provide music and sing for us. Master was supposed to sing next, but we heard his throat is really sore." Mama Anat fluttered her hands in the air and looked very distressed.

"That leaves us without anyone at the worst possible time," Inez finished for her.

"Of course, we're terribly worried about Master," Mama Anat added, looking at Ambrie. "I do hope everything goes all right with him. Player would do this for us, but he has other commitments." She looked helplessly around the table, as if one of the women would suddenly become a singer.

"Isn't Seychelle singing for you?" Savage asked.

Doris' smile was that of a proud mother. "Yes. With her beautiful voice. But all the music is for duets. A man and a woman. We'd have to change the entire program."

"Mama Anat wrote all the music herself. It's so beautiful," Lizz said, her voice shy.

Savage heaved a sigh and looked as if he'd rather pull out his fingernails one by one than stand there at the table with them. "This church is small? As in *really* small."

"Yes."

He glared at Mama Anat. "Woman, you get me in more trouble than anyone I know. And that includes Seychelle, which is saying a fuck of a lot."

Mama Anat beamed at him. "You'll do it, then?"

Savage swore under his breath, threw his hands into the air and stalked across to the table, where he sank into a booth. "I swear you're going to drive me to drink."

"You already drink, honey," Mama Anat said, her voice brimming with laughter. She was in no way perturbed with his not-so-gracious attitude. "Maybe I'll make it so you never drink."

"Keys, this is what comes with associating with older women. They put curses on you. You find yourself agreeing to do things for them you'd rather be tortured before you'd ever do, and you don't even know why."

Even Ambrielle found herself laughing at Savage's mournful tone. He was supposed to be the big, bad, scary one of Torpedo Ink. Seychelle looked at him lovingly, and Mama Anat and Doris seemed to as well. They didn't even wince when he cursed.

"Are we super late?" Three more women joined the table, one scooting in close to Ambrie, the other two on the side of the table close to Lizz. "I'm Anya. I bartend with Preacher at the Roadhouse. And this is Lana; she owns Label 287. Tessa is apprenticing at Label 287. She fills in occasionally at Alena's restaurant. We all kind of rotate and help each other out at the various businesses."

"Hi, Ambrie," Lana said. "I wanted to officially welcome you to Torpedo Ink." She reached over to Seychelle and touched her hand briefly. "I wasn't so welcoming to a sister when she needed it, and all of us have learned to do much better. We're a family. Everyone here. And you're part of that family. We've got you covered."

Doris looked shocked. "Wait. Lana, you didn't welcome Seychelle? Honey, you never said a word to me. Seychelle, you were having such a difficult time and you were so ill. Lana?"

"I know, Doris. I was wrong to question the relationship," Lana said.

Seychelle smiled at Lana. "It was no big deal. We cleared everything up."

Lana shook her head. "You were very hurt. It was a big deal. One of the things Alena, Tessa and I are talking about quite a bit with Blythe is taking responsibility for our mistakes and owning up to them. I really hurt you and contributed to the breakdown of your relationship with Savage. At least I could have. I hate that I did that, and I think about it every day."

"Lana." Seychelle was gentle. "You know there were extenuating circumstances. I love that you've taken me into your circle, but I don't want you to feel guilty over something that was out of your control, and it was."

Sabelia arrived, her wild hair pulled back in a ponytail and a wide smile on her face. "Ladies, what will it be today? I see you have a newcomer with you. I'm Sabelia, and I just managed to kick Preacher's bossy butt on the challenge of the week, so I'm in a very good mood. May I suggest the lavender-honey tea as one of your choices? It's especially wonderful today. And the apricot scones are yummy."

Ambrielle couldn't help herself. "Were there *real* toads in Preacher's truck? Live toads?"

"You bet there were toads. Hundreds of them. Very large ones too. Croaking away, announcing a loud messy triumph that said, 'Sabelia kicked your bossy butt.' He might make me work overtime at the bar this weekend and yell at me, but he'll know I might retaliate in a way he won't like. The next time he goes to bed, the toads might join him." She did a little dance right there in the aisle.

Savage and Keys groaned in unison.

"We're right here, Sabelia," Keys announced. "You know we can hear you. Aren't you the least bit afraid one of us might decide to strangle you?"

She looked at him over her shoulder and gave a little sniff. "Aren't you afraid I might decide that little shop of yours you love so much is next on my hit list?"

"You wouldn't dare."

"Try strangling me and see what happens, Keys."

"This is what comes of letting riffraff work at the bar," Keys stated, overly loud.

Ambrielle looked around the tea shop, blinking back tears. Master. He had arranged this. While he was in a doctor's office having biopsies done to determine whether he had throat cancer, he had made certain she wasn't sitting in a waiting room. Ambrie had been so certain she wanted to be right there, as close as possible, not to be supportive but because she was afraid to be away from him. He had given her this—these wonderful crazy people. He had surrounded her with funny, real people of all ages, willing to laugh at themselves and give her their time in order to distract her from the reality of her parents' deaths. From the violence surrounding her from those moments on. That was the man he thought so unworthy of her. So which one of them was really unworthy?

FOURTEEN

"I'm pretty sure she used to be a quiet little thing," Keys whispered to Savage loud enough for Ambrielle to hear when Sabelia had taken their orders and walked away.

The two Torpedo Ink members were joined by Destroyer. He was so large he seemed to take up the entire store. That didn't stop him from sitting in one of the empty chairs at the table beside Keys.

"Who was a quiet little thing? Not the new bride," Destroyer asked.

Ambrielle blushed for no reason. The spotlight was back on her just like that.

Seychelle reached for her hand. "The rings are beautiful. Anything Ice creates is amazing."

"May I see them?" Mama Anat asked. "I love his work. Every piece he does is different and so beautiful."

"He puts such love into his craft," Lana said. "He always has. He has a group of other designers he trades gems with. They've been doing it for years. He manages to get just what he needs through them. They keep their circle very small and know which mine each stone comes from."

"You put love into every garment you create," Tessa said.

"That's why everyone wants your clothing. It's so popular we can't keep up. The coolest thing you do, though, is when Darcy or Kenny brings some kid to the shop and you custom design clothes for them and tell them they got them on a scholarship, or whatever it is you say. I love that you do that. Those kids have nothing at all. You give them the best clothes, and it changes how they feel about themselves. You don't just give them clothes; you talk to them while you measure them. All about life and getting knocked down and standing back up and never letting other people's opinions stop you from pursuing your dream because you're different."

Lana waved the compliments away. Ambrielle looked at her in a whole new light. She was fairly certain Master had said it was Lana on the roof of a building with a sniper rifle covering him when he was on the patio of the restaurant. If Lana had been the one trusted to keep Master from being killed, she had to be a dead shot with that rifle. Yet she was clearly compassionate with teens needing clothing, and she took the time to talk to them when they needed someone to hear them and give them advice. She also wasn't afraid to apologize and admit when she was wrong in front of others. There was a lot to admire about her.

"That's wonderful, Lana," Mama Anat said. "Zyah keeps telling me I have to go by your shop, but I'm always so late when I go to the market. I sew, but I'm not nearly as good at design as you are."

"Thank you," Lana murmured. "Tessa is beginning to come up with some wonderful ideas. I'm really excited for her."

Tessa flushed a beautiful rose. "I love to create new looks. I especially would like to come up with ideas for young people to make them have confidence the way Lana does, but so far, I haven't managed to do that. I think I've designed a couple of vests and jackets that are pretty cool, but nothing else. Nothing that would sell."

"That's not true, Tessa," Lana denied. "Your designs are

going to be huge sellers, especially those little camisoles. They're almost perfect. You just need to decide on the right material and how you want each one made. If you're going to do custom clothing, you can't think in terms of mass production. Under Label 287, everything must be custom in order for us to afford to give away the clothing for the kids who don't have anything. Later, if we want to get into mass production, we'd need a partner and a different label."

"What do you do, Ambrielle?" Seychelle asked.

Ambrielle had known the question would be asked sooner or later. "My profession is probably boring to most people, but I love it. I'm a financial advisor. I help my clients with planning and with their investments and building their retirements. I happen to love numbers the way Lana and Tessa love design. I enjoy helping my clients feel safer about their futures. It's also very satisfying to get them out of debt."

"You do sound enthusiastic, dear," Inez said. "I have terrible debt. I'm not afraid to admit it in front of everyone. It's not like my friends don't know. I was solid at one time, but I helped a friend and then the bottom dropped out of the market and things went downhill fast. I should have known someone like you then." Her laughter was a little hollow. "I don't regret helping my friend, but I do worry about our future. I'm getting a little too old to be running the store every single day."

"Don't you have anyone looking at your portfolio for you? You should have someone going over your income/ debt/retirement and investments now, Inez. It isn't too late to get back on track and start pulling everything out of the fire fast."

Inez shook her head. "I tried to do it myself, but I just look at the numbers and they look so dismal I've given up."

"You don't know me, but my firm has a good reputation. I'll give you the name and number and you can look it up. Seriously, I'd like to help you," Ambrielle said. "You shouldn't have to worry about your retirement or anything else at this stage of the game. Master can look over my shoulder. He's good with numbers too."

Inez looked down at the table as Sabelia returned with several teapots and placed them in front of them, naming the various teas for them to try. When Sabelia left to retrieve the three-tiered trays of scones and sandwiches, Inez cleared her throat and then looked directly at Ambrie.

"I would have to look at what your firm charges before I agreed to hire you." Her voice was tight with pride.

Before Ambrie could say anything, Anya spoke up. Her brows were drawn together in a little frown as she consulted with Lana. "Doesn't Torpedo Ink still owe Inez a huge debt?"

Lana nodded. "That's correct. Inez, you know the club owes you big-time. Ambrielle's married to Master; that makes her Torpedo Ink. We all pool resources to pay down debt. She can help you out, and her time can take off part of what we owe you." She made it sound like it was a done deal.

Inez gave a little shake of her head as Doris poured tea into her cup. "I'm sure you paid that debt off, Lana."

"I know we didn't, Inez. You don't pay any attention when Czar talks money to you, do you?"

Ambrielle was suddenly certain Torpedo Ink didn't owe Inez money, but it didn't matter—they were going to convince her they did.

Inez looked a little embarrassed. She took an apricot scone and a strawberry one off the tray and put them on her plate. "Well, actually, no. I trust Czar. When the money's right, he'll let me know."

"Then as soon as I can, I'll look things over and see if I can straighten your finances out for you," Ambrie said. She loved helping her clients, especially if they thought the task was impossible. Often, their financials appeared to be in such a mess, the task seemingly impossible, but then, unraveling the tangle one step at a time, she always managed to find a way to build retirement, pay down debt and even invest. Once she could invest, her clients made money.

Inez tried to look very sober, nodding her head. "That sounds good. I'll have to talk to Jackson, just to be sure."

"Jackson?" Ambrie's eyebrow shot up. "The deputy sheriff? Is he related? Your son?"

Before Inez could answer, Doris chimed in. "Oh no, dear, but he may as well be. Jackson has always treated Inez as if she was his mother. They never admit it though. They just pretend they're distant friends, but no one has believed it for years."

Mama Anat nodded in agreement. "I haven't lived here the number of years everyone else has, but even I know that."

Lizz smiled at Inez. "I'm afraid your secret is well-known throughout the village."

Inez sipped her tea. "It isn't my secret. I tell the world I love that man. He's very good to me. And not just me. He looks after Donny Ruttermyer, and Donna and the Dardens. Just like Savage does."

"You're such a saint, Savage," Keys whispered overly loud. "Right up there with Jackson Deveau."

"Shut the fuck up, Keys," Savage snapped.

"Savage, language," Mama Anat cautioned, her voice very gentle. "Keys, all of the boys have been helping lately. Master hasn't been feeling good and yet he's been out every day working on fixing Talia and Lars Barber's home in Caspar. That huge tree fell on it after the storm. Lars can't possibly repair the roof or bedroom. We bring food to them, or Alena does. I haven't seen you there, and you're amazing working at carpentry."

Savage folded his arms across his chest and stared at Keys. Destroyer did the same. It was completely forbidden to lash out in any way at Mama Anat. The rule was unspoken, but everyone knew that not only was she Player's grandmother-in-law, but Savage and Destroyer claimed her for their own. She might be sounding sweet, but she was calling Keys out, taking Savage's back.

"Sorry, Mama Anat. I do plan to help out the Barbers. It's been my week at the Caspar Market helping Zyah. By the time the store closes, it's too dark to get to the Barbers' and be of any use."

"Well then, that's perfectly fine. You should try the apricot scones. They're just delicious," Mama Anat advised, her tone forgiving. Keys was once again back in her good graces.

Keys looked relieved. "I'll do that." He took an apricot scone off the tray.

Ambrielle thought the dynamics of the club and these women were interesting. She would have to ask Master how they fit in with Torpedo Ink. The little hat bells tinkled merrily, and Blythe, Czar, Maestro, Reaper and a little boy came into the store. The little boy looked to be about six. He had shaggy thick blond hair and blue eyes, and one side of his jaw appeared to be swollen. He looked miserable. Blythe looked as if she'd been up all night.

She and Czar brought the little boy up to the counter, all three holding hands. Ambrielle thought Czar looked very cute holding his son's hand. It was obvious the boy was growing his hair longer in order to look like his father.

"Sabelia, is Hannah here today?" Czar asked.

Sabelia nodded. "She's in the back with Preacher. Master's throat is pretty bad, and she's showing Preacher the mixture of ingredients to use in order to soothe it and promote faster healing. I can get her if you need her."

"How long do you think she'll be?" Blythe asked. "Jimmy had to go to the dentist with a bad tooth infection. I thought Hannah might be able to make something to help him."

"She's almost finished, but she'll put what she's working on aside for a child," Sabelia assured them.

"He's numb at the moment," Czar said. "We have time for a cup of tea and scones. I'm sure Reaper and Maestro just can't wait for tea."

Reaper had already backed all the way to the door and was standing to one side of it, leaning a hip against the wall, chin down, his gaze on the street and up on the rooftops. "I'm good."

A little giggle escaped Anya, and she hastily pressed her fingertips to her lips to stifle real laughter. "He's a man of few words."

Maestro took up a similar position on the other side of the door, hip to the wall. Ambrielle studied both men. The way they stood, sideways, their feet under their shoulders, they presented a slimmer target. Anyone looking into the shop would have a difficult time seeing them, yet they had great visibility, taking in the entire street as well as the buildings across from the Floating Hat.

Ambrie was trying to learn everything she could from these men and women. Her parents had taught her so much. They'd put her in self-defense classes almost from the time she was a toddler. They'd had her shooting guns and learning to handle other weapons, but she recognized the caliber of those club members surrounding her from Torpedo Ink. They were trained from childhood as assassins. They moved in shadows and had knowledge even her father didn't have. She wanted that knowledge for herself. She was determined to find and kill the men who had murdered her parents.

"When I bring your tea and scones, I'll bring something for Jimmy to drink that will help him now," Sabelia said. "I'll just be a minute. Let me consult with Hannah."

Blythe, Czar and Jimmy sat at the table across from the large table where Ambrielle was seated, but one table ahead of Savage, Keys and Destroyer.

Ambrie listened to the animated conversations swirling around her in the tea shop. Two women came into the shop and began to wander around the aisles, looking into the various tempting baskets of lotions and oils. She watched them as she inhaled the wonderful healing fragrance of the shop, aware that the scent had changed subtly. How? When?

It was different now, soothing and yet clarifying at the same time.

The two women appeared to be in their late forties, although Ambrie thought they could have been a little younger or older. She took another sip of the lavender-honey tea, her favorite of all the teas she'd sampled, while she contemplated the age of the women. They wore pencil-slim trousers, one in a black houndstooth with a white blouse and black cardigan, the other in simple black and a black-and-white-checked blouse with a black cardigan. Both women had short haircuts, although the similarities ended there.

The shorter of the two had her hair in soft brown waves that fell to her chin in an attractive bob. The taller woman was a dirty blonde with very short hair that she wore almost in spikes. It should have looked masculine, but on her feminine face, the hairdo looked intriguingly timeless and even elegant. She looked like a trendsetter. Both wore drop earrings and sparkling bracelets. The shorter of the two wore nearly three-inch heels on her boots. The taller woman wore two-inch strappy heels.

"Tourists," Seychelle whispered in Ambrielle's ear. "The lifeblood of Sea Haven."

"How can you tell?"

"The way they're dressed. They're artfully casual. We're just casual. They have money; their clothes are designer; so are their purses. Look at the jewelry they're wearing." She put a hand over her engagement ring. "Savage insisted on this diamond. He says it matches my eyes. The stone in your ring is very special as well. I wouldn't be surprised if those women would recognize Ice's work if they saw it."

Instinctively, Ambrie followed Seychelle's lead and put her hand in her lap, ensuring if the women happened to glance toward the large table, they wouldn't see her wedding and engagement rings.

"Czar," Inez said. "I don't want to take advantage in any way of Torpedo Ink, so if Lana is wrong, you let me know. Ambrielle is a financial advisor, and she offered to untangle the mess of my finances for me if it is at all possible. Everyone knows I have no money to pay her, but Lana said Ambrie is Torpedo Ink and the club still owes me a debt. I'm sitting here trying to figure out how that could be true."

Her tone was painfully proud. Doris and Mama Anat, facing Czar and Blythe, looked as if they were going to fall out of their chairs to try to warn the president. Lizz leaned toward Inez as if she could somehow shield her.

Czar gave Inez a faint smile. "You really didn't pay any attention at all to the paperwork I sent you, or anything said at the meetings, did you?"

"Czar." Blythe's reprimand was gentle. "No one likes those stuffy meetings, with the exception of Master."

"I like them," Jimmy said.

Ambrielle could tell by the shocked reaction of the members of Torpedo Ink that no one had expected the boy to talk. Even Reaper and Maestro flicked their gazes from the street to the boy for one brief moment. Blythe pressed her lips together, but not before Ambrielle could see that they were trembling. Even Savage, Keys and Destroyer reacted by slowly turning to look at the boy. Lana gripped Tessa's wrist and Seychelle and Anya held hands hard enough that their fingers turned white.

"You do?" Czar's tone was very casual, his voice pitched low. "What do you like about the meetings, Jimmy?"

"The numbers, mostly. Master explains them to me. He knows I like them. Inez has part interest—one-third, so she gets one-third of the profits. The profits should be reinvested back into the store, but only a percentage. Master invests part of Inez's profits for her, so she makes more money."

"Wait," Inez interrupted, leaning across the table toward the aisle and Jimmy. "Does someone at the meeting say the Caspar market makes a profit?"

Jimmy nodded. "Master says it does. The numbers do, I mean." He frowned and looked up at Czar. "Am I getting it mixed up?"

"No, that's what Master tells us at the meeting. The

market has been making a profit, and Miss Inez is a part owner, just like you said. I'm glad someone was paying attention." Czar smiled at Inez. "I believe Ambrielle can straighten out your financials for you, Inez, without worrying. If the Sea Haven store isn't turning a good profit for you, perhaps you might have Zyah take a look at what you're doing there. She worked internationally for a large chain and has impeccable credentials. You should be making even better money in the Sea Haven store than we do at the Caspar one."

Sabelia set the tea and scones in front of Blythe and Czar and a drink in front of Jimmy. "I know absolutely nothing about numbers, Jimmy. When I have to make my bank account add up correctly, I'm going to ask for your help. Do you charge money? Is that going to be your regular job?"

Jimmy shrugged and fell silent. Ambrielle had the feeling the child could maintain his silence for long periods of time. She looked to Seychelle for an explanation.

Seychelle leaned in close. "He doesn't speak to anyone. Sometimes Emily—that's another one of Czar and Blythe's adopted children. But he doesn't speak."

Jimmy had indicated he'd spoken to Master, or rather Master had spoken to him, explaining how profits and investments went.

"How old is that boy?"

"He just had a birthday and turned seven."

The two women had finished their shopping, paid for their lotions and oils and then found a table a little apart from the Torpedo Ink group, more toward the front near the bay windows. As Sabelia took their orders, two men entered. They hesitated just inside the doorway, suddenly noticing Reaper lounging against the wall. The bells shook and danced, the music a wild symphony of welcome. For no reason other than that hesitation, Ambrielle felt a small frisson of alarm creeping down her spine.

The men didn't look at any of the members of Torpedo Ink after that first quick glance of alarm. They clomped in their heavy boots up the main aisle straight to the counter. Sabelia called out to Hannah that she was needed. Almost immediately, Hannah stuck her head out from behind a closed door in the far back and smiled at the two men.

"I'll be right with you."

Her smile could have charmed a raging saber-toothed tiger. Those large blue eyes and generous mouth were enough to make anyone want to do exactly what this woman asked. Ambrielle couldn't imagine her husband winning any arguments. Hannah was so beautiful, and with her voice, how could someone have managed to slash her to ribbons with a knife? Couldn't she have just cried out, *No*, and her attacker would have been compelled to stop?

Ambrielle had said no. Her parents had said no. There wasn't any way to stop men like Walker Thompson. When they wanted something and they ran into opposition to get it, they simply mowed down anyone or anything in their way. She could smell the faint scent of blood and gunpowder and was instantly nauseated. Had Gleb and his partner, Denis, found Master? He would be groggy from whatever they were using to numb his throat. It would be so easy to kill him.

The conversation swirling around her receded even further. She heard laughter as if in the distance. Czar's voice. The low murmur of a woman's voice. Mama Anat answering. Her lungs burned from lack of air. She wrapped her arms around her middle, cold invading until she thought she might freeze.

Was Ice watching over Master? How did the doctor biopsy the polyps in Master's throat? She hadn't asked. She pictured the doctor numbing his throat. Pressing one hand deep to her stomach in an effort to stop the churning, she pressed the other to her forehead, hoping she would remember what he'd said or done the night before. He'd been quiet mostly. But he'd been taking pills. He never did that. He'd been in the bathroom often. Most of the night. He hadn't eaten anything. That was unlike him. Why hadn't she asked more questions?

Ambrielle was nearly in a full-blown panic attack. Her blood thundered in her ears, drowning out the voices and laughter swirling around her. Her eyes burned. She didn't have panic attacks. She didn't cry in public. She didn't need a man to lean on. She wasn't clingy. Master was in the middle of a procedure, totally vulnerable, and he was in danger. She felt the danger creeping up on him. She had to get to him. Where was the doctor's office? Why hadn't she asked?

Ambrielle pressed a hand to her churning stomach. *Master. I have to find you.*

The air in the room was stuffy. There were too many people in the small space. She had to find a way to reach him. To get to him.

"Ambrielle." Seychelle's voice was very soft, but extremely compelling. "Look at me. Open your eyes and look at me."

She hadn't realized her eyes were closed. She lifted her lashes and saw that several members of Torpedo Ink had crowded around the table, their large bodies cutting off the view from everyone else in the room. No one could see her but those at the table and the men surrounding them.

"I have to get to Master. He's in trouble," she whispered, willing them to believe her.

Czar stood closest to her, Savage beside him. Czar rested his hand very gently on her shoulder. "Ice is with Master, and he would never, under any circumstances, leave his side. He's protected, Ambrie. He wanted to ensure you were protected and that you were having a good time." He glanced at his watch. "I've texted Ice, asking when Master will be recovered enough to join you."

"I have this feeling in the pit of my stomach that just won't go away," she said. "I know it sounds ridiculous, but I know he's in danger. I need to get out of here. I can protect him."

None of the men laughed at her or even exchanged looks over her head.

Lana reached out and gripped her hand. "I'm so grateful

you married him. He deserves someone in his life who puts him first."

"Ice just texted me back," Czar announced. "They're on their way here, Ambrie. Master said to wait right where you are; he's coming to you. He wants you to ask Hannah to have one of her special soothers waiting for him."

Ambrielle should have been happy. It wasn't that she thought Czar would lie to her. She had her own phone. She could text Master herself and ensure he was out of the doctor's office. She didn't like that there was only Ice to protect him. She *really* had a bad feeling. Biting down hard on her lip to keep from blurting out that the entire Torpedo Ink club should go to him, she forced herself to nod and sat there while they all sat back down in their seats as if the matter were resolved.

The older women smiled at her as if, because she was a new bride, they understood perfectly that she would be worried about her husband under the circumstances. It was only Lana, Seychelle and Anya who seemed to catch the fact that she was still feeling a terrible sense of dread.

"You'll feel so much better when you see him," Seychelle whispered. "Savage had a hit put out on him, and I was terrified to let him out of my sight." She flicked a quick glance at Lana. "I still feel terrified at times."

Anya gave a small, almost imperceptible nod. "When they go out on those missions and I have no idea where Reaper is, what he's doing or when he'll get back, I feel the same way."

"I'm ashamed to say I never once thought what it must be like for you," Lana whispered.

Hannah's aura reached them before she did. Calming, soothing, a powerful presence, she seemed to exude tranquility, even managing to tamp down the feeling of impending danger as she placed a tall frosted glass on the table in front of Ambrielle. "This is for Master. It should help his throat as the numbness wears off."

"Thank you," Ambrie said.

Hannah smiled and turned to Czar and Blythe's table. "Jimmy, it's nice to see you again. I hear you have a very bad toothache."

Jimmy nodded solemnly and pointed to the swelling on the side of his jaw.

"We managed to get him an emergency appointment," Blythe said. "He has an abscess. His teeth have been such a problem for him. The baby teeth have been stubborn about coming out before his adult teeth want to come in."

"We can take care of that pain for you, Jimmy," Hannah reassured him. "We've done it before, haven't we?"

Jimmy glanced at Czar and then at Blythe. Both smiled encouragingly. He clutched at Blythe's hand before he nodded.

"Do you have a preference on a flavor you would like me to make your special drinks?"

Again, Jimmy looked to his parents. Ambrielle found herself, just like the other members of Torpedo Ink, willing the little boy to voice his choice. It took patience on Hannah's part not to hurry him. Blythe and Czar were quiet, allowing Jimmy to make up his mind whether or not he would speak on his own behalf.

"I like the cherry a lot." Jimmy stated it in such a low tone he could barely be heard.

Ambrielle wanted to cheer. She couldn't imagine how his parents felt with that small victory. Hannah beamed at the boy. "Cherry it is. It will only take me a couple of minutes, Czar, and I'll have six of them made up for him."

"Thank you, Hannah. I'd like to get my family home as soon as possible."

Czar's tone didn't convey urgency, but Ambrielle remembered the threat hanging over his head. The Russian woman wanted to kill him. Not only him, but his wife and children. Czar was keeping them in lockdown, where they were safe from her assassin squads. He wouldn't have brought his son into town unless it was an emergency.

The bells jingled merrily, announcing more visitors to the shop. Ambrielle looked around. There were quite a few members of Torpedo Ink at the tables. Reaper and Maestro remained standing near the bay windows. The tables were filling up for teatime. The Floating Hat was popular with tourists and locals alike.

Jonas strode in, nodding to Czar and a few others, but not breaking stride as he went straight behind the counter to his wife. One arm slid around her waist. "I'm off for the day, Hannah. How can I help? I saw you had deliveries that weren't unpacked. Would you like me to take care of that?"

"Are you sure? You've been working overtime, Jonas," Hannah said, leaning into him. "You should go home and sleep for a little while. Abbey took our little naughtiness for the day. The house is quiet for once."

"I'd rather be here helping you. Give me something to do, baby doll."

She tried frowning at him but laughed instead. "If you really don't mind unpacking all the crates for me and shelving everything. You know where it goes. You've done it enough times. You make prettier baskets than anyone, so if you finish . . ."

"Hold up there, woman, you don't need to say that where anyone can hear you." He bent down to bite her neck.

Hannah yelped and glared at him. "I swear you're a vampire."

Jimmy burst out laughing. "He can't be a vampire," he whispered, overly loud. "It's daylight, Mom. Wouldn't he burn up in the sun?"

"Jonas is a cop, Jimmy." Savage leaned over Blythe's shoulder. "They don't burn in the sun. They can walk around harassing the crap out of innocent bikers and biting beautiful women on the neck. You have to watch out for them."

"Savage." Blythe glared. "Stop filling his head with your nonsense. That's not true, Jimmy. Jonas is a friend. He's married to Hannah. She loves him even when he bites her neck."

"*Especially* when I bite her neck," Jonas corrected and winked at the boy.

"*Not* when you call me 'baby doll,'" Hannah declared firmly.

Jonas just ruffled her hair, laughed and disappeared into the far back room where no one could see him.

Jimmy looked up at his parents, his eyebrows drawn together. "Why does he call Miss Hannah 'baby doll'?"

"I don't know," Blythe said. "You'll have to ask her if you want to know." She poured herself another cup of tea and put a scone on her plate.

Czar glanced out the window and then at his watch. "Blythe." There was warning in his voice.

"We're already here, honey, and Jimmy's having fun."

Ambrielle didn't blame her. If the boy hadn't really talked before and all of a sudden he was interested enough to engage, she wouldn't want to leave either. They were surrounded by Torpedo Ink, and Jonas was there as well. Still, Ambrie had that dark dread in the pit of her stomach that refused to go away.

"What are you thinking, Inez?" Mama Anat asked. "We can't possibly host everyone. Could we?"

"Someone has to do it. I was texting with Jackson, and he thought it was a really good idea. You wrote all those beautiful songs, and we have Seychelle. Now Savage. Seychelle has the voice of an angel. Everyone always brings potluck, but we could ask Alena to cater. This is our chance to show the others that we might be small, but we still have what it takes to host something of that size."

Ambrielle turned her head to look at Seychelle, who had gone pale. What had she missed? The little hats over the door danced merrily, announcing more visitors with a happy tune, and she felt Master's presence instantly. She nearly climbed over Lana, who laughed and stood, allowing her to get to the aisle.

Ambrie didn't run, she just stood looking at Master. His size was shocking to her. He wasn't as big and dense with muscle as Destroyer, but he was close. He was ripped, and every muscle showed beneath the tight black tee he wore stretched across his thick chest as he moved toward her. His thighs were twin columns of muscles encased in blue jeans. He wore his vest open over the tee. His dark hair, cut short on the sides, spilled onto his forehead, covering a scar she knew was there.

His eyes met hers. Dark. Compelling. Moving over her, seeing everything. Seeing right into her. There were little white lines around his mouth. Creases that hadn't been there in his face when he first left her. She waited until he was standing in front of her and, uncaring of their audience, reached up with the pads of her fingers and gently smoothed those lines.

Her heart turned over. He moved her every time with the way he looked at her. With the way he seemed to see inside of her.

He slid one palm around the nape of her neck under her fall of hair. "You have to stop worrying about me, princess."

"That's never going to happen, so you'll have to get used to it." She realized it was the truth. They had a bargain. He had those eyes, and he was capable of things she needed desperately. She'd seen the killer in him, and she had wanted that man. Right there, in that moment, Ambrielle realized she didn't want Kir "Master" Vasiliev, her husband, to kill anyone for her. Not him. He'd been used too many times by too many people who should have seen that he needed care. That he was a good man and was vulnerable. Now he was hers to look after. She was not going to use him like everyone else had.

Who, then? Because Walker Thompson, Gleb and Denis had to die. Savage? He was capable. Reaper? Maestro? Savage had Seychelle. She would never risk Savage when he belonged to Seychelle. Reaper belonged to Anya. Maestro, then? He was a stranger to her. She didn't know what kind of man he was. None of them, then. It was up to her to rid the world of men like Thompson, Gleb and Denis. She had known that all along. Her father would have been horrified at the idea that she wanted someone else to do her dirty work for her.

Master leaned down, his mouth close to her ear. "Never play poker, baby, at least not with me. You're an open book. I'm tired and want to lie down. Let's go home."

Ambrielle slipped her arm around his waist and turned back to the table to say her good-byes. As she did, outside on the street, a song played obnoxiously loud, the guitars and drums blasting, filling the air between the various stores and climbing to the clouds.

The women see me comin'

That silver truck of lovin'

That no one can deny

They need a red-hot hero

Not a poser or a zero

Deputy desire

You know I'm your live wire

Of fun . . .

Red Hot Jackson

Get your 911 of fun

And I'll let you hold my gun

Because I'm . . .

Red Hot Jackson

There was dead silence in the Floating Hat and then a burst of laughter from everyone inside. Even Hannah laughed as Jonas came out from the back room.

"What the hell is that ruckus?"

"I think your deputy is looking for attention," Keys said, tapping the beat on the tabletop with his palms.

Jonas listened as the words and music repeated themselves, growing even louder. Jackson's silver truck came into view, slipping into the parking slot right in front of the shop. Several shop owners and their customers stepped out of their stores to see what the commotion was all about. They began to tap their feet to the beat or clap their hands. Jackson shut off the engine and the song stopped playing abruptly. He jumped out, slamming the door.

"Uh-oh. He's armed," Jonas warned. "He looks pissed."

"You're the sheriff," Czar pointed out. "Why would he be pissed?"

Jackson ignored the hats swinging as if a seismic event had taken place as he stalked through the door and straight up the aisle to stand in front of Savage. "A man's truck is *sacred*," he announced.

Savage nodded. "I agree. Just like my bike. No one touches it."

"You put your hands on my truck."

Savage put his hands in the air, palms out in surrender. "I didn't."

"I recognize the voices, Savage. Seychelle. Even Blythe." Jackson pinned her with an accusing gaze. "I never would have thought you would be involved in something like this."

"I'll admit I sang the song—several times. It's so catchy," Blythe said. "Rashad was there, and we were all . . . drinking and it was just fun. Your truck wasn't anywhere near the place."

Sabelia all but danced around. "Do you mean to say someone actually rigged your truck to play that song?"

"Not even through my radio. When I step on the gas, it

starts to play and gets louder and louder until I hit about twenty miles an hour. That ensures when I'm in town it plays where everyone can hear it. If I'm at a stop sign, it plays."

Sabelia clapped her hands together. "That's better than toads. I have to learn how to do that."

"Oh, hell no," Preacher protested, throwing both arms out in front of her, blocking her view of Jackson and Savage as if that would stop her from learning anything that had been done. "This little hellion would unleash some unholy power by mistake."

"What's a hellion, Mom?" Jimmy asked.

"I'm not exactly sure, Jimmy," Blythe said. "Preacher will have to explain that one to you."

All eyes and ears were on Preacher. He didn't hesitate; he indicated Sabelia with her glossy black hair that all but over-powered her delicate pale features and too-large eyes for her small oval face. "Right there. A wild thing, Jimmy. A woman so attractive she lures you in and then—bam—she knocks you on your ass when you least expect it because she's doing some crazy thing she shouldn't be doing. Pure trouble. That's what a hellion is. Always getting into trouble. Always will be trouble. Lives for it."

Jimmy turned his wide blue gaze on Sabelia as if seeing her for the first time. He looked at her very admiringly.

"Get rid of it, Savage," Jackson demanded.

"I wouldn't know how." Savage was complacent, sprawling back in his chair as if he didn't have a care in the world.

Ambrie thought he looked like a wolf.

Jackson pulled out his cell phone and began rapidly text-ing. Inez's phone began to sing. He glanced up at Savage, satisfaction on his face. "You're going to be very, very sorry that you ever decided to mess with me."

Savage raised an eyebrow. "I never touched that truck."

"Where're Mechanic and Transporter?"

"I imagine they're hard at work," Keys answered for Savage.

Jackson looked around until he spotted Jonas, who hastily wiped a grin from his face. "I'll need a ride."

"Sure." Jonas kissed Hannah on her temple. "I'll be back in a few minutes."

Jackson paused beside Master, who had stepped to one side to allow the two lawmen to move past him. "I know you're probably armed most of the time, but I'm warning you ahead of time, I'll be stopping any Torpedo Ink member for any infraction. You're a felon. That means I can search you and your vehicle. Don't have any weapons on you."

Savage scowled at him. "You don't get to use your position to retaliate when you don't like the way you get pranked, Jackson."

"That's beneath you," Czar said, standing, signaling to Blythe that they were leaving as well. She held out her hand to Jimmy.

"I have to agree," Jonas said. "You two started these ridiculous pranks. You keep them as gentlemen rules."

"Did you hear what he did to my truck?" Jackson demanded.

"I understand it was a masterful stroke to pull off," Jonas said, "and why you'd be upset, but it isn't like you to mix professional with civilian."

Jackson sighed. "Damn it, you're right. I apologize, Master. It's just that it's my truck. My truck is sacred."

"So was my bike," Savage pointed out. "Although I'll admit, you pulled off a hell of a great prank. My bike wears it proudly."

A small smile broke through the dark veil of anger on Jackson's scarred features. "Yeah, I do like the way that hat sparkles when the sun hits it just right."

"We'll just have to call it even," Savage suggested.

"Not quite yet," Jackson denied and abruptly strode out of the shop.

"Brilliant," Jonas conceded and followed him out.

Czar nodded to Blythe as he preceded her to the front

door. She tugged at Jimmy's hand. He went with her, but only because she had a firm grip on his wrist. Maestro fell into step behind Czar's family.

Master swept his arm around Ambrie's waist, indicating she cut short her good-byes and they follow Czar's family out.

"It was so nice meeting everyone," Ambrielle called. She wanted to leave, to get Master home, where she felt he was safe. Where they could talk, just the two of them, not surrounded by so many people.

They stepped outside onto the old-fashioned, quaint cobblestone walkway. Torpedo Ink motorcycles lined the street just down from the Floating Hat. One of the prospects, Hyde Kedrov, stood at attention, watching as Czar, Blythe and Jimmy walked toward the RAV4 parked just to the right of Master's truck. Ink shadowed behind them.

Blythe laughed at something Czar said, and leaned down to listen to Jimmy as he tipped his head up to speak to her.

Reaper suddenly tensed and the entire Torpedo Ink club went electric, as if each member were on the same nerve pathway and that one telling move alerted them.

"Cover! Cover!" Reaper yelled.

FIFTEEN

The instant Reaper yelled a warning, gunfire erupted, a hail of bullets striking all around them, hitting the concrete, buzzing like angry bees past Ambrielle and Master to lodge in the thick walls of the building behind them. Reaper's large body tackled Czar, who had flung himself over Blythe, taking her to the ground. Czar tried rolling with her beneath Master's truck. Blythe resisted, fighting him, reaching for their son as he wrenched himself out of her grip.

"Jimmy," she called, her voice filled with desperation.

"Mommy, my drinks." Jimmy turned back toward the Floating Hat, running on his little legs to get to the door.

Instead of seeking the refuge of the tea shop, Master shoved Ambrielle toward the building. "Get inside and stay on the floor."

Ambrielle, her heart in her throat, stumbled backward from the shove Master had given her, watching the scenario play out in slow motion. Master was so big. He was already in motion, his large body running the few steps, arms out, making himself even larger to cover Jimmy completely before wrapping him in his arms, lifting him, turning toward the street and the cover of the cars.

She saw him wince. Stagger. That galvanized her into action, and she sprang forward, ignoring the yells of Jackson, Jonas and the outraged Torpedo Ink members who poured out of the Floating Hat, creating a human wall around Czar and Blythe as they located the shooters and sent a storm of bullets back.

She ran to Master, tried to make herself larger, taller, tried to take him to the ground and cover him with her body. Anything. Any way to keep him safe. The sound of gunfire was loud, the whine of bullets sounding like angry bees as they whined past her. Something burned along the top of her shoulder, and another tore a strip of skin from the side of her thigh as she leapt onto Master's back.

"Damn it, Ambrielle, what the fuck do you think you're doing?" Master snarled as he went to the ground, wrapping Jimmy in his arms. He pressed one knee down and then the second one, trying to turn to take Ambrielle from his back. She stuck like a second skin, refusing to allow him to detach her.

Both the sheriff and deputy sheriff identified themselves and ordered the shooters to put their weapons down and surrender. They were answered with another volley of bullets. Jackson returned fire and a body dropped from the roof onto the street.

Czar swore. "Who are they shooting at, Jonas?"

"Everyone," Jonas replied. "Hannah, stay the hell inside and keep down."

Ambrielle turned her head enough to see Hannah standing just inside the doorway of the shop. Sabelia stood beside her. Both lifted their hands and looked toward the ocean, or more precisely toward the Drake home where it sat on the cliff overlooking the ocean. The wind began to pick up, blowing in from the sea, turning a vicious cold as it washed over them in a rush that lifted all loose debris in the street and sent it swirling in the air like a mini tornado.

Chaos reigned as Jonas and Jackson returned fire and the wind hurled itself at the shooters on the buildings across

from the tea shop. The wind was so forceful that debris from
the street was flung up onto the roof. Signs shook loose from
chains and flew like Frisbees, spinning up and over the roof,
seeking targets like missiles. They were faster than they
should have been, hurling through the air at incredible
speeds, going straight for the shooters.

One of the snipers flung up his arm to deflect a thick
board coming at his head. A shot rang out, and he rolled
across the roof to the very edge, where he hung half on and
half off, upside down. The third shooter crawled toward the
back of the roof away from the street side. Jackson was up
and running toward the alley between the buildings.

Master swore and pried Ambrie's hands from his shoulders. "You cover this boy, Ambrielle. Don't let him squirm
out from under you, no matter what he does. No matter what
kind of fit he throws."

She caught at his vest, trying to hold him to her. "Don't
go. Where are you going?"

"Jackson has no backup. Jonas went around the other side
of the building. He's got Maestro with him."

"You don't have a gun."

"Can't carry. I'm a felon." He'd already extracted himself
from her clinging hands and forced her arms around the boy.

It didn't matter that Master was a big man, he was light
on his feet, up and running in a crouch after the deputy,
sprinting fast to catch up with him before he emerged between the buildings and out into the open.

"Coming behind you, Jackson," he warned.

"Damn it, Master. Leave this to the cops," Jackson
snapped, looking over his shoulder, his eyes narrowed.

"Jonas went around the other side. No one has your back.
I'm not engaging unless I have to, Deveau, so shut the fuck
up. You think I want to save your ass?"

"You can't have a gun."

"I don't have a gun. I have a pocketknife."

Jackson laughed as they ran out from between the shops
into the open area. The wind hit their bodies hard, tearing

at their clothes as they made it halfway across the street. Bullets sprayed across the asphalt right in front of Jackson's boots, and Master knocked him sideways out of the line of fire.

The two men went down in a tangle of arms and legs, but both rolled onto their bellies, Jackson's gun extended toward the shooters, firing steadily. Master landed half over the top of the deputy, partially covering his body.

"What the fuck are you doing?" the deputy demanded.

"Taking a nap, what do you think I'm doing?"

"If I knew that, I wouldn't have asked." Jackson hadn't taken his gaze from the upper-story window of the small studio apartment where the shooter had taken refuge.

"Your wife is paying me big bucks to guard your ass," he said drolly. "You ever heard of a personal protector?"

Jackson laughed again. "I can see that pocketknife of yours is going to come in really handy."

"I'm damn good with it." He was. He'd killed several men with knives much smaller. "The shooter's hanging back in that room, about five feet from the window. Can you take the shot?" Master asked.

"Can you actually see him?" There was worry in Jackson's voice. "A kid lives in that studio. Donny Ruttermyer. Doesn't look good for him if there's a sniper in the kid's home."

"Savage sponsored Donny to a cooking camp for kids with special needs. Seychelle and Savage took him there last week," Master assured Jackson. "If you can make the shot, you're clear."

Jackson steadied his hand on his wrist and squeezed the trigger without any further hesitation. Correcting his angle by a hair, he did so a second time instantaneously, so the sound blended into an easy one-two reverberation.

"He's down, and he's not going to get back up," Master said, sliding easily off Jackson to allow him up.

"You're a little insane, Master."

"You're not the first person to tell me that."

Master sat up slowly, cautiously, his body still shielding the deputy from the building. There were several shooters. Jackson had killed one of them. Where were the others? The wind shrieked and moaned. The sound of a gun being fired twice in the distance told him someone was shooting at Jonas and Maestro.

He hurt like hell. Everywhere. Not just down his throat, in his stomach, but everywhere. Every muscle. His bones. His skin hurt. He was bleeding in a couple of places, but he wasn't about to check them out in front of Jackson. The man would start asking questions he didn't want to answer.

He just wanted to go home and crawl into bed. That was after he had a long talk with his new wife and laid down the law. Damn her anyway. What the hell did she think she was doing, leaping onto his back in the middle of a gunfight? He didn't understand women, and he never would. It was one thing for him to protect the kid and Jackson, but for Ambrielle to use her little body to try to cover him was sheer lunacy. He swore under his breath. He'd nearly had a heart attack when she'd attached herself to his back like a second skin.

Jackson rested a hand on his shoulder for a brief second, then it was gone. "Thanks, man, for taking me down when you did." Then he was up and sprinting toward the alley again.

Master could read people easily; he'd grown up having to do so in order to survive. He'd known the moment Jackson lifted his head and took a cautious look around that he would be on the move quickly. He matched him step for step.

Jackson didn't bother to snarl at him for inserting his body between the deputy and the buildings. Master was used to protecting Czar and the others. That was his purpose—taking care of the others.

"You must drive that woman of yours out of her mind," Jackson observed when they managed to reach the alley without incident.

They paused just inside, both leaning against the wall of Donna's Gift Shop.

"I think I do," Master conceded. He didn't mean to. He didn't know the first damn thing about relationships. He did know how to keep people alive. One way was to keep them from leaping onto his back during a gun battle. "My little fairy princess turns into a fiery little hellcat sometimes. Restraining her is a full-time job."

Jackson again looked at him over his shoulder, his eyes piercing, seeing too much. "You love that woman."

"Shut the fuck up."

"No, you really do. Your marriage to her is the real deal. I thought maybe you two got together in order to find whoever murdered her parents, but it's clear she's the real thing for you. I should have seen that right away. I was too busy trying to get Savage back with our pranking feud. She's beautiful, Master. Ambrielle is really beautiful, and she's gone on you. She didn't hesitate to protect you when the shooting started."

"I'll be having a few words with her about that." Master knew he sounded grim, but he couldn't help it. He felt grim. "She could have been killed. She's a financial advisor. She doesn't know the first thing about some asshole deciding to shoot up people going about their everyday lives just for the hell of it."

"No, but she's learning fast. She just lost her parents. She doesn't want to lose you too, Master," Jackson warned.

Master didn't need to be reminded. He looked up at the body hanging from the roof. One arm dangled down just past the head. The wind had died down enough that only a few leaves were swirling around the dead man's chest and face. Master paid attention to his hand and the tattoo on his index finger—the one with the snake coiled around it. He was careful not to look too closely at it. The man had tattoos concealing the tops of his knuckles, fingers and hand and a heavy sleeve that nearly covered every inch of skin.

"You ever see him before?" Jackson asked.

Master hadn't. He shook his head. "No, but he's Russian. We attended a school there, as I'm sure you're aware. He wasn't part of it, but there were other schools. I've heard a rumor that there're some graduates who banded together to form a business. He might be part of that."

He looked closer to see if there was a gold ghost worn on him anywhere. The man wasn't wearing a suit, so there weren't any cuff links, and he didn't see a gold ghost pin on him. The snake tattoo told him this man had been part of Helena's, or whatever she was calling herself, hit team. Jackson had killed three of them. If they were lucky, Jonas had killed one or more. Helena was going to run out of assassins if she wasn't careful.

"Do you have any idea who these men were shooting at?" Jackson asked, easily climbing up the side of the building to the roof.

"How the hell would I know that?" Master demanded. "I just had a procedure done on my throat. I'm tired, hurting and want to go home and go to bed. If you think you can manage to stay alive all by yourself, that's where I'm headed."

"You need to stick around and give your statement."

"I need to go to bed before I fall on my face. You know where to find me. Ink has to drive me home. I was put under so I can't drive. My statement is I don't know a fucking thing, Jackson. I walked my wife out of the tea shop and someone started shooting at you. Or Jonas. Or just at everyone. Hell if I know who they were shooting at." He stopped as if just having the thought. "You don't think they were shooting at Hannah, do you? She was standing right in the doorway of her shop. Jonas will lose his mind. My head hurts so fucking bad I can't think straight."

He ran all his words together so Jackson would have a difficult time separating truth from lies. If he was very lucky, the deputy would give him a pass, thinking the anesthesia had scrambled his brain. He'd already turned away, striding back toward the Floating Hat.

Master could see Torpedo Ink members surrounding Czar and Blythe as they came out from under a truck. Blythe looked as if she was crying. That got to Master. She tried to break away from Czar, but he held her firmly, bending his head to hers and saying something she clearly didn't agree with. She shook her head several times, but Czar was insistent.

As Master neared them, he could hear Czar's low tone, the one that was a warning to anyone listening. He rarely used it with Blythe.

"He has to learn, Blythe. He could have been killed. He put your life in jeopardy along with his. He put Master's life in jeopardy and then Ambrie's. He's old enough to learn the rules, just like the rest of the children had to learn them. You're too soft and you know it. You have to let me handle this."

"He's just coming out of his shell and learning to trust us," Blythe pleaded.

Czar put his hands on her shoulders and gently moved her behind him. "Do as I say, baby." As gentle as he was, Czar meant business, and there was no getting around him.

Reaper put his hand on Blythe's shoulder as Czar approached Jimmy and Ambrielle. Jimmy was squirming, wriggling and even outright trying to twist his wrist free of Ambrie's grip. She held him in front of her, refusing to allow him freedom.

"You better let me go or I'm going to kick you again, only harder," Jimmy threatened.

"Stay still until your father gets here," Ambrielle said.

A flash of unexpected anger erupted in Master. It shocked him that he could feel wrath at a boy that young, but the little shit had kicked Ambrielle, and all she'd done was protect him.

Jimmy turned his head toward her arm and opened his mouth to put his teeth on her arm.

"You bite her, kid, and you won't have any teeth left to

eat with," Master proclaimed, not caring what Czar might say or think.

Jimmy froze at the threat. Ambrielle looked up at him, her eyes lighting up, but she remained silent, focusing on keeping Jimmy corralled. The boy wasn't intimidated for long. He wanted his freedom and was intent on getting it. He tried to yank himself free and once more pulled his foot back in a threatening manner.

This time it was the sight of Czar approaching, grim faced, eyes flashing silver, that stopped the boy from fighting.

"Did you just kick the woman who kept you from getting shot, Jimmy?" Czar asked, his voice lower than ever.

Master came up behind Ambrielle and circled her waist with one arm, drawing her back against his solid form.

"She wouldn't let me go," Jimmy said.

"She wasn't supposed to let you go. She's an adult, and in a situation where there's an active shooter, someone threatening your life or the lives of your family, what do you do?"

Jimmy hung his head.

"I asked you a question, and I expect an answer. Someone was shooting at us, and you were supposed to stay with your mother, but you didn't. What do you do in the situation you found yourself in?"

Jimmy continued to hang his head. He remained silent. Master knew how to use silence. He'd been doing it all his life. He also knew from experience that Czar would never let Jimmy get away with it, not when survival was at stake.

"We can stand on this street all day and all night if that's what you want to do, Jimmy, but you will answer me. I'll send your mother home with Reaper. I need to know that you have the skills to survive in any situation, and that means you answer every question I ask you. Do you understand me?"

Jimmy barely nodded his head.

"Then look at me, son."

Master thought adding "son" was a stroke of genius because Czar didn't change his tone. It was demanding and warning at the same time. Somehow "son" softened that lethal warning.

Jimmy tilted his head slightly. "I wanted to get my drinks from Hannah."

Czar was silent for a moment as if contemplating the explanation. Master thought it more than likely he was counting to ten to keep from exploding. The kid had placed his life in jeopardy for some drinks he could have gotten at any time. He just didn't know he could have those drinks anytime. He was young and still learning.

"Jimmy," Czar said softly, using the same voice. "Would it matter to you if you had the drinks and Mommy was dead?"

Blythe gasped and shook her head, a fresh flood of tears tracking down her face. Reaper squeezed her shoulder. Master wasn't certain if he was trying to comfort her or stop her from running to her son. Czar flicked her one glance, and she covered the lower half of her face with her palm and stayed very still.

"Are those drinks more important to you than your mother?"

Jimmy shook his head adamantly and for the first time looked up, not at Czar but at Blythe. "No. Mommy, no."

Blythe pressed her hand harder over her mouth. Ambrielle turned her face into Master's chest. As upset with her as he was, he couldn't help bringing his palm up to cup the back of her head.

"What about Master? He deliberately risked his life to save you. You would have been shot, Jimmy, but Master wrapped his arms around you and put his body between yours and the gunmen. Instead of you getting your head blown off, he took a bullet, didn't you, Master?"

Ambrielle gave a low cry of alarm and jerked out of his arms, stepping back to look up at his face. "Where?" she demanded. "Tell me now. We have to get you to the doctor."

"We're not making a big deal out of it," Master snapped, unable to keep the annoyance out of his voice. He glared at Czar. "The last thing I want is for Jonas or Jackson to force me to stick around and see a medic. Steele can drop by the house. In case no one noticed, Ambrielle's bleeding as well. We're leaving now, Czar. And, kid, you're damn lucky I didn't see you kick my wife the first time you did it. I'm not nice like your father."

Master caught Ambrielle's hand and signaled Ink that he needed to leave right that second. He wasn't feeling nice. Ambrie started to protest, and he tightened his hold on her.

"It would be best if you kept quiet this one time, princess. I'm in a damn foul mood, and you just ran out the cuteness factor to get you out of trouble."

She could barely keep pace with him as he stalked with long strides to the truck. He didn't slow down as he normally would, not even when Czar and Blythe called after him. He knew they were going to thank him for saving the kid. Right that moment, he didn't feel he'd done the world—or them— that big a favor. He might even say so if he stuck around.

Shit. The kid risked his life to run back for the drinks Hannah made for him. Okay. He could accept that. He could accept the fact that he got kissed by a bullet meant for the kid. But Ambrie jumped onto his back and clung like a fucking monkey. She was bleeding on her leg and on her arm. The kid had the gall to kick her. He was going to bite and kick her again. Czar needed to box the brat's ears. He hadn't held back down in the dungeon when he thought one of them had gotten out of line, that was for sure.

Master yanked open the door to the truck's back seat, turned, caught his fairy princess around her waist and all but tossed her inside. "Put your seat belt on."

He saw that stubborn little chin of hers go up. Before she could say anything, he slammed the door closed and yanked open the door to the front passenger side. He had planned to sit in the back with her, where he could examine her body to see how bad any wounds were, but he knew he was too angry. It would be better to wait until they were home alone together. He didn't need Ink thinking he was going to strangle his wife.

Ink had the truck moving down the highway before Ambrielle dared to speak. "Master, I know you're upset with me—"

"You think?" He cut her off. "Let it go until we get home."

"Will you at least tell me how bad it is?"

He wasn't going to tell her anything, not with Ink there. Not when he was so angry, and he didn't know how to express himself. He didn't do arguments. That wasn't how it worked in prisons. Arguing got you nowhere. You laid down the law. You did it in a soft voice, so the guards didn't hear you. So other inmates didn't overhear. No one else was privy to your business, because if you had to defend your honor or your life, you wanted to make certain no one ever suspected you unless you were proving a point. That point would be: *Don't fuck with me.*

Master reached over to flip through some channels until he was satisfied, choosing one, flooding the interior with music. He put his head back and closed his eyes, letting the sounds of the various instruments soothe him. *Bog*, but he hurt like hell. It had been a long time since he'd felt that every muscle in his body was in pain.

Prison sucked, but he knew the rules. He understood the mindset. He knew the kinds of people on every level. The ones who came and went. The lifers. The guards. The games that were played. He'd been in that world from the time he was a kid. He knew how to barter. He could pick out gang members with one quick assessing look and instantly identify those in positions of power. It was his world, and once he was there, it was nearly impossible for anyone to maneuver him into a position he didn't want to be in. He was the master, the most skilled at moving around in any of the prison systems.

"Home, Master," Ink said. "You need me to help you into the house?"

Master jerked awake. "I'm good." He said it out of habit. He was used to being alone. Used to taking care of his own wounds. He looked out the window of the truck. He was back in his sanctuary, the woods, surrounded by trees. The forest made him feel as if he could escape into it whenever he needed to breathe. There were plenty of trails leading away from his home, and he knew every one of them. He would never be trapped here.

He shoved open the door. "Thanks for the ride, Ink. I appreciate it."

"I'll park the truck in the garage and take my bike home," Ink said. "Text Steele if either of you need him."

Master turned to help Ambrielle out of the truck. She looked tired as well, even though it was still midafternoon. He indicated she precede him to the door. He rarely used the front entrance. It was a huge glass door with a screen. The great room was beamed construction with a massive two-story real fieldstone fireplace. The open loft upstairs served as his music room, but he had a couple of futons up there just in case Keys or Maestro stayed over after working on songs.

One of the selling points of the house had been the unique open-concept master bedroom and bathroom, a claw-foot tub and curbless shower with solid granite walls. The panoramic views of the woods and access to a private patio overlooking the pool, yard and forest as well as the hot tub all made the property even more desirable.

"Go on through to the bedroom and strip. I want to see where those bullets kissed you." He sounded as gruff as he felt.

She tilted her chin at him. "You know my wounds are superficial, Master. I don't know if yours is. Why don't you let me take care of yours first? You should be in bed after that procedure anyway."

"You like what you're wearing? You remove your clothes or I do. It isn't as if you have a lot of things to wear, Ambrie." It was a warning. Clear and simple.

She stood looking at him for a long moment and then she sighed and began to unbutton the little tiny pearls down the front of her shirt. "I can see you're still very angry with me."

He didn't bother to address the obvious. Instead, he crouched down in front of the double sink to find the emergency medical kit he kept on hand. By the time he walked back into the bedroom, she was sitting on the bed in her bra and panties. He paused in the open doorway to drink her in, to savor the fact that she was his. He didn't know what to do with her, but he liked the fact that he had her.

There was a stain of blood on her shoulder, up high, close to her neck. He really didn't like that and cleaned it with an alcohol wipe, knowing it burned like hell. She didn't so much as flinch but kept her gaze steady on his. When he cleaned the second wound, the one that had taken a chunk of her skin from her thigh, she gasped and her eyes watered, but she refused to cry. She blinked rapidly in order to keep from shedding tears.

"You could have been killed, Ambrie," Master said in a low voice. "You fucking could have died pulling that stunt."

Her small white teeth worried at the corner of her bottom lip, scraping back and forth. "You could have been killed, Master. You're a much larger target than I am, or than Jimmy. You deliberately stood there instead of getting under cover. Why? Why did you do that?"

"Czar didn't have Blythe under the truck yet. The shooters would concentrate their fire on me instead of trying for them." He kept his tone flat. Matter-of-fact. He knew she wasn't going to like his answer, but it was the truth.

He'd lied to Jackson. Those men had been there to kill Czar's family. Blythe and Jimmy had been the targets. Czar maybe. He doubted it. The Russian woman wanted Czar to suffer. She wanted him to see his family dead before he died. That was the entire point of sending her assassins. She was losing her men though. Too many of them. She couldn't afford to lose too many more. The bad news was, she knew where Czar lived. She knew where his family was. That changed things in a big way.

Ambrielle shook her head and jerked away from him. She had her back to him because he was trying to spread antibiotic cream over the wound where the flesh was gone. He caught her arm.

"Stay still."

"No. I want to leave. I'm leaving." She sounded on the verge of tears. Or she was already crying. Or fighting mad. He couldn't tell because she wasn't looking at him. Again, she tried jerking away from him.

"Damn it, Ambrielle, stay still. You aren't going anywhere. Let me put this cream on you and we can talk about it."

"There isn't anything more to say, is there, Master? You're willing to throw your life away for all of them, but you aren't willing to live for me." She dashed at tears on her face, but she didn't move, and she didn't turn around.

He'd been furious with her. Now he didn't know what to feel. There was a mixture of hurt and anger in her trembling voice, and he really didn't know what to do with that. He slowly applied the cream, buying himself a little time. The moment his stroking fingers had applied a gauze bandage over the wound, she threw herself across the bed and rolled to the other side. Immediately, she stalked to the closet and yanked out a pair of leggings from the drawer where he'd put them when Ink had brought a small suitcase filled with clothes.

"I wasn't throwing my life away."

"I'm not talking about it with you. You lied to me. You promised me you wouldn't lie to me, and you did." She pulled a long sweater from the shelf and jerked it over her head. "I'm going for a walk." She sat on the floor and yanked on her boots.

Her dark hair fairly crackled with anger, and yet he felt the weight of her tears. The pressure in his chest increased.

"Princess, you aren't making any sense. How did I lie to you?" He eased his arm out of his vest. Using care, he folded his colors and set them aside. "Ambrielle, answer me."

She looked up from where she was still sitting on the floor and then pressed her forehead into her palm. "You took an oath when you married me. You're supposed to protect me. You're supposed to put me first. Not Czar or Blythe. Not your club. You didn't give me a thought when you were so willing to die right then."

"I think of you every minute of the day since I laid eyes on you. I think of you when I take a breath. Don't tell me I don't think of you, princess, because you don't know shit if that's what you think. What you don't know is how the club works or the rules we live by. The rules, by the way, you agreed to when you married me."

Her head snapped up and she looked up at him for the first time, a little frown making her look more lost than ever. He had an insane desire to kiss her until that frown was gone. Instead, he began to take off his shirt.

"The rules of the club? Of Torpedo Ink? I agreed to rules?"

Those long lashes of hers fanned down, blinking. Making his heart ache. *Bog.* She was beautiful beyond belief. Inside, where it counted. She shook her head. "I don't remember that, Master." Her hands came up to rub her temples. "I know I get confused. After what happened with my parents, and I still can't force myself to really look at that head-on yet, I have entire blocks of time gone. Entire conversations. I may have agreed to rules and then forgotten them."

That was his woman. Honest to a fault. "Yeah, babe, when you married me, you became part of Torpedo Ink. Czar is president. Blythe is his wife. We're sworn to protect the president at any cost, including our lives. We protect one another after that. Does he like it? No, he does not. But that isn't up to him. You don't have to like it either, but you do have to abide by the rules, just like the rest of us."

She looked up at him with stricken eyes. "You don't even hesitate, Master. You just throw yourself right in front of God knows how many guns shooting. You terrify me. You sat out on the patio of the restaurant like a sacrificial lamb, surrounded by men who intended to kill you. You didn't even flinch."

"I flinched when you left the safety of the others and came outside, where it was going to be much harder to protect you. I wasn't worried about those men surrounding me. I knew I could kill them. I'd already worked out exactly how it was going to go down. Lana was my backup. Then you came out and I had to make sure Lana protected you, not me."

"You tapped on your chest. In code. That was what you were doing, telling her to look out for me. I was there to protect you."

"You were in that restaurant to learn. You're supposed to be keeping your eyes open and watching how everyone positions themselves. How they interact. What they say. You keep your mouth shut and pick up how we weave our nets and collect our prey. I made a hell of a mistake today because I was tired and pissed as hell at you, maybe still under the influence of the anesthesia they put me under. You never want to lie to Jackson Deveau. He's a human lie detector. When you talk to him, you word everything carefully so there isn't a lie for him to hear. There at the end, he asked me if I knew who the shooters were after. I told him I didn't know a fucking thing. I went so far as to ask if they could have been after Hannah. But I stated I didn't know who the shooters were after. He let me walk, but he'll give that some thought and he'll be coming around—and soon."

He sat on the edge of the bed and bent to take off his motorcycle boots. He'd had them a long time, and they were worn, but comfortable. Right now, he felt the solid weight of them, but it was too damn much trouble to get them off. Bending wasn't his favorite move.

Ambrielle got up and came to kneel at his feet. "Let me, Kir, you lie back. I'll do this and help you get your jeans off. That's why you were so angry about me jumping on your back to protect you. You wanted me to see what all of you were doing."

He groaned and threw one arm over his eyes as he carefully stretched his body across the bed from his knees up. With his free hand, he unbuckled his belt and unzipped his jeans. "At that point I wasn't thinking about you learning how to blend in with the club, Ambrielle, I was thinking about losing you. So no, I didn't want you to see what anyone was doing. I wanted you to get your ass under the truck where you'd be safe. You nearly gave me a heart attack. I almost spun around, which would have put the kid in harm's way. As it was, I half turned, shoving him toward the truck as I took us down."

There was real pain in his voice he couldn't conceal. The thought of losing her when he'd just had her for such a short period of time had been paralyzing.

"Why do you get to protect me and everyone else, but no one gets to protect you?"

That damn voice of hers was back to trembling. She had his boots off and was working his jeans off his ass, so he had to lift up to make it easier for her to slide them over his hips and down his legs.

"That's the way it is, Ambrielle. You have to accept that in me just the way you have to accept the rules of the club. It's who I am. If you can't accept who I am, you married the wrong fucking man. And you can never, under any circumstances, ever pull a stunt like that again. I have to have your word of honor."

"Master . . ."

"I mean it, Ambrielle. You knew there was going to come a time when you saw who I was, who you really married. Well, babe, you're looking at him. If you can't live with me as I really am, you'd better know now. I protect you. You don't leap on my back and fucking take a hundred years off my life. I know what the hell I'm doing. I have a plan. You do what I say. When you're good at this shit, we'll discuss what you're going to be doing ahead of time. What you'll never be doing is leaping in front of guns. Do you get me?"

He didn't look at her. Either she got it or she didn't.

"Yes."

"Then give me your fucking word, and I expect you to keep it."

"I give you my word, I won't do that again."

She didn't hesitate, and that was a good sign. It meant she got him, and she could live with him.

"Don't screw up again. When I tell you to do something, you do it. I won't be able to take you with me if you mess up, promises or not, Ambrielle. You do what I say. You can't be a loose cannon when we're working. Understand?"

"Yes."

"Good. I'm going to sleep."

"I'm calling that doctor of yours. You're bleeding."

"I don't give a fuck." And he didn't. He was too damn tired to protest.

SIXTEEN

Leonard Stoddard, Reese Fender's parole officer, lived in a modest three-bedroom house at the end of a quiet cul-de-sac in a family-friendly neighborhood. His car wasn't in the least flashy, and most of his furniture came from IKEA. Master studied the large picture window off the front porch. He could look right through the glass into the living room, straight to the stone fireplace.

"If he's taking money, he's not spending it on his home," he observed.

"If he was married," Ambrie said, "she's been gone awhile or she's a slob. The laundry is piled up on the sofa and another chair. He's got dirty dishes sitting on the coffee table in front of the television screen. There's a pizza box on the floor."

Master pulled his gaze from the house he was watching to the woman lying on her belly beside him on the rooftop of the home directly across the street from Stoddard's. She wore black leggings, a tight-fitting tank under an equally tight-fitting jacket, thin black gloves and soft-soled dark boots. Her hair was woven into a braid. Just looking at her put a lump in his throat—not a good thing when his throat still felt raw and swollen.

He'd slept all day, all night and most of the next two days while she looked after him, doing everything Steele had told her to do.

"Probably had a good woman like you looking after him," he said gruffly. "Probably meant the world to him and she walked out when she realized he wasn't all that easy to live with."

She turned her head, her eyes deepening to an almost indigo blue. "I heard what you said yesterday, Master. All of it. You laid out the rules for me and I understand them. I'm willing to follow them in order to be with you. I don't think you're asking too much."

"You understand you can't fuck up tonight. Torpedo Ink is all over this one. You're in a training program, princess, and you have to be able to follow orders. Czar runs a crew and Steele runs another one. Steele usually runs my crew. If you want to be a part of it, he has to know you're solid and he can count on you—that every single member can count on you to be where you're supposed to be. You can't be a wild card, Ambrielle."

She looked him straight in the eye. "I absolutely understand. I asked you to teach me and you gave me your word. I know you don't like it but you're still doing it. I swore to you I wouldn't throw my body between yours and bullets again, and I meant it. I also meant it when I said I'd listen and learn. I don't make the same mistake over and over."

He nodded, those knots in his gut tightening even more. She had married him for a reason. She was learning the ropes, and he knew Code was getting closer to tracking down Walker Thompson. The man couldn't hide forever. As soon as they knew where he was hiding, they would devise a plan to rid the world of him.

Master didn't want Ambrielle to go with them when they killed Thompson because it might not be as clean a kill as he would want it to be in front of her. They needed information to find the others hiring the Ghost assassins to murder innocents. He'd promised her, and he was a man who kept his promises.

He'd never had anyone looking after him before. She'd stuck it out all day. Both days. Insisting he drink Hannah's soother. Changing the dressing on his wound the way Steele had shown her. Sitting on the edge of his bed, talking softly to him and pushing back his hair as if he meant something to her when he woke up restless. She hadn't flinched when he had a nightmare and he'd awakened, tangled in the sweat-soaked sheets, half-crazed, fighting, thankful he didn't have a weapon when he realized he had her hair bunched in his fist and she lay passive under him, looking up at him and murmuring soothingly.

Ambrielle had simply changed the sheets again while he took a shower. Then she changed the dressing on his wound a second time before getting him the soother and soup Alena had sent over. She fed it to him a spoonful at a time, then told him to go back to sleep. A man could get used to that kind of care.

When he woke this evening, the house didn't smell stale and airless. Ambrielle had managed to bring the fragrance of the outdoors inside. His house smelled of fresh pine and juniper. Cedar. The woods. More, it smelled of *her*. Ambrielle Vasiliev, his beautiful princess of a wife. She had transformed his sanctuary into a home almost overnight. He wasn't ever going to go back to living without her.

"You're frowning, Master." Very gently, with the pads of her fingers, she smoothed over his lower lip. "What's wrong?"

Her touch shook him, but he kept that to himself. "He had a wife once. Why did she leave him? Is he corrupt? Did he make a deal with the devil and get in over his head?"

"If he did, he sure isn't spending the money at home. Maybe he has another woman and that's why his wife left." She tipped her head up to look at him. "I wouldn't just leave. I'd make sure the other woman knew you were mine and she shouldn't have poached. You'd go to sleep and wake up minus one ball."

He choked. His cock twitched. His balls drew up, tried to hide. He was a big man, and it wasn't like he could put that junk just anywhere. She wasn't kidding, as sweet as she sounded. She raised an eyebrow and reached down to stroke between his legs.

"Don't worry, honey, I'd be humane about it." This time she gave him her sassy little grin. He could swear he saw her teeth gleaming.

"You mean that shit." He made it a statement. Looking down into her eyes was a mistake. Even knowing she'd cut off his balls, he wanted her.

"You bet your life on it, honey. You cheat on me after all this, I'm going to do something permanent to your ass. Since your entire body is a statement to the torture you've already gone through, I had to think of something really diabolical and nasty that you'd remember me by." She gave him another sweet smile.

He couldn't stop himself. He was on the job. Working, damn it. Still, he curved his palm around the nape of her neck and dragged her in close to him, his gaze moving hungrily, possessively, over her face. That little haughty princess face that told him she was far too good for him.

She gave him the smile she reserved just for him. "What is it, honey?"

He leaned over and brushed a kiss on top of her silky head because if he kissed her the way he wanted to kiss her, he wouldn't stop and they'd be going at it right there on that rooftop instead of watching the house like they should be.

"It's nice not to feel alone. Thank you for giving that to me." He should have felt like a fucking idiot for saying that to her, but they'd promised each other the truth, and there it was.

Her incredible blue eyes darkened to violet and moved over his face, taking in every inch as if committing him to memory. Her dimple appeared, sexy as hell, making him hard as a rock on a stakeout, for fuck's sake—when she'd just threatened to cut off his balls. Who wouldn't love a woman like that?

"I intend to give you the world, Kir, if you'll let me."

He could only hear truth in her voice. See it on her face. "I've done nothing to deserve you. A few nights ago, I killed several men, and then I sat down to dinner like nothing happened. You know that, right? I did that. You know what I thought about while I was in the restaurant? It wasn't the men I'd killed. I put them out of my mind. I thought about you and all the ways I wanted to fuck you. I thought about picking you up and carrying you out to the truck and throwing you on the back seat. Just looking at you makes me crazy."

"That's good."

"No, princess, that's bad."

"I'd be open to back-seat sex in the truck."

"Don't encourage bad behavior. I'm trying to clean up my act just a little for you."

Her smile vanished. "Don't you dare. Well . . . you can clean up your astonishingly shocking dirty mouth, if you have to clean up anything, but not during sex. I rather like it then, especially when you're coming and all you can do is shout the F-word at the top of your lungs in that raspy, sexy way you have. I really like that, so keep that."

He could only stare at her for a moment, and then he found himself laughing. Really laughing. *Bog.* His woman. She was going to be the death of him. She brought more than a feeling of companionship to him. She brought the joy of living. The feeling of being alive.

He was very aware of the night breeze on his face, just touching his skin. The sound of a dog howling and another answering with a short warning bark. Something small rustled in the garbage can. Over his head was the night sky, stars visible, doing their best to peek through the heavy purplish clouds that streaked through the dark sky. It was a beautiful night.

"If you're going in, Master, you'd better get to it," Ink's voice said, using the small radio to caution him. "I've got a feeling."

Everyone participating in the mission was using an inserted earpiece that was nearly impossible to see if someone came across them. Mechanic was a genius when it came to making new gear for them.

Master had that same urgent feeling growing as well. Still, he hesitated taking Ambrielle with him. He'd promised her, but seeing things go south wasn't the same as discussing it. She'd blown it twice now when she thought he was in trouble. And more than that, if he had to kill Stoddard or get information out of him fast, it wouldn't be pretty.

"This is your last chance, Ambrielle. You can stay back, keep eyes on us from here. You have to be absolutely certain you can stomach anything that happens in there. I might have to kill him. Worse, I may have to question him in a way you won't like. I tell you to walk out of the room, you do it. Understand me? You do it, and you don't look or listen."

She swallowed visibly without taking her eyes off him, but she nodded. "I want to stay with you, Master. I can't explain it, but I *need* to be with you. I'll follow directions. You have my word."

"It's a go," Master reported to Steele. "Heading in."

"Car's coming up the frontage road slow," Ink reported, using the small radio to warn them. "I've got that feeling. You aren't going to have much time."

Ambrie looked up at him as she scooched backward toward the other side of the roof. "You called it. You said Stoddard was going to get a visit if Reese didn't make the call or meet with him."

Master remained expressionless as he stayed close to her, ensuring she didn't slip. She was enjoying the stakeout just a little too much. Just as she'd taken the deaths of so many of the men who had come to kill them. She was just a little too accepting, when she hadn't been born into the life. He'd known no other life. Death and killing were all he knew.

"I've been around these kinds of people since I was a kid. I know how they think. It wasn't all that difficult to know what the next move was going to be. They're not rocket scientists."

Ambrielle had grown up in a military family, and her parents had prepared her to defend herself, but she hadn't seen the kinds of violence that would enable her to be so accepting of what had happened to her in the last few weeks. He suspected she was so deeply traumatized that she was living in a reality she'd chosen for herself—one she had created in order to survive. He'd seen it in children where he'd grown up. They anchored themselves in a part of their mind so they could function, whereas others simply gave up.

Hell, he did it. When Master was in prison, he allowed that part of him that felt little or no emotion to take over. He could do whatever he had to in order to live in that world and get whatever information was necessary in order to get out as fast as possible. If he had to torture someone, he did so as efficiently as possible. If he had to kill them, he did so. He'd learned as a child to separate himself from what was happening and just do whatever was necessary to get through—get through and survive.

"What do we do? We haven't had a chance to talk to Stoddard. We don't know if he's part of this, or even why they're trying to control Reese." Ambrielle's gaze moved over his face, and then switched back to the house. "Do you think they're coming to kill him?"

So casual. Too casual, he noted. She wasn't Lana or Alena, raised from childhood in blood and death.

"I don't know, princess, but we aren't going to do him any good up here. Let's go. Wait for me to get on the ground and I'll help you down." More and more he considered that it was a mistake to bring her along, but he'd given his word. He didn't break code. It was all he had left. His word. His honor.

It was easy enough to slide off the roof and reach up and guide her legs down until he could catch her around the waist and simply lift her free. "Stay behind me and follow in my exact steps. It isn't only Stoddard you don't want to see you. Be aware of cameras, alarms, neighbors' cameras, the video doorbells on their front doors. Anything that will pick you up and identify you." He whispered the caution to her as he began to move toward the Stoddard property.

A thick hedge divided the properties between Stoddard and his closest neighbor on his right side, and a tall wooden fence provided privacy from the neighbor on his left. Both the hedge and the fence were set at angles, giving Stoddard a very large wedge-shaped piece of property.

At one time someone had taken great care of the yard. It had been landscaped, the bushes and flowers carefully planted and maintained. Now he could see weeds pushing their way up through the ground, and the plants hadn't been cut back in anticipation of the winter storms and chill. It was too bad. This was the kind of yard Reese would love to get his hands on. He'd be in his element working here. Stoddard had to know that. He'd seen enough of Reese's work and knew he had a good work ethic.

Shit, Stoddard must really be on someone's payroll not to have given the job to Reese. As they approached the side door, Master glanced back at Ambrie. She wore a very serious expression on her face. She was following in his exact footsteps, concentrating on making certain she was stepping in his prints. When he stopped, she did as well, her gaze lifting to his eyes. He turned fully around to face her, his heart beating overtime. It was strange to him that it was such a short time he'd been with her. It felt a lifetime, as though she was already a part of him. Somehow her soul had slipped into that empty place inside him where his had been torn out. She'd filled that space to make him complete.

He framed that little beloved face, such perfection, his thumbs sliding over her cheekbones, knowing he was stealing from another realm and he'd have to pay for it sometime, most likely in some horrific way. He'd learned there was always a price, but she was worth kingdoms. Worth anything.

He bent his head and pressed his forehead against hers, murmuring to her softly.

"If I never get the chance to say this again, Ambrielle, I fell hard for you. From the moment you pushed that knife into me and it broke, all the while looking me straight in the eye. I could see right into you, and I fell hard. I know why you're with me, and it's okay with me. That's who I am, and I've accepted what I was shaped into a long time ago. Looking at you, if that's what it took in order to have the privilege of serving you, then it was worth everything I went through in order to be this man, even if you're mine only for a short time. I just wanted you to know."

Before she could reply, protest, say anything at all, he kissed her. Her lips were soft and pliant. Opening for him to give him that cleansing fire that swept him away to paradise. He let the flames burn through him until he couldn't think, just feel. Until her body was imprinted on his and she somehow had wound her way inside him, branding his bones and organs with her name, with who she was, so there was never going to be room for anyone else. Just her. Just his fairy princess. Ambrielle.

Abruptly, he lifted his head and dropped his hands from her, stepping back. "Do what I tell you." His voice was gruff. All business now.

He didn't wait to see her nod. He made short work of the alarm system and even shorter work of the lock. Stoddard should have had a dog. His security sucked. If he was going to be in the business of shaking down his clients, he needed to know how to survive. He wasn't very good at it.

Easing the door open to ensure there was no secondary alarm or creaks that would give them away, Master went through first, entering sideways to present the smallest target. Shadows lengthened along the hall, but there was no movement that he could detect. His internal warning system told him there was no one waiting to take his head off. He moved down the hall toward the living room, the place he'd last spotted Stoddard.

The man sat in a recliner staring off into space. There was no smell of alcohol, nor did he have a glass in his hand. He just sat there, as if waiting for someone, yet he didn't look toward the front door. He just stared straight ahead. Master held up his fist to indicate to Ambrie to stay in the hall. He stepped into the living room but stayed out of sight of the windows, not an easy thing to do when the glass was so expansive.

"Came to talk to you, Stoddard. You might want to sit very still and not reach for anything like a phone or a gun. Either will get you a bullet in your head very fast."

Stoddard's gaze flicked to him. He didn't look particularly shocked to see him. "I've been expecting you. There's no need to drag this out. Just get it over. Shoot me. I didn't do what you told me to do, and I'm not going to. I know you're holding my wife, and you've said you're going to send her to me in pieces, but you've had her so long and the last three times I've asked for proof of life you've refused. I don't think she's alive. Reese has a wife and daughter. I'm not going to ruin his life on the chance of keeping her alive anymore."

Stoddard's speech was the last thing Master expected. The bit about someone holding his wife and threatening to cut her into pieces was far too close to what the Ghosts had their assassins for hire do to the women they kidnapped to bring the motorcycle clubs in line.

"Reese thought you were acting out of character, and he asked me to stop by and see if you were under duress. I would say having someone kidnap and threaten to cut your wife into pieces would qualify. What do these people want you to do?"

"He has to go back to prison. Reese. They want him back in prison."

"His family?" Master persisted, because that didn't make any sense. Why would they have waited so long? Things were beginning to click into place. The Russian assassins had taken Stoddard's wife. He didn't believe in coincidences.

Stoddard frowned. "Reese's family? I doubt it. Why would they? No, whoever is behind this is powerful and ugly. He made an enemy, and I have no idea who it is or why they want him back in jail. I figured he did something there, and once he's back in they intend to even the score."

Ink's voice was soft in Master's ear. "Car coming around the block and moving slow again. I think you're going to have company. Wrap it up."

"Did you see the men who took your wife? Were they Russian? Did they have tattoos?"

Stoddard nodded. "Yeah. A lot of tattoos. Weird ones on their fingers. Snakes."

"Reese knows or has seen Helena," Master said quietly into his mic. "Get him, his wife and his daughter to a safe house now. She wants him dead. This isn't his family after him. That's a red herring. This is Helena tying up loose ends. He's a loose end."

He beckoned to Stoddard. "You want to live and try to find your wife, you need to get away from that window now. They're coming for you."

He gestured toward the kitchen. He would need this man to be strong. Already, his brothers were sliding into the house, moving to cover him. They would have to allow one of the assassins to get away and hopefully lead them to Stoddard's wife. Code would have to stay close to him to jam all communication so there was no chance for him to call ahead or text and send word to kill her if she was still alive.

"Go into your bedroom and close the door. You can't see or hear anything, so you won't have to testify, but we need information if we're going to get your wife back."

"That doesn't seem fair that you're assuming all the risks."

"Go." Master poured command into his voice. He already knew the risks, and this wasn't the one he was concerned with. If Reese knew Helena, if he'd seen her in prison and the assassination crew was waiting for him there, that meant, no matter what, Master would have to go back. He knew one more time and he was done. Right now, he couldn't think about that. He had to face the men pulling into the driveway and getting out of the car.

"Ambrielle, at least two of these men will be coming through that door behind you. I want you to come to me and tuck in right behind me just the way you did when we made our way here. Give me plenty of room to maneuver. The idea isn't to fight. We're going to kill all but two. One will escape and the other will answer questions. You stay very still. Do you understand those orders?"

"Yes." Ambrie was already moving, a whisper of sound, her hand gliding over his ribs as she came up beside him and then went on past to do just as he said. She slid into the shadows behind him and went very still.

Master found himself proud of her as always. The military upbringing her parents had given her had prepared her for orders and stealth. She slipped into that mode when needed. The five-man team entered the house, using two at the front door, two at the back door and one at the side entrance.

As the two entered the living room via the front door, Master allowed them to move past him. He stepped up behind the last man, matching footfalls, not a whisper of sound, his knife in his fist. He wrapped his hand around the man's head, covering his mouth, at the same time slamming the blade into the base of the skull and lowering the body to the floor. Leaving his knife, he pulled a second one as he came up with blurring speed just as the first man pivoted. Master slapped his arm down, deflecting his weapon, and cut up with his blade, severing the arteries in both thighs, and continued up the body in a figure-eight pattern, cutting arteries and veins as he went until he slashed through the throat, dropping the body on the floor.

The two men were dead in seconds. Master stepped back,

took a breath, refusing to look at his woman. Instead, he wiped his blade clean, using the clothing on his first victim, and then removed the knife from his skull. That was never an easy retrieve. When he'd cleaned that blade, he signaled to Ambrie to follow him, again without looking at her.

The third man had entered via the door they had come through. He had a good view of the living room and would see his dead companions. He would try to talk to the two men coming in through the back, the ones who were already dead or captured. Maestro and Keys were in position with orders to kill one and take the other prisoner. The man in the hall wouldn't get a response. He would have to decide to go forward or retreat.

The man had his weapon drawn and took a step to bring him into the living room, but he paused, staring at the two dead men and the blood pooled around them. He backed stealthily into the hallway all the way to the door. Once there, he eased it open and was gone, sprinting for the vehicle, talking into his radio. Clearly, no one answered, because he yanked open the door and fired up the engine, backing out quickly. Master didn't pay him any more attention. He was Code and Preacher's problem. They would follow him and hope he led them to Stoddard's wife. It was Maestro, Keys and Master's job to question the remaining assassin for information.

"Ambrielle, now is the time you join Steele outside. You know where he is. I expect you to avoid all cameras. You can't make a sound or alert any of the neighborhood dogs. You wait with him."

His heart accelerated in spite of his efforts to keep absolutely calm and dispassionate. He didn't look at her. He didn't want the others to think he didn't trust her. He wanted them to believe he had absolute faith in her. There was no sound until she moved up behind him and the whisper of her fingers trailed over his ribs as she passed him to go down the hallway to exit the house. No protest and no hesitation. She kept her word to him. His woman. His princess. His hand went to his aching throat. He had the best of the best, and just like that, fate took her away from him. He was headed back to prison. There was no getting around it, and this time he wouldn't survive.

Maestro dragged the prisoner into the living room while Keys drew the blinds to ensure any neighbors couldn't see in. "You recognize this one?" Maestro asked as he shoved the man into a chair facing the two dead bodies lying on the floor.

"He looks a little worse for wear," Master observed, pacing in front of him, then circling around the chair. "But I've seen him. He was wearing orange. It was years ago. In a small private prison. We were in Crawley together." He continued the circle until he was standing in front of the man again. "I see you remember me. They called me Master for a reason, didn't they? She sent you. The devil woman. That snake on your finger tells me you work for her."

Master pulled off his thin gloves and showed his bare skin. His hands were big and scarred and covered in tattoos, but they were significant tattoos, ones gotten in prisons all over the world. None was of a snake. "I never allowed a woman—or a man for that matter—to own me. I don't dance to anyone's tune. Didn't you get enough of that shit in the schools we were in?"

He pulled his gloves back on and flexed his fingers and then looked up at Maestro and laughed. "Of course, he went to the school for pussies. We used to laugh at the way they thought they had it so rough."

"What the hell do you want?" the man demanded.

"Tell me your name. You were a little pissant in Crawley, and I didn't bother to learn your name, only your number."

"Karlin," he mumbled through his swelling lower lip. "What do you want? We left you alone. You can't possibly care about Stoddard or Fender. They have nothing to do with you."

"Give up the wife. Where is she?"

Karlin swore under his breath in his native language.

"You. You're the one. You and Viktor and all the rest of you. You've been going after the women and taking them back."

"Don't like anyone making war on helpless innocents. Had enough of that shit in the school. Took a vow, Karlin, and we don't break the code. You need to tell me or you're going to take a long time to die and it's going to fucking hurt like hell."

"I don't care if you take back the bitch. Garry got away and he'll kill her before you get to her anyway." There was a wealth of satisfaction in his voice. Bragging even.

Master's eyebrow shot up. "Really? You think we didn't know he was there? I could have cut his fucking throat a dozen times. We have men on him. No matter where he goes, he isn't long for this world, and he certainly isn't going to have the opportunity to kill Stoddard's wife. You don't look too happy, Karlin. If that information changes your mind and you want to hold out, I'll give the brothers the go-ahead to go to work on you."

"Fuck you, Master."

"You're not my type, Karlin."

"She's in an empty house in Fort Bragg. She's been there all along. No one ever checks those empty houses." He gave the address without so much as hesitating.

Master passed it on. "Tell me about Helena and Crawley Prison. How many she has working for her there. She wants Fender dead because he knows too much about her business. She talked too much, made mistakes." He poured contempt into his voice. "She likes to control men by sleeping with them, but sometimes she just can't control herself and she talks too much, isn't that right, Karlin, and then you have to clean up after her."

Karlin's back straightened and his shoulders went rigid. "She doesn't make mistakes. She always knows what she's doing. Fender is the pitiful one. Drinking too much. Making a mess out of his life. He had a chance to serve her, and he didn't see her greatness. Fuck him. He deserves to die, and he will. So will Viktor. You can't save him, Master, or his family. They're marked for death. His wife. Every child. He'll see them dead and then he'll die."

Master didn't react. Didn't change expression. He continued to stare down at Karlin with cold, flat eyes. "You think Helena is infallible and yet I was there at Crawley the same time as Fender. She tried to recruit him because of his fighting abilities. She was behind trying to get him to throw the fights. When it didn't work and he ended up in prison, she thought she had him. But I was there too, and she didn't even notice me. Did you, Karlin?"

Karlin took a breath and let it out. "Yeah. I saw you. In the yard. But you flew under the radar. The guards didn't single you out as a troublemaker. No one saw anything unless they got close and knew what to look for. Then Lance Picard was found dead in his locked cell. Strung up, his intestines wrapped around his throat. Someone had done a number on him. He was a pedophile and had raped a number of children, always bragging about it. There was no one caught on the security cameras. No prints. Nothing at all. A couple weeks later, you got out, and then two weeks after that, Fender went. Helena was furious. She had no idea how Fender got out. But it was you, wasn't it? Both Picard and Fender."

"She has a boss. She isn't the head of this. Someone runs her, Karlin, who is it?"

Karlin shook his head vigorously. "No, she hires out her services, brokering the teams for jobs, but no one runs her."

"You know that isn't true. She may be trying to break away from him, but he's all over her. Someone from her past. Someone from Russia. He won't let her go, no matter what he tells her. She's too valuable to him. She's the perfect front." Now Master sounded almost solicitous, as if he worried a little about Helena.

Karlin scowled. "He's a monster. He likes little kids. Boys and girls. He likes movies. He wants her to provide the people he knows with those things, and then he films them and blackmails them."

"And she does it for him," Master confirmed, trying not to let his stomach turn.

"She has no choice."

"Is he after Viktor? Did he send her after Viktor?"

Karlin drew back. "No. She found out about Viktor at one of the clubs she frequents and has been hunting him ever since. She thought he was dead and was horrified to find out he was still alive. The thing with Viktor is personal to her."

"Who is the man in Russia she works for?" His throat hurt like a son of a bitch. It felt raw and sore, like it was burning and swelling with every word he spoke. He was afraid if he kept it up he would start bleeding, but they needed this information.

"I have no idea. Helena keeps her own counsel."

"Who does she have at Crawley?" Master returned to the original question. Helena wasn't alone there. She wasn't the one running the prison, but she had too much freedom. She'd planted a team in another prison, so someone had shown her the ropes.

Karlin looked stubborn again, remembering he had taken an oath to protect his mistress and he was giving out too much information. The moment he hesitated, Maestro slammed a two-inch blade into his left thigh, up high near his groin. At the same time, from behind him, Keys covered his mouth with a gloved hand to muffle his scream.

Master just looked bored. "We can go at this all night, but it's really kind of useless. You know what's coming next. They've got the tools laid out. Blowtorches. Drills. You've done this a million times. When that doesn't work, they start slicing you to pieces. I know you've done that, because you seem to like to do it to women."

Karlin knew enough to deny that accusation adamantly. "No, it's a job. It's how he wants it done if we're hired. A signature. He suggested it. He called it 'a bit of home.' The Russian. He's the one who came up with that punishment. He likes it filmed and the film sent to him. Helena always handles that."

Master filed away both pieces of information. Helena might not know his real identity, but she had an address for Torpedo Ink's enemy. The "bit of home" was a familiar torture. All of them were forced to learn it. They'd practiced over and over until they'd perfected the technique.

"I want the name of the man at Crawley that helps Helena. It isn't the warden, so don't give me that crap, Karlin."

"You're going to kill me anyway."

"Yep. You're going to die. Difference is, I kill you fast and painless or you die slow and in agony. You can make that choice. This is the last time I'm asking the question."

"The warden sits in his office all day. He doesn't mingle with the prisoners or guards. He doesn't know shit about the prisoners. The chief deputy warden doesn't either. But the deputy warden, he hears every complaint, investigates, talks to the prisoners, talks to the guards. Makes the rounds. He knows everyone, doesn't he?"

Master had been half expecting the answer. No doubt Helena had seduced the warden to get access to the prison, but it was the deputy warden who held the power she was looking for. He had the information on the prisoners, and he would be able to house her assassins. Let them slip in and out when needed. He would handpick others for her.

"Anton Elin is the deputy warden."

Master raised his eyebrow. Elin was a common last name in Russia. The origins of the meaning were rooted in English, but there was a biblical origin as well—Helen. He remembered Anton Elin. He had never spoken with the man, but he'd seen him speaking to a few of the other prisoners. He'd talked to Reese on more than one occasion.

"The names of the assassination squad housed in Crawley."

Karlin swore in his native language. Master recognized the signs. He wasn't going to give much more information. This was about all he would get out of him.

"A five-man team. They rule the prison. Everyone's afraid of them, and they should be. Two brothers, Filip and

Mark Gusev, Nil Gorkey, Stas Krupin and Timothy Garin. They're always together in the yard."

When he'd been in Crawley, Master had seen the men. There were always the ones that everyone had to stay away from or in some way bow down to. Master hadn't been in Crawley to make trouble. He was there to bring justice to Lance Picard. He'd avoided the rulers of the prison, always staying a distance from them and keeping a low profile so he remained off their radar.

Master nodded to Karlin, but he really was giving Maestro the go-ahead to kill the man. There was nothing more to get out of him, and pushing him would only make him clam up. Master didn't want him to see it coming. He'd given them the information, and Master was a man of his word. He didn't want Karlin to see death coming or to feel it.

He went to the bedroom and opened the door to confront Stoddard. "Got word from the others. Your wife is alive, but she's in bad shape. She's being airlifted to the hospital in San Francisco. I'm texting you the details so you can get there fast. We'll clean up here. When they ask you questions, you don't know about us, understand? You talk about us, really bad things can happen to you."

Stoddard nodded. "I get it. Thanks for everything."

"She's in bad shape, and if she survives, she's going to need understanding, counseling and a lot of patience and care." He felt like an idiot standing in the doorway in his colors and motorcycle boots dictating to the man.

Stoddard nodded again, this time with tears in his eyes. "She's everything. I've got to get to her."

"Then go."

SEVENTEEN

Ambrielle rarely found anyone to be intimidating. She hadn't been raised that way. Her parents had brought her up to believe she was equal to anyone. She had plenty of self-confidence, and right at that moment, the only person who mattered to her was her husband. Still, for all that, as many times and in as many situations as she'd seen Czar, she'd never felt more power radiating off a person than she did from him right at that moment. His energy filled the room until it was a tangible thing, shimmering in the air and making the walls bulge with it.

"Breathe, princess." Master wrapped his arm protectively around her and drew her body closer to his. "There's no need to be nervous."

Did she look nervous? She was. She was about to take on the fight of her life, and she knew it. Master, as always, was going to sacrifice himself. She knew he was. She could feel it. She wondered how this powerful man commanding the room and everyone in it didn't realize that Master would never come back whole and sane if he did what Czar expected him to do. He would never be the same wonderful, amazing man that was her husband.

"I'm fascinated by him," she admitted softly and inched even closer to Master, inhaling his fresh, woodsy scent.

They sat in a little love seat together in Czar and Blythe's great room along with most of Torpedo Ink, Reese and Tyra. Sandree, Reese's little girl, was being taken care of by Darby and her sisters in another room.

"Reese." Czar's voice was pitched very low, but it was compelling. "We know this has nothing whatsoever to do with your family. It never did. You refused to throw the fights when you were told to. Helena manufactured a way to get you put in prison. She may have used your family to do it, but she was behind it. She uses sex to bind men to her and make them loyal to her. That was what she was trained to do. It's what she's very, very good at."

Reese looked nervously at his wife, tightening his hold on her hand. Already, he had put her through so much. He would be asking her to accept so much more. "Yeah, I remember her," he admitted. "From the prison. When I was in Crawley. She was always coming around. She had full access to the prison. The warden gave her anything she wanted, and all the guards deferred to her."

Czar nodded. "Helena told you things about herself. Personal things. I want you to think back and try to remember every single detail you can and tell me what she told you."

Ambrielle sized him up as her father had taught her, pushing all emotion aside. This man was her enemy—no, not her enemy. He was her opponent. She could hear the power in his voice. He was compelling. She felt his power. Every single person in that room wanted to do his bidding—apart from her.

It wasn't that she didn't want to fall in line with everyone else and be part of the Torpedo Ink family. She absolutely did, but she knew what was coming. She knew what Czar would demand of Master, and she wasn't having that. She had to be calm and come up with an excellent plan or nothing she said would matter. Czar was extremely intelligent. Far more so than people around him ever saw, mostly because they took him at face value. She wasn't going to make that mistake.

"Reese," he prompted.

"Yeah, I'm trying to remember the details. It isn't like I want to remember her."

"Start with her description. Tell me what she looked like."

"She's tall, dark hair, wears it so it curls around her chin. I don't know what women call that kind of hairstyle, but it never looks messy. She was always put together. Her clothes, her makeup, her jewelry, even her shoes. She seemed always aware of how she looked. She had this interesting snake ring that she wore on her index finger."

Reese curled Tyra's hand closer to him as if holding on to her was holding a lifeline. "What else? She didn't really have any curves to speak of. She looked like a model and walked like one. Like you'd see in a magazine. Like you could hang her on a coatrack. She was beautiful but cold. She had tattoos on her back. They covered scars she had. They were the oddest scars I'd ever seen. I asked about them."

Reese brought Tyra's hand, locked in his, to his chin and rubbed. "She laughed, but it came out almost a cackle. A weird, strange sound I'll never forget. She called them loom scars and said the children of today would benefit from them. That they would learn their lessons so much faster if they knew the loom would activate if they weren't prepared and hadn't studied properly."

Czar's head came up abruptly. That meant something to him. Ambrielle looked around the room and then up at Master's face. *Loom scars* meant something to all of them, yet she'd never heard of such a thing. She'd seen odd scars on Master's back. He had a multitude of scars, but there were some she couldn't identify. She should have asked him.

Czar's sharp gaze collided with Destroyer's and then with some of the other men of Torpedo Ink. "You're certain she used the term *loom scars* when she addressed the scars on her back?"

"Yeah. I asked her to elaborate, but she refused."

It was very clear to Ambrielle that the Torpedo Ink members knew what a loom scar was. All of them. Did they all bear those same scars? The ones on Master's back?

"If she has scars from the loom, Czar," Code said, "she had to have been a survivor of our school. No one in the other schools had the loom used on them."

"You're certain?" Czar asked. "You know that for a fact, Code?"

"I've checked over and over. The original idea was for the loom to be used in the school Gavriil and some of the others went to as well, but it was too large to move and a second one was never built. After it was destroyed, Sorbacov never had it replaced—at least, I've never come across any evidence of it."

"Then we're definitely looking for a girl from the same school we were in. One who managed to survive," Czar said, his tone thoughtful. He looked around the room again. "How? How did she manage to get out alive, and we didn't know?"

"Did she get out?" Absinthe asked. "She still works for the Russian. It seems to me the Russian took over for Sorbacov, possibly even when Sorbacov was alive."

Czar's gaze narrowed on Absinthe. "Sorbacov would never have stopped using small children for his pleasure. He was seriously addicted to the rush he got from watching the torture and abuse. That was how he became aroused. He wouldn't have stopped just because we had all disappeared."

Mechanic drummed his fingers on the edge of the end table beside his chair. "He was under a tremendous amount of scrutiny once Uri, his son, became interested in politics. He wouldn't have taken a chance of continuing to be the one running the ring, but there would be one. He would need someone in place who would be too afraid to betray him."

Master's voice was strained and hoarse as he chimed in. "The Russian might not have run the schools, but he's a pedophile, and he runs the largest ring in the world."

"I agree, Master," Czar said. "He controls that industry—and it has become an industry, thanks to him. He also seems to have found a way to get the free independent assassins trained in various schools to work for him. I think it's very probable this Helena never truly got out."

"If that's true . . ." Alena paced across the room, her hair fairly crackling with energy. She looked so alive, her skin and eyes bright and shining with vitality. "She had to have been one of the girls taken from the school by a patron. That's the only way she could have survived without our knowledge. Some of the girls were sold to Sorbacov's friends or given to them to pay off a debt of some kind."

"Very few," Lana added. "We can eliminate the ones that were sold to any of his friends who kept coming back for more. We knew those children, male or female, didn't survive."

Czar shook his head. "We can't rule them out, Lana. That isn't a certainty. We assumed that. We were children, and all around us, all the kids were dying. We figured if the bastards came back for another kid, it meant they'd killed the one they had. Now we know they also sell them when the child grows a little too old for their liking. We didn't understand the rules of human trafficking back then. A child can grow up serving in that world all their life."

"Damn it," Alena exploded. "Just damn it. This is going to be impossible to figure out."

Storm put his arm around her. He was much taller, the muscles in his arms and chest nearly overwhelming her, but his hair, platinum, gold and silver, along with his glacier-blue eyes, declared him without a doubt Alena's birth sibling. It was easy to see he was being very gentle and comforting toward her.

"We'll figure it out because we have to." Czar stated it as fact, his voice as compelling as ever.

Ambrielle was fascinated by him. She didn't have a doubt that they would figure out who the woman was. Czar gave them all that kind of confidence with his quiet manner and his sheer will. No doubt his personal strength of character was how he got them through their darkest times and why they all followed him. He would not be defeated, and if he ever was, he would go down fighting. He wasn't a man to ever surrender.

"Reese, what else can you tell us about this woman? Anything at all you remember. You've given a good description of her. Dark hair and eyes. Tattoos." Once more, Czar fixed his compelling gaze on the man.

"Thin. Model thin. Tall. She had no lines on her face at all, but her face was rigid, as if it didn't really move when she smiled. She said and did all the right things, but it seemed more as if she was an actress playing a part. She always seemed sad to me. I also had the feeling she didn't like men, which was strange because she came on to me. I mean, *really* came on to me."

Reese looked at his wife and then away as if ashamed.

Tyra leaned into him. "It's okay, Reese. We've gotten past all of this. Just tell them everything you can about her."

Ambrielle admired Tyra. She was giving her man courage and support when he clearly was afraid he might lose her.

"She talked about her mentor sometimes. She said she didn't have anyone else but her, and she taught her everything and was good to her most of the time as long as she cooperated."

Ambrielle noted the difference in the room immediately. That meant something to Torpedo Ink. Whoever the mentor was, she wasn't particularly a good person. She may have been good to Helena in a child's eyes, but whatever she was forcing the child to do wasn't a good thing.

"You're certain Helena's mentor was a woman?" Czar asked.

Reese nodded. "Absolutely certain."

Ambrie closed her eyes and rested her head against Master's side. The things these people had been through were horrific. Even now, she was barely able to assimilate the murder of her parents. Slowly, a little at a time, the reality would slip into her brain, and she would instantly reject it. She couldn't imagine what it must have been like for each of these men and women to have seen their parents murdered in front of them when they were children, some toddlers, and then taken to another place and used so cruelly for so many years. It made her sick to her stomach.

"Did she ever name this mentor?" Czar persisted.

Reese frowned and looked up, clearly trying to remember. "She did. Once. She'd brought some Jack with her. She knew I liked to drink, and she brought me whiskey. She drank with me that night, which was unusual. Most of the time, she poured and I drank. She was upset with something one of her clients wanted her to do. She didn't exactly tell me what it was, but she drank way too much, and she started talking. That's when she said she detested men. Of course, she tried to cover it up and said not me, but most men. At the time I thought she was talking about this client. Later, I knew she really meant what she said—she didn't like men."

He took a drink of water from the glass his wife handed him and smiled his thanks at her. "I asked her what this client wanted her to do. When I did, I called her Helena. That was the name she always went by. Everyone called her Helena. She said her name was Mila, but Dellicia said she was never to say that name again. Dellicia cared for her so much she allowed her to use her own last name, so she was called Helena Devin. Of course, she couldn't use Dellicia's last name now."

Czar looked around the room. "Dellicia? Mila? Anyone recognize either name?" When there was silence, he indicated for Reese to continue.

"She wasn't making any sense, and there were so many names I was confused. Mila. Dellicia. Helena. Devin. Then she began to say this man was bad and he wanted this child so he could do bad, bad things to her. That freaked me out. I might have been drunk, but I understood what she was saying to me. I told her she couldn't help him get a child. I think I got belligerent with her. I demanded to know if her client had asked her to get him a child because he was a pedophile. I told her if she helped him, she was every bit as bad as he was."

"What was her reaction?" Czar pushed.

"She got really upset and started crying. I never saw her like that. She left. I didn't see her for a couple of weeks, and when she came back, she asked me if she had said anything strange or inappropriate. I had a bad feeling that if I said yes, I might end up dead, so I said no. I told her that she just started crying because I wouldn't agree to be her sex slave. We'd joked about that a few times, so that seemed the best way out of it."

"That was smart," Czar said. "I think you were right. I think you would have been killed for hearing that information about her."

He looked around the room. "That's it, everyone. Her real name is Mila. That's what we would have known her by when she was at the school with us. Her mentor is or was Dellicia Devin. Code, you need to jump on that, see if anything pops here or in Russia. All of you, think back. I know it was years ago and you probably tried to block as much as you could, but this is important. This is the woman who wants to kill my family."

Czar curled his arm around Blythe's shoulders to comfort her. "We'll find her, baby. There's no way she's going to hurt our children or you."

"I know," Blythe said with complete confidence. "I'm well aware you and the others would never let anything happen to the children or to me."

Ambrielle shook her head. She had never believed anything could happen to her parents. They were very well trained in self-defense. Their house had a very good security system. What did Blythe intend to do? Never go out of her house again? Never allow her children outside? They had to know a sniper could be a mile away and still manage to kill one of the children—or Blythe. There was a glassed-in room just off the great room. The glass wall of the sunroom opened onto the porch. Ambrielle had noticed two spinning wheels set up. Clearly, Blythe spun yarn on one of them. Possibly one of her daughters spun on the other. She could see there was a long, low cabinet with many small drawers. Through the clear fronts of the drawers, Ambrielle could see various colors of yarn. A good marksman could shoot Blythe as she sat spinning with her daughter. And what about emergencies like little Jimmy with his abscess? Would Blythe and Czar ignore a child's injury or illness? She couldn't see either of them doing that.

Master felt her shake against his side and tightened his hold on her. "It will be all right. We're figuring out who she is, princess. Once we do, she won't get away. Most of her teams are already gone. Now we know where her main go-to team is."

Her stomach clenched. She knew what that meant. He had to know she knew what that meant. She'd known the moment she entered the house and all of Torpedo Ink was there. She had a premonition that Czar would be sending him to another prison.

He wasn't going back to that prison in order to assassinate that horrible woman's main go-to team, or whatever Master wanted to call them. She knew what that did to him. Czar should know. He seemed able to read everyone in the room. Why couldn't he read Master? See that he was right on that edge? If he went back to that place, he wouldn't be returning, not as the man they all knew. Not as the man she had already fallen in love with.

The realization hit her hard—so hard she could barely catch her breath. How had it happened and when? She wasn't a woman to ever get emotionally involved with a man. She didn't like them touching her as a rule. Kissing was out—until Master. She couldn't get enough of him. She would never get enough of him. But it wasn't the sex.

She had looked into Master's eyes on her supposed

wedding day to Walker Thompson. There were dead bodies all around them. There was blood on her wedding dress. Thompson had gotten away, but she wanted to know that Master would find him for her so she could see him dead. She had looked into Master's eyes and she saw exactly what she needed. He could hunt and kill for her. She also knew he was a man of honor. She had recognized certain qualities in him immediately. He had been her chosen weapon.

She'd made a bargain with him. She would marry him, be his wife and never take that vow back if he would hunt down Thompson and the Russians who killed her parents. She meant every word she said. *But.* There was a big *but* in her mind. She no longer wanted Master to be the one to kill Thompson, Gleb and Denis. There were two others, Stas and Simon, she wouldn't mind including in her vengeful plot, *but* . . . There was that word again. The hesitation in her mind. She was certain Master would hunt them down and find them, but she absolutely no longer wanted him so he could kill them.

Unforeseen circumstances changed everything. Master was far more than the killing machine everyone seemed to see and expect. He was the most unexpected, sweetest, even most loving man, and she didn't deserve him. But—that word again—she wanted to be his wife for the rest of her days. She wanted to be able to have a family with him. Children. Watch them grow just as Czar and Blythe were doing. She wanted that same thing with Master.

"Reese, thank you for the information. It will help quite a bit. We may be able to figure out just who this woman is and why she's fixated on my family. In the meantime, now that you know she coerced your stepfather, mother and brother into cooperating with her, you know you aren't safe. I can offer your family the protection of our guesthouse. You're already staying in it and know it's large enough if you want to continue to stay here until the situation is resolved. I'm certain that will happen very quickly."

Reese and Tyra looked to Master as if he were the person

to answer the question. Master nodded his head slowly. "It's best just to make certain you're safe. We can make it right with your landscaping clients if that's your worry. You'll still have Ink when you need him. Any groceries can be delivered. Call the Caspar store or even the one in Sea Haven."

"Thank you, Czar, we accept the offer." Reese looked relieved.

"As you're aware, Blythe stocked the guesthouse with food for you, but if you need anything else, just call one of us."

Czar stood, forcing Reese and Tyra to do the same when he offered his hand, clearly dismissing them. Ambrielle admired the way he was able to maneuver the pair into doing what he wanted. He wanted them out of the room while the rest of the discussion took place.

The members of Torpedo Ink went to the buffet Blythe and Czar had laid out on the sideboard. The silver warmers were full. Beans, rice, shredded steak, avocado, cheese, olives, even grilled tofu were laid out with hot tortillas. They talked quietly while they ate, trying to remember a girl who had grown into a monster of a woman, willing to sacrifice lives in order to get her revenge on a man who didn't even know what he'd done.

Once Reese and Tyra had collected their little girl and gone to the guesthouse, Torpedo Ink pulled the chairs into a circle. Ambrielle could tell by the easy way they did it that they were used to talking together in Czar and Blythe's home. Master made her a part of the circle by simply wrapping his arm around her and guiding her to the buffet table and then to the chairs. He selected one and pulled her down with him into the comfortable love seat.

"We have to go far back, not just a few years," Steele reminded them. "Think in terms of Helena, or Mila, being a young girl, not the woman we're looking for today. Mechanic, Transporter, you two might have better memories. You've been with Czar the longest of any of us. Think back to why a girl would have a grudge against Czar. Or Viktor. Let's think of him as Viktor."

"Maybe it was a young girl who fell in love with you and you ended the relationship," Blythe ventured, turning to her husband.

Czar slid his arm around the back of the seat and dropped his hand on her neck. "I didn't have time to flirt with girls, Blythe. No one was going to fall for me, not even in my teens. It was hell down there. I thought of it as a dungeon, a torture chamber, and it could be called those things. No one fell in love."

Alena cleared her throat. "That's not altogether true, Czar. Some of us needed to think someone down in that hellhole actually did care. I was one that needed that kind of reassurance, and I made up fantasies. When I was eight and nine, I was sure Destroyer, a much older boy, who at the time was kind to me, was going to be my prince. He betrayed me by saving his sister instead of allowing Ice and Storm to win the challenge so they could save me. That's what a real prince would have done—thrown the race so I could go free."

Alena blew Destroyer a kiss. "I held a grudge for a long time, the way children do. But then I did find love. Maybe it was teenage love, but Demyan was my hero over the next few years. I sometimes felt as if I couldn't get through a single hour without him." She swallowed hard, as if there was a huge lump in her throat as she turned her gaze to Absinthe. "I loved him so much. When he died, I honestly didn't think I'd live through it."

"I know you loved him, honey," Absinthe murmured. "He loved you. You were his world. He told me often that his number one goal was to get us out of there so he could give you everything you deserved."

Tears glistened in Alena's eyes for a moment, but she blinked them away. "I just want you to understand, Czar, you're a rock—you're *our* rock. Demyan leaned on you too.

All of us did. There may have been a girl you barely noticed who wanted to lean on you."

"I'm sorry I'm having all of you bring up memories that hurt," Czar said quietly. "I'd never ask you, but it's Blythe and the children in danger, not just me."

"Demyan is a good memory," Absinthe said.

The others nodded.

Steele took a deep breath. "He should have made it out with us. We were so close. For years I blamed myself that I took my eyes off him, and they killed him. It's the reason I hold Breezy too close."

"Steele." Absinthe's voice was pitched low. "We put this right between us. You were a prisoner, just as he was. They tortured you both. You were tied up. The things they were doing to you—to him . . . That wasn't on you. Sorbacov allowed them to kill him. I thought for years it was because I wasn't strong enough to hold the bridge between us. Demyan broke the bridge. He knew he was dying, and he spared me his death. He would have spared you if he could have."

Ambrielle could hear the raw heartbreak in Absinthe's voice. She could see it on Alena's face. Demyan had been loved by these people. All of Torpedo Ink had loved the man. They'd all been through so much, over and over and at such young ages.

Master leaned down and put his mouth against her ear. "You're too compassionate, princess. You have tears in your eyes."

His voice was so low and raspy. He shouldn't be talking. Shouldn't be reassuring her. She needed to be taking care of him, not the other way around. Did she have tears in her eyes? She blinked back the terrible burn and found herself snuggling deeper under Master's arm. He felt safe.

"You weren't there for a lot of this because you were at the prison, right?" she whispered.

He nodded. "During the day, but at night, I was always

back with Viktor and the others. I was a bloody mess. We all were."

"Czar," Lana asked. "Could you have ordered a hit on the mentor? On this Dellicia? Or a member of the family? I mean when she knew you as Viktor? Someone this girl cared about?"

Czar shook his head and ran both hands through his hair. "I don't remember sending anyone after a Dellicia."

Mechanic snapped his fingers. "Wait. Transporter." He turned to his brother. "She was tall and thin, almost emaciated. Like a skeleton. We called her the skeleton. She had dark hair that hung to her chin and she was always with Sorbacov if she came to the school. She was very rigid. Preacher, you must remember her. She kept looking at Lana. We were afraid Sorbacov was going to give her to the woman. Lana was just a little thing, maybe four."

Preacher stood up and paced across the room to the window, turning his back on everyone, but not before Ambrielle caught a glimpse of his face. Easygoing Preacher wasn't quite as easygoing as he seemed. The memory of nearly losing his baby sister was stark on his face, putting lines in his smooth skin and the stamp of the killer in his cold blue eyes. Preacher had always seemed so gentle, the one who laughed and so easily deterred any arguments. That glimpse of the glacier in him, that well of rage that roared to the surface, usually buried beneath a glacier of dense blue ice, was shocking.

"Yeah, I remember her. Dellicia Devin. Sorbacov called her DeeDee to annoy her. She was very stiff and formal all the time. She only wanted female children, and they had to be just as formal when they were with her. Her punishments were very severe. She had her eye on Lana, and I told Viktor straight up that if Sorbacov gave Lana to her, I would find a way to kill her before she took her out of the school."

He turned and glanced over his shoulder at Czar. Ambrielle tried to interpret that look. Had Czar not agreed to defend Lana? Was there some animosity toward their leader?

It didn't seem so. More like despair. As if Preacher had known they wouldn't have been able to stop Sorbacov and the woman from taking Lana from them.

Czar sighed. "I remember, Preacher. It was a constant worry. We did our best to hide her from Sorbacov and Dellicia. I remember that horrid woman now. She didn't come often, but when she came, she always wanted a little girl."

"This girl, this Helena, could she have been with us briefly, and we weren't able to keep her from Dellicia?" Lana ventured. "Maybe, even though she claims the woman is her mentor, she's resentful."

Ambrielle found herself shaking her head. They were off track and getting more off track by the moment. This was about Viktor. Not Czar. Not Dellicia. Viktor. He had done something to a young girl. The girl wasn't Helena. She was named Mila at the time. Mila became Helena when she went off with Dellicia. Originally, when she was at the school with Viktor and the others, her name had been Mila.

"What are you saying?" Master asked.

Ambrielle became aware the others were looking at her. She swore under her breath. "I'm sorry. I have a bad habit of thinking out loud."

"We can use all the input we can get," Czar encouraged.

She hesitated, looking up at Master. He nodded. She pressed her fingers over her lips for a moment, wishing she'd kept her mouth shut. "It's just that I think you're getting off track. This is about you, Czar, when you were Viktor. And about this girl when she was Mila. Mila obviously was given to Dellicia by Sorbacov. Do you remember this little girl at all?"

Czar pressed his fingers to the corners of his eyes, shaking his head. "I don't. There were so many, and God help me, I don't."

Again, there was a short silence. Ambrielle was the one to break it. "If you don't mind me asking, what kinds of decisions did you make for everyone, Czar? I'm talking about when Lana was four or five. When Alena was four and five. Think back to what was happening around that time and the decisions you were making. What were they, and who did they affect?"

Czar pushed his hands through his hair again. He had a lot of hair, and now he looked wild. Blythe leaned into him, and instantly he turned to her, his body language intimate and loving. She tamed the wildness of his long hair into a semblance of order.

"I had to make harsh decisions. There was never enough food. It was cold, and we had to conserve heat. Our part of the basement was down by the kitchen pipes, so we had some heat that the others didn't know about. We had to defend our territory. We shared everything. We worked out and practiced our psychic talents no matter what shape we were in. I drove everyone to do those things. I planned out protection of our territory and food storage as well as killing an instructor who was particularly violent. They all were violent, but some of them enjoyed being brutal beyond imagining. I made those calls. No one else. I didn't want anyone else to have that on them."

"You didn't do the actual killing?" Ambrielle persisted.

"Not as a rule. Sometimes in the basement, if I had to defend our territory, but usually, if we were going after instructors, my body was too big."

"So you couldn't have killed someone Mila liked. What other decisions did you make that could have in any way affected an outsider to your group?" she continued, deliberately using the little girl's name again in hopes it would trigger a memory.

"Wait a minute," Mechanic said. "Wait just a minute. Lana and Alena were called upstairs for the first time with that horrible toad who liked to use a crop before he raped them. They were four. Alena had never been exposed to anything like that before. There was another little girl from Galina's group called up as well, and two girls from Vas' group. The girl from Galina's was a year or so older than Lana and Alena. Maybe five. Pretty little thing. Lana, do you remember?"

Lana wrinkled her nose and frowned. "I do. I remember being so scared and holding Alena's hand. We were taken to a room and made to put on these dresses so we looked like little dolls. They combed our hair and then made us go into another room, where a man was."

Her tongue touched her lips to moisten them. Ambrielle could see she was struggling to stay in the present. The memory was a trigger for PTSD. Her face was very pale, and she looked as if she might explode into violence or shrivel up into a little ball right there in front of everyone.

"Gurin," Czar said. "Gaston Gurin. He was a monster." He scrubbed his face with his hands and looked at his wife. "The things he did to little girls were despicable. The thought of Lana or Alena in his hands . . ." He shook his head. "We had to do something."

Ambrielle closed her eyes for a moment, seeing the naked pain on Czar's face and feeling the helpless rage of that young boy who took the responsibility for all the men and women in the room when they were just little boys and girls. Children. He'd been a child himself. She realized the enormity of what he'd done for them and why they were so loyal to him. That loyalty had been earned a thousand times over just from the glimpses she could see.

"We didn't have the time to plan, to keep everyone safe the way we normally did," Czar murmured, sounding as if he were going back in time as well. "I had to weigh losing everyone against losing our girls. They were our heart and soul. I knew I wouldn't have made it if we lost them. I didn't think the others could have either. So I just went with my gut and came up with a plan to kill the bastard. It had to look like an accident, and the other girl, the one who wasn't ours, couldn't witness that we did it. The timing had to be right. It was going to be close."

Alena let out a hastily choked-back sob, and Lana went to her. They clung to each other, arms tight, foreheads pressed together.

"Demyan, Reaper and I went upstairs to the room where

the girls were," Czar continued. "We went in through the vents. Demyan and I barely fit. Guran wanted to know who the new girl was. Alena had never been used, and he wanted her. Mila pretended she was the new girl and stepped forward. He tried to use the crop on her, and she fought him. He knocked her out, which was terrible but helped us. Then he went after Lana and Alena. Reaper hit him with a statue."

"Mila wanted to join our crew down in the basement. Galina was such a liar. She didn't treat her people very well, but Vas was worse," Mechanic said. "You kept us small. Tight. I understood the need for that, but Mila had proved she would sacrifice for others. I didn't understand why you turned her down."

"I didn't either," Lana said. "It wasn't like she asked us, but I asked you. I'd never asked for a favor before, and I was really upset with you when you said no, and you didn't give an explanation. She saved Alena."

All the members of Torpedo Ink watched Czar carefully. He heaved a sigh. "Do you remember when Sorbacov was determined to get it out of us that we were the ones killing the instructors—that it wasn't accidents or other instructors? They tortured Reaper for days. They took Savage and tortured him. They lied to Reaper and said Savage broke and confessed. They lied to Savage and claimed Reaper broke and admitted everything. Neither of them said a word to Sorbacov. They would have died first. Why? To protect all of you. Mila has turned over countless children to men and women to be raped, tortured and murdered for her to continue with her lifestyle. She hasn't tried to break away from the Russian. She would have betrayed us if Sorbacov got to her, and he would have. He always recognized the weak link."

Ambrielle recognized the stunned silence. Sorbacov may have known who the weak link would be, but he was an adult. Czar had been a child and he had known. He had carefully chosen the children he had brought into his circle. There had been a reason for those choices. He had known they would show unwavering loyalty and they wouldn't break no matter how difficult the circumstances.

He sighed. "She never asked to join our group, but I wouldn't have allowed her entry. I suppose she wanted us to invite her, and she blamed me for not doing it."

"That makes sense, especially in a child's mind," Preacher agreed. "Over the years, for everything that happened to her, she would place the blame squarely on your shoulders."

Czar pushed his hand through his hair again. "Now we know who. We know where her main crew is." He looked at Master, and Ambrielle's heart dropped. "You'll have to go to Crawley Prison and take them out, Master. She'll be cut off from her teams. If she wants to hire assassins, she still can, but that will mean she'll have to let the Russian in on her revenge plans. She won't like that."

Ambrielle waited for Master to object, but he didn't. He didn't say a word. She took a deep breath. She'd known all along it would come to this.

"Czar, everyone here has a clean record apart from Master. I know all of you have been in and out of prisons for various reasons, yet you look as clean as Snow White. You can carry weapons and even have a shop where you sell and repair them. Why is it that you didn't wipe Master's slate clean as well?"

"Ambrielle . . ." Master cautioned. "Now's not the time."

"Now is exactly the time. I want an answer to that question." She couldn't help the challenge in her voice.

"Why are you asking?" Czar's tone was mild.

"Because Master believes the reason you didn't bother to give him a clean slate is that you don't think he's worth it."

Czar's head snapped up, and he looked straight at Master in shock. "That can't be true."

Master shrugged and stood up, pulling Ambrielle with him. "It doesn't matter what I believe. I've got a job to do. Absinthe will have to get me into the prison."

"You're not going," Ambrielle said. "I mean it, Master. I

know if you go this time, you won't be coming out. You'll either die there, or you'll be different. You know it too. I'm not willing to lose you. So yes, I want that question answered for both of us. I think you deserve to hear the truth one way or the other." She was firm, but she didn't raise her voice, and she didn't give in to the insistence of Master's warning grip on her wrist. She kept her gaze fixed on Czar's.

A murmur of dissent rippled through the members of Torpedo Ink. Blythe looked horrified.

"I absolutely never thought that about you, Master," Czar denied. "You can hear lies just like the rest of us. Absinthe, I want you to confirm everything I'm saying. This is far too important not to."

Czar waited until Absinthe made his way across the room and took Czar's wrist in his hand, fingers resting on his pulse. "You are worth the same as every man and woman in this room. You're loved the same. You're my brother. I didn't wipe the slate clean because Torpedo Ink needed your expertise in prison. No one else had your skills. I also had this vague feeling that you would meet someone through those skills that would be important in your life. I believed—obviously incorrectly—that you would come to me when you'd had enough, and Absinthe would wipe your record clean at that time."

Master stared at Czar as if he'd grown another head. Ambrielle could feel shock moving through him. Rejection. He'd spent a lifetime believing Czar thought of him as a throwaway. He thought that of himself. To try to turn that opinion around in that one moment was impossible, although, like Ambrielle, like the others, he had to have heard that ring of truth.

"We'll find another way to get that assassination team. I won't risk you going in. Ambrielle seems to have a very good read on you in such a short time with you. I think my radar was particularly on point as far as the right someone coming into your life, Master."

"I've got to eliminate them," Master said. "I'm not willing to take the chance that she'll send them after Blythe and the children. In fact, Czar, you know she will. She's going to come at you soon. We've taken her other teams. She'll have to use them. She believes in them, and she'll want to see the results firsthand."

"Exactly," Ambrielle confirmed. "I've had quite a bit of time sitting here thinking up a plan I think is going to work, depending on my man's skills. I think pretty highly of him and all of you, so I think you can pull this off with no problem."

"You have a plan?" Czar asked.

Ambrielle knew she looked smug. She couldn't help it. "I do. My father was in the service, and the one thing he taught me was to always have a really good battle plan."

"Master, sit down. I want to hear your woman's plan."

EIGHTEEN

It didn't matter that Master was going into Crawley Prison as a free man; the moment he entered, he felt that same stink. His skin was instantly covered in slime. Poison ran in his veins. Hatred. He remembered every single time he'd been beaten into submission as a child. Every gang rape. It happened every time. Rage washed through him. Not anger. Rage. It swirled in his gut, threatening to eat him from the inside out.

He felt the change coming over him, that other part of him moving to take over. The killer was strong in him, far stronger than the husband who had managed to find a degree of tenderness in him he hadn't known existed. He had to bury that shit deep. It didn't belong anywhere in this shit-hole. That kind of thing could get him killed fast.

He walked with total confidence past the guards, giving one the finger when the man went to say something to him. He was not Kir Vasiliev, shuffling into the prison with cuffs on his wrists and ankles. He was Titus Ustrashkin, Helena Smirnov's closest companion, that man who accompanied her to Crawley Prison each time she came.

Fortunately, the real Titus had a big build, much like Master. He was ripped, and his purpose in life was to intimidate or kill. He carried his muscle in his arms and chest, but he wasn't muscle-bound; he could move fast. Like Master, he had trained in one of Sorbacov's schools and had been doing assassination work from the time he was a teenager. Master wore thin gloves over his hands to cover the fact that he didn't have the snake tattoo. He wore rings on his fingers under the gloves just as Titus wore. If, for some reason, he had to remove the gloves, he had a fake replica of the snake drawn in perfect detail by Ink. There was no doubt in his mind it would pass muster.

Beside Titus, Helena appeared to stroll down the hall, placing one foot in front of the other as if strutting down a runway. Her glossy dark hair swung around her chin, drawing attention to the fact that she had perfect skin. She had beautiful dark eyes and perfect lips. She was dressed in a slinky skirt that fell below her knees yet clung to her, so that every step appeared sensual and wholly feminine. On her index finger, she wore a gold ring, a snake coiled around the finger with vicious fangs and striking eyes of glittering diamonds.

Even with Lana walking so confidently beside him, nothing could remove the stink of prison from his mind or his skin. The stench slowly invaded until it coated his bones and began to wrap around and pierce every organ. Lana suddenly looked up at him as if she knew what was happening to him, her eyes wide with too many memories. She slipped her hand into the crook of his arm.

Like Ambrie. Pushing at his killer. He inhaled her fragrance. She was wearing Ambrie's scent. What the hell? No one smelled like Ambrielle. He leaned down. Lana was tall, and it wasn't far. Ambrielle was a tiny little thing. His fairy princess barely reached his pecs.

"What the fuck, Lana? You smell like her." He whispered the question in her ear, a furious demand, because really, it gutted him to take his princess into that hellhole with him. She'd asked to come. Even had a cover for herself to be there, but he'd absolutely shot that idea down.

"She knew you'd have a difficult time, and she wanted you to come back to her. You, Master. Not some other version of you," Lana replied easily.

She wasn't afraid of him any more than Ambrielle was. Lana had grown up with him. She regarded him as a sibling. She'd seen him at his worst—when he'd been brought back from the prison and the guards had tossed him down the stairs. Viktor and Mechanic would carry him down through the narrow opening to their side of the basement, the little territory they had carved out for themselves. All the children would gather around trying to ease his suffering if they hadn't been tortured that day.

"She'll leave me after I kill Walker for her. She'll come to her senses and leave. She should. She's too good for someone like me."

Lana stopped midway down the hall and turned to look up at him, forcing him to meet her gaze. "Stop talking like that about yourself. Stop thinking like that. Ambrielle loves you. You have to start thinking you're worth her love or you *will* lose her. She suffered trauma, yes, and she's working her way through it, just like we did and are still doing, but she put all her cards on you. She's not going anywhere. You're her everything, Master, and that's a hell of a load for you to carry. If you want out, make sure it's because you really want out. Because you don't want her. Otherwise, stop whining about what a fuckup you are and be glad the woman has blinders on and adores you."

Lana spun back around and began her strut again. Damn. The woman could deliver a lecture. And she meant every word. She spoke the truth. "Whining?" He hissed it at her when he wanted to laugh.

"Hell yeah, Master. A whiny little baby wanting to look at yourself like a poor little martyr not good enough for your woman. Isn't that what you're doing?"

He didn't laugh, but he did smile. How could he not? "You're messing with the big, bad killer impression I've got going, Helena."

"You are a big, bad killer, crazy man. It isn't that difficult to see. You wear that look every damn day." Lana sent him a smile over her shoulder. "She's way cool, Master. You got lucky when you landed her. Don't be an idiot and lose her. I mean it. She's someone special. They don't come along that often. She fits with us, just like the others do. That's a miracle. She just accepts us. There's no judgment."

Master turned Lana's observation over and over in his mind as he made his way to the room where the two guards had taken the prisoners to meet with Helena and Titus. The guards and Anton Elin, the deputy warden, were meeting with Helena as well. She had a lot of clout at the prison, and when she made the request through the warden, Elin jumped at the chance to accommodate her. She made it clear only Elin and the two guards were privy to the meeting.

They didn't care if the cameras recorded Titus and Helena striding down the hallway as if they owned the place, or if the warden had complied with the order to keep the meeting private. Titus and Helena would be blamed for the bloodbath that would occur at the meeting.

"Where are you going?" The voice was harsh and demanding.

Master turned to see Mechanic dressed in a guard's uniform. His face was covered in a thin mask, making him appear much older. He was blond and balding. His uniform showed a bit of belly. At once Lana put on her flirty smile and sidled up to him, running her finger up his arm.

"I've got an appointment to see the deputy warden, Anton Elin. Do you know him? He's so sweet. We're to meet him in the lower basement workout room. I don't think we got turned around. We didn't, did we?" She batted her eyelashes at him.

He cleared his throat several times, staring at her. Then he shook his head and called out to another guard who had just rounded the corner. "Have a situation here, Roy. Need to know where the lower basement workout room is. I'm new and never been there."

Keys, dressed in a guard's uniform and sporting a new face and hairpiece, strode up to them using a walk that could only be duplicated by a true movie cowboy. He even put his thumbs in his belt as he sauntered up to them. Master had never seen anything quite like it. His family was doing everything they could to make it easier on him to go back inside the prison. That was due to his woman talking to them. Making them aware. He didn't know whether to kiss her or strangle her.

"You look ridiculous," he hissed at Keys to keep from laughing.

"You don't look very intimidating," Keys pointed out.

"I told you," Master snapped at Lana.

This was a shit show. If they were going to carry this off when they went down to the basement, it had to appear real to the men waiting. Not so much Elin or the two guards. But the five assassins from the school in Russia had been with Helena and Titus a long time. They knew them. The five men were trained killers, and they were experienced in their profession. Master and the other members of Torpedo Ink would have only seconds to carry out their plan. They couldn't afford to be recognized or show that anything was off.

"No one is going to think you aren't Titus, Master," Lana assured. "We all look Russian because we are. They're expecting Titus and Helena. They know we're bringing extra guards with us, and those men are Russian as well. We walk like them, talk like them and they aren't going to question it in the fifteen seconds, if that, they'll have while we set up."

They were continuing down the hall, Keys leading the way as if he owned the place. Master walked with Lana and Mechanic brought up the rear. Keys went straight to the narrow stairway that led to the basement.

"Why are you so worried? You've done this a hundred times, Master," Lana said.

He'd been given many assignments in prison by Sorbacov, long before he'd taken any for Torpedo Ink. He'd been Sorbacov's secret weapon. His enemies weren't ever safe behind bars. He killed with precision. Once he was inserted into the same prison, he was like a heat-seeking missile. He never stopped until he got his target.

"I work alone. You work in teams. I studied these men. They're different than some of the others I've gone after. Did any of you take the time to study them? To get to know how they move or fight? Which weapons they prefer? How they kill together?"

Master couldn't prevent the edge to his voice. His brother and sister in the club weren't amateurs, but they believed they were going to walk in and easily kill five trained assassins because they went to a better school and were more experienced. Did they know that for certain? They *assumed* it. He knew better than to assume. He'd learned a long time ago and had the knife scars to prove that one should never make an ass out of themselves.

Lana stopped walking, and the smirk faded from her face. "You're right, Master. We didn't prepare for this one at all. We had the plan, but not the prep." Deliberately, she caught his arm with one hand and gracefully, with the other, bent to adjust the strap on her high-heeled designer shoe as if she had a problem. "Tell us now. Give us everything you have on them. We'll absorb it. You know we don't forget details."

The knots in his gut unraveled a bit. They were taking his warning seriously. "Filip and Mark Gusev run the team. They're brothers and are extremely cruel. They both like knives. Little, big, doesn't matter, and given the chance to keep someone alive so they can play, they do. They don't care if the victim is a man, woman or child. They always work in tandem. One holds your attention while the other circles around behind you. Never trust either of them."

Lana nodded her head as she unbuckled the thin leather strap.

"Nil Gorkey looks short but has a long reach, and he is crazy good at capoeira. Not only can he leap over objects, but he can also leap over you and slice off your head while he does it. He carries weapons on him, mostly long blades, but always guns."

"The ones that really know capoeira move like lightning," Keys observed. "He's got to go first thing."

Master agreed with Keys' assessment. "Stas Krupin favors a garrote, but he's armed with several guns and will shoot first. He'll always be the one to fire his weapon first. More than once the Gusev brothers have threatened to kill him because he fucked up. Even in the prison yard he overreacted. He doesn't want to die, and he's fearful in a fight. He'll have to be watched closely."

"Great, and Timothy Garin?" Mechanic prompted.

Master sighed. "Timothy is their ace in the hole. He looks like a young kid. He's been in prison with them the entire time but always looks young. Gives off the nice vibe. The other prisoners tend to tell him things. They go to him all the time because he's the one that might do a favor. The other prisoners don't seem to see his connection to the Gusev brothers. He's good at talking, and when they least expect it, he guts them with a smile on his face. His specialty is murdering women. He likes to get in close so he's staring right into their eyes."

"Nice," Lana said. "How did you think you were going to kill them all?"

"I had a plan. I wasn't going to make it out, but they were all going to die," he said with complete confidence, because it was the truth. There were eight men to kill. Helena's five-man team, the two guards and Anton Elin. He would have killed them, but there was no way that he could have survived and gotten out of the prison alive. He knew he would have been severely wounded. How could he have walked away from that without anyone noticing?

"Maybe your plan is better if I get to keep Ambrielle." He tasted the idea of that for the first time. The realness of it. Could it be real and not a fucking fairy tale? His breath caught in his throat. He'd even trade the ability to talk for her. Give up anything for her. Was Lana right? She saw things clearer than most people, and she wasn't one to bullshit him.

He moved in front of her as they went down the dark, narrow steps to the basement. These were stairs made for an ambush. Back stairs, never used by the prisoners. The metal door they came to was unlocked.

Keys pulled open the door, looked inside to assess the situation and then nodded, moving to one side, all business, his features set and hard. He moved directly behind the two prison guards who sat on a metal table looking bored. They were paid a great deal of money, but they had no real loyalty to Helena or her assassins. They did what they were told by Anton Elin.

Anton turned to watch Titus and then Helena strut into the room. Her dark eyes moved over him with her usual expression, somewhere between lust and amusement, a combination that drove him half-crazy with need for her. Titus kept walking straight across the room, ignoring him the way he did, as if Anton were beneath his notice, taking up a position behind the Gusev brothers. Anton didn't care if Titus never noticed him. The Russian was a psycho.

The last guard entered and carefully closed and locked the door, peering through the small glass window to ensure no one had followed them before he moved around to the side close to Nil Gorkey.

"Helena," Anton greeted. "We're all here. What's the emergency?"

Out of the corner of his eye, he saw Titus move. The man was a blur of speed so fast it was like lightning. It looked for a second as if he'd simultaneously slammed knives into the back of Filip's and Mark Gusev's skulls, severing the spinal cords. Could anyone do that? Before either man could drop,

Titus pulled another knife out and slashed Stas Krupin across his throat.

Helena stepped up to Timothy Garin and, staring him straight in the eye, shoved a knife through his heart and a second one in his throat. At the same time, the guard next to Nil Gorkey slammed a knife into his kidney, twisted and then cut his throat.

Everything happened so fast Anton didn't have time to process. Seconds. Maybe three. Five at most and Helena's elite assassination team was down in a bloodbath. He tried to back up and stepped in a pool of blood. His immaculate brown Italian leather shoes were coated with the substance, and his stomach lurched. He turned to the guards behind him. They were lying across the metal table where they'd been sitting with their throats cut, and blood ran toward him in long streaks of red.

Anton found himself staring at Helena and her Russian bodyguards. They were looking at him as if he were nothing at all. Not the powerhouse at the prison. The man who could make things happen for her.

"Helena, what are you doing? I've always helped you. Always." He held up his hand to ward her off as she approached him slowly with her runway walk. "Anything you wanted, I gave you. You wanted to kill a prisoner, he was gone."

"Yes, you did do that, didn't you, Anton," Lana agreed. "And you made so much money agreeing to kill whoever Helena wanted dead."

Anton reached behind him for the table, looking more confused than ever. "You're Helena." He looked around the room at the others. Titus. The guards. They had moved to the door. The guard looked out the window to ensure no one was close.

"I'm not. Helena is doing her best to kill my friend's family right now. She's not going to get away with it. You shouldn't have taken her money, Anton."

"The warden . . ."

"She slept with him to get his cooperation and then you got involved. You got very greedy, didn't you?" Lana continued to stalk him, careful of her shoes. "The warden went to you to try to get out from under her, but you wanted money. And you liked sleeping with her."

Anton couldn't deny it. Lana looked just like her. She was close to him now. Looking him right in the eye. He didn't feel the knife until it was too late. Until he looked down and saw blood running down his chest. He shook his head.

"Helena, no. You owe me. I allowed you to work out of the prison. Your men stayed here and had every luxury. We brought women and booze in for them. We protected them." He told her. He was certain he spoke aloud, but she didn't seem to hear him. She was walking away, her ass swaying the way it always did in the tight skirts she wore deliberately to arouse men. To arouse him.

The metal door opened, and the two guards passed through first. Anton found himself on his knees, watching them curiously. He held his hand over the blood spurting out of his chest. It was weird, like a geyser. Helena went next. She didn't even look back at him. She just kept walking. None of them seemed to have blood on them. That was impossible. He looked around the room. There was blood everywhere. There should have been shoe prints at least. Tracks. He needed to get out his cell phone and call for help. Call someone. Tell them that Helena had gone completely insane and murdered everyone. That Titus, the big brute who had paused in the doorway and watched him with cold, dead eyes, had helped her. Titus seemed to fade. Anton couldn't stay on his knees. He slumped over and fell face-first into that red pool. He wanted to scream but was afraid to open his mouth. It was too late to do anything but breathe the blood in. Then there was nothing at all.

Master locked the door to the basement, that little room no one ever used anymore, and they went back up the stairs and through the hallway: Helena, Titus and the prison guards that the warden had personally assigned to her. They walked right out of Crawley Prison, got into the vehicles they would ditch and drove away.

Blythe carried the tray with the pot of tea on it into the room, looking so calm and serene Ambrielle wasn't certain she really understood who her visitor was. How could she? Mila Devin sat in the great room with her perfect posture, wearing her smug expression as if she had them all fooled. She gave Ambrielle the creeps. Mila wore a tight red skirt and a silk blouse that buttoned up to her neck, with a large bow that tied just under her chin. To Ambrie the outfit looked ludicrous, as if Mila were trying to look like a doll rather than a real person. Her high heels were nearly stilettos, and Ambrielle would bet her last dollar Mila was adept at using them as weapons.

The man she introduced as Titus stood to the right of the window, his attention on the outside of the house, not on the inside. He didn't see any of the women or children as a threat. He was clearly Russian, a big man with a lot of muscle that didn't stop him from moving fluidly. Ambrielle watched him closely. He was the one she knew she would have to take out fast when the time came.

Darby sat very quietly on the long couch with her sisters, Emily and Zoe, on either side of her and Jimmy, the newest member of the family, in her lap. Beside Emily was Kenny, a gangly teenage boy, staring at Mila with watchful eyes. He had strict orders from every member of Torpedo Ink not to provoke either Mila or Titus.

Blythe poured tea for their guest first and then for Ambrielle and herself. "What do you take in your tea, Mila? It's so lovely that you've come to visit Viktor after so many years."

"I prefer milk in my tea, thank you," Mila answered.

Blythe obliged her and added milk to her cup as well. "Perhaps you'll be able to straighten out whatever happened between you."

"Perhaps," Mila said. "The two of you certainly have enough children. Who knew Viktor would want so many."

Ambrielle noticed Blythe's fingers move on her thigh, tapping out a rhythm. The code. Czar must have taught the Torpedo Ink code to his children, and Blythe was communicating something to them.

"I'm unable to give birth to children, so we've taken in survivors of human trafficking. It would be such a coincidence if you had handed over one or more of our children to the pedophiles who tortured and raped them before Viktor and the others were able to rescue them and bring them home. My sisters, who also live on the farm here, have taken in children, some rescued from ships where they would have been killed and thrown overboard after being used. You may have had a hand in turning those children over to those men and woman as well. That certainly would be coming full circle, wouldn't it?"

Ambrielle couldn't believe the sweetness. The absolute serenity. Blythe could have been discussing the weather, not the fact that her guest turned children over to pedophiles. There was no one sweeter than Blythe when she wanted to be, and her face was relaxed, her expression friendly.

Ambrielle couldn't help feeling horrified at the way Blythe so casually discussed the children's backgrounds. She glanced at them. They appeared as stoic and unaffected as Blythe. She realized their mother had warned them of what she planned on saying using the Torpedo Ink code, so they were prepared.

While Blythe's features never lost their calm demeanor, Mila's took on a deep horror as color blossomed, darkening her skin. "No, no, that isn't true. Who told these terrible lies about me? Did Viktor tell you that?" Her serene voice rose to a note of near hysteria. Even the fine china shook in her hand.

Titus turned around and took a step toward Mila. Ambrielle inhaled deeply to clear her mind, her hand remaining loosely over the revolver she intended to kill Titus with. Just not yet. They had to stall for time. Try to get the children out of the room if possible. That was the ultimate goal. They were banking on the fact that Mila would want Viktor to witness his family dead before he died. To exact the revenge she wanted, Viktor had to be present.

"No, of course Viktor would never make such an accusation without proof. Another young man told us he was certain you provided young victims for pedophiles."

"That would be impossible," Mila assured calmly, bringing her teacup to her lips and sipping delicately. "I was a victim myself."

"I'm so sorry," Blythe said immediately. "You can relate to these children, then." She gestured around the room at the silent watchers.

"I had no idea they weren't Viktor's biological children," Mila admitted. "It never occurred to me that he had taken in victims of human trafficking." She frowned as she replaced the delicate cup in the saucer. "The tea is excellent, Blythe."

"Thank you. Tea is so calming. My mother was . . . difficult. She murdered my unborn daughter in a drunken fit of rage, and I've had to come to terms with the way I handle my temper. I never want to be like her. Never. I meditate. Run." She gestured toward the glass wall where the porch housed her spinning wheel. "I spin my own yarn. And I love to experiment with various teas to get them just right."

Mila lifted her chin and looked straight at Darby. "How is she at handling her temper? What kinds of work are you all expected to do? Are you given to the club members to entertain them?"

Darby and her sisters looked not only shocked but angry. "No way. They rescued us from that kind of thing. They protect us," Darby snapped. "We're loved here and treated as members of a loving family. We have our own rooms that we clean, like pick up our clothes. I can do my own laundry, but Blythe helps the girls with theirs. Kenny can do his, but Blythe does Jimmy's. She cleans the house. We help if we're not in school. We love our classes, if you're going to ask about that. No one hits us. Since I've been in this home, I've never been struck. No one raises their voice to us. The entire club protects us, but Blythe and Czar love us and treat us as their own children."

Kenny nodded. "They rescued me from a situation I never would have lived through. I was practically forced on Blythe, but she didn't even flinch. She took me on when I had a chip on my shoulder. I hadn't gone to school in years, and she tutored me herself to help me catch up." He smiled at Darby. "Darby helped me too."

"I did too," Zoe said.

"Yeah, you did." There was affection in Kenny's voice as he ruffled Zoe's hair.

Ambrielle loved the fact that the children were interacting so naturally in front of Mila. She'd asked for it too. It was clear from her expression she hadn't expected the answer she got from Darby or the additional information from Kenny. The idea of the children all being human trafficking victims had thrown her.

Mila sipped at her tea until it was gone. She placed her cup in the saucer again and looked at Blythe. "I would very much like another cup of that delicious tea. Perhaps a scone to go with it. Did you make them yourself, or are these from the Floating Hat everyone seems to talk about so much? I have yet to go there, but I plan on it very soon."

Blythe rose immediately. "Let me make a fresh pot. I like my tea very hot." As she walked away, she continued the conversation. "Hannah and Sabelia at the Floating Hat make excellent scones. You'll have to try their apricot scones if you like apricot. They're so good. I do like to bake, especially treats that go with tea, so I made these scones. I'm pleased that you're enjoying them."

"The fresh berries are particularly wonderful," Mila said, "but I can't place them. What are they?"

"Olallieberry. The berries grow here, and if the bears don't get them first, we pick them fast so we can make pies, scones and cobblers."

"Bears?"

"The forest is right behind us. We have brown bears. They aren't as scary as the mountain lions," Blythe revealed. "The bears tend to stay on the same routes and don't come near our homes. Mountain lions, on the other hand, are unpredictable. We have to watch for signs of them getting close."

The teakettle whistled. "It's amazing that you're so unafraid that you'd go running." There was a note that said Mila didn't quite believe Blythe.

"Nearly every night for the last five years," Blythe confirmed.

"This is insane," Titus snapped. "Get it over with, Mila. I don't understand what you're waiting for. The longer we're here, the more we have to worry that someone else will show up."

Mila spun around, scowling at Titus. "Don't embarrass me," she hissed, sounding like the viper she had on her finger. "I'm doing this my way. I've waited years and I'm not just going to be fast about it. I'm waiting for Viktor."

"Since we're waiting for Viktor, Titus, can I offer you tea or coffee? I can make both the Russian way."

For the first time, Titus looked interested. "You can?"

Blythe nodded. "Yes, both. Viktor prefers them made that way, so I learned. Which would you prefer?"

"Coffee."

"Cappuccino or Turkish? I can do either."

"Turkish, then. I can get cappuccino anywhere. I like mine with milk and some spices." He said it like a challenge. "I wouldn't mind a scone with those berries."

"Yes, of course. Mila, your tea is ready. I'll bring that to you while his coffee is brewing."

"Do you need any help, Mom?" Darby asked.

"I'm doing fine, honey," Blythe said. "You keep the kids together. That's the biggest help."

Ambrielle tried to keep her face expressionless. They were stalling to wait for Master and the others to get there.

Then Czar would come. Everyone was certain that Lana's appearance would throw Mila just a little. Once Czar arrived, she would be even more shaken. But something in Blythe's voice checking her daughter's movement set Ambrielle's warning system blaring. Blythe was up to something. She was deviating from the plan. That was never a good thing. Ambrielle didn't know Blythe well enough to predict what she was up to.

She watched closely as Blythe fussed with Mila's tea, making certain everything was just so. Mila was very particular about her tea ritual, and Blythe seemed to know the exact way to make the tea to Mila's satisfaction. Once she had Mila happily drinking tea and eating scones, she brought Titus his coffee in a to-go mug to make it easier for him to drink where he was stationed. She also brought him two of the scones to try.

Ambrielle thought she was being far too good of a hostess as she sat back down and resumed the conversation. Thankfully, Czar and Master came in when Mila was nearly finished with her tea. Ambrielle had gotten to the point that she couldn't stand her smug, proper ways.

The moment the two men entered, Titus had his gun on them and insisted on searching them for weapons. Neither man had brought a weapon into the house with them.

"You're holding my wife and children hostage. I'm not going to take chances with their lives," Czar said. He moved into the room, giving his children a quick look to make sure they were all right before seating himself beside Blythe. He took her hand.

Master sat beside Ambrielle, threading his fingers through hers, his arm resting on the gun hidden in the material of her sweater.

"What is it you want from me, Mila?" Czar asked. "I recognize you now. Why in the world would you be so angry at me that you would send your assassination squads after my wife and children? That makes no sense."

"No sense? After what you did to me? Ruining my life?"

Mila's voice swung out of control, and she took several deep breaths to get it back. She coughed, her hands shaking. Her body trembled. "You took away my life. That's what you did."

"How? I don't understand how I had anything to do with your life," Czar objected. "I barely knew you. You lived with Galina's crew, not mine."

Mila's scowl was that of an accuser—of a child. "Galina was a liar and she made deals with Sorbacov all the time. She made them with the guards, with the Kozlovs, with everyone. She did it by using us. She would lend us to them in exchange for food or clothes. Sorbacov wanted a spy in your camp. She was certain she'd come up with the perfect idea. You had passed over me once already . . ."

Czar held up his hand. "You chose Galina immediately. You had choices given to you when you first arrived at the school, and the moment you saw her, you wanted to be with her faction. It was larger and they had clothes and looked as if they had supplies."

Mila shrugged, refusing to be sidetracked. Ambrielle could have told Czar Mila wasn't a woman who would take responsibility for anything. She blamed everyone but herself for the choices in her life. Perhaps Czar already knew that.

"Say whatever you want, Viktor, to make yourself look good in front of Blythe and these children. You don't deserve them. I've gotten to know them, and you don't deserve them." Her voice hissed with venom. Once again, she coughed, and her body slumped a little back against the chair. She tried to straighten, but it seemed too much of an effort.

"Please continue, Mila," Blythe coaxed gently. "I'm very interested in what happened."

"Galina came up with an idea to insert me into Viktor's group. She said I couldn't just ask to be taken in because he'd be suspicious. She claimed I would have to do something heroic, like save one of the girls from a monster. She arranged with Sorbacov to have a horrible toad of a human being, Mr. Gaston Guran, come to the school. He beat girls with a crop before he raped them. Galina told me all about him. She delighted in telling me. It wouldn't be my first time with such a man, so she said it would be easy for me. He would want whichever of the girls hadn't been with anyone. I could save the girl and they would go back and tell Viktor what I'd done. He would invite me to be part of his faction."

There was a long silence while Mila drained the rest of her tea and Titus the coffee Blythe had thoughtfully put in a to-go mug for him. He had remained with his gun in plain sight, covering Viktor the entire time. Blythe didn't seem to be in the least worried about Titus, perhaps counting on Ambrielle and Master covering him from their position. Titus knew Master was without a weapon; he had never once checked to see whether she had one.

"He didn't invite you?" Blythe prompted, glaring openly at her husband.

Mila shook her head. "Galina made my life hell after that. She took every petty revenge on me. The Kozlovs were angry with her, and so was Sorbacov. It was a relief when I was given away. At least . . ." She stopped talking as if she'd run out of breath. Her face was very flushed.

Blythe removed the tray with the tea things and took them to the kitchen. "Mila, would you care for a glass of water?"

Mila opened her mouth. Coughed. Her eyes went wide. She slumped back in her chair, for the first time losing her perfect posture. Titus seemed to realize something was wrong, and he gripped his gun—or tried to. His fingers refused to curl around the grip, and the gun clattered to the floor. It was Ambrielle who got up, calmly walked over to him and stripped him of his weapon.

Blythe returned to the chair beside her husband and took his hand, threading her fingers through his. She leaned toward Mila. "Did you really think you could come into my home and threaten my husband and children and I wouldn't do anything about it?" She gave Mila her sweet smile and then turned her head to look at her oldest daughter. "Darby, would you please take the children out of the house? Take them to Airiana's house. Kenny will go with you."

Darby rose obediently. Mila looked as if she wanted to protest, but she didn't speak, just squirmed a little on her chair. Titus slithered down the wall to sit on the floor. He looked surprised to find himself there. The shock on Czar's face made Ambrielle want to laugh.

Once the children had gone out the front door and it was firmly closed behind them, Blythe turned back to Mila. "I even told you what my mother had done. I told you I had to fight my temper every day. You didn't understand the warning I was giving you. There was no possible way you were going to leave this house alive after threatening the people I love. Either of you. It was not up to my husband to end your miserable life, Mila. He did nothing to you."

"Blythe," Czar said gently. He looked at Master and Ambrielle.

Ambrielle knew what he was thinking. Two potential witnesses. She was proud of Blythe. Ambrielle would have done the same thing had she thought of it. She still wasn't quite certain what Blythe had done, only that it was very effective.

Blythe shook her head at her husband, keeping her attention on Mila. "I wasn't going to allow you to take my children from me or the best man I know, the best of the best. The one person in my life I hold above all others. You don't get to do that. Did you really think I'd let you? You were so wrong. You have about twenty more minutes, and then you'll be gone, and I have to say, the world is going to be a much better place without you. Czar is going to worry that I'll lose sleep over this, but I can assure you, Mila, that I won't. I warned you about my temper and I even told you I liked to experiment with various teas. I all but told you I was going to poison you. Had Titus not asked for coffee,

Ambrielle was going to shoot him. Both of you were dead either way."

Blythe stood up, leaned down and kissed her husband. "Honey, would you and Master do me a huge favor and take out the trash while I show Ambrielle my gardens? I don't want any evidence of them ever having been here if possible. When I come back in, I'll do up the dishes."

"Consider it done, baby," Czar assured her.

Ambrielle stood as well and followed Blythe out. She wanted to be just like the other woman, standing up for her man quietly, without fuss, just getting the job done.

NINETEEN

Ambrielle found herself up against the wall on the front porch. Master opened her blouse and then just impatiently tore it off her, tossing it aside. Her bra followed, spilling her breasts free. The way he did that, as if he couldn't wait another minute, not even to get inside the house, to have her body, was so hot, she found herself nearly drowning in liquid desire.

"Skirt off, princess, if you want to save it. Otherwise, it's gone."

His voice was husky. Needy. She *loved* his voice like that. A part of her wanted him to just tear her skirt off. It was thrilling to have him be so insane for her. She did her best to comply, dragging the material down her hips, taking her soaked panties with it, stepping out of it and kicking it away.

He lifted her easily with his big hands, stretching her legs around his hips. "Lock your ankles, princess."

She was slick and hot and pressed tight against his hard shaft. She felt him pulsing against her, and she groaned, rocking her body against his. His mouth caught hers in a bruising kiss. There was nothing gentle about the way Master touched her. His hand on her breast was possessive, kneading and tugging. His mouth was hot and wild. Her back was up against the hard exterior of the house, so there was no give. Nowhere to go to escape.

His taste was nearly feral. His kisses driving her past insanity. She couldn't think, only feel, only want more of him, her fingers sinking into his hair, her tongue tangling with his in a wild duel. She was desperate for him. *Desperate*. At the same time, his erection was a monster and more than intimidating. Frightening. She was never sure she could take him, especially when he was like this. Wild. Out of control.

He trailed kisses down her chin. Down her throat. The bristles on his jaw scraped over her tender skin, but that only added to the fire building in her body. Then his mouth was on her right breast, so hot and wild, pulling strongly. The line from her nipple, where he tugged and pinched with his teeth, created a lash of fire that went straight to her clit. She yanked at his head, pulling him closer to her. Wanting more. Needing it. She ground her slick entrance against his hot, pulsing shaft, all the while rocking her hips.

She found herself chanting his name, begging him to take her, and yet trepidation had already set in, and she found herself staring down at him, at the giant erection he had already begun to push into her body. The burning sensation alarmed her. The way he stretched the walls of her sheath in spite of how wet and welcoming she was.

"Master. You're too big like this. It isn't going to work. You aren't going to fit."

He dropped his head onto her shoulder, his teeth sinking into that spot between her shoulder and neck, biting down until she cried out and goose bumps broke out everywhere. A fresh flood of hot liquid poured around his shaft. He lapped at the stinging bite mark.

"You like that, don't you, princess? And you like my big cock. Take a breath. You're getting more. You're going to take all of me."

His eyes stared straight into hers, as if he'd fused them

together with his piercing intensity. He looked at her as if she were his entire world. His everything. He looked at her as if he would die if he couldn't have her.

"Look at you, baby. So fucking beautiful. You're a miracle, and you don't even know it." He kissed his way back up her throat to her chin and then to the corner of her mouth. He didn't let up on the pressure between her legs, slowly forcing his way through her folds.

Her body tightened against the invasion, wanting to fight him. His hands dropped to her hips, fingers digging in.

"You've got this, Ambrielle. You've taken me dozens of times now. It always burns at first. But it's a good burn, remember. First that stretch and heat. Then the fire. We want to burn together, don't we?"

He was temptation. He was sin. She would follow him straight to hell and walk beside him. She never wanted him to stop. It was that good. But it was that scary. It was always scary when he took her like this.

"Kiss me, Master. I can't think when you kiss me." It was the truth. Once he kissed her, she would be gone. Totally gone. He could do anything, and she would be under his spell so deep it would be just fine with her.

He always gave her what she wanted. His mouth took hers. Hot. Wild. He poured flames down her throat, sent them blazing over her skin and roaring through her veins. The inferno grew until it was a wildfire burning out of control. He never once stopped his steady invasion, pushing through her tight folds with relentless determination until he broke off kissing her.

"Fuck. Fuck. Fuck." He chanted it like a prayer. "You're so damn tight. You're killing me, woman. Strangling me. Nothing like you in the world." He threw his head back as he sank into her. Burying himself until he was so far inside her, she felt like he'd crawled so deep she didn't know how she could possibly get him out. The burning and stretching were beginning to give way to something else—something far more pleasurable.

He pulled back, gripping her hips, tipping her body slightly. Her back was wedged against the wall, preventing movement. When he drove his cock hard into her, holding her still with his hands, he had positioned her perfectly so that he scissored over the sensitive bundle of nerves. The friction sent fiery streaks coursing through her body in waves. Over and over. Rough. Tender. Fast. Slow. He never allowed her to adjust to the rhythm. He didn't stop, driving her up, taking her right to the brink so that she was sobbing for release, clutching at him desperately, begging him.

He was wickedly trying to keep her on edge, but her body refused to obey his silent command. Not so silent. He swore under his breath. That prayerful, crude chant he rasped out as he stared into her eyes, keeping her captive, claiming her. Possessing her. *Owning* her, body and soul. And her heart. He didn't know or believe it, but he owned her heart. He kept up the chant. Kept hammering into her until the tsunami came, wave after powerful wave, rolling through her body.

He was so large she felt every vein, his heartbeat, every pulse and jerk. His extraordinary heat. So hot, a scorching furnace. Then she was clamping down on him, a wet silken embrace, sucking at his cock, eager to milk him dry, feeling his reaction, hearing his roar as he threw back his head and called to the heavens. His powerful cock erupted in a violent frenzy, coating her sheath with ropes of his hot seed, triggering more answering waves in her body.

Ambrielle had no idea how long they were on the porch, the sound of their ragged breathing and the wind matching the tune of the branches shifting in the trees. She clung to his strong neck, her only anchor, her legs wrapped around his hips. His body shuddered while hers continued to have strong rippling aftershocks. His face stayed buried between her head and shoulder, the bristles on his jaw sliding along her skin with every small movement.

Eventually, Master lifted his head. "You all right, princess?"

Was she? She wanted to tell him so many things. All the revelations she had. The realizations she'd come to. She could only stare at him, shocked at how in love with him she actually was. "I'm perfect."

He slowly lowered her legs to the floor of the porch and allowed his cock to slip out of her. Okay, maybe she wasn't so perfect. Maybe she wasn't going to be able to walk after all. She found herself laughing as she caught at his arm, steadying herself.

"Um, babe, I think I need a bath with salts. That's the only way I'm ever going to be able to walk normally again. At this rate, I'm going to be walking bowlegged."

His gaze jumped to the hot mess that was the vee between her legs. He never seemed to notice she was a mess. He just viewed her with absolute lust, as if he could never get enough of her. It was impossible to feel embarrassed by her naked state when he was still mostly fully clothed, not when he was looking at her with that look.

She held up her hand. "Not again. I need the bathtub. I'm serious. You are exhausted and need a bed. Let me take a bath and we can sleep for a little while."

He woke her twice, once with his mouth between her legs and once to drag her up on her hands and knees. He seemed insatiable. Ambrielle didn't mind because sex with Master was nothing short of fantastic, but it did require maintenance and aftercare—which he was always careful about.

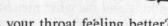

"Is your throat feeling better?" Ambrielle had been very careful to avoid the subject of Master's throat over the last few days. She'd regarded their time together as a mini honeymoon. Walking on the property hand in hand. Talking quietly on the porch, just the two of them, chairs side by side. Making meals together in the kitchen. He was very good at making her laugh. Mostly, it was his droll humor. In the evenings they went upstairs to his music studio, and he played for her. He didn't sing because he couldn't, but she looked forward to the nights when he could.

They spent a lot of time in the bathtub, one of her favorite places. They were there once again, after a marathon sex session. He'd turned out the lights again and lit the candles on the tall pillars, joining her.

"Master." Ambrielle laid her head back on the cushion and watched the candlelight flicker on the ceiling above her head. The water moved back and forth, giving the illusion that the flame was burning on the surface. She dipped her fingers in the water and idly chased the flame.

"Right here, baby." He picked up her foot and began a massage.

As always, he wasn't the gentlest when he dug his fingers into the knots that had formed, but his attention felt good.

"I've changed my mind."

His head jerked up and she felt his dark, compelling eyes like lasers on her. She tried not to look at him, but she couldn't help it. At once, her gaze was held captive by his. It was difficult not to be taken over, to drown there in him.

"What do you mean, princess? Changed your mind about what?"

His voice. That husky sound that penetrated every cell in her body. His fingers never stopped moving on her feet and ankles, moving up to her calves so that she felt so cared for. Master had a way of paying attention to detail.

She touched the tip of her tongue to her lips to moisten them. "Our bargain. I know we both made a vow, but I really would like to change just a portion of it. I mean, not the entire thing."

She was stumbling over her words, making a poor job of explaining what she meant, because he was staring right into her soul. He *owned* her. He didn't know it, but he did. It was all the little things he did for her and for everyone else.

"Keep talking, princess."

"I don't want you to kill Walker Thompson." She said it fast, the words tripping over one another. She meant it. She didn't want him to be the killer, not for her. He was her lover. Her love. He had to know that was how she saw him. That was who she needed in her life. Who she wanted. Not the killer.

He stared at her in silence. His hands never faltered. His eyes didn't blink. He reminded her of a predator. All of a sudden, she was in the bathtub with a very dangerous marauder, and she was telling him to call off the hunt.

"I'm in love with you, Master. I'm so in love with you I don't know what to do with it. I don't want you because I know you can find and kill a man for me anymore. I don't even want you to do it. I realized when I saw you go back to that prison, that doing something like that takes a toll on you. I don't want that for you. I just want us to have a life together. You and me. A future. Hopefully a family." She waited for his reaction, her heart pounding. She meant every word. Confessing she loved him when she wasn't certain how he felt emotionally about her was a huge step for her.

His gaze remained locked with hers. "It's a damn good thing you love me, Ambrielle. I don't know how that happened, but I'm not tempting fate to ask you. I'll just thank my lucky stars and do my best to keep you happy."

He dug his fingers into her calf muscle and massaged. "Are you giving up on the idea of seeing Thompson dead?"

She took a deep breath. She couldn't lie to him. "Not exactly. I know Torpedo Ink is chasing after him for their own reasons. They're close to finding him. I've been talking to Code. Once they do, I'm a good shot, Master. From the very beginning, I always was going to shoot him myself. He gave the orders to kill my father and mother. As for Gleb and Denis, I'll get them eventually. It isn't like I'm not going to come across them. You know as well as I do that they'll seek me out."

She watched his reaction carefully. His jaw hardened. His impossibly long lashes swept down and then up, and she was looking into eyes the color of obsidian. "No."

Ambrielle frowned. "I don't know what that means."

"It means no. You aren't going to put yourself in that position. You aren't bait for Gleb and Denis, and you aren't going to kill Thompson. That's my job. We had a deal, and I keep my word. It's a matter of honor."

"I'm supposed to go with you. You were teaching me," she protested.

"I have been teaching you, and you've been a good student. I don't have any complaints. Do you?"

He carefully replaced her feet in the tub and stood up, reaching for her hands to help her up. Those little things he always did for her. Small courtesies. Where had he learned them when he'd spent his childhood in prison? She knew he thought he wasn't a good partner.

"I don't have complaints, Master," she had to say. "You taught me so much already, but we aren't finished talking about it." She took the towel he held out to her and began drying off. "I really meant it. I have changed my mind about you being the one to kill Walker Thompson. You aren't my killer. You're my beloved husband."

He dropped his towel down his chest to his groin and looked at her with his dark, velvety eyes. "That's where you're wrong, princess. I'm no one's killer but yours. No one runs me. I won't go back to prison for Torpedo Ink. I'd already made up my mind about that before Mila made her run at Blythe and the kids. But for you, that's different."

She shook her head. "I don't ever want you to think that's why I'm with you."

He gave her his ghost of a smile, the one that told her he was finished arguing with her. "Get dressed in dark clothes. Something you can move in. Those boots I bought for you. Put those on as well, the ones with the soft soles."

She studied his face. "This is the real deal. You have news. Code was supposed to inform *me*."

He flashed her a little grin. It was brief, barely there, but sexy as all get-out because he so rarely genuinely smiled. "You had to know that wasn't going to happen. Damn, woman, you are put together fine. If you don't cover up those tits and that ass, we're going to be late. When there's a briefing on running a takedown, being late is frowned on."

Ambrielle had to admit hot blood rushed through her veins. Pure adrenaline. He loved her body. She had his marks all over her to prove it. How could she not bask in the way his eyes went hot with pure lust when his gaze moved so possessively over her? Deliberately she turned and strutted to the closet, knowing he was very fond of her backside. Hearing him groan was very gratifying. She laughed softly to herself.

"The last anyone heard of Thompson, I thought they'd said he'd tucked his tail and run back to New Orleans," she called as she adjusted her very generous breasts into a sports bra. She followed that with a T-shirt and jeans.

"He would have been a lot safer if he'd stayed in New Orleans," Master declared.

"He's not in New Orleans?"

"No, he came back looking for you. Hired an army and thinks that's going to save his ass. He's gearing up for war. I don't know what he thinks he's going to do, drive tanks into Caspar and demand we turn you over to him?" He gave a short, humorless laugh. "We're going to take the war to him so there's no chance of any bystanders getting hurt."

He sounded close, so she lowered the dark sweater she was considering wearing to find him towering over her. He wore a loose-fitting pair of jeans and a tight tee stretched across his thick chest. He held out a tactical vest to her.

"You need to wear this. It's heavy, just so you know, if you haven't used one before."

He put it into her hands, and she nearly dropped it, not expecting the weight of it, even though he'd warned her. Just seeing and feeling the vest suddenly made everything in her life all too real. There was no pushing her parents' murders away, or the fact that she'd been in training so she could retaliate and kill the man who had ordered her parents dead. The smell of blood was strong in her nostrils, and even the coppery taste was there in her mouth. She wanted to vomit all over the soft-soled boots Master had bought for her.

"Ambrielle?" She heard his voice calling to her from far away.

Forcing air through her lungs, she steadied herself. She couldn't faint or have a panic attack, not now, when she was so close to her goal. She shook her head. "I think I need to eat something. My blood sugar is low. Otherwise, I'm fine."

He cupped her face in his large hands and forced her to look at him. "Listen to me, Ambrielle. Whether you're there or not, he's a dead man. I give you my word on that." The pad of his thumb slid across her lower lip as his dark eyes stared intently into hers. "There's no need for you to go with us. You've seen how we work. You know you can trust me. You know I'll get this done for you."

There was no way to prevent him from feeling her shaking, so she didn't try. She dug her fingers into the tactical vest and looked Master in the eyes without flinching. "I can do this," she assured him, her voice barely a thread of sound. "It's hitting me harder than I thought it would, everything coming back at once, but I've got you for my anchor, to hold me safe, and I'm counting on that. I need this, Master. I won't be able to live with myself if I don't see this through."

He nodded his head and took the vest back from her, sliding it over her shoulders and fitting it over her breasts. "Tighter fit than I thought. Is that too uncomfortable? I gave the measurements to Mechanic. He gets our gear for us."

She could deal with the tightness, and clearly the vest was supposed to be worn snug. She shook her head. "It fits just fine. The jeans fit fine as well." That had surprised her. She had a small waist and full hips and butt. It wasn't easy to find any kind of pants other than leggings that would accommodate her figure.

He handed her a belt. "You'll need this. You'll be carrying a gun and several rounds of ammunition. You have those loops on that vest for a reason." He began handing her various objects. A small penlight. One a bit larger. A knife. Definitely a garrote. She wasn't going to try using that, but she'd pass it over to him if he needed it. By the time he was finished weighing her down, she was a walking arsenal.

"What happens if a cop stops us?"

"We have a rabbit."

"I don't know what that means."

"If a cop spots us, Transporter takes off and leads them away. He stays just out of reach. When we're safe, he loses them. He's our rabbit."

"What if he gets caught? Cops have a way of trapping runaway cars."

"Not Transporter. No one outdrives him. In any case, Code would be telling him where every cop car was or was setting up to be. He'd also be wreaking havoc with their dispatch."

His hands were suddenly framing her face again, thumbs wiping away tears. "You're still crying, princess. You don't have to do this. Killing a man isn't easy, and it's worse to live with. I don't ever want that for you, and there's never going to be that need, not as long as you're mine. You decide I'm not the man for you, that's a different story, but you want me as your man, princess, you gotta know, in our family, I do the killing. You back me up, but I'm always the one pulling the trigger."

His dark eyes compelled her to answer. She understood what he was telling her. This was who he was. Her heart turned over. She just nodded her head because she did understand, and he was her man. She was going to back him up. But she was going with him.

⌐

The night was dark with very little moon. Ambrielle understood that the members of Torpedo Ink thought it was a good thing, although she didn't think it was. Master handed her a pair of night vision goggles as they exited their vehicle about a mile up the road from the turnoff to the property where Walker Thompson had his private army protecting him. From there they'd jogged through an olive garden and then begun a mostly uphill scramble through brush and trees until they were above the main house, where their quarry was staying.

Thompson had rented a twenty-acre ranch that was used mostly for destination weddings. The property rented for thousands a day and had a vineyard and a small winery on it. There were several guesthouses, a main house, swimming pool and sauna and spa. She wanted to tear off the tactical vest and most of her clothes by the time they reached the hill overlooking the place. She was that hot despite the cool night air. She needed to work out more. To lose weight. Not a single member of Torpedo Ink appeared to be breathing hard when she was all but wheezing. And she'd always thought she was fit.

"I'm going to the gym the minute we get home," she muttered to Master. "And I'm losing fifty pounds." She lay stretched out next to him in the dirt and grass. "Can I take this vest off? I'm hot and sweaty."

"No. And you don't need to lose weight. You want to work out more, we can run together." He put his hand to his ear. "We're about to pick up live feed. Code is finally able to tap into his cell."

Ambrielle waited, trying to control her breathing. She hadn't enjoyed the way they installed the little gadget in her ear, but it was a miracle of perfect sound. She could hear everyone clearly when they spoke, yet the communication was only in her ear and didn't go beyond it.

"Yeah, Crandell, I was careful," Walker Thompson said. "I've got this covered. We've got another shipment coming in for the Billowses. They're preparing to handle it. They can take up to fifteen and get them ready. They'll move them fast for us."

The other voice interrupted. It was nearly as clear as Thompson's. "Why so few? Jonesy takes twenty, and don't we send the same to Prosper?"

"So far, the Billowses have been the most efficient at training and moving the product. They've never lost any. The others aren't so successful. We lose too many with the others. I've told you that before. It isn't good business, Mike. You can send Jonesy fifty, but if he turns over ten, what good does that do you? And we get complaints later. I'd rather use him as a supplier than a trainer. He has no finesse."

"Where the hell are you? I dropped by the casino to see you, but you were gone, and no one seemed to have a clue where you are."

"Taking a little vacation," Thompson said. "Needed to breathe some fresh air."

There was a short silence and then a laugh. "You're with a woman. Don't tell me the mighty Walker Thompson actually has fallen for a woman."

Again, there was a short silence. Finally, Thompson sighed. "Don't give me shit over this, Mike. I met her, yes, but I haven't reeled her in."

"Because you have a reputation. She's smart. You look at women and they fall all over you. You get that anytime you want. She's got to know that. She'll know you're never going to be faithful."

"That doesn't matter. She'll be faithful. She's going to be my wife, and she'll do what I want her to do."

Crandell burst out laughing. "That sounds like the man I've known all my life. You get to carry on as usual and do whatever the hell you want, but she must live up to your standards or what? You'll break her neck?"

"She'll wish I'd break her neck," Thompson said ominously.

Ambrielle wanted to go shoot him right then. He was so decisive. Absolutely convinced that he was entitled to dictate to his wife while he went on to keep his life exactly how he wanted. She must have made a move as if she was going to crawl over the ridge, because Master dropped a hand on her bottom, his palm curving around her left cheek. He leaned close to her.

"Down, princess. He'll get his." There was amusement in his voice. It came in on the channel built into the little radio that looped in all the Torpedo Ink members.

"He's making my head explode."

"I can imagine."

"You're not alone," Lana said. "Scarlet is with me, and both of our heads did explode."

"I'm with Lissa," Alena chimed in. "Our brains are splattered all over the ground."

Ambrielle laughed. She couldn't help it, the tension building in her dissipating because she was part of these people already. "Where're Seychelle and Soleil?"

"They never take part in something like this, honey, and have to be protected," Czar said. "They're very sensitive. I can't explain exactly what I mean, but it has to do with the mind and the ability to process and get rid of images. Particularly violence."

"To answer your question," Savage said, "Soleil won't go to the clubhouse when Ice is gone. She wants to stay at her home, so Seychelle asked to stay with her there. Anya is with them as well. Blythe, Lexi, Breezy and Zyah are all at Blythe and Czar's. We've got everyone locked up tight. No worries."

She knew that members of another chapter had arrived to guard the clubhouse and the women while they carried out this "mission."

Crandell chuckled into the phone. "We'll see if your woman has enough sense to wiggle off any hook you've dangled in front of her. Get that shipment to the Billowses and get home. We've got to work out these glitches we keep running into. We need a face-to-face meet."

"Give me a couple more days. I'll wrap this up, put a ring on her finger and get home."

"That fast? This isn't a love match. You've found some

old lady with money. You'll marry the bitch, then off her a month later and play the part of the grieving widower. You clever bastard."

"She's young and hot as hell," Thompson said. "I'm hanging up now."

Crandell laughed and ended the call.

"You *are* hot as hell," Master said. "Only thing that man said I agree with." He rolled over, caught Ambrielle's chin and kissed her.

It wasn't his usual take-no-prisoners kiss. He nibbled on her lower lip tenderly, nearly making her heart stop. Suddenly, he angled his body, so his chest was across hers, his hands cupping her face gently. His thumbs slid over her skin as if he were absorbing the texture of her into him. He kissed the side of her mouth. Her upper lip. Trailed kisses to her chin.

"I love you, Ambrielle. In case I forgot to mention that to you this evening before we left the house. I'm so fucking in love with you I can't think straight."

His mouth settled on hers, once again with exquisite gentleness, not at all like his crazy, out-of-control kisses, but that didn't seem to matter. Her stomach immediately reacted with a wild roller-coaster somersault, and electricity sparked over her skin. She tried to pull him closer, to settle her mouth tight against his, but he pulled away, just a breath away but out of her reach.

"That means you're worth more than revenge, Ambrielle. Staying alive is always worth more than dying because you have me to get back to." His intense eyes bored straight into her, piercing her soul. "Every one of us in Torpedo Ink is needed. Our women are needed. I need you just to breathe the fucking air. You can't take chances. We can't get him this time, we pull back and go after him later."

He took her mouth again. This time he was all Master. His lips commanding. Demanding. Possessive. Rough. A takeover. This time there was the roar of flames rushing through her veins to center in her sex, building a wildfire so fast it threatened to burn her from the inside out. She didn't care. She wrapped her arms around his neck and held on for the wild ride that always ensued when Master kissed her. The ground disappeared, and then the world, until there were only the two of them.

"Absinthe, I think it's time you began working on cleaning up Master's record," Czar said. "Knock it off, you two. You can take your honeymoon after we rid the world of a monster."

Czar's voice was very clear in her ear. So was the laughter from the other members of Torpedo Ink. Master lifted his head slowly. He didn't seem to care that everyone heard his declaration. He took his time. His eyes searched her face.

"You hear me, princess?"

She ran her fingers lightly over his bone structure. All those sheer planes. All those hard angles that made up his beautiful, masculine features. So tough. Scary tough. Only not to her. Never to her. "I heard you loud and clear, Kir. We go home alive. Both of us. And for the record, I heard you too, Czar. Thank you."

Master continued to look into her eyes and then very slowly he smiled. When that smile reached his eyes and lit them up, turning them a shade of turquoise she'd never seen before, her heart turned over. Melted.

He went to his knees, sobering, that gorgeous smile fading. He stood, pulling her up with him. She always marveled at how strong he was, how easily he just tugged her weight around. She might be on the shorter side, but she had weight to her. Muscle. She was fit. Solid. Master could easily pick her up, and he did it often.

"Stay close," he ordered.

She got that from the last few times they'd gone places in the dark together. Practices. The real deal when they'd helped Reese. She knew what was expected. More than anything else, everything he'd said to her, she wanted him. Keeping close meant she could watch over him. She wasn't going to take the chance of losing him. In the short time she'd been with him, she'd come to understand just what mattered to her. It wasn't keeping her husband so he would kill for her. She didn't want him as her weapon. She wanted him forever as her man.

If she could have, she would have put her hand in his back pocket, but suddenly, they were all business, moving like silent wraiths down the hillside and entering the vineyard that separated them from the house where Walker Thompson thought himself so safe. She was used to military operations, and at first, she thought this one was carried out as a mission would be—but it wasn't. She began to realize they were more like a very efficient pack of wolves hunting together. They spread out and surrounded their prey.

The outer perimeter was guarded by four roving patrols, two men with two dogs each. The men patrolled in a circular route that allowed them to cross paths every so often, but because the area they were assigned was so large, it took time before they actually saw one another.

Ambrielle didn't understand how the Torpedo Ink members could slip up on the four crews right under the dogs' noses and kill them, but they did it with seeming ease. They worked in silence, rising off the ground right behind the guards and driving knives into the backs of their victims' skulls with the dogs right there. The dogs were taken to one of the guardhouses and left with a command to stay while the Torpedo Ink members continued their forward assault.

The vineyard held several men with automatic weapons. These men seemed to be randomly placed in groups of two, staggered throughout the small acreage. She didn't have time to do more than catch a glimpse of them because they were already being taken down by the time she even spotted them. Master didn't even slow down. There were no stops or starts. They just kept moving forward in that silent, stalking way that was more predator than human. It was as chilling as it was exhilarating. They were a machine, flicking hand signals or tapping a code out, but never making a sound. The enemy never saw them coming. They didn't leave evidence of their passing, other than the kills they made.

There were alarms on every door and window of the main house. The alarms didn't seem to slow them down either. She saw Mechanic move up to the front along with his brother, Transporter, and then the Torpedo Ink members were slipping inside the beautiful home through every conceivable entrance, both upper and lower stories.

Master and Ambrielle went through the front entrance as if they were guests of Walker Thompson. The house was only dimly lit, amber lights glowing in the halls and on the stairway. Master, Ambrielle and Ink converged with Maestro and Player, and then, as they rounded another corner, Keys and Preacher. She saw more of the Torpedo Ink members descending the stairs. Again, they gave the impression of a wolf pack converging on prey.

"Mr. Thompson, I think we need to go. Now. I've got a bad feeling."

Ambrielle recognized the voice immediately. "That's Gleb," she whispered.

"We're surrounded by an army, and no one knows we're here," Thompson protested. "I don't want to hear another word on the subject."

"Whatever you say, Mr. Thompson," Gleb answered. He spoke in Russian.

Master interpreted for her. "He's ordering his team to leave now."

Master swept her back into the shadows. She knew to go still just as all of Torpedo Ink did. They became shadows. Ambrielle couldn't let herself breathe in the presence of the four Russian assassins who wore the little ghost cuff links to signify they were part of the organization Czar's Torpedo Ink had been tracking for a long time. These men hired themselves out to torture and kill for the traffickers, but they were independent contractors, and they were leaving Walker Thompson since he refused to listen to their advice. They had left him with his own hired bodyguards, four other men who thought they were tough but had no idea of the caliber of men who had just walked out on them.

Gleb and Denis led the way. They were six feet into the wide expanse of the living room when Gleb suddenly halted, instincts warning him they were in trouble. Ambrielle pressed her hand over her mouth, terrified for Master, but he was already behind Gleb. Maestro was behind Denis. Keys and Preacher had crept up behind the other two as well. There wasn't a single sound to give away the fact that four men died right there, not twenty feet from where Walker Thompson watched a basketball game in the game room.

Heart pounding, Ambrielle slumped against the wall. It seemed anticlimactic that Gleb was really dead that quickly after he had murdered her father at Thompson's demand. His death had been without any real struggle. He hadn't had the chance to fight back. She thought he was nearly invincible, and yet Master had killed him in seconds.

Master turned to her, his eyes moving over her face, and then his hand followed where his gaze had traveled. "You doing all right?"

"It's just that I thought he would put up a huge fight."

"The idea is to never give your opponent that opportunity. He started the fight. We're finishing it. Unless we need to interrogate someone, what's the point of talking to them? Get the job done. Don't make it personal."

"It is personal to me."

He cupped the side of her face, his thumb sliding over her lips, his gaze turning soft. "I know it is, princess. That makes it personal to me. Stay behind me."

She knew to do that, so she nodded, attempting a smile to show him she was going to be just fine. She had no idea how they were going to go into a lighted room with four, possibly five armed men in it. She should have known better. Torpedo Ink always had a plan.

"On three," Czar said.

Master counted down. He entered the room, stepping to

one side to allow Maestro and Ink entrance. Guns were blazing. The windows were open, and Czar, Savage and Reaper had also gained entrance, firing at the four bodyguards. The men had no chance, dropping to the floor unmoving.

Walker Thompson stared at the bodies, mouth open, uncomprehending. Savage searched him none too gently for weapons, pulling out several as well as taking his phone. He tossed it to Code, who pocketed it.

"Before you die, Thompson," Master said, walking up to him, looking him right in the eye. "I want you to know you fucked with the wrong family. You never should have issued the order to kill the Moore family. That was a big mistake on your part. Then you were too damn stupid to leave it alone."

As he spoke the last, he caught the back of Thompson's head in his giant palm and jerked him forward as he thrust his knife through his throat, all the while staring directly into his eyes. They stared at each other, Thompson shocked and uncomprehending, blood bubbling up around the wound and then streaming down in earnest. Master didn't let him go, not until his legs turned to jelly and his eyes went glassy and then lifeless.

Walker Thompson went down to the floor as his knees buckled and then he face-planted. Master had stepped back to avoid getting hit with the body. "He's dead, princess. You're safe, and your parents are avenged. We've got the information we needed to get to the next rung in the ladder. Let's go home." He held out his hand to her.

"Don't you need to collect the weapons?"

"The others will do that while we make our way back. It's a bit of a trek, remember?" He brought up her hand to kiss her knuckles. "I keep my promises, babe."

Ambrielle smiled at him. "You do. So do I. We're in this together." And she meant it.

TWENTY

~~

"Um, Master." Ambrielle couldn't keep her eyes off Savage, who looked as if he might actually explode any moment. She'd never seen anyone so wound up. He was on the edge of the grass, pacing back and forth. "Savage doesn't look too happy."

Seychelle shrugged her shoulders, turned away from Savage and headed toward the two of them as they sat at their picnic table with Ice and Soleil.

Master and Ice exchanged a knowing grin, but when he looked at Ambrie, Master was perfectly somber. "He does look upset."

Seychelle marched up to the table and took the bottle of water Ice held out to her. "That man is impossible sometimes."

"What's he upset about?" Ice asked.

"Apparently a text was sent to every member of Torpedo Ink, all the Red Hat Ladies, members of law enforcement and all the members of the various churches in the area that Savage and Seychelle were singing Mama Anat's song today in an interfaith get-together. Everyone was invited and told to bring food. They would appreciate the support for Mama Anat. He thinks he was set up. This was supposed to be a small gathering of her church alone, which is usually just a few people." Seychelle looked over her shoulder at Savage. He was still pacing. She sighed. "He's really paranoid about this."

Master stood up, looking resigned. "I'll talk to him. It isn't fair that he's stuck singing with so many people around. He was taking my place because I'm supposed to rest my voice for a few weeks. I don't think it would hurt for me to sing just this once."

"You can't." Ambrielle caught his arm in a firm grip. "I'm sorry, Seychelle. You're the best of the best, but I can't let Master take a chance of hurting himself like that. He just had surgery on his throat, and he is not wrecking it. No one can sing, or you can sing alone if he won't do it."

"He'll sing. He's just so certain that there's a massive conspiracy against him."

Ice grinned at Soleil. "See, baby? I told you it would be fun to come and watch him lose his mind."

Soleil shook her head. "He really did say that, Seychelle. He expected Savage to get upset when he saw that text. Who sent out the text in the first place? We couldn't tell."

"Savage even asked Code, and Code couldn't figure it out. The sender bounced around from so many towers and even went out of the country."

"That's crazy. Maybe it *is* a conspiracy," Ambrielle said. She looked around the park. The entire picnic area was taken. Every single site. Every place on the grass that could hold a chair had been claimed, and that section was massive. There was seating in the amphitheater. Every seat was filled. The low stone wall surrounding the park had people sitting on it, and in front of the wall, people had placed folding chairs and seemed prepared to stay, with picnic baskets placed at their feet. "Do you even know these people?" she asked.

Master shook his head. "No doubt Czar will see this as an opportunity to get to be really friendly with the community." He sounded so mournful even Seychelle laughed.

Savage walked up to them. He glared at Master. "This is totally fucked."

"These are churchgoing people," Seychelle reminded him.

"And it is Sunday," Blythe added, coming up behind them. She put several baskets of food on the table to add to what Soleil and Ambrielle had brought. Czar and Kenny carried a second picnic table to put with the first one to add more room.

"Do you see what's going on here?" Savage demanded.

"Don't whine," Czar ordered. "It isn't becoming. It's a beautiful day, and people turned out to celebrate Mama Anat. She deserves it. Just think of it as paying tribute to her. You never say the L-word, but we all know you love her, so just think about that while you're singing and nothing else. It's one song."

"You'd think I'd get a little sympathy," Savage groused. He slung his arm around Seychelle. "Just you, babe. You're the only one who knows I'd rather pull out my fingernails one by one than do this."

Music reached them first. A catchy tune, the notes building in strength. Then the words sung next by the popular artist Rashad Perry, the singer for the Troubled Sons.

I'm a legend of a lover

A man for undercover

A thirst trap in disguise

The women see me comin'

That silver truck of lovin'

That no one can deny

They need a red-hot hero

Not a poser or a zero

Deputy desire

You know I'm your live wire

Of fun . . .

Red Hot Jackson

Get your 911 of fun

And I'll let you hold my gun

Because I'm . . .

Red Hot Jackson

On the chorus, more voices joined in. As Jackson Deveau's silver truck pulled into a parking slot, some of the people in the park picked up the verses of the song and began to sing the catchy little tune.

Savage swung around and watched as Jackson sat in the truck for a moment, allowing the song to play out before shutting off the engine. He slipped out from the driver's seat and strode toward them, appearing relaxed and confident, nodding toward a few people but not stopping. Jonas Harrington drove up beside the silver truck and parked. He followed the deputy at a much more leisurely pace.

"He was the one who orchestrated this," Savage said. "He arranged all of this. Jackson Deveau is going down for this one."

"If he managed all this, he's downright brilliant," Czar observed.

"He's a cocky son of a bitch," Ice had to admit. "Can't help but admire the bastard."

"Language," Blythe reminded him, exchanging a look of pure amusement with Soleil. "The children."

By the time Jackson made it to the table, Savage's entire demeanor had changed. Czar greeted him, but Savage seemed welcoming, although he didn't crack a smile. He simply wrapped his arms around Seychelle and nodded to the deputy, waiting until Jonas arrived before he spoke.

"Good you both came to support Mama Anat. Don't know why she's so worried about this silly gathering, but she's got herself in some kind of tizzy. Zyah's got her hands full trying to calm her down."

Ambrielle had to hand it to Savage, the man should get an Oscar for his performance. He appeared genuinely concerned for Mama Anat and pleased that the two law enforcement officers were attending the church benefit, not in the least as though he'd just been threatening Jackson.

Ambrielle caught a flicker of dismay on Jackson's face, and then it was gone, and he wore his usual expressionless mask. Had she not been studying him so closely, she would never have caught it. Yeah, he definitely had something to do with the turnout of the large crowd. That didn't stop the Torpedo Ink members from making room for them at the table.

Jonas added a picnic basket filled with baked goods from the Floating Hat. "Hannah isn't feeling very well, so she's staying home and resting, or she would have come," he explained.

Blythe and the others immediately murmured their concern.

"We'd better get set up, Seychelle, Savage," Master said. He held out his hand to Ambrielle and enveloped her hand in his. His voice still sounded very husky, but she knew the moment they were away from everyone, he would once again volunteer to sing despite what the doctor had ordered. He couldn't help himself. He didn't like others to be uncomfortable, and he felt guilty that he'd put Savage in this position. He knew Savage didn't sing in public.

Sure enough, they hadn't gotten more than thirty feet from the picnic tables when Master immediately made his pitch. "Look, Savage, this turned into a huge shit show. I get that Jackson pulled off a cool prank, but this is one you don't have to follow through with. I was supposed to handle this with Mama Anat, not you. I can sing the duet with Seychelle and get you off the hook. One song isn't going to ruin my throat."

Ambrielle wanted to protest that it could. The doctor had been very specific. But she didn't say a word. She didn't even raise her gaze in protest to Seychelle or Savage. They had already been told. They knew. She just waited, squeezing Master's hand tighter. He brought her hand to his chest, his thumb rubbing over her knuckles as if he could ease the tension in her. Nothing could, but she didn't voice that either. She simply waited.

"Not gonna happen, Master. I'll sing with my woman. Just look at her and no one else. Seychelle will get me through it. When I look at her, the rest of the world disappears. And when I hear her voice, there's a kind of magic that happens. Jackson can't know that."

"He'll get the audience to demand more songs," Master warned.

Savage shrugged. "All I ask is when I go to prison for murdering him, you look out for Seychelle. And when she comes to visit me, come with her. Don't want the other prisoners ogling her."

Seychelle burst out laughing. "You're so crazy. You aren't going to murder Jackson just because he thought up an awesome prank and one-upped your prank. He still hasn't figured out how to stop that song from playing. Everyone in the village is singing it. Once we're done here, that will be the end of it."

Ambrielle loved the sound of her laughter. Savage followed her up to the platform, where the band had assembled. They'd all come to support Mama Anat—or torture Savage. Ambrielle wasn't certain which.

"I'll wait for you at the picnic table with the others, Master," she said, gesturing to the now-very-large group assembled. Some of the Drake sisters had joined them.

"Wait right over there," Master said, indicating the few seats closest to the platform. A few of the Red Hat Ladies were there, surrounding Mama Anat and Inez. "I want to see your face."

Ambrielle wasn't going to protest. She didn't even consider it, not when he slung his arm around her neck and kissed her right in front of the ladies and a good portion of several churches until she was bright red.

"Just want you to remember who you love. That would be me," he said as he walked her over to the Red Hat Ladies.

They laughed and hugged her, moving over to give her the center chair. "That man is a good man," Mama Anat said.

"Yes, he is," Ambrielle agreed. "And I'm madly in love with him."

No.1 *NEW YORK TIMES* BESTSELLING AUTHOR

CHRISTINE FEEHAN

'The queen of paranormal romance...
I love everything she does'
J. R. Ward

PIATKUS

Do you love fiction with a supernatural twist?

Want the chance to hear news about your favourite
authors (and the chance to win free books)?

Christine Feehan
J.R. Ward
Sherrilyn Kenyon
Charlaine Harris
Jayne Ann Krentz and Jayne Castle
P.C. Cast
Maria Lewis
Darynda Jones
Hayley Edwards
Kristen Callihan
Keri Arthur
Amanda Bouchet
Jacquelyn Frank
Larissa Ione

Then visit the *With Love* website and
sign up to our romance newsletter:
www.yourswithlove.co.uk

And follow us on Facebook for book giveaways,
exclusive romance news and more:
www.facebook.com/yourswithlovex

PIATKUS